"A THOROUGHLY BELIEVABLE HEROINE DEALING WITH CORRUPTION, GREED, DECEIT AND DANGER."

—*Booklist*

"FULL OF MENACE AND VIOLENCE."

—*Kirkus Reviews*

"KEEPS THE TENSION HIGH."

—*People*

P9-AZV-670

Also by Nancy Taylor Rosenberg

NANCY TAYLOR ROSENBERG

sullivan's law

PINNACLE BOOKS
Kensington Publishing Corp.
http://www.kensingtonbooks.com

PINNACLE BOOKS are published by

Kensington Publishing Corp.
850 Third Avenue
New York, NY 10022

All Kensington Titles, Imprints, and Distributed Lines are available at special quantity discounts for bulk purchases for sales promotions, premiums, fund-raising, and educational or institutional use. Special book excerpts or customized printings can also be created to fit specific needs. For details, write or phone the office of the Kensington special sales manager: Kensington Publishing Corp., 850 Third Avenue, New York, NY 10022, attn: Special Sales Department, Phone: 1-800-221-2647.

Pinnacle and the P logo Reg. U.S. Pat. & TM Off.

First hardcover printing: May 2004
First mass market printing: April 2005

10 9 8 7 6 5 4 3 2 1

Printed in the United States of America

ACKNOWLEDGMENTS

I would like to thank my editor and friend, Michaela Hamilton, along with the wonderful staff at Kensington Publishing Corporation. My agent, Arthur Klebanoff, has done a fine job of organizing my complicated professional life.

I would also like to mention my beautiful family: Forrest Blake, Jeannie, Rachel, Chessly, Jim, Jimmy, Christian, Hoyt, Barbara, Remy, Taylor, Amy, Mike, and Nancy Beth. I attribute my creative talent, such as it may be, to my amazing mother, La Verne Taylor.

To Dr. Christopher Geiler, my medical expert, friend, and personal physician for the past six years, your time and efforts are sincerely appreciated.

I owe a special debt of gratitude to Daniel Conrad Hutchinson. All I can say, Dan, is that someone who jokingly refers to himself as the Ultimate Specimen of Manhood should be able to take on the role of two characters in one fictional book. I doubt if you have anything in common with the one named Daniel, though, and the professor is not nearly as persnickety as you. Also to Christina Hutchinson and Sarah Bostick, for their tips on today's teenagers.

To the others who love and support me: My brother and sister-in-law, Bill and Jean Taylor, as well as my nephews, Nick, Mark, and Ryan; my sister and brother-in-law, Linda and John Stewart, as well as Sharon and Jerry Ford; my assistants, Thomas Villani and Geronima Carrillo, who keep my bills paid, food in the refrigerator, and my clothes clean. For the technical expertise of my friends at SDSI Business Systems: John Paul Thomas, Patrick Thomas, Jean Barnett, and Nancy King. They've done a great job redesigning my new Web site, as well as continually calming a panicked writer when her computers go on the blink. To Heather Ehrlick, a true friend and wonderful therapist, who helped keep my pain under control while I was writing.

To my special friends at the Immaculate Heart Center in Santa Barbara: Joann, Ann, Pauline, Carol; to Father Virgil at the Old Mission, a remarkable and inspiring man. To Barbara and Rabbi Bernard King: I'm proud to be considered even a small part of your loving and spiritual family. To their son, Neil, whose name I also used for a character.

To my many angels, saints, and muses, I don't know all of your names, just that we all work for the same employer.

Chapter 1

Danger lurked among the plush California greenery, under the bright midday sun. A grouping of cumulus clouds could easily be mistaken for a snowcapped range of mountains. According to the weather report, a rainstorm would be moving in by nightfall. The white clouds were deceptive, laden with moisture. They would soon turn dark.

Everything in his world was deceptive.

What had first caught his attention were her shoes. When she walked, lights flashed inside the tiny heart-shaped cutouts. Following children wearing fancy shoes was a new game he'd been playing. It came to him one day while he was eating a corn dog and sucking on a lemonade at the mall. Sitting around and waiting for someone to call drove him crazy. Even worse was having to report in at a specific time. This broad was flakier than most drug dealers, and dealers always made a guy's life miserable. At least they had a reason for leaving you hanging. They were either out of product, their supplier didn't show up on time, or they were so doped up they didn't even remember you'd called. The lady changed the times he was supposed to call every time they spoke.

He followed the kids with the fancy shoes to the parking lot, curious as to what types of cars their parents drove. During a four-hour period the day before, he'd followed nine kids wearing the same kind of shoes. Not the same exact style. The only criteria was that the shoes had to light up. He didn't care if the cut-outs were animals, hearts, flowers, baseballs, or footballs. He knew the discount stores made knock-offs. No matter where the parents bought them, though, the shoes with lights still cost more than your average pair of children's sneakers.

Flipping through his three-by-five notebook, he added up the two rows of numbers. If the make and model of a car was any indication of a person's income, there were far more poor kids wearing the fancy shoes than there were rich kids. The ironies of life had always amused him. Of course, he knew his game wasn't an actual survey. Checking kids' shoes wasn't his job or anything.

He hated waiting. At present, he was looking for a place. He'd checked out several houses a few blocks away, but none of them fit his needs. He liked trees, houses set back away from the street, the kind of neighborhood where people didn't pry into a person's business.

He'd never had a woman tell him what to do before.

Leaning against a tree, he was inhaling the smoke from his cigarette when he saw her open the front door of her house and walk out onto the patio. God, she was beautiful. What kind of parent would let a little girl go out alone? Sometimes she rode her bicycle with the pink streamers. Other times she skipped. At least her mother had set some restrictions. She could not leave the block. He had seen her ride to the end and stop, then turn around and head off in the opposite direction. He glanced at his watch. It would take her eight minutes to reach the vacant lot behind him.

The entire brood had left for church at nine-thirty that morning. He'd seen them leaving, all decked out in their Sunday clothes. They'd come home around one, parking their rusted-out Volkswagen van in the driveway. Must have stopped for lunch somewhere.

All week long, he had kept his eyes peeled for a man. He was almost certain the woman didn't have a husband. Damn, he thought, the youngest couldn't be more than six months old. The baby cried all the time, and the two boys were always fighting. The oldest was a girl. She must be in her teens— she had a set of knockers he could spot a mile away. Maybe the baby was hers, although he never saw her pay it much attention. Every evening she sat on the steps of the front porch, staring into space. A few nights ago he'd heard a lot of yelling. When the big sister came outside, he could tell that she'd been crying.

The mother didn't work, so he assumed she lived on welfare, probably the Aid for Dependent Children she collected for each of her five offspring. He assumed she paid for her groceries with food stamps. At least no one in the household smoked. They couldn't use stamps for cigarettes or booze. People traded them to their friends for cash, probably at half their value.

Flicking the ashes from his cigarette, he gave the mother extra points because she cooked. He knew she cooked because he'd spied on them through the kitchen window one evening. The aroma was good enough to make him want to knock on the door and ask if he could join them.

The children appeared fairly clean, and he could tell the mother didn't spend whatever money came her way on herself. She wore rundown shoes and the same black rayon dress to church every Sunday, and carried a beat-up black plastic handbag. A thief would have to be nuts to try to snatch that old purse, he thought with a chuckle. He suspected it was stuffed full of cash. She was a big woman who could put a hurt on a man if she got riled up. No matter what was happening, she never once set down that purse. One of the boys had fallen off his skateboard and broken his arm two days back. His mother had rushed out to help him, the purse shoved under her armpit. It would take a crowbar to pry those arms apart. The purse was a clutch type of thing with no straps. Purse snatchers preferred straps. Most women didn't have that kind of insight.

Everywhere he looked he saw the distinctive signs of poverty. Broken down cars on the street that had to be pushed every seventy-two hours to keep the police from towing them. The cops added to the misery of poor people. They didn't have enough money to register their car, so they got a ticket. How could they pay the ticket? If they had any money, they would have registered the car. And car insurance was out of sight. More tickets. Pretty soon the person ended up in jail. When he was freed, there were more fines to pay and new court dates. Why even try? Stay at home and collect welfare. Nobody slapped a ticket on your ass walking to your mailbox. He spent his childhood in the same kind of neighborhood.

Holding the Gideon Bible he'd stolen from the motel in front of his chest, his body surged on adrenaline. Five minutes and counting. He could already hear her singing. It was hard to make out the words, but he recognized the song. Like everything else about her, her voice was pure and sweet. No heavy cologne, no sticky makeup, no body odor, no open sores or needle tracks.

"Jesus loves me! This I know, for the Bible tells me so."

"That's my favorite song," he told her, stepping up beside her. He hated it that her new shoes were making contact with the dirty concrete, and that she lived in that rundown old house. She was a princess, his beautiful princess. Her curly brown hair framed her adorable face. Her skin was a rich, warm brown, and her eyes sparkled with joy. How long before the singing stopped? Would she end up sobbing on the porch like her big sister?

He had intended to wait another week, hoping he'd get caught up in his new job and forget what he had convinced himself was a harmless game of counting shoes. He wanted her too bad. He imagined holding her in his arms, smelling her freshly washed hair, stroking her warm and flawless skin.

She stopped skipping and glanced over at him. For a few

moments she was silent, then she saw the Bible he was holding. "Do you go to our church?"

"Yes, I do," he lied, smiling. "I was talking to your mother this morning. She asked me to keep an eye on you. You know, make sure nothing bad happens." He turned and pointed down the adjacent street. "I don't live that far away. How's your brother's arm? Your mother told me he fell off his skateboard."

"I want a cast too," she said, fiddling with the ruffles on her flower print dress. "Then all the kids can sign their name on it and my mom won't make me set the table for dinner. The plates are too heavy. I'm not strong enough."

"I bet you're a lot stronger than you think," he told her, squatting down on one knee. "Put your hand in mine and push as hard as you can. You might even be stronger than me."

"Really?" she said excitedly.

Her small, perfect fingers wrapped around his own. He felt a jolt of electricity, a taste of the pleasure she would provide him. Tears welled up in his eyes. The dark cloud was above him. He had to move fast. As soon as it started to rain, someone would come looking for her.

She deserved a palace and all he could offer her was death.

The April rain was coming down in transparent sheets. Because she'd driven her two children to school, Carolyn Sullivan was twenty minutes late to work. She parked her white Infiniti in the closest spot she could find. When she got out and opened her umbrella, it snagged on the car door.

Another Monday from hell, she thought, tossing the ripped umbrella onto the backseat and covering her head with the newspaper as she jogged toward the front of the building.

Fifteen minutes later, Carolyn was sitting in a chair in her supervisor's office at the Correction Services Agency in

Ventura, a small city on the outskirts of Los Angeles. Her hair was dripping wet, the soggy newspaper was clasped in her right hand, and she'd been called on the carpet before she'd even had a chance to grab a cup of coffee.

Why had Brad Preston left a message on her voice mail demanding that she report to him the moment she arrived? Something big must be happening. Carolyn hoped it was good news—a long overdue promotion perhaps. As a single parent, her decision to get her law degree had placed a serious dent in her already strained budget.

She walked to the outer office. Brad's assistant, Rachel Mitchell, had informed her earlier that he was in a meeting with the agency's chief and had left instructions for her to wait. "I'll be right back," she told the woman, pulling her damp shirt away from her chest. "I'm going to the break room for some coffee."

A tall, handsome man with blond hair and blue eyes caught Carolyn by the elbow. "You're not going anywhere," Brad Preston said abruptly, steering her back into his office and kicking the door shut behind him. He released her and stared at the newspaper in her hands. "Did you get a look at the headlines?"

"No," Carolyn said, depositing the wet papers in the trash can. "My umbrella broke. I used the paper to stay dry. What's going on?"

"Eddie Downly raped an eight-year-old girl!" he said, tossing his copy of the *Ventura Star Free Press* at her. "She's alive but he did his best to kill her. This was your probationer. When did you last see the bastard?"

Carolyn's fingers trembled as she stared at the rapist's picture. On the street, they called him Fast Eddie. His real name was Edward James Downly. At sixteen, he'd been sentenced to serve a year in the county jail, then placed on four years' probation. Since the crime had been sexual in nature, Downly had been tried as an adult and ordered to register as a sex offender. Under the DNA Forensic Identification Data Bank and Data Bank Act of 1998, all registered sex offenders had to provide a DNA sample. At present, Fast Eddie was only nineteen years old.

"I . . . I . . ." Carolyn stammered, slowly raising her eyes. "I don't remember, Brad. I'll have to check his file."

"Of all people," he said, dropping down in the leather chair behind his paper-strewn desk, "I never thought I'd be having a conversation like this with you, Carolyn. How long has it been?"

"I told you," she said, her voice shaking, "I'm not certain. His probation is due to terminate any day. Eddie never gave me any indication that he was a rapist or pedophile. In the underlying offense, all he did was slide his hand up the dress of the fourteen-year-old who lived next door. Eddie swore she was his girlfriend. He claims the only reason he was prosecuted was due to some kind of vendetta between the two families. The last time I talked to him, he was engaged to get married."

Brad leaned forward, his face frozen into hard lines. "The media's beating our door down. You're one of our best officers. Tell me what I want to hear, Carolyn."

She rubbed her forehead, covering a portion of her face with her hand. He wanted to be reassured that she'd seen Downly that month, that she'd monitored his every move, that there was nothing the agency could have done to prevent him from brutalizing a child. "The truth? Do you really want to know? It's not what you want to hear."

"Of course I want the truth," Brad shouted, standing and removing his jacket, then yanking off his tie. "We have to back up our statements with documentation. I promised we'd get copies of everything in Downly's file to the police within the hour. The address they have for him is no good. How long has it been, Carolyn?" He walked over until they were only a few inches apart. "Christ, we can't play twenty questions while a rapist is on the loose. Tell me where we stand, damn it."

"A long time," she said, nervously rubbing her palms on her skirt. "Nine months . . . maybe as long as a year."

"A year!" Brad exclaimed, his hot breath on her face. "You haven't seen this man in a freaking year?"

"Don't forget," Carolyn told him, "I'm not assigned to field services. I had over forty pre-sentence investigations to complete last month. On top of that, I now have a caseload of over two hundred offenders. To stay on top of everything is humanly impossible. You know that, Brad."

"When I heard it was your case," he said, pacing around the room, "I didn't think there was going to be a problem." He shook his hands to release the tension. "Get everything you have on Downly to the PD. Don't answer your phone, and don't leave the building until we figure out what we're going to tell the press."

Carolyn pushed herself to her feet, then stood with her arms limp at her side. "There's nothing to figure out," she said. "As soon as I hand over Downly's file, they'll know I let the case fall dormant. Even if the brass decides to fire me, I refuse to falsify information."

Brad pointed at his chest, even more agitated than before. "Did I ask you to falsify information? Are you trying to blackmail me?"

Carolyn fell silent, linking eyes with him. They'd been lovers until Brad's promotion six months ago. The affair had been doomed from the onset. He was thirty-nine and had never been married. A decent man in most respects, Brad had a wild streak, probably what made him so irresistible to women. He raced cars in his spare time, liked to hang out and drink with the guys, and his temper was notorious. Carolyn could never understand how he maintained a perfect physique and didn't look a day over thirty. Good genes, she told herself, thinking his lifestyle would eventually catch up to him.

"I don't want a repeat of the Cully case," she told him. "It blew up in our faces, remember?"

The situation with Jerry Cully had been similar, yet far more serious. Cully had been placed on probation for indecent exposure. In most instances, men who exposed themselves were not sexual predators. The nature of their crimes was passive. They tended to be introverted, almost pathetic individuals who weren't known to commit acts of violence. Jerry Cully had been an exception. He'd raped a student the previous year on the same campus where Carolyn attended law school, a few months before Brad had been promoted. His probation officer, Dick Stanton, had been counting the days until his retirement. Unlike Carolyn, who had supervised Eddie Downly diligently for over three years before falling lax, Cully's probation officer had only seen him on one occasion.

When the rape occurred, Stanton had doctored the files so it appeared that he'd been routinely monitoring the man's activities. As it turned out, Cully had been a serial rapist. Dick Stanton had unknowingly provided his probationer with an alibi for one of his crimes. Stanton had come forth with the truth, then turned in his resignation. During the time he and Carolyn had been seeing each other, Brad had confessed that he was the one who'd encouraged Stanton to alter the files. He knew what he'd done was wrong, yet he'd defended his position as protecting not only his fellow probation officer, but the reputation of the entire agency. Carolyn wanted to make sure he wouldn't ask the same thing of her.

"To expedite things," Brad told her, "bring the file and let Rachel copy it and get it to Hank Sawyer at the PD. If there's anything you left out, e-mail it to Hank later. I'll call the boss while you're gone and deliver the bad news. I have another case I want you to handle."

"What do you think?" Carolyn asked, worried that she could lose her job once the truth came out regarding Downly.

Brad Preston reached across his desk for the phone. "Do what I said," he told her, gesturing with his free hand. "The sooner they catch Downly, the quicker things will die down."

At nine-forty-five, Carolyn handed Rachel the thick file on Eddie Downly. Before she returned to Brad's office, she darted into the ladies' room, then burst into tears. Opening her purse, she removed a tissue and dabbed at her eyes. She tried to tell herself that even if she had seen Downly every month for the past year, it wouldn't have prevented him from raping an innocent child. When an offender began to disintegrate, however, telltale signs generally appeared. This wasn't always the case with a sex offender, though. Many times they came across as model citizens. A pedophile was like a crack in the wall, hidden behind a piece of furniture. Regardless, she would have to live with this for the rest of her life, never knowing if she could have somehow stopped it.

Carolyn propped the paper up on the mirror above the sink. An eight-year-old girl, for God's sake. Her daughter, Rebecca, was twelve. Downly had not only raped the child, he'd strangled her. When the girl had fallen unconscious, he'd mistakenly thought she was dead. Yesterday while Carolyn and her children were enjoying a cookout with her mother in Camarillo, Luisa Cortez was in a ditch behind an abandoned building that had once been a Dairy Queen.

Carolyn wadded the newspaper up in a ball and hurled it across the room. Years ago, she'd enjoyed her job. Now she woke up every morning with a knot in her stomach. They had to stop giving her more work than she could handle. Before Brad had taken over the unit, she'd lost it one day. The eleven-year-old victim in the case she'd been investigating had been made to bend over the toilet every morning before school while her stepfather sodomized her. When she fought back, he'd twisted off her nipples with a pair of pliers. The case alone had been horrifying. During the investigation, Carolyn learned that the social services agency had failed to provide the child with psychological counseling. While the stepfather remained in the home pending trial, the girl had been placed in foster care, leaving behind her friends, her school, and even her mother. Her mother continued to reside with the defendant under the belief that he was innocent. During the trial, Cheryl Wright had tried to kill herself.

Carolyn had stormed into her supervisor's office and demanded that the case be reassigned to another officer. She was investigating four other crimes against children and she couldn't handle it. On the verge of a nervous breakdown, she'd thought of going to the stepfather's house and shooting him. Irene Settle, the woman in charge of the unit at the time, had told her that she must finish the case or turn in her resignation. When Carolyn had asked why, the woman had looked her squarely in the eye and told her she was the only one in the unit who was qualified to handle a case of that magnitude.

Carolyn continued to work at her job for the benefit of the victims. In her first year at Ventura College of Law, she attended classes every Monday and Wednesday evening. She was fortunate that her fifteen-year-old son, John, was responsible enough to look after his younger sister. She had enrolled in law school to better herself and increase her income. She was also looking for a way to escape.

At thirty-seven, Carolyn was small in stature, yet possessed a curvaceous and feminine body. Her chestnut hair fell to her shoulders in natural waves, her skin was flawless, and her eyes were the color of molasses. Dressed neatly in a pink cotton shirt and a simple black skirt, she'd draped the matching jacket over a chair in her office so it could dry from the rain. Two identical suits hung in her closet at home, differing only as to color—one navy blue, the other beige. Carolyn varied her wardrobe with six pastel shirts which she ironed every Saturday morning. Now and then she wore a dress, something simple yet tasteful. Her only accessories consisted of a sterling silver cross with a flower in the center given to her by her mother, a Swiss Army watch, and an antique pair of pearl cufflinks that had been in her family for over a hundred years. During the thirteen years she'd been a deputy probation officer, the cuff links had become her trademark.

Carolyn kept her head down as she darted down the hall toward Brad's office. Rachel wasn't at her desk, and the door to his office was standing open. He looked harried, yet not to the extent he had earlier.

"Wilson took it fairly well," Brad told her, referring to the head of the agency. "I just got off the phone with Hank Sawyer at the PD. He was amazed at the amount of work you put in on Downly. You've got all his known associates, local haunts, relatives, employers." He flashed a confident smile, displaying a row of gleaming white teeth. "My bet is Downly will be behind bars before the day is over. Sawyer didn't even mention anything related to the supervision problem. The average term of probation is thirty-six months. We may luck out on this one. The press certainly doesn't know what we do. The idiots don't even know the difference between concurrent and consecutive sentences."

"You mentioned a new case," Carolyn said, concerned that there might be repercussions. Brad Preston was a proverbial optimist. And all his emotions were out in the open. If you made a mistake or pissed him off, he pounced on you like a cougar. On the other hand, if he caught sight of a solution, he instantly moved on to the next problem. Although she'd resented the fact that he'd been promoted over her, she had to admit that Brad had been the better candidate for this stressful position.

"Yeah, the case," he said, handing her a file. "The last thing we need is another parolee, right? The knuckleheads in Sacramento should take the heat for what happened with Downly. As soon as the maximum case levels are reached at the district parole offices, the overflow is dumped in our laps. We work for the county, not the state."

"Why doesn't field services handle the parolees?" Carolyn asked him. "Our job is to write court reports, reports that are mandated by law. That's why the unit is called Court Services, even though no one seems to care."

"Same problem," Brad told her. "Field services can't possibly supervise the number of people we have on active probation." He paused, then a moment later continued. "Okay, here's the deal. After twenty-three years, they paroled the man who killed Charles Harrison's son. This is a famous case. You must have heard about it."

Carolyn's jaw dropped. "Are you referring to the deputy chief of the LAPD?"

"Harrison, yeah," Brad said. "But when his son was killed, he was the chief here in Ventura."

"But why would you want me to handle this case?" Carolyn asked, glancing through the prisoner's release sheet from Chino. "Even though the PD didn't spot the problem with the Downly matter, that doesn't mean it won't come back to bite us."

"You're the bomb, sweetheart," Brad said. "Look over the particulars. I'll get us some coffee." He leapt out of his chair and disappeared through the doorway.

Carolyn looked up to ask him a question before she realized he was no longer in the room. Another one of the man's unique traits was that he moved like a bolt of lightning. Where did all the energy come from? She knew he wasn't on drugs. Brad always said he'd trade his frenetic energy for her ability to concentrate. When Carolyn put her mind to something, a person could drop a brick on her foot and she wouldn't notice.

She stared at the photo of her new parolee. Whereas Brad looked remarkably young for his age, Daniel Metroix appeared ten years older than his forty-one years. His skin was ashen, his dark brown hair was matted and dirty, and his eyes were lined with dark shadows.

When Brad returned and shoved a steaming cup of coffee into her hand, she accepted it eagerly. "You know why I stopped seeing Eddie Downly, don't you?"

"We've already gone through it," Brad said. "I was in your shoes until recently. I know how overworked you guys are. Downly left a ton of evidence at the scene. How do you think they fingered him as the rapist so fast?"

Carolyn closed the Metroix file. "I have to take work home with me every night as it is, and I've never put in a request for overtime."

Brad gave her a chastising look. "Now isn't the time to complain."

"I'm not complaining," she said. "I'm attending law school, in case you've forgotten. The reading alone is killing me. Last night I fell asleep at the kitchen table in my clothes. And I'm not spending enough time with my children." She stopped and sucked in a breath. "You don't assign me thefts and burglaries, Brad. If you want me to do a decent job on the serious cases, you can't expect me to ride herd on a bunch of probationers and parolees. And especially not a case as sensitive as this one. I know you're my supervisor, but shouldn't you rethink this?"

"You're our top investigator," he told her, riffling through his desk drawer and pulling out a bottle of Tylenol. "Never drink tequila on a weeknight." Once he washed the pills down with his coffee, he continued. "What would take another officer several months to complete, you can knock off in a few days. Sometimes I think you know more about the law than half of our judges. When you recommend a fifty-year sentence, it's a done deal. If you told the court a defendant should be taken out and shot, a few of the judges would start shopping for a shotgun."

"Don't be asinine," Carolyn said, her face flushing in embarrassment. "My recommendations are imposed because they're well researched and appropriate. The judges know me, that's all. They know I take my work seriously."

"No," he argued. "That's power."

"Wielding power in the courtroom doesn't pay my bills," she told him. "Why do you think I'm working so hard to get my law degree?"

"Put in for overtime. Are you that much of a martyr?"

"You know what's going on, Brad," Carolyn told him, surprised that he'd make such a statement. "With the budget cutbacks, if we start putting in for overtime, they'll start laying off people. Then we'll have more work than we have now."

"I admit I assign you more difficult cases," he said, bracing his head with his hand. He hadn't taken the time to get a haircut, and with his blond hair almost reaching his eyebrows, his face took on a deceptive look of innocence. "Sure, it's not fair. I don't have a choice. You're one of the few people who understands the complexities of sentencing. Assign one of our other officers a twenty-count case, with multiple victims and dozens of enhancements, and I'll end up doing most of the work myself."

The cases kept coming like bullets, and the only way Carolyn could meet the mandatory deadlines was to start plowing through them as soon as they hit her desk. Officers who procrastinated either did a lousy job or ended up putting in twenty-four-hour days. With her outside commitments, Carolyn couldn't afford to let her work stockpile.

Supervising a parolee was not anywhere as complex as handling a pre-sentence investigation, however. Unless the individual violated, the only obligation was to monitor his activities on a monthly basis. On the other hand, supervision was dangerous. After glancing through the file, Carolyn knew Brad was placing her in a precarious position, the last place she needed to be at the moment. "Everyone and his dog are going to be looking over my shoulder with Metroix."

"Good observation," Preston said sarcastically, tapping his pen against his teeth. "Metroix killed a kid, Carolyn. The kid's father is a high-ranking law enforcement official. He falls into a sewer and fifty cops will nail down the lid."

"I'm aware the victim was Charles Harrison's son. I even dated Liam Armstrong when I was in high school."

"Who's Liam Armstrong?"

"One of the two boys who survived," Carolyn told him, bringing forth images of the egotistical football player who'd tried to force her to have sex with him on their second date.

"Small town," Preston said, gulping down another swig of his coffee. "I'm glad I didn't grow up in this place. Bring me up to snuff on your other work."

Ventura was a unique city, Carolyn thought. The community had sprung up around the San Buenaventura Mission, and in many ways still maintained a Spanish flavor. Houses with boat slips were now crammed along the ocean side of the 101 Freeway, and the real estate in the foothills offered fantastic views. An hour north was Santa Barbara—home to millionaires, polo fields, and pristine beaches. The citizens of Ventura, however, were mostly hardworking, middle-class people.

"Well," Brad said, "are you going to tell me or do I have to beat it out of you?"

Carolyn was tempted to lie, tell him that if he persisted in assigning her Metroix, the same thing would happen that had occurred with Downly. There were other competent officers in the agency. No matter how heavy the workload, though, someone had to do it. Knowing it was Carolyn gave Brad a sense of security. After the Downly incident, she would have expected him to back off. Obviously, that wasn't the case, and it wasn't how the man operated. He liked to live life on the edge. Doing things the easy way, he'd once told her, was boring.

"I finished dictating the Dearborn shooting yesterday,"

Carolyn answered. "I recommended the aggravated term as we discussed. The Perkins robbery has already been filed. As for the Sandoval shooting, I've summarized the facts of the crime. I interviewed the defendant at the jail last week. I'm seeing the victim, Lois Mason, this afternoon. Since Sandoval has two priors for assault with a deadly weapon and the DA filed under three strikes, he's going down for the count."

"Great," Preston said, one side of his mouth curling into a smile. "That means one less asshole on the street. I can't believe Sandoval shot an old lady to steal her purse."

"She fought back," Carolyn reminded him. "I have a few other minor things on the burner, and that's it." Being efficient had its drawbacks. She ended up doing twice as much work as many of her fellow officers. "I guess you can slap me with anything that comes in, Brad. You will anyway."

"I don't have a choice," he said, relieved that he'd heard at least some good news for the day. He had twelve new cases that had to be assigned, and no officers available to handle them. At least four of the twelve would end up with Carolyn Sullivan's name on them. Now all he had to do was find someone to investigate the remaining eight.

"Keep me posted on Downly," Carolyn told him, standing to leave.

"Everything's going to be fine, baby," Brad tossed out. He began thumbing through a thick stack of phone messages from the week before. He stopped and looked up. "The file said Metroix tried to get himself transferred to the prison hospital by claiming he was a paranoid schizophrenic. Every psycho I've ever run across knocks himself out trying to convince you he's sane. A man who's been in prison this long is dangerous. Watch your back." He paused and then added, "And start carrying your damn gun."

"I'll start carrying my gun when you stop calling me baby and sweetheart," Carolyn snapped back. "You're my supervisor now. Whatever happened between us is history."

"Cut me some slack," he said, placing his hands behind his neck. "We may not be seeing each other anymore. That doesn't mean I don't care about you. I can't sleep with someone I supervise."

"I hear you've been putting the make on Amy McFarland," she told him. "Doesn't the same rule apply to her that applied to me? I suggest you clean up your act before you get hit with a sexual harassment suit."

Carolyn had worked with Brad Preston since the day she'd been hired. Before making the mistake of sleeping with him, she'd wondered why he had never married. After their affair had ended, she'd noted a specific pattern. Preston liked the thrill of the chase. Once he got the girl in bed, it was only a matter of time before he lost interest. Amy McFarland had been on the job for less than three months. Carolyn didn't trust her.

"I'm not chasing after Amy McFarland. Amy and I kid around now and then. What's the big deal? You used to be fun, Carolyn. Are you jealous because I got promoted? I've got five years' seniority on you. I should be running this agency. Instead, I'm not much more than a glorified clerk. I'd change places with you in a minute if it wasn't for the money."

"That's baloney, Brad," Carolyn said, her face set in defiance. "With all the real estate you own, you could walk out the door right now and live better than the average person. Your father was a wealthy man."

"Cheap shot," he told her. "Nothing says we can't have lunch together. Stop by around noon." She was about to walk off when he raised an arm to stop her. "Oh, I scheduled Metroix for two. We need to get a fix on this guy right away. Harrison's up there in years. That doesn't mean he isn't a tough son of a bitch. We screw up on this one, and both our careers will go down the toilet."

"Forget lunch," Carolyn said, glaring at him over her

shoulder as she was about to step through the doorway. "I don't have time for lunch. I have a maniac for a boss."

Brad tilted his pencil toward her. "You're feisty. I like that in a woman. Maybe I'll ask to be reassigned and we can pick up where we left off."

"Not on your life," Carolyn said, pulling his door closed behind her.

Chapter 2

Back in the cubicle that served as her office, Carolyn's stomach began gurgling with acid. She glanced at her watch and saw that it was already past one o'clock. She'd consumed six cups of coffee and hadn't eaten since the night before.

Opening the bottom drawer of her desk, she reached for her emergency rations—a stash of protein bars, along with a six-pack of bottled water. She only liked the protein bars that contained peanut butter, and they were hard to find. Her phone rang and she answered it, dropping the Balance bar on her desk. She heard the distinctive voice of her thirty-one-year-old brother.

"I'm having some people over tonight," Neil said. "Nothing fancy. Some wine and cheese. We're trying to decide what paintings we should put in the show next week. I'd like your opinion."

"You know I have school on Monday nights," Carolyn told him. "Why weren't you at Mother's yesterday? You didn't even call. I tried your cell. It was busy."

"I'm sorry," Neil told her. "It completely slipped my mind. Was Mom upset?"

"Not really," Carolyn told him. "You're the golden boy, the contemporary Michelangelo. The only way you could have risen higher in Mom's eyes was to become a priest."

"God forbid," he said, laughing. "I'll call her now and try to make amends. Are you all right? You don't sound good."

The previous year, the county had issued everyone headsets. Carolyn pulled hers out and put it on so she could eat while they talked. "Did you read this morning's paper? The man who raped the eight-year-old girl was my probationer."

"Jesus," Neil said, "how can you work with these bastards?"

"Working with them isn't the problem; it's controlling them."

"Don't worry, sis," he said. "You'll be a lawyer before you know it. Another five years and you can be a judge. Then you can make all the decisions. You know that client of mine, Buddy Chambers, the big divorce lawyer? I was talking to him the other day. He knows all about you. He thinks you'd make a great judge."

"I was joking when I said I wanted to be a judge," Carolyn told him, embarrassed. "Please don't talk about me to your friends. I'll be lucky if I pass the bar exam."

She depressed the off button on her headset. They were so close that they both knew when a conversation was over. To save time, they seldom said good-bye. People thought it was strange. Their father had been dead for five years. Since his death, the family had developed a heightened awareness of one another. When either Carolyn, her mother, or her brother had some type of problem, one of the three would invariably call. Several of their friends thought they communicated over the Internet, using Instant Messenger or some other similar computer program. No, she told them. They didn't use the Internet and they weren't psychic. Their ability to sense one another's needs arose from the oldest and most powerful force in the universe—love.

Neil's world was very different from Carolyn's. He might not be another Michelangelo, as her mother boasted to her lady friends, but he was an extremely talented artist. His career was finally taking off, and Carolyn was happy for him.

Yanking the headset off and returning her attention to Daniel Metroix, Carolyn read through the file again. He'd attacked three teenage boys outside of a bowling alley. Two of the boys had incurred minor injuries. Metroix had allegedly caused Tim Harrison's death by intentionally pushing him in front of an oncoming car. Metroix had been unarmed at the time, and there were no eyewitnesses outside of the victims. The driver of the car hadn't seen anything until the moment of impact. Metroix had been tried and convicted of second degree murder.

A crime of this nature, basically a fistfight among four young men in the same age bracket, Carolyn thought, should have been pleaded as involuntary manslaughter. The boy's death had more than likely been an accident. What made it a crime, regardless of who was responsible, was that the death had occurred during the commission of a felonious assault. The DA, however, was charged with determining what type of offense would be filed against the perpetrator. The two surviving boys had sworn under oath that Metroix assaulted them and intentionally shoved the victim into the path of the car.

One of the things Carolyn couldn't understand was why the three boys hadn't overpowered Metroix. Three to one was pretty good odds, and these particular boys had been football players. She reached inside an envelope affixed to the back of the file and brought forth a stack of mug shots taken the night of the crime. Metroix's face had been a mass of bloody pulp, the look out of his eyes dull and disoriented. The police reports indicated the only injuries the surviving boys had suffered during the fight were a few minor bruises.

"Your two o'clock appointment is here," Kathy Stein said over the intercom. "Where do you want him?"

"Oh," Carolyn said, "put him in room four. His name is Daniel Metroix, right?"

"Yeah," the woman said gruffly, her voice deeper than most men's. "That's what he said. Want me to check his ID?"

"No, no," Carolyn said. "That won't be necessary."

She waited a few moments, giving the receptionist time to walk Metroix to the interview room. The Court Services Division of the Ventura County Corrections Services Agency encompassed the entire third floor of the building, and was located directly across from the courthouse. The jail was under the same roof, but there was no entrance inside the main building. Prisoners, however, could easily be moved from the jail to the courthouse via an underground tunnel.

The partitioned offices where the probation officers worked overlooked the parking lot and courtyard. On the opposite side of the floor were rows of small rooms. Each room contained a table and four chairs as well as a phone that the officers used for on-line dictation to the word processing pool. The rooms were also used to conduct interviews. In most instances, the individuals interviewed were not on probation or parole. They were convicted offenders released on bail pending sentencing, victims, or other persons related to the specific crime the officer had been assigned to investigate. If the defendant had been denied bail, the probation officer would interview the subject inside the jail. Having the jail located in the same complex saved time for everyone involved in the criminal process.

The officers assigned to court services generally possessed different skills than the officers who supervised offenders. Of vital importance was the ability to interpret complex laws related to sentencing, as Brad Preston had emphasized. The laws in the state of California were becoming increasingly more convoluted. An officer assigned to court services must be proficient at writing. On serious cases involving multiple offenses and victims, reports averaged somewhere between twenty and fifty pages.

The Field Services Division, whose primary duty was to supervise offenders, had satellite offices scattered throughout the county. The officers in field services had enormous caseloads, to the point where they were clearly unmanageable. Failing to properly investigate a case could cause serious problems, yet in supervision, an oversight might leave an officer responsible for the death of a child, a battered spouse, or any number of tragic situations like the one that had occurred with Eddie Downly. Everyone in the agency was aware of the problem—there were simply not enough officers to supervise the constant influx of offenders.

The situation in state parole was even worse as parole officers supervised individuals who had been released from prison, and the majority of these individuals had committed acts of violence.

Carolyn thrust open the door to the interview room where Daniel Metroix was waiting. Once she was inside, she pulled the door shut behind her, her right hand still clasping the doorknob. Photographs didn't always offer a good representation of a person's appearance. The man seated at the small round table was wearing a light blue denim shirt, jeans, and a black leather belt. His feet were clad in what appeared to be new tennis shoes. His light brown hair was neatly cut. He'd obviously lifted weights while in prison, as she could see sinewy muscles beneath the fabric of his shirt. A far cry from the frail young man in the arrest photos, Carolyn thought. The look out of his eyes was flat and cold, then she noticed a spark of excitement.

"How have you been?" he said, standing and extending his hand.

Carolyn had no idea what he was talking about. Did she know this man? Although they weren't that far apart in age, his records stated that he'd attended Tremont High, not Ventura High, the school she'd attended.

Daniel dropped his hand to his side, obviously disappointed. "I'm sorry," he said after some time. "We used to live in the same apartment building. It's been so long, I guess you don't remember me."

"No," she said, curious now. "Where did you live?"

"The subsidized building on Maple Street," he told her. "I

think it was called the Carlton West. Pretty fancy name for such a lousy building." He dropped his eyes. "Anyway, that's what my mom used to say. You lived a few doors down from us. You always wanted me to play with you."

"You're mistaken," Carolyn said curtly. "I never lived in that building."

She pulled out a chair and sat down at the table, gesturing for Metroix to do the same. She had kept her maiden name when she'd married. Brad was right about Ventura being a small town, but something about Metroix set her hair on end. The number of people she'd pushed along the road to prison was enormous. Metroix couldn't hold a personal grudge against her, though, as she was in high school when he'd been convicted. Her picture was occasionally in the paper. Perhaps she'd investigated one of his former cell mates. Had he called one of his prison buddies and told him the name of his new parole officer? Could his talk about knowing her have been a way to cause her to let her guard down? With the Internet, you could find out information about anyone. She had lied when she said her family had never lived in the Carlton West apartments. But Metroix couldn't have remembered her. She'd only been five years old at the time.

Carolyn saw him staring at her left hand. She'd been divorced for seven years now.

"What did he do?"

"Who?"

"Your husband," Daniel said. "What did he do to make you stop loving him? You used to be married, didn't you?"

"I don't discuss my personal life at work," Carolyn said, knowing she needed to establish a position of authority at once. She placed his file on the table and opened it, removing a piece of paper listing the terms and conditions of his parole. "You've been placed on parole for a period of thirty-six months," she said. "As a condition of your parole, you are to report to this office on a monthly basis. Do you understand?"

Daniel nodded, tilting his chair back on its hind legs.

"You are to submit to home visits with or without advance notice."

"What if I don't have a home?"

"Where are you living?"

"I just got into town," he told her.

"But you were released two weeks ago."

"I wanted to do some sight-seeing," Daniel said. "I spent some time in L.A. My release papers said I didn't have to report here until the end of the month. All I had to do was call and set up an appointment. When I called, a lady told me to come in this afternoon."

Great, Carolyn thought, reminding herself that this was a parolee. After spending most of their life inside an institution, some of them committed suicide. "You can't live on the street. If you don't have a place to stay or necessary funds, you'll have to stay in the shelter."

Daniel reached into his pocket and pulled out a crumpled piece of paper. "A guy on the bus gave me the address of a motel. As soon as I leave here, I'll get a room. It's called the Seagull, over on Seaward Avenue. What do you think? Is it worth checking out?"

"I'm not a travel agent. Call and let me know if this is where you'll be staying. I'll need to check your living situation." Carolyn pulled out her Palm Pilot. She had a paper to turn in tonight at law school, and she doubted if she'd have time to complete it. She had planned on working on it during her lunch break. "We'll set the appointment for five-thirty tomorrow evening." That way, she thought, she could stop by on her way home from work. And with daylight saving time, it would be light out.

"Fine," Daniel said with the disinterest of a man who was used to having people order him around.

Leaving her Palm Pilot on the table, she read off another condition of his probation. "You have both alcohol and drug terms."

"What does that mean?"

"It means you're not allowed to frequent bars or any establishments where alcohol is served."

"I don't drink."

"Then you won't have a problem," Carolyn said. "You also have to consent to drug testing whenever I feel it's necessary."

"You mean illegal drugs?" Daniel asked, placing his chair upright. "I'm taking medication for my illness."

"What type of illness?" she asked. Brad had mentioned something about him feigning mental illness while at Chino, although she hadn't found any mention of it in his paperwork. Of course, she'd only had a few hours to review his case.

"Schizophrenia," he answered. "I have the prescription, if you want to see it. It's a new drug. I give myself an injection once a month. I mean now that I'm out. At the prison, they gave me the shots in the infirmary."

"When were you first diagnosed?"

"My junior year in high school," Daniel answered, his cocky, almost menacing demeanor replaced by a look of sadness. "I spent three months at Camarillo State Hospital. I'd rather go back to prison than that hellhole."

"I need to see your prescription." Carolyn stuck out her hand, waiting until he fished out another crumpled piece of paper. "Stay here," she said, standing. "I have to make a copy for the file."

After using the copy machine a few doors down, she quickly returned to the interview room and handed him back his prescription. She didn't recognize the drug—decanoic acid phenothiazine—but she wasn't that familiar with psychotropic medications. She jotted down the letters DAP, reminding herself to check out the drug on the Internet. A new treatment for schizophrenia was interesting.

The fact that the medication was administered in a syringe, though, presented a problem. She'd run it by Brad before she decided how to proceed. Glancing at his terms and conditions, she was surprised that he hadn't been ordered to undergo regular psychiatric treatment. He had drug terms, yet no psych terms. They saw this type of idiotic mistake every day. She'd petition the court to have the term added.

Carolyn reached over and grabbed his left forearm. Daniel jerked away, looking as if he were about to slug her. "Roll up your sleeves."

"Why?"

"I have to check for tracks."

She examined both arms and didn't find anything. Even in prison, narcotics were readily available. Some of the things criminals came up with were mind-boggling. Pretending he needed treatment with an injectable drug would be the perfect way to cover up a heroin or methamphetamine addiction. He'd have to bring his medication in when he came for his monthly appointments. After she verified it wasn't narcotics in the syringe, he would then have to administer the drug in her presence. Not finding tracks on his arms didn't mean he wasn't an addict. She'd known men who would shoot the stuff in their penis. "You can pull your sleeves down now," she told him, thinking she might have stumbled across a way to avoid supervising him. If he required a full body search every month, he'd have to be reassigned to a male officer.

"Let's complete the formalities," Carolyn continued. "You must not associate with any known felons. You must secure gainful employment. If you commit any type of crime whatsoever, your parole will be automatically violated."

She shoved the document across the table for him to sign. "This is standard procedure, Daniel. If you fail to comply with the conditions set forth, you'll be charged with violation of parole and returned to prison. Since your sentence was twelve years to life, I don't think you want that to happen. Any questions?"

"Yes," he said, signing the paper without reading it.

Carolyn ignored him and picked up her Palm Pilot again,

quickly scheduling appointments for the next four months. She then jotted the dates and times down on one of her business cards. "If an emergency comes up and you have to reschedule an appointment, you must call me as soon as possible. Are we clear?"

"Yes," Daniel said. "About the employment . . ."

She tried not to look into his eyes. Something in them frightened her. Besides, in supervision cases, it was better to remain impersonal. When preparing pre-sentence reports on rapists, murderers, or other violent offenders, she tried to convince them she was their best friend. She even wore short skirts and high heels, hoping to walk away with admissions that could tack another twenty years on to their sentence. "Have you already lined up a job?"

"I have almost seventy thousand dollars," he told her, his confidence returning. "I don't need to work right now."

Carolyn blinked several times. Fresh out of prison and the guy had more money in the bank than she did. She felt like filing a violation against him for spite. "Where did you come up with that kind of money?"

"I inherited it," Daniel said, smiling. "My grandmother left me ten thousand dollars. She passed away right after I was shipped off to the joint. A lawyer put it in a trust fund for me. Now I have seventy grand. Pretty sweet, huh?"

Carolyn gave him a phony smile, then fell serious again. "I'll need to know the name of this attorney. I have to verify that you came across these funds legitimately."

"No problem," Daniel said, scratching the side of his face. "I don't have his phone number with me. He's listed in the Ventura phone book. His name is Leonard Fletcher."

"You have to work," she said, staring at a spot over his head. "Holding down a job is one of the conditions of your release in the community. Weren't you listening when I read off the terms and conditions of your parole?"

"I guess not," Daniel said, shrugging. "I've never worked. I was only seventeen when they arrested me. I don't really have any skills. I got my GED while I was in prison. Other than that, most of what I know I learned on my own. I'm pretty good at physics and math. I can draw, but mostly conceptual stuff for machines and devices. What kind of job do I have to get?"

"Anything," Carolyn explained, fiddling with the cuff link on her left wrist. Did he really say he was good at physics or was she hearing things? "You can pump gas, wait tables, sweep floors."

The reality of his situation was beginning to sink in. Daniel's voice elevated. "Why do I have to work if I don't need the money?"

"Because maintaining employment is one of the conditions of your release," Carolyn told him. "If they inserted a clause that said you had to sit on top of a pole for the next three years, you'd either sit on a pole or get shipped back to prison. I'm not the person who made these rules. I'm only charged with enforcing them."

"Then I guess I'll get a job," he said. "How long do I have?"

"Thirty days," she said. "You should be gainfully employed by the time I see you next month. I don't like the idea of your living in a motel, no matter how much money you have. In addition to getting a job, I'll expect you to find a suitable place to live by your next appointment."

He looked perplexed. "Why can't I live in a motel? Was that in those conditions you read me?"

"No," Carolyn said. "It doesn't have to be. Certain things fall into the area of judgment—my judgment. I suggest you look for an apartment. If you live in a hotel, your money will run out and you'll end up on the street." She started gathering her paperwork to leave. The interview with the victim on the Sandoval rape case was scheduled for four, and Carolyn had agreed to drive to the woman's house as a courtesy. She glanced at her watch and saw that it was almost three. "When you call in later today, leave the phone number of the motel, as well as your room number. As soon as you secure a permanent address, you need to notify me. The same holds true as to your employment. I have to know where you are and what you're doing at all times. You can't quit your job, move, or leave town without my permission."

"Being on parole is almost the same as being in prison," he said, cracking his knuckles. "Prison might even be better. At least they feed you and give you a place to stay. I even had my own lab so I could work."

Carolyn scribbled Seagull Motel in his file. If he didn't report in, she would know where to start searching. She looked up when she heard him say something about a lab. "What did you mean, you had your own lab?"

"Oh," Daniel told her, "the warden let me convert a storage room into a makeshift lab."

Sure, Carolyn thought. The man was a raving lunatic. Now he'd spent the past twenty-three years doing physics in his own lab. No prison she'd ever heard of would set an inmate loose in a lab.

"I'll see you tomorrow night at five-thirty. Don't forget to leave word where you're staying." Carolyn wanted to call the hospital and check on Luisa Cortez's condition. She wondered what terrible crimes Daniel Metroix might be capable of committing. Fast Eddie had been a wake-up call. She would do everything in her power to keep it from happening again. If one of her people slipped so much as an inch, she'd have a warrant issued for his arrest.

Daniel fixed her with an icy gaze. "As long as I'm on parole, you basically own me. Isn't that what this is all about?"

"You got it," Carolyn told him. "Sweet, huh? I'd rather own a puppy. Stay out of trouble for the next three years and you'll be home free."

Chapter 3

A handsome young man with long blond hair dropped down on one knee beside Carolyn's desk before the start of her Criminal Law and Procedure class Monday evening.

"A friend of mine is having a party Saturday night," David Reynolds said, grinning flirtatiously. "Why don't you come along? If the party's a dud, we can split and go to my place."

Carolyn turned around to make certain no one was listening. She made it a habit to sit in the front row, believing she learned more when she maintained eye contact with the professor. She wasn't a note taker. Listening served her better. David sat directly across from her. Most of the class went for the seats in the back, making it easier for them to finish assignments or find answers to questions on their computers. She asked, "How old are you?"

"Thirty-one," David said, brushing a strand of hair out of his face. "What difference does it make? Age is only a number."

"We had this same discussion last week," Carolyn told him. "You only look a few years older than my son. If you're thirty-one, I'm twelve."

"You're making a mistake," he whispered, seeing the professor entering the room. "I know how to have fun."

David had transferred in from UCLA Law for the spring quarter. Ventura College of Law was basically a cram school, the curriculum geared toward passing the bar. Since UCLA was a far more prestigious university, she assumed he'd made the move out of financial necessity. Either that, or he'd done more partying than studying. The school was full of intelligent, good-looking young women. Carolyn had to admit she was flattered by his advances. She'd never expected her relationship with Brad to become permanent. He'd been the first man she'd slept with since her divorce. A flush spread across her face. The sex had been incredible.

The professor, Arline Shoeffel, was also the presiding judge of Ventura County. At forty-six, she was a tall, willowy redhead, her fair skin sprinkled with freckles. Her hair was cropped close to her head, and she wore tortoiseshell glasses. Her manner of dress suggested a person who had no concept whatsoever of fashion, and no desire to do anything other than to cover her body. She was wearing a flower print dress that Carolyn suspected she'd had for twenty years.

"Good evening," Shoeffel said, leaning back against a podium in the front of the class. "Leave your papers on my desk during the eight o'clock break. Tonight we're going to briefly review the differences between criminal and civil law. Mr. Reynolds," she said, "can a crime be defined or created by the court?"

"Sure," David said, laughing as he glanced across the room at Carolyn.

"Incorrect," the professor told him, giving him a stern look. She scanned the room, then rested her eyes on Carolyn. "Ms. Sullivan. . . ."

"Crimes can't be created or defined by the courts. This must be accomplished in the state legislature. It's then up to the courts to decide on a case-by-case basis whether a crime has been committed by an accused defendant." Carolyn paused, collecting her thoughts before continuing. "Interpretation of the statutory criminal law resides with the court system in each of the states."

"Excellent," Shoeffel said, turning to the blackboard to

write down their next assignment before she continued her lecture.

When the class ended at nine, Carolyn lingered behind to finish her paper on her laptop. She'd worked on it during the break and had only a paragraph or two left. She couldn't print it out, so she saved it on a disk and wrote her name across the front with a black marker. Placing her computer inside her backpack, she left the disk on Judge Shoeffel's desk, hoping she might think she had accidentally missed it when she'd picked up the other students' papers.

Heading to her car in the parking lot, Carolyn spotted Arline Shoeffel standing in front of a silver Acura, anxiously checking her watch. The rain had stopped before she'd left the courthouse. The evening was chilly and damp, though. She continued walking, then made her way between the cars to speak to the professor.

"I never know whether to call you professor or judge," Carolyn said timidly. "This isn't the safest place for a woman alone. Are you waiting for someone?"

"My car won't start," Arline Shoeffel told her. Wearing a tan trench coat, she was tapping her umbrella on the asphalt. "I called Triple A almost thirty minutes ago."

"Do you think it's the battery, Judge Shoeffel? I could try to jump it for you. I carry jumper cables in my trunk."

"Please, call me Arline," the woman said. "I appreciate your offer. I'm sure they'll show up any moment."

"I've waited over an hour before," Carolyn told her. "Why don't you let me take a look? A girl was raped in almost this same exact spot last year."

"Oh, yes," the judge answered, "Maggie McDonald. I recall her being attacked in the parking lot. I wasn't aware it was in this particular section." She scanned the lot. "The school needs to put in more lights. It's far too dark. This should have been taken care of last year. I'll call the board of regents tomorrow and have a word with them."

"Can I try to get it started?" Carolyn asked, slipping her

backpack off her shoulders as she reached for the door to the Acura.

"Certainly," Judge Shoeffel said, handing her the keys. "I intended to wait in the car with the doors locked. I was afraid the tow truck driver wouldn't see me. I guess I don't set a very good example for a woman in my position."

Carolyn turned the key in the ignition. All she heard was a clicking sound. She tried again. This time the engine sputtered, then died. Depressing the gas pedal several times, she waited a while, then gave it another shot. The engine finally engaged.

The judge was peering in through the window. "Let's make sure it doesn't die before you take off," Carolyn told her. "I think your starter needs to be replaced. Either that or the fuel pump. Wait about five minutes before you cancel your road service, then I'll follow you home."

"I really hate to inconvenience you this way."

Carolyn gave her a warm smile. "I left a disk with my paper on it on your desk. I stayed late to complete it. I'm a single parent. Between my children and the job, getting my law degree is probably more fantasy than reality."

"Say no more," Arline said, holding up a palm. "If you hadn't stopped to help me, I might have been assaulted. Did you hear about the young girl who was raped this past weekend?"

"Yes," Carolyn said, reaching inside the car to retrieve her backpack. "They believe the man who did it was one of my probationers."

"Good Lord," Arline said, a look of shock on her face. "No wonder you didn't have time to finish your work. At least you can relax now that the police have apprehended him."

"When?" Carolyn asked, excited. "Are you certain?"

"I heard a report on the radio a few minutes before class this evening. His name was Edward Downly. Is that the name of your probationer?"

"Yes." Carolyn was grateful that she could go to bed with

the knowledge that Fast Eddie wasn't roaming the streets looking for another victim. She wondered why Brad or someone at the PD hadn't notified her. Maybe the judge was mistaken and they'd only released Downly's identity. Pulling out her cell phone, she checked her messages and heard Brad's voice. "Told you they'd get him," he said. "The PD busted Downly at that barbecue joint on the corner of Clairmont and Owens that you listed as one of his favorite hangouts."

"Thank God," Carolyn told the judge, slipping the phone back into her purse. "It's hard when one of the people you're responsible for does something this despicable."

Arline placed her hand on Carolyn's shoulder. "How's the girl?"

"The doctors think she'll make a full recovery," she answered, the two women connecting on a more intimate level. "Physically, anyway. Because he strangled her, they were worried about brain damage. She'll never feel safe again, that's for sure. I had the guy. I didn't see it." She touched her finger to her left eye, wiping away a tear. "I'm sorry. I didn't mean to unload on you. You carry fifty times more responsibility than I do."

"If only we could find a way to prevent these dreadful crimes from happening," Arline told her, behind the wheel of her car now. "One day, instead of streetlights on every corner, there'll be surveillance cameras."

Carolyn was still thinking about Eddie Downly. She finally responded to the judge's statement. "Is that where you think we're heading? I know a few European cities have tried it with considerable success."

"I don't know of anything else that will work," Arline told her. "The death penalty isn't that effective, at least not as a deterrent. Individuals who commit acts of violence seldom consider the consequences. When people realize their every move is being monitored, crime rates rapidly diminish."

It was after ten and Carolyn needed to get home. Her

daughter was generally asleep by now, but she could spend some time with her son. "Where do you live?"

"Skyline Estates," Arline told her. "You're going to follow me, right? All you have to do is get me to the gate. From there, I should be fine."

"I'll get my car," Carolyn told her. "I drive a white Infiniti."

"I'd like to buy you dinner," Arline said. "Maybe one night after class. I usually have conferences during the lunch recesses."

"Don't worry about it," she answered as she walked off.

"Wait, Carolyn," Arline yelled out the window. "You're doing very well in my class. And I'm not saying this because of tonight. You'll make an excellent attorney."

"Thanks," she said, waving as she jogged toward her car. It was nice to know that a day that had started disastrously was ending on a positive note. She couldn't wait to recommend a prison term for Fast Eddie. Already, she was stacking the counts in her head. What she couldn't accomplish by law, the prisoners themselves would handle. Not even hardened criminals could tolerate a man who raped a child, and their punishment would be far more fitting than anything the court could administer. Downly would be lucky if he survived.

"Get used to bending over, Eddie," Carolyn said, depressing the button on the alarm and climbing into her Infiniti. At nineteen, Fast Eddie was a slender young man. His skin was smooth and his features were slightly on the feminine side. The line would be a mile long. The inmates would love him. First, however, they would beat him and sodomize him.

The two-story house was located in the North Hollywood section of Los Angeles. The driver parked his black Jeep Cherokee at the curb, making certain to engage the emergency brake so the vehicle wouldn't roll down the hill. The two passengers got out of the car and made their way up a stone walkway to the front of the house. The taller one, a dark-haired man in his late forties with a neatly trimmed beard and mustache, was smacked in the head by a tree branch. "This place is a jungle, Pete," Boyd Chandler said in annoyance, snapping the thick branch in half as if it were a twig. Chandler was dressed in a blue knit shirt and dark slacks. "You'd think the chief would at least have the trees trimmed."

"He's drunk out of his mind half the time," Pete Cordova told him. A short, olive-skinned man, Cordova had graying hair and was wearing jeans and a black sweatshirt. "He probably can't even see the damn trees."

"So he dips into the sauce too much," Boyd tossed back. "He's still the deputy chief of the LAPD."

They stepped onto the porch and Pete rang the doorbell while Boyd removed a pack of chewing gum from his pocket and popped a piece in his mouth. "I'd die for a cigarette right now."

"I don't remember," Pete said. "How long has it been since you quit?"

"Three years."

"That long, and you want to smoke?"

"Yeah," Boyd told him, "some urges never go away. Know what I mean?"

Pete laughed.

A pretty Hispanic housekeeper answered the door, lowering her eyes as she gestured for the men to enter. "You can go into the study," she said. "Would you like coffee, water, a cold soda?"

"Bring us a couple of beers, sweetie." Boyd's eyes swept over her body, coming to rest on her ample breasts. She was dressed in a white cotton dress, and he could see her nipples through the flimsy fabric.

"I'm sorry," the woman explained. "Chief Harrison's doctor had me remove all alcoholic beverages from the house."

The two men exchanged glances. "Things change," Boyd whispered. "If he's sober, we're gonna be in even more hot water." He watched the woman's hips sway as she walked into the other room. "Think the chief is doing her? Mighty fine body, don't you think?"

"Nah," Pete said. "That woman's a lady, man. What would she want with a burned-out drunk like Harrison?"

They entered a dimly lit room. A fifty-eight-year-old male was slouched in a brown leather recliner, his legs splayed out in front of him. He peered out at the men through watery hazel eyes hidden behind thick glasses. He was dressed in pajamas and a terry-cloth bathrobe, and his feet were encased in fur-lined slippers. A stack of newspapers was tossed on the floor beside him, and the end table was cluttered with prescription pill bottles.

"Sit," Charles Harrison said, glancing toward the sofa. He fixed the two men with an icy stare. Finally he spoke, his words low and measured. "I trusted you to take care of things. Metroix was never supposed to see daylight."

Boyd cleared his throat, almost swallowing his chewing gum. Plucking it out of his mouth, he deposited it in an ashtray. "We got to most of the parole board, Chief," he told him. "The problem was they appointed three new people this year."

"Did you talk to them?"

"We tried," Pete interjected, finding the man in front of him more pathetic than menacing. He remembered Charles Monroe Harrison in his prime—good-looking, educated, articulate, a shining star in the world of law enforcement. Then his entire life had crumbled. His seventeen-year-old son had been murdered. His wife, Madeline, had been hospitalized for years with some type of peculiar illness. He believed they called it chronic fatigue syndrome. These days, Pete thought, people had a fancy name for everything. The wife had cracked up, plain and simple. Harrison's career had advanced but the man had drowned his sorrows in the bottle. From the way he looked tonight, Pete was certain the booze was going to kill him.

"We did everything we could, Chief," he said. "We wined and dined them . . . told them how dangerous Metroix was, that his psychological profile indicated a high probability that he'd kill again if released. We even showed them Tim's picture in his football uniform." He stopped speaking, seeing the deputy chief's chest expand and contract with emotion. "Things were looking pretty good until we met with this woman, one of the new people on the board. The first thing she asked was to see our credentials. As soon as we admitted we were no longer officially employed by the police department, she slammed the door in our faces."

"Yeah," Boyd added, his right shoulder twitching with nervous energy. "I called her up later and convinced her to talk to us again. This time we leaned on her. Her husband chased us off the property with a shotgun."

Charles Harrison's eyes flashed with rage. "I told you fools that those kind of tactics would only work against us. What did you do? Tell her you were going to break her legs?"

"Not exactly," Boyd told him, making a waving motion with his hand. "She's got a son who's a senior in high school. So I follow him one day, see, catch him smoking pot with some of his friends. I'd already checked out his school records. The little snot had won a scholarship to one of those fancy schools back east. Harvard, I think."

"Princeton," Pete said, a look of envy on his face. He imagined what it would be like to start his life over. The day he'd been sworn in as a police officer had been one of the proudest moments in his life. Several members of his family had gone into law enforcement as well, quickly moving up through the ranks. A Hispanic cop carried a good deal of status. All Pete had was a high school diploma. Unless a person became a security officer, ten years as a cop didn't account for anything, and his situation was far worse than most. Pete and Boyd were convicted felons.

"All I did was tell the kid's mother that the university might have some pretty strict rules regarding the use of narcotics," Boyd explained. "You know, that her boy could lose his scholarship."

"Metroix had already served a longer sentence than most people convicted of the same offense," Pete added, fidgeting in his seat. "Not only that, the guy became buddies with the warden. His report listed Metroix as a model prisoner."

The older man's face froze into hard lines. "That bastard killed my son. And you two morons have the balls to sit in my house and tell me he was a model prisoner. Get out of my sight," he shouted, a trickle of saliva running down the side of this mouth. "You disgust me. You were both worthless when you wore a badge and you're worthless now."

Pete coughed, glancing over at Boyd as he tried to decide what they should do next. They'd tangled with a cranked up burglar one night and Boyd had beaten the man so severely, he'd suffered permanent brain damage. Pete had altered his report to cover his partner, unaware that there were several witnesses to the incident, one of them a reporter for the local newspaper. During the majority of the beating, the prisoner had been in handcuffs. Both officers had been convicted and sentenced to three months in the county jail. The day they were released, Chief Harrison had been waiting outside in his car with a suitcase containing twenty thousand in cash. Somehow, every year, the chief had come up with another twenty grand to make certain Daniel Metroix remained in prison.

Over the years, the two former officers had moved into the shadows, rubbing shoulders with organized crime and narcotics traffickers. Pete and Boyd didn't steal or deal; however, they served as extra muscle with a few remaining contacts inside law enforcement. The money Harrison paid them was peanuts. They had continued to work for him out of respect.

"Forget it," Harrison said, his voice trailing off. A shaky hand reached for a bottle off the end table as he poured several pills into his palm. He popped them into his mouth, then washed them down with water. "My liver's shot," he told them. "Alcoholics aren't placed at the top of the transplant list. I can't go to my grave knowing this man is on the street. Do you understand me? I've got two hundred grand in my brokerage account."

"We're glad you've got some money to keep you comfortable," Pete said, pushing himself to his feet. "Problem is, Chief, Boyd and I don't kill for money."

He started to walk over and shake the man's hand, thinking this might be the last time they saw him. Harrison wasn't an evil person. He was a dying man who'd never come to terms with his grief. Pete took several steps forward and then stopped, terrified that he might be looking at a future vision of himself. What would he do if someone killed one of his children? He quickly spun around and followed his partner to the door.

"Two hundred grand is a lot of money," Harrison told them, his voice strong now. "Do you think I haven't kept tabs on you? I can document every crime you've committed, as well as every crook you've associated yourselves with since you were booted off the force in Ventura. All I have to do is make a few phone calls, and you'll spend the rest of your lives in prison. Of course, if you turn your back on me and walk out that door, you may not live long enough to go to prison."

Pete Cordova had feared all along that it might end this way. He had a wonderful wife and two darling daughters. The underworld people they dealt with couldn't afford to be exposed, and Harrison had nothing to lose and everything to gain. "Come on, Boyd," he said, tugging on his sleeve. "We're not talking to a rational person anymore. You're on your own, Chief."

"You'll be back," Harrison told them, bending over at the waist as his face contorted in pain. "Even if you don't, someone else will take me up on my offer."

Once the two men left the house, Boyd said, "I wanted to take out Metroix the night he killed Tim. Greenly was chicken. Would have saved everyone a lot of grief if he'd listened to me."

Pete Cordova kept his mouth shut and walked ahead to the car. The time had come for him to turn his life around. He owed it to his family. One of the first people he needed to distance himself from was Boyd Chandler. He doubted if Harrison would follow through on his threats and report their illegal activities to the authorities, but Boyd might go behind his back and take the chief up on his offer. Two hundred grand was a sizable sum of money, and Boyd was a habitual gambler.

Chapter 4

Carolyn resided in a modest three-bedroom home located near Ventura College. Before she began attending law school, she'd spent her weekends gardening in the California sunshine. The walkway leading to the front door was lined with blooming rosebushes, and the beds along the exterior of the house were filled with rows of vibrantly colored perennials.

Pulling her white Infiniti into the driveway at ten-thirty that night, Carolyn rushed into the house, hoping her son was awake. Because John cooked dinner and helped Rebecca with her homework on Mondays and Wednesdays when she attended classes, Carolyn had given him permission to convert the garage into his own private apartment. All three of the bedrooms were located on the same side of the small house, and at fifteen, John needed privacy.

Rebecca was a rambunctious, popular twelve-year-old. She played her stereo at deafening levels, constantly had one girlfriend or the other over visiting, and only cleaned her room when her mother threatened to ground her. Unlike most teenage boys, John was fastidiously neat. He spent his time reading and studying, and detested any type of noise whatsoever. Outrageously handsome, he stood over six feet and had thick dark hair and luminous green eyes. At present, though, the opposite sex played an insignificant role in her son's life. He would occasionally take a girl to a school dance or a movie. Afterward, the girl would call or drop by the house, but John was too busy to put up with the demands of a steady girl-friend.

Carolyn's son aspired to go to MIT and major in physics. Providing for her children's needs was not easy. She certainly couldn't depend on her ex-husband. Frank had been a compulsive liar, and had cheated on her repeatedly. When he'd started using drugs, Carolyn had finally put an end to the marriage.

She found John in the kitchen stacking the dishes in the dishwasher. He was wearing a pair of jeans and a white tank top. His skin was tan and his body taut and muscular.

Carolyn walked over and kissed him on the cheek. "You're looking good, kid," she told him, knowing he worked out every day now in his new garage apartment. Lifting weights, John told his mother, helped him to sleep at night. Like herself, her son found it hard to quiet his constantly churning mind. After years of sleepless nights, Carolyn had finally resorted to medication. She hoped her son didn't end up following in her footsteps.

"I'll finish cleaning up," his mother told him. "You need to get to bed. I've told you a dozen times not to bother with the dishes. You do enough as it is."

"Bed?" John said, an anxious look on his face. "I have hours of homework left to do." He wiped his hands on a dish towel. "Paul Leighton bought a house down the street. I saw him outside today. I was going to walk over and introduce myself. I decided it wouldn't be polite to bother him until he gets all his furniture and stuff moved in."

Carolyn opened the refrigerator and removed a pitcher of lemonade, pouring herself a glass and taking a seat in a wooden chair at the round oak table. "Am I supposed to know this person? The name doesn't sound familiar."

"He's a physics professor at Caltech," John told her. "Mr. Chang showed me all of the books he's written. He thinks

Leighton is going to be another Richard Feynman, the guy I've been studying."

"Impressive," Carolyn said, bracing her head with one hand, then kicking her shoes off. "So he's both a writer and a physicist?"

The boy shook his head in frustration. His mother was an enigma. In the past, she could solve a math problem he'd worked on for days in less than an hour. Since she'd been attending law school, though, she'd turned into a space cadet. He knew she was tired. He could see it on her face. "Leighton doesn't write novels, Mom, like Dad tried to do. He writes textbooks. Not only that," her son continued, "he graduated from MIT."

"Now I'm really impressed," Carolyn said, smiling. "There are other schools besides MIT, you know. What's wrong with Caltech? Even Long Beach State is a good school. A California university wouldn't be as costly."

"You don't understand," John argued. "MIT is the best. Maybe Professor Leighton could write a letter for me. Since I went to summer school last year, I'll be able to graduate when I'm seventeen. That's only two years away. All I need to do is ace my SATs."

"Sounds great," his mother said. "When I can free up a night, we'll invite the professor and his wife over for dinner."

Her son had a sheepish look on his face. "He doesn't have a wife. He's divorced. His daughter is the same age as Becky. That means she'll go to the same school. I've already talked to Becky and she promised to introduce Leighton's daughter to some of her friends."

"Your sister doesn't like to be called Becky," Carolyn reminded him. "She says it sounds too babyish now that she's in junior high."

"What do I care?" John tossed out. "I do all the work around here. I can call her anything I want."

"I had a similar conversation with Brad today," Carolyn told him, finishing her lemonade and carrying the glass to the sink. "Call her Rebecca, okay? I've got enough problems without listening to you two squabbling over a name."

"What did Brad do to make you mad?"

"He called me sweetheart."

"What's wrong with that?"

"It's not appropriate for a supervisor to use terms of endearment at the office. He also called me baby."

"I'm glad you stopped seeing him," the boy said. "He's a prick, if you ask me. The thought of him shacking up with my mother made me want to puke."

Carolyn slapped him on the shoulder. "Talking about your mother shacking up is unacceptable, got it? I was lonely. Brad and I've been friends for years. We went out to dinner and took in an occasional movie."

"Right," John said, smirking. "You can't feed me that bullshit. I saw you sneaking in at two in the morning."

"Stop using bad language," Carolyn corrected him. "Regardless of what Brad and I did, it's none of your business. It's over now anyway."

"Professor Leighton isn't old and ugly," John told her, excited. "He might be a few years older than you. Smart guys don't always look like movie stars. He's better looking than Dad."

"Speaking of your father," Carolyn said. "Has he called or stopped by lately?"

"No," the boy said, averting his eyes. "Even if he did, I wouldn't want to see him. He doesn't care about us. We don't even have his phone number. The last time we talked, he said he was calling from a phone booth. I'm sure he was lying. I heard some chick laughing in the background. He lies about everything now."

Carolyn remembered the sensitive, romantic young man she had fallen in love with. They'd had picnics and made love on the beach. He wrote her love letters and brought her flowers. Curled up together in his bed, many nights they'd talked until the sun came up. Her son was wrong. Frank had been a handsome and appealing man. It was amazing what alcohol and drugs could do to a person's looks. Not yet forty, her former husband looked like an old man. Their marriage had started coming apart ten years ago.

Because of the baby, only one of them could continue their education. Carolyn had placed John in day care and worked as a secretary to pay Frank's tuition. He'd taught English while he struggled to complete his first novel. When he wasn't able to get the book published, he bolstered his ego by sleeping with other women. Then, even his sexual escapades had failed to appease him. He'd allowed drug dealers to come to the house around her children. During the divorce, Carolyn had tried to keep the truth from John and Rebecca. The psychologist they'd only recently stopped seeing insisted that she tell the children why she had divorced their father. When a person became involved with hardcore narcotics, there was no room for anything else. Frank no longer loved anyone. The only thing he loved was the drugs.

"My teacher says Professor Leighton's a fun guy," John told her, breaking the silence. "You might like him."

"Oh, I see," Carolyn said, smiling. "It's all right if I shack up with a physics professor as long as you get a recommendation to MIT. Is that what this is all about?"

John chuckled. "Sort of," he answered. "At least I'd learn something. I can't imagine learning anything worthwhile from Brad. I admit I thought he was cool with the race cars and all when I was younger. I bet the guy couldn't even pass my calculus class. I *know* he doesn't have the brains to ever do physics."

"I'm too busy to get involved with another man right now," Carolyn told him, using a sponge to wipe down the counter. "Is Rebecca asleep?"

"Yeah," he said. "I had to help her with her homework again. She's lazy, Mom. She could have done it by herself. I have my own work to do."

Carolyn had heard this complaint before. She made a

mental note to talk to Rebecca in the morning. "Did she pick up all the junk in there like I told her?"

"You know Rebecca never cleans her room. She gets her friends to do it for her. She's a spoiled brat, Mom. You should see how she acts when you're not here. She won't even pour herself a glass of milk. She treats me like I'm her slave."

Carolyn braced herself in the doorway. "Who got the whole garage to himself? Besides, I thought you wanted me to hook up with this physics professor. Perks are perks, guy. Everything in life comes with a price."

A tall brunette with dark eyes and a round, friendly face looked up from her desk when Carolyn swept into the office Tuesday morning. Behind each partition were two workstations. Since Carolyn had seniority, her desk was located next to a window. Veronica Campbell's desk was on the opposite side of the partition, but since she had the desk near the wall, the two women could see each other and converse. Veronica had a tendency to talk too much, one of the reasons she had trouble staying on top of her work.

"I'm so sick of this job I can't even think straight," the woman said, scowling. "Preston assigned me two new cases this morning." She picked up a stack of files, then tossed them back down on her desk. "There's no way I can finish these reports on time, even if I stay here every night until midnight. I've got a husband and three kids. I think Drew has a girl on the side, and my two-year-old thought I was the babysitter last night. No wonder the agency makes so many mistakes. We're not machines, you know."

"Tell me about it," Carolyn said, walking into her cubicle and placing her purse and briefcase on the floor next to her chair. The two probation officers who shared partitions with Carolyn and Veronica were seldom around. Blair Ridgemore, who shared a space with Carolyn, was one of the small group of people in California who were still addicted to nicotine. When Ridgemore wasn't interviewing victims or defendants, he dictated his reports into a tape recorder while sitting on one of the concrete benches outside in the court-yard where he could smoke. Sandra Wagner, who shared Veronica's space, had been on maternity leave for the past six months.

"So when do you think you'll graduate from law school?" Veronica piped up again. "Then you can leave this drudgery and become rich and famous. I can't wait to see you on those TV shows talking about all the slimy bastards you'll be defending."

"Thanks," Carolyn answered, sighing as she pulled out the file on Daniel Metroix. "Even slimy bastards are entitled to legal representation, Veronica. It's not like I intend to represent child molesters, rapists, or murderers. That is, unless I'm convinced they're innocent."

"Right," Veronica told her. "That's what everyone says. Why don't you become a divorce attorney? Then you can stick it to all those cheating husbands. If I catch Drew fooling around, I may be in the market for a divorce attorney my-self."

"I'd rather defend criminals. Domestic law is the worst. Not only is it maddening, half the clients can't pay. Criminal law is what I know best. Who knows? I might become a prosecutor."

"You go to class tonight, don't you?"

"Not tonight," Carolyn answered, thinking once the children were in bed, she might be able to catch up on her reading. Thank goodness, Judge Shoeffel, or Arline, as she'd asked Carolyn to call her, hadn't assigned them another paper to write this week.

"I don't know how you do it," Veronica continued. "My kids would burn the house down if I left them alone for more than an hour. Jude is almost fifteen, but she's a rotten baby-sitter. Micky was a goof, you know."

"You mean the baby?"

"Yeah," the woman said. "I'll be raising children until I retire. Besides, I could never tackle law school. You don't even have a husband to help you."

"It isn't easy," Carolyn admitted, gazing out the window. "As far as the kids go, I'm lucky that John is so responsible. Rebecca can be difficult. I hope I can finish school before she starts getting involved with boys."

Carolyn went into a room with the intention of dictating a report on the Sandoval shooting. She kept thinking of Daniel Metroix, though. Since she would be seeing him that evening, she decided to search the computer archives to see what kind of additional information she could dig up on his case. The man's claim that he knew her had spooked her. He'd left his room number at the Seagull on her answering machine the night before. She didn't want to end up fighting off a rapist, or have the guy whip out a gun and shoot her. And then there was all that crazy talk about physics and having his own lab at the prison.

Ah, she thought, slipping on her headset and dialing the number for Chino. She could clear up at least one delusion.

"Warden Lackner here," a deep voice said. "My secretary told me you had a question regarding a former prisoner named Daniel Metroix."

"Yes," she said, relating what Daniel had told her.

"Metroix is a decent fellow. We never experienced any behavior problems during the time he was here."

"Wasn't he being treated for schizophrenia?" Carolyn asked, riffling through the file and pulling out the paperwork from the prison. "People with schizophrenia generally exhibit a myriad of behavior problems. Who made the diagnosis?"

"He claimed he was hearing voices," the warden said. "Our staff psychiatrist checked him out and felt he could benefit from medication. Then Metroix heard about some new drug. We couldn't get the board of prisons to approve it, so Metroix paid for it himself. If I remember correctly, one of his relatives left him some money."

"Did you verify that?"

"I can't keep track of everything that happens inside this facility," Lackner answered defensively. "Why don't you call and speak to Dr. Edleson?"

"Forget the money for the moment. Did you provide Daniel Metroix with a lab?"

"Oh, that," the warden said, emitting a nervous chuckle. "Prisoners have a way of exaggerating things. It was an old storage closet. Daniel was good at fixing things. You know, appliances and things we use here at the prison. He was a trustee, so I let him set up a little shop. A few other trustees worked there as well."

Carolyn was about to conclude the call when she glanced down at a report written by the warden in Daniel's behalf. Having a warden on your side should have made the prison gates instantly swing open. In a twelve-year-to-life sentence, most individuals were paroled after approximately eight years. Unless they tried to escape or killed a guard or another inmate, all prisoners received good time and work-time credits, credits which cut their prison terms almost in half. Daniel Metroix had been incarcerated for twenty-three years, a sentence that was equivalent to forty. She'd known multiple murderers who'd served less time.

"Why was this man repeatedly denied parole?" she asked. "You recommended that he be released over fifteen years ago, citing him as a model prisoner."

"You'll have to speak to the parole board," Lackner said. "I have to take another call now."

Carolyn disconnected, then looked up the number for William Fletcher, Daniel's attorney. After she emphasized her credentials, the man's assistant patched her through to him at his home. Fletcher was semiretired and specialized in estate management.

"I can't divulge information without a signed consent from Mr. Metroix."

"Come on," Carolyn prodded. "I don't need numbers and details. All I want is a yes or no. Did Daniel Metroix receive an inheritance from his grandmother?"

"You're a smart lady, Ms. Sullivan. The fact that I'm his attorney should tell you something. Don't call me again until you have a signed release from my client."

Carolyn made an exception and ate lunch in the cafeteria. Then she spent most of the afternoon in front of her computer screen, reading through every document she could find related to the arrest, trial, and conviction of Daniel Metroix. She was puzzled as to why the public defender who'd represented him hadn't pleaded him not guilty by reason of insanity. The fact that Metroix suffered from schizophrenia and had spent three months in a state psychiatric hospital had never been mentioned during the trial, nor were any records from his psychiatrist forwarded to the authorities at Chino. She couldn't ask his public defender what happened as the man had been killed in a car accident fifteen years ago.

When she finished reading through the trial transcripts, Carolyn managed to extract Metroix's original arrest and booking sheet from the computer's archives. Among his personal belongings had been an appointment card from a local psychiatrist, along with a small white envelope containing four pills, which the crime lab had identified as a drug called Levodopa.

She'd never heard of this particular medication, which wasn't surprising considering what little she knew about psychotropic medications. She first tried to track down Walter Gershon, the psychiatrist listed on the card, but was unable to find his number. Assuming the doctor had either retired or died like the public defender, she typed in the drug Levodopa on the Internet, then hit the search button.

The on-line *PDR,* or *Physicians Desk Reference,* indicated that Levodopa was primarily used in the treatment of Parkinson's disease. Why would a schizophrenic be given a drug used to treat Parkinson's? The medication dramatically increased the levels of dopamine in the brain.

Carolyn decided to call a psychiatrist who frequently served as an expert witness. Once she told Dr. Albert Weiss's secretary that she could bill the county for an hour of the doctor's time, the woman transferred her to his cell phone.

"I need to ask you a question," Carolyn said, telling him the name of the medication and a brief outline of the circumstances.

"Any psychiatrist," Dr. Weiss said, "or even any physician, for that matter, would never treat a known schizophrenic with Levodopa. Are you sure you got the name of the drug right?"

"It could have been a typo," she told him. "Was there a medication with a similar spelling which may have been prescribed for this condition over twenty years ago?"

"I've been practicing psychiatry since you were in grade school," Weiss told her. "As far as I know, there's no such animal."

"What kind of effect would the drug have?"

"Oh, nothing much," the psychiatrist said sarcastically. "The patient would more than likely become psychotic not long after the drug hit his bloodstream. You caught me on the golf course. I'm about to tee off. Did I answer your question?"

"Thanks," Carolyn said. "Enjoy your game."

Heading to the break room to get a soda, Carolyn ran into Brad Preston as he was chatting and laughing with Amy McFarland.

"I've come across some major discrepancies in the Metroix case." Carolyn pulled back the tab on her can of 7UP and took a swallow. "As soon as I get all the facts straight, we need to talk."

Brad smiled at Amy McFarland. "See the guy once a

month," he told Carolyn. "I assigned you four more investigations this morning. The Metroix case is ancient history. You don't have time to be concerned about discrepancies."

Carolyn gave him a look that would drop an elephant. His new girlfriend didn't seem to be pressed for time. She turned and smiled sweetly at the woman. "Have you met Brad's fiancée, Amy?" she asked. "You should see the ring he gave her last week. Looks like about three carats. Not only that, he's taking her to Paris on their honeymoon. Isn't that romantic?"

Carolyn watched the woman's face twist in anger. She stormed out of the room, whacking Brad in the stomach with her purse as she passed.

"I knew you were sleeping with her," Carolyn said.

"You're not only nuts," Preston said, coffee spilled down the front of his shirt, "you're a first-class bitch."

"Keep your dick out of the office," Carolyn told him, a look of satisfaction on her face.

"You didn't mind."

"You weren't my supervisor then, remember?"

Back at her desk, Carolyn read through Metroix's trial transcripts again to make certain she hadn't missed anything. Something didn't add up. Brad had originally told her how sensitive the case was, and warned her not to make any mistakes. In the break room, he'd told her the case was ancient history, that all she had to do was see the man once a month.

Carolyn was now determined to find out everything she could about the death of Tim Harrison. As a law student, she was intrigued by numerous elements of the case.

Confirming her suspicions that Brad was sleeping with another woman hurt, particularly since Amy McFarland was twenty-five and a knockout. Obviously, he hadn't ended their affair simply because of his promotion. Had he been seeing Amy even before she'd been hired at the agency, possibly helped her get the job? A probation officer didn't make a great deal of money, but as in most civil service positions, the number of people who applied was staggering. The benefits were excellent and the pay increases came like clockwork. Most of the new people were college graduates, and many held master's degrees.

Carolyn stared out the window, trying to keep herself from crying. The older a woman got, the harder it became to accept rejection. Her thoughts turned to David Reynolds. Should she accept his advances, then somehow manage to parade him in front of Brad? She rushed into an interview room and called her brother. "What are you doing?"

"Eating a bowl of cereal," Neil said. "What are you doing?"

"Contemplating suicide," his sister told him. "Brad dumped me for a young blonde. Not only that, I have to work with her. I feel like a fool."

"Told you the guy was an asshole," Neil said calmly, knowing she was being melodramatic. "Is she a young blonde, or is she a gorgeous young blonde? If she's got a decent face and a dynamite body, I'll give you fifty bucks if you get me her number. Tell her I'm a famous artist. I'll paint her and immortalize her beauty forever."

"I hate you," Carolyn said, kicking a chair and knocking it over. "I don't know why I called you. When I'm upset, you never try to comfort me. All you ever do is insult me."

"That's the point," Neil said, laughing. "Now you're mad at me instead of Brad."

Leaving the interview room, Carolyn decided to get out of the office and pay a visit to the property room at the jail. Nothing related to the psychiatrist or the pills had been introduced during Daniel's trial. Could someone have suppressed this evidence because they knew it would support either a diminished capacity or an insanity defense?

"Is this date right?" asked Jessie Richards, a deputy assigned to the property room. He peered out at her from a window in the door.

"The date's right." She handed him the computer printout, listing the items that had been in Daniel's possession at the time of his arrest, hoping against reason that they were in a box somewhere collecting dust. Procedure called for the prisoner's belongings to be forwarded to whatever prison he was sent to in order that they could be returned upon his release. Sending an inmate his property wasn't a high priority; therefore, it was occasionally overlooked.

"I was in diapers when this dude went to prison," Richards said, typing in the case number from the printouts she'd given him. "I didn't know they even had computers in those days."

"They had cars too, Jessie," Carolyn told him. The man was an avid surfer and had probably spent his teenage years in a fog of marijuana. Ironically, the lower spectrum in law enforcement had numerous individuals with his type of background. Years ago, things had been different. Potential officers had to consent to a lie detector test. Any drug use whatsoever and they were sent packing.

"Our records show his stuff disappeared a few days after his arrest," Richards said.

Carolyn was confused. "That can't be," she said. "The drugs were sent to the lab to be analyzed. I found the report in the archives. It doesn't say anything about the property being lost." Almost every computer had its own access codes and many of the files were encrypted. Security was particularly tight as to evidence, but the situation had been entirely different twenty-three years ago. "Call the lab and see if they forgot to return it."

"You must be joking," Richards said, spinning his chair around to face her. "All the guy had on him were some prescription pills, a few bucks, and a business card. They make a bonfire every year and burn up mountains of pot. Trust me, Sullivan, it ain't worth a phone call. Not only will nobody at the lab know where it went, they won't even take the time to talk to me."

Carolyn's suspicions were mounting. On the walk back to her office, she asked herself if the person who'd stolen Metroix's property had failed to realize that the items in his possession at the time of his arrest had already been entered into the computer system. The crime had occurred when the entire criminal record system was being overhauled. Even if the person who'd swiped Metroix's property had checked the computer, the information might not have shown up due to the confusion of trying to computerize such a massive amount of data.

Daniel Metroix was only four years older than Carolyn. It was ironic that they'd lived in the same apartment building. She only remembered the name of the complex because her parents had told her about it. Her father had been unemployed for a number of years, causing the family to have to move into a subsidized building on the west side of Ventura. Soon afterward, things had improved and he'd secured a job as a high school math teacher. Her mother later went back to school and obtained a master's degree in chemistry. Until five years ago, Marie Sullivan had taught at a junior college in Ventura. She now lived in an exclusive retirement community in Camarillo.

Neil was the baby of the family and his artistic talents and easygoing manner had caused her mother to idolize him. Carolyn had possessed the brightest future academically until she'd gotten pregnant during her second year at Stanford. So, she thought, she and Metroix shared something else in common—unforeseen obstacles had prevented them from meeting their full potential. According to his high school records, several teachers had recommended Metroix for a scholarship, and one had classified him as a near genius in the areas of math and science.

Carolyn didn't think twice when recommending a maximum sentence for a violent offender. She was not only one of the most respected probation officers in the county, she was also the most punitive. But something had gone terribly wrong in the case of Daniel Metroix. Suppressing or tampering with evidence was a felony.

With an objective viewpoint, Carolyn thought, returning

to her desk, a person realized that the pendulum swung both ways. Some offenders who served only a short stint behind bars posed a serious threat to society. Daniel Metroix's case didn't appear to be merely sloppy and unconcerned work on the part of his attorney.

The system had been manipulated.

Chapter 5

En route to her appointment with Daniel Metroix at the Seagull Motel Tuesday evening, Carolyn retrieved her cell phone out of her purse and called her house. "Where have you been?" she asked when her son answered.

"Here," John told her. "I called you back. Didn't you get the message?"

"No," his mother said. "I must have already left the office when you called. I took off early. What's going on? Did you defrost the meatloaf like I asked you to this morning?"

"Rebecca hates meatloaf," John told her. "That's why it's been in the freezer for two months. When are you coming home?"

"I should be there by seven at the latest," she said. "If you're hungry, go ahead and eat without me."

"What are we supposed to eat?" John asked, his voice tinged with annoyance. "You need to go to the grocery store. We don't have anything to make for our lunches tomorrow, let alone any food for dinner."

"I'll pick something up," Carolyn told him. "Where's your sister?"

"Holed up in the bathroom," John said. "She's dying her hair purple."

Carolyn shouted, "Get her butt on the phone!"

"I'm kidding," her son said, although he sounded despondent. "You're never here, so what do you care? I've been stuck on this calculus problem for over two days. We're going to have to figure something out, Mom, or my grades are going to slide. I can't handle everything by myself. I cook, do laundry, tutor Rebecca."

"I understand," Carolyn told him. "We'll talk about it this weekend. I only called to tell you I was going to be late. Don't eat, okay? I'll call you back in five minutes." She started to hang up, then realized she was being insensitive. "I appreciate everything you do, John. I promise I'll find a way to lighten your load."

"I'm sorry I complained. I guess I'm tired tonight."

"I love you," Carolyn told him. "You don't have to apologize, sweetheart. Your complaints are valid. I may take this semester off anyway. I'm tired too."

She hit the auto dial on her phone. Neil picked up on the fourth ring. "I'm glad you're home," she said. "I need you."

"God's always home when you need him," her brother quipped. "What's going on now?"

"Are you busy?"

"I have a show next week," he said. "I also have a gorgeous naked model in the bedroom panting for my attention. Even you'd fall in love with this girl. She has the face and body of an angel."

"I'm not interested in girls," Carolyn told him. "Put the naked chick on ice and take my kids out for dinner. I have to do a home check on a parolee. John claims there's no food in the house. You owe me for not showing up at Mother's on Sunday. She had me make you a damn pie, for God's sake."

"Was it that layered banana thing you make with vanilla wafers and whipped cream? That's my favorite."

"Yeah," she said. "We ate it, or I would have driven over and smashed it in your face. You know I don't have time to make pies. I barely have time to go to the bathroom."

"I'll pick John and Rebecca up in fifteen minutes."

"Thanks," Carolyn told him. "Call and tell them to get

ready. If you bail me out tonight, I promise I'll make you another banana pie."

"I'm afraid the show is going to be a disaster."

Here we go, she thought. She'd been expecting a meltdown. "Everything will be great."

"You don't understand," Neil said in hushed tones, not wanting the girl in the other room to hear. "The economy sucks right now. People aren't investing in art. Because I sold a lot of paintings last year doesn't mean this year will be the same. I've been thinking of selling the house."

As confident as he came across, Neil was emotionally fragile. Carolyn assumed it was his artistic temperament. He always got nervous before a big show. "Relax," she said. "Didn't you sell a painting last month for thirty grand?"

"Yeah," he said. "But that was an exception. The guy was so stupid he would have bought a blank canvas. He had a lot of money, that's all. I think he's some kind of gangster who's trying to pass himself off as a society guy. When he figures out I've never sold a painting in that price range, he'll probably come back and chop me up into pieces."

Oh boy, Carolyn thought, now she was talking to the twelve-year-old Neil. When her brother got upset, he started regressing. "Didn't the *L.A. Times* do a feature on you?"

"Yes, but—"

"Listen to me," she said. "You're a wonderful artist. As long as you don't go hog wild, you have enough money to carry you for at least five years. And that's if you don't sell any paintings, understand? You bought Mom that expensive condominium in Camarillo. Since you bought it outright, we can always get a mortgage on it. You've loaned me money more times than I want to admit. I love you, Neil. Everyone loves you. Your show is going to be fantastic. You're going to make a ton of money. If you don't, it doesn't matter."

"I don't know what I would do without you," Neil said, letting out a long sigh. "You're the string that holds me together."

"Same here," she said. "You spend too much time in that shack behind the house that you use as a studio. Call John and Rebecca. Go somewhere fun. They'll make you feel better."

Looking at the clock on the dashboard and seeing that it was already past five-thirty, she tossed her phone back into her purse and stepped on the accelerator.

Carolyn pulled into the parking lot of the Seagull Motel a few minutes before six. She'd always been a timely person. It made her nervous to be late. She thumbed through her keys and found the one that unlocked the glove box, then reached inside and pulled out her gun and shoulder holster. Removing the 9mm Ruger, she felt around until she found the ammo clip, then quickly inserted it. She hated guns. Although probation officers were sworn peace officers with a right to carry a firearm, until a year ago, probation officers in Ventura weren't armed. After a field officer was killed when he paid an unexpected home visit to a probationer who was in the middle of a major drug transaction, the department changed its policy. The fact that they were now supervising more parolees from prison was also a factor, as it intensified the danger.

She flicked on the dome light inside the Infiniti, checking the safety and making certain nothing was lodged inside the barrel of the gun. Five months had passed since she'd so much as unlocked the glove box, let alone carried the Ruger on her person. Because she'd accidentally left her jacket at the office, she felt stupid wearing the shoulder holster. Opening her purse, she dropped the gun inside, tossing the holster on the passenger seat. She had a bulletproof vest in the trunk. She wasn't even certain it fit, as she'd never gotten around to opening the box.

Carolyn was uncertain if she was safer with or without the gun. She'd investigated too many crimes involving firearms. Legislation regarding the registration of handguns was nothing more than a Band-Aid. The greatest majority of guns used in crimes were stolen from citizens who purchased them legally. People thought owning a gun would protect them. Nine times out of ten, the perpetrator used the victim's gun in the commission of the crime, or someone in the household got their hands on it and either killed himself or a family member.

She was no stranger to this type of tragedy. Her uncle had put the .38 caliber pistol he'd purchased at a pawn shop to protect his family to his head and blown his brains out. Carolyn and his fourteen-year-old daughter had been the ones to find him. These were the types of memories that stayed with a person for a lifetime.

She got out of her car and depressed the button for the alarm. The parking lot was almost empty. All she noticed was a black Chevy truck parked near the office. The location was good, she thought, but the hotel was badly in need of repair. Since they didn't appear to have many guests, she assumed they wouldn't be in business much longer. As she crossed the parking lot, she experienced an eerie sensation. Several times she turned around, certain she heard footsteps behind her.

Daniel had written down his room number as 221. Most of the rooms on the upper floors appeared to be dark, yet she clearly saw a man sitting in a chair in front of an open window.

Carolyn climbed the stairs two at a time. When she reached the room, she saw the key protruding from the lock. Standing to one side, she reached around and knocked, her hand resting on her gun inside her open purse. Daniel opened the door. "Why did you leave the key in the door?"

He ran his fingers through his hair. "I was working," he said, gesturing toward a stack of papers on the table next to the lamp. "I leave the key in the door so I won't lock myself out. Sometimes there's no one in the office. It's not like I have anything to steal in here. I mean, I have my work. I can't see a thief running off with a bunch of papers he'll never be able to decipher."

Carolyn wondered if he would ever adjust to the outside world. He had on the same shirt from the previous day. One side was protruding from his jeans, his hair was standing on end, and he was wearing only one sock and no shoes.

"I enjoy having a window," Daniel said, walking over and placing his hands against the glass. "I didn't have a window in prison. When my eyes get tired, I can rest them by looking out at the ocean. Isn't it beautiful?"

While his back was turned, Carolyn quickly checked the closet and bathroom, looking for signs of weapons, drugs, or alcohol. Damn, she thought, she'd have to do another home visit once he found an apartment. "Did you find a place to live today?"

"No," he said, turning around. "I don't have a car. I have the money to buy one, but I don't have a driver's license. I took the bus and tried to look at some apartments, then I got lost. No one knew where the bus stop was. I had to come home in a cab."

Carolyn walked over to the cluttered table and picked up a piece of paper. On one side was a complex drawing, which she couldn't make out, and the other side was covered with equations. "What is this?"

"Oh," Daniel said timidly, "I've been working on this for about eighteen years. It's an exoskeleton."

"You didn't answer my question." She recognized the word, but she didn't associate it with something a person could build. Eddie Downly had been a rapist and she'd failed to see it. The more Metroix rambled, the closer she would get to assessing the risk he posed in the community. "Refresh my memory. What exactly is an exoskeleton?"

"Certain animals have exoskeletons," he explained. "A crab has one. You know, an exterior shell. I tried to build an exoskeleton for a guard's daughter who was partially paralyzed."

Three parts delusion, one part science, Carolyn thought. It almost sounded like one of her mother's off-the-wall home chemistry projects. Baiting him, she continued, "So this is one of the projects you worked on in your lab at prison?"

"It didn't turn out very well," Daniel told her, responding to her interest. "A human exoskeleton is an extremely complex device. The problem is developing the right material for the suit. That and figuring out how to provide a power source that's lightweight and portable. I think the government is working on the same problem. They want to enhance the performance of combat soldiers. They call it HPA, Human Performance Augmentation."

Carolyn held up her hand. "Slow down," she said. "Let me get this straight. Are you telling me you invented something eighteen years ago that the government is now developing for national security?"

"Yes, but I didn't invent an exoskeleton," Daniel told her. "The only person who holds a patent on an exoskeleton is God. All homo sapiens are doing is trying to copy and adapt something that's part of nature."

"God, huh?" Carolyn said, stunned that he'd maintained his religious beliefs after twenty-three years behind bars. Religious ideation, however, wasn't uncommon in schizophrenia.

"Yeah," Daniel said, smiling. "And we'll probably never get it right. I could have the greatest lab in the world, the most brilliant minds, the best equipment. Do you think for one minute that I could create an ant, a dog, a horse, let alone a human being who could think and reason? God is the ultimate inventor." He paused and rubbed his forehead, deep in thought.

"Did you invent anything else while you were in prison?"

"Sure," Daniel said, having already had the same discussion with his attorney. "I invented all kinds of stuff. The first thing the prison used of mine was this multiscreen monitoring system, which also recorded on tape. They really liked that one because they could cut down on the number of guards on duty."

Carolyn was at least familiar with this particular device. Businesses everywhere used video surveillance. "Was the VCR already around when you developed this?"

"The early prototype for the VCR was developed by a man named Charles Ginsburg while he was working at a company called Ampex. It was huge, though, almost as big as a piano. They later sold it to Sony. The first commercial VCR was released in 1971. I began working on the machine I made for the prison before I was arrested because some of the television components related to a communications system I was designing. I got it up and running about fifteen years ago."

The time coincided with the dates on the first letter the warden had written recommending his release. "Did you ever sell one of your inventions?"

"I've never sold anything," he answered. "To tell you the truth, I never even thought about making money off the things I invented. To me, it's work. It's what I do, you know. I see some kind of problem, and I do my best to solve it. Besides," he added, not in the least concerned, "I signed over all rights to anything I invented while I was at Chino. That was the provision for me getting my own lab."

Carolyn tried to think like an attorney. She didn't know anything about patent law. She would have to find out who legally held the rights to his inventions. From what she'd seen, he hadn't been making license plates. Her fatigue had vanished, and she felt alert and stimulated.

"Did you repair appliances?"

"Are you serious?" Daniel answered. "The warden didn't want me to work on anything but the exoskeleton. I kept telling him that I didn't have the right equipment."

Deciding she'd let him ramble long enough, she asked, "Do you remember what happened the night you were arrested?"

"Not much," Daniel said, sighing deeply. "I was having problems then. I remember because my mother got worried and called my doctor."

Carolyn asked, "Was the doctor's name Walter Gershon?"

"Yeah," he said. "I wrote him tons of letters from prison. He never answered me."

"I tried to find him as well. He isn't listed. He either retired, moved away, or he's dead. Do you recall ever taking a drug called Levodopa?"

"No, why do you ask?"

"When you were arrested, this medication was listed among your possessions. I checked with a psychiatrist and he informed me that this was the worst drug anyone could give to a person with your condition."

Daniel's eyes drifted downward as he tried to remember. "I carried my pills in an envelope when I was at school or away from the apartment. Were the pills in an envelope?"

"Yes," Carolyn answered. "How long had you been taking them?"

"A week maybe," he said. "Dr. Gershon changed my medicine. I don't remember what it was called. I know I was upset when I picked up the prescription from the pharmacy."

"Why were you upset?"

"Because it had a different name than what the doctor had ordered," Daniel told her, making small circles on the surface of the table with his finger. "I even got in an argument with the pharmacist, thinking he'd given me some other person's prescription by mistake. He brushed me off, telling me it was a generic form of the same drug. You know, that's why it had another name."

"How did the drug affect you?"

"Everything fell apart," Daniel said, tears glistening in his eyes. "I was doing really well in school before I started taking the new drug. Then I started having problems again. When I called the doctor, he told me to double the dose. As soon as I did, things got even worse."

This was a vital point, Carolyn thought, not that either the psychiatrist or the pharmacist had made a serious error, but that someone related to the crime had kept this information from the court. "Can you tell me the name of the pharmacy?"

"O'Malley's," he said. "But the store isn't there anymore. I passed the street on the bus today. There's a new shopping center where the drugstore used to be. All the drugstores are big chains now. The O'Malleys were a family."

"I know," Carolyn said, sad at how their world had changed. Family businesses were rare these days. "Why did the doctor change your medication to begin with?"

"Because I was only a few months away from graduating," he said, blinking repeatedly as he continued to move his finger in circles on the table. "Stress can set off an attack. I'm sorry. Talking about this disturbs me."

Carolyn forged ahead. She'd caught a glimpse of his illness. Now she wanted facts. "Have you ever committed an act of violence during an acute attack?"

"Never," Daniel said. "I've walked naked in the middle of the street, along with some other bizarre things. I'm not a violent person. Even when I first got to prison and the inmates went after me, I didn't fight back."

"Let's concentrate on the night of the crime. Do you remember the three boys at all?"

"I know what they looked like from the courtroom," Daniel told her, clasping his hands together tightly. "When they jumped me, it was dark and I couldn't see their faces that well. I'd been studying at the library."

"The crime occurred in an alley behind Rudy's pool hall," Carolyn said. "What were you doing in the alley?"

"It was a shortcut to my apartment. I wanted to get home so my mother wouldn't yell at me. She treated me like I was—"

"Try to focus, Daniel," she said. "You need to tell me what happened."

"I remember seeing these three big jocks standing out the back door of the bowling alley. I kept dropping my books. The strap on my backpack had broken, so I was trying to carry them all in my hands. Some of the books were textbooks. The others I'd checked out at the library. Every time I tried to pick up a book, one of the boys would kick it. I got really upset. It was dark and I couldn't find half of the books. I knew they were expensive. I didn't want my mother to have to pay to replace them."

"Keep talking," Carolyn said, wondering how upset he'd become that night. She could imagine a jury asking themselves the same question. This may have been the reason his public defender had not allowed him to testify at the trial. "What else do you remember?"

"I tripped and fell on my stomach," he said, his eyelids fluttering again. "I remember them laughing at me, calling me names. I tried to get up when they started hitting me. A black guy turned me over and forced my mouth open. Things get fuzzy after then. The last thing I remember was one of them urinating in my mouth."

Carolyn placed her head in her hands. If what he was saying was true, it was a travesty. Had he spent twenty-three years in prison while the three obnoxious thugs who had beaten and humiliated him went free? She corrected herself, as Tim Harrison, the chief's son, had lost his life.

"Did you intentionally push Tim Harrison in front of a car?"

"No," Daniel said, standing and pacing as he relived the events of that night. "After they started beating me, I'm almost certain I never got up off the ground until right before the guy got run over. By then, I'd convinced myself the entire thing was a delusion. Why fight people who don't exist?"

"Where were you when Tim got killed?"

"When they began fighting among themselves," he said, wrapping his arms around his chest, "I crawled over to a corner and hid behind a trash barrel. I was in pretty bad shape. That's where I was when the police arrested me. One of the boys swore I'd threatened them with a knife. The police never found any kind of knife. My mother would have never let me out of the house with a knife, even a table knife." He smiled briefly. "With the kind of problems I had, even I knew better than to carry a knife."

"Were the boys fighting among themselves before or after Tim got hit by the car?"

"Before," Daniel told her. "One of the guys got mad. I may be mistaken, but I think it was Harrison. He kept talking about his father, saying his friends shouldn't have hurt me, that they were all going to get booted off the football team and his father was going to beat the shit out of him."

Carolyn generally used first names when referring to victims. Parents and loved ones didn't call each other by their last name. "Did you see Tim get struck by the car?"

He stopped pacing and faced her. "I'm not sure," Daniel said, sucking in a deep breath. "When you think something isn't real, you try to pay as little attention as possible."

"Tell me precisely what you heard," Carolyn said, her pen poised over her pad.

"Precisely isn't going to work," Daniel told her. "We're talking twenty-three years and a mind that wasn't right. All I can do is tell you what I *think* I heard. Are you sure you want to know? When I explained it this way to my attorney, he told me that whatever I saw or heard was basically worthless. That's why he wouldn't let me testify."

"I'm aware you didn't testify," Carolyn told him. "I'm not your attorney, Daniel. And Tim's death wasn't a delusion."

"Fine," he snapped. "I heard a car engine, tires screeching, and people yelling. The next thing I remember I was being booked at the county jail." He dropped down in the chair, his face twisted in bitterness. "What difference does it make if I was guilty or innocent? I've already served my time."

Carolyn realized that most people would have trouble comprehending the complexities of the criminal justice system. "Your sentence was twelve years to life. As long as you're breathing, they can send you back to prison."

The shrill ring of the phone startled her. When he walked over to the nightstand to answer it, Carolyn's instincts kicked in. Her eyes swept across the room. She saw wires running along the top of the ceiling. Two FBI agents had been killed recently when they'd walked inside a booby-trapped room. "Don't answer it."

"Why?"

"Who did you give this phone number to?"

"Only you," he said, picking up the receiver. "It's probably a wrong number."

Carolyn snatched the phone out of his hand, dropping to the floor beside the nightstand. In addition to the standard phone cord, there was another thick black wire similar to the ones on the ceiling. She wondered briefly if it was a cable for a modem. Whatever it was, she wasn't going to wait around to find out.

"We have to get out of here!" she told him, grabbing a handful of his shirt as she frantically tried to get him to follow her. "Hurry! This may be a trap. The call was to make certain you were here."

"My papers," Daniel said, reaching back for them.

"Come now, we can't waste time," Carolyn yelled, halfway through the doorway.

They got a few feet down the corridor before they heard the explosion. An enormous ball of fire burst through the hotel window. Both Carolyn and Metroix were hurled to the ground. The concrete walkway was swaying as it would during an earthquake. "Are you hurt?" Carolyn shouted, coughing from the smoke.

"I don't think so," Daniel said, looking back in the direction of the room.

"We have to get down the stairs before the building collapses. Here," she said, ripping off a piece of her cotton blouse with her teeth and handing it to him, "put this over your mouth and nose. Don't stand up. Stay as close to the ground as possible."

As shards of glass and pillars of smoke flew through the air, Carolyn and Daniel crawled as fast as they could in the direction of the stairwell. The smoke became so thick that she couldn't see. Her arms and knees were scraped and bloody. She heard him coughing and gasping behind her. Another explosion occurred, and Carolyn was terrified that the concrete walkway on the third floor would come crashing down on top of them.

Off in the distance, she could hear the sirens. They couldn't wait to be rescued. Finally, she found it. By extending her right arm and patting the ground as she crawled, Carolyn felt the first step at the top of the stairs. She reached behind her and grabbed his hand. "Turn around," she yelled. "We have to go down the stairs backwards."

"I . . . can't . . . breathe," Daniel said, flopping over onto his back.

Carolyn straddled him, lifting his arm and letting it drop in an attempt to find out if he was unconscious. She used her fingers to open his mouth, then sucked in as much air as her lungs could hold, trying desperately not to cough. If she succumbed to smoke inhalation, they would both die. Pinching his nose closed, she sealed her mouth on Daniel's and began ventilating. When he didn't respond, she jerked her head in the direction of the stairs. John and Rebecca's faces flashed in her mind. Her children needed her. What good would it serve if they both died?

She had to decide.

Carolyn sucked in another breath and exhaled into Daniel's mouth. She was lightheaded from lack of oxygen, and her eyes were watering profusely. As soon as she heard him coughing, she grabbed his left leg and started her descent down the stairs, pulling him along with her. A short time later, Daniel began moving on his own. They made it to the bottom of the stairs at the same time the fire trucks and emergency vehicles arrived on the scene. Carolyn collapsed face first on the grassy area next to the parking lot.

She heard men's voices barking orders, and felt herself being rolled over onto her back. Her eyes opened as a paramedic placed an oxygen mask over her face.

"We need a gurney over here," the man called out. "I've got another victim."

Carolyn pushed the oxygen mask off her face. "A man was with me," she whispered, her throat almost too parched to speak.

"Your friend will be fine," the paramedic told her as he ripped open a package containing an intravenous needle. "I'm going to insert an I.V. in your arm. Try to relax and breathe normally."

Carolyn closed her eyes. A few moments later, her head slumped to the side. Sounds disappeared as she floated in a sea of darkness.

Chapter 6

John reached through the bars of the hospital bed and gently stroked his mother's hand. "You're all right, Mom," he said, concern etched on his face. "You're in the emergency room at Good Samaritan Hospital. The doctor said you can go home in a few hours."

Carolyn tried to sit up and then collapsed back on the pillow. Her knees and elbows smarted, and she saw an I.V. bottle hanging on a pole by the bed. She was on oxygen, and her throat felt as if she'd been drinking acid. "Can you give me some water?" she asked, her voice barely audible.

John picked up a cup of ice chips from the table and used a spoon to place them in his mother's mouth. "The nurse said you could only have the ice chips," he explained. "They gave you a shot when they stitched up your knees and elbows. They don't want you drinking a lot of water. The nurse said you might throw up."

Carolyn's hand flew to her chest. "Where's my mother's cross?" she asked, fearing it had been lost in the explosion.

"I have it," her son told her. "They also gave me your cuff links and watch. Here, take some more ice."

The ice chips eased the burning sensation in her throat. They must have given her morphine, Carolyn decided. Her muscles felt like spaghetti and she was having trouble focusing her eyes. "Did you come with Neil?"

"No," John told her. "I called him. You know he turns off his phone at night when he's painting. Professor Leighton drove me."

It took her a few moments to figure out where she'd heard the name. Sounds and smells from the explosion were blocking everything else from mind. She gazed lovingly at her son, grateful to be alive. "The man down the street?"

"When the hospital called," John said, "I didn't know what to do. I tried calling Dad, but his phone has been disconnected again. I was going to call a cab, but I only had a few dollars. Rebecca ate lunch with Professor Leighton's daughter today, so she had their phone number. He's really a nice man, Mom."

"Where's your sister now? You didn't leave her alone, I hope."

"No," he told her. "Professor Leighton has a live-in housekeeper. Rebecca's sleeping over at his house. Everything's fine. Try to rest, or the doctor won't let you go home."

"What happened to Daniel Metroix?"

"You mean the psycho guy?" John said, grimacing. "Professor Leighton couldn't understand why you would go to his motel room. You're lucky he didn't kill you."

A complete stranger had suddenly become entangled in her life. "What I do at work is confidential," Carolyn said. "Because I don't usually supervise a caseload of offenders, you don't know how this part of my job works. Probation and parole officers make home visits all the time. We have to check out their living situation. This man was staying in a motel until he found an apartment."

"Maybe you should get another job then," John told her. "We need you, Mom. What would Rebecca and I do if something happened to you?"

"Nothing bad is going to happen, honey," she said, clasping his hand. "I just got banged up a little tonight. And Mr. Metroix didn't try to hurt me. It was probably an accident.

Promise me, though, that you'll never repeat anything I tell you again about my work. Are we clear?"

The muscles in the boy's face stiffened. "You're not being fair," he told her. "What was I supposed to do? The hospital called and said a responsible party had to come and pick you up. Don't you know how embarrassed I was having to turn to a man I'd never met? Professor Leighton asked me all kinds of questions in the car. Where's your Dad? Where're your grandparents? Why doesn't your uncle answer his phone?"

"You didn't call my mother, did you?" Carolyn said, not wanting to worry her.

"No," he answered. "I know Grandma doesn't drive at night anymore."

"You could have called Veronica Campbell," she said, concerned that he had so much pent-up hostility. "Her number is on the bulletin board by the phone. Brad's number is there as well. Jane Baily would have helped you. She's looked after you and your sister for years."

"Mrs. Baily moved away," the boy said. "Professor Leighton bought her house. The house was up for sale for six months. Don't you remember, Mom?"

Carolyn was ashamed. Once again, her son was right.

"I've only met this Veronica lady one time," he continued in the same distraught tone. "I might not want you to marry Brad, but it was kind of nice to have a man around. Since he became your boss, all you do is complain about him. He used to stop by now and then, have us over to his place for barbecues, let us swim in his pool. He might be a jerk, but at least he seemed to care about us. We never have anyone over to the house anymore."

Carolyn sighed, too weak and weary to continue. "I need to rest," she told him. "Tell Mr. Leighton that he can go home. We'll take a cab."

"He's a professor, Mom," John reminded her. "Why waste money on a cab?"

"Thank the *professor* and tell him there's no reason to stay here. In fact, why don't you go home with him?"

Tears pooled in John's eyes. "You're mad at me, aren't you?"

"Not at all," Carolyn said. "We'll talk tomorrow when you get home from school."

John started to leave the room, then turned around and walked back over to his mother's bedside, leaning over and kissing her on the cheek. Carolyn cupped the side of his face in her hand. "I expect a lot from you," she said. "I'm sorry. Sometimes I don't have a choice. I heard everything you told me tonight loud and clear. Go home with this nice man from down the street. Tomorrow will be a better day."

Carolyn had dozed off when she heard a male voice speak her name. She saw Detective Hank Sawyer and a younger, uniformed police officer standing beside her bed. The clock on the wall read two-fifteen in the morning. She wondered why the hospital hadn't sent her home. Rubbing her eyes, she assumed the nurse had looked in and saw her sleeping, believing she was too sedated to be released.

"We need to ask you a few questions," Hank said. "This fellow is Trevor White. Doc said you got out of that mess at the motel with nothing more than some nasty cuts. You must have the luck of the Irish."

Carolyn peered up at the two men. She'd worked with Hank for years. He was not only a detective, but a sergeant in the crimes against persons division. At forty-five, he was slightly under six feet and about twenty pounds overweight, most of it in his midsection. He had thinning brown hair and a ruddy complexion.

The detective was a shrewd and highly esteemed investigator. He'd tracked down and apprehended the murderer in a case Carolyn had investigated several years before. In the process, he'd taken a bullet to the abdomen, one of the most painful places in the body to incur a gunshot wound. While handling the case, she was amazed that he'd been back at work in less than three weeks.

Officer White looked to be in his mid-twenties, and displayed the rigid demeanor of a soldier. He was probably a rookie, she thought. When a police officer made a point of trying to appear authoritative, he was generally covering up for lack of experience.

"Tell me what happened," she said, pushing a button to elevate the head of the bed. "Was it a bomb?"

"Let's call it an explosive device," Hank told her. "Until our bomb squad completes their investigation, we can't be certain."

"How many people were injured?"

"You and a guy named Daniel Metroix. Records list Metroix as a recent parolee from Chino. He claims you're his parole officer. Is that true?"

"Yes," Carolyn said. "Where is he now?"

"The prisoner's being booked at the jail," Officer White said, resting his hand on the butt of his gun. Several inches shorter than his superior, White had closely cropped hair and small gray eyes.

Hank shot the officer a stern look. "Get me a cup of coffee," he said, promptly putting the other man in his place. "And while you're at it, get me a Snickers." He reached in his pocket and tossed over a handful of quarters. White wasn't quick enough to catch them, so he had to bend over and pick them up one by one off the floor.

Once the officer had left the room, the detective turned back to Carolyn. "Kids," he said, scowling. "I'm getting too old for this training bullshit. What did my boy do wrong?"

"He volunteered information," Carolyn said, not concerned about the personnel problems at the police department in light of what she'd heard. "Why did you arrest

Metroix, Hank? He had nothing to do with what happened. I had to check out his living situation. I scheduled a visit at his motel room."

"How did you get out before the place blew?"

"The phone rang as I was about to leave," she said, staring up at the ceiling as she tried to remember the sequence of events prior to the explosion. "When I saw wires running across the ceiling, I knew something was wrong. Then I saw the same kind of wire coming out of the back of the phone. I told him we had to get out of the building. We almost made it to the stairway when Metroix stopped breathing. I administered CPR, and he came around." She reached over and picked up a pitcher of water off the end table. He took it out of her hand and poured the water into a cup, handing it to her and waiting until she finished drinking it. "My throat, you know," she said, hoarse.

"Smoke has a tendency to do that," Hank told her. "I started out with the fire department. I've swallowed my share of that stuff."

"What are you charging Metroix with?"

"At present," he told her, "violation of parole. The DA may file attempted murder charges by tomorrow afternoon, depending on what kind of evidence we can produce. We're hoping you can help us put this case together."

"Metroix didn't violate his parole, Hank," Carolyn told him, placing the plastic drinking cup back on the end table. "The man almost died."

The detective pulled on the lapels of his jacket, adjusting it on his shoulders. "You know what a suicide bomber is, Carolyn?"

"Of course," she told him. "Daniel Metroix isn't a suicide bomber." She paused to think, listening to the patient behind the curtain next to her moaning. "Why weren't there more injuries? What happened to the rest of the people staying at the motel? I was afraid the whole structure was going to collapse."

"I'll be honest," Hank said. "We've got a peculiar situation on our hands. The motel wasn't open for business. That's why no one else was injured. The building was scheduled to be demolished this coming Monday. They stopped renting rooms over a month ago."

"How were they going to demo it?"

"By implosion," he told her. "There were several signs posted by the demolition company, Barrow and Kline. They even had a security guard patrolling the premises. We spoke to him earlier and he insisted the motel was vacant. Didn't you see the signs?"

"No," Carolyn said. "I was running late. There was a pickup truck near the office. I thought the place was in such bad shape, nobody wanted to stay there. When the phone rang, I asked Metroix if he'd given anyone the number. He said he hadn't. After I saw the wires, I remembered the incident with the two FBI agents and freaked. Things didn't feel right from the time I got there. I felt like someone was either watching me or following me."

"Did you see this person?"

"No," Carolyn told him. "If there was a security guard, why didn't he realize Metroix was staying there? As soon as I drove into the parking lot, I saw him sitting in front of his window on the second floor. He had the lights on and the drapes open. Your security guard is lying."

"Anything's possible," Hank said, glancing over his shoulder as White slipped back into the room, handing him his coffee and candy bar. "Maybe the guard went to get something to eat. What time did you arrive at the motel?"

"Around six," Carolyn told them, giving a sympathetic glance toward the young officer the detective had intentionally humiliated. "I remember because I looked at my watch. I was late, like I said. I was supposed to meet Metroix at five-thirty. I was afraid he'd think I wasn't coming and leave."

"The security guard worked twelve to eight," Hank said, placing the Snickers bar in his pocket and then taking a sip of his coffee. "He took his break around six. That explains why you didn't see him. How long had this Metroix guy been squatting at the motel?"

"I don't know," she said, shoving a strand of hair behind her ear. "He was paroled two weeks ago from Chino. He claimed he got into town Monday when I conducted the initial interview. I doubt if he was squatting at the motel, Hank. The man inherited seventy grand from his grandmother. Something else is going on here."

"Oh, yeah?" he said. "I'm all ears."

Carolyn turned away, her hands closing into fists. She had to be extremely cautious now. Although she felt certain Hank was an honest cop, he had to know who Daniel Metroix had been convicted of killing. Everything related to the motel could have been an elaborate setup to make certain the man who killed Charles Harrison's son would go away forever. If so, this was worse than what she'd feared, as far too much planning had been involved. "Why would Metroix allow his probation officer to visit him if he'd illegally entered a building? I could have had him shipped back to prison to serve out a life sentence."

Even if Daniel had seen the signs, Carolyn thought, he might not have read them. Discounting the fact that he was schizophrenic, this man lived in a different dimension than most people. Someone had obviously rented him the room, and under the circumstances, the only thing that made sense was that the room clerk was a plant.

"Whoever was behind this could have removed the signs on Monday when Metroix checked in," Carolyn reasoned. "As for the security guard, you know about these guys, Hank. He may have been drunk or stoned."

Daniel Metroix had claimed to have known her from the past. He'd seemed disappointed when Carolyn didn't remember him. Did she have a connection with this man somewhere? On the other hand, she'd been making a lot of inquiries. Word would have gotten out that she was looking into the circumstances of Tim Harrison's death. Could Charles Harrison have decided to use her as a means to ensure that if Metroix didn't die in the blast, a jury would sentence him to death for her murder? Too callous, she told herself. To step out of bounds to keep the individual responsible for your son's death off the street was understandable, particularly if Harrison was convinced the two surviving men had told the truth. To want Daniel Metroix dead would be the ultimate revenge, but nowhere near as maniacal as taking a probation officer with him. Another fact to consider was that the kind of people who set off explosives didn't care if innocent people were injured or killed.

Carolyn heard Hank speaking to White and turned to face the two officers, grimacing in pain as an excuse for her prolonged silence. "Why did they leave the electricity on if they were going to blow up the building next week?"

"Probably so the demo company could see what they were doing," Hank said, crunching the empty Styrofoam cup in his hand. "The gas was turned off several days ago. Your buddy didn't even have hot water. If he was paying good money to stay there, why didn't he complain?"

Hank had a point. He also didn't know Daniel Metroix. A schizophrenic might go weeks without showering. Now that she thought of it, he'd been wearing the same clothes he'd worn at the interview. "What do you think happened?"

"Not sure yet," the detective said, tossing the pieces of the Styrofoam cup into the trash. "My guess is Metroix figured out how to detonate one of the explosive devices near the room where you met him. We checked his prison record. He was known at Chino as the Engineer. The wires were already in place, so a guy with Metroix's type of expertise could have rigged the thing up pretty fast."

"Your premise is shit," Carolyn lashed out. "Metroix got a phone call right before the explosion. He swore he hadn't told anyone else he was staying at the motel. If he blew the place, who called him?"

"Anyone can make a phone ring," Hank told her, smiling smugly. "The motel switchboard was automated. All Metroix had to do was set up a wake-up call for a specific time. He could have been working with another ex-con, or even some-one still serving time at Chino. Metroix's a psycho. Nothing those people do makes sense."

"You're prejudging this man because he has a mental ill-ness," Carolyn said, annoyed at the detective's narrow-mindedness.

"Maybe his voices told him you were the devil and he had to kill you."

Seeing a young doctor speaking to a nurse outside in the corridor, Carolyn decided it was time to put an end to their conversation. Anyone connected with the Ventura police had to be considered a possible ally of Charles Harrison. By aligning herself with Daniel, however, she may have placed something far more valuable than her job at risk. She needed to get home to her children as quickly as possible.

"I don't feel well," she said, reaching for her stomach. "I'd appreciate it if you'd leave now so I can speak to the doctor."

"No problem," Hank said. "Will you be at your office to-morrow in case we need to ask you a few more questions?"

"I'm not sure," Carolyn said. "My office knows how to reach me."

The detective moved closer to her bed. "You're playing a dangerous game here, Carolyn," he said, a look on his face that said he knew she was terminating the interview for rea-sons other than her injuries. "Daniel Metroix is a violent criminal. You were his intended victim. The phone call was pro-bably a ruse to get him out of the room. When you saw the wires on the ceiling, he lost several minutes. This thing was timed to the second. He was going to leave you there to die."

"Let's say he did attempt to kill me," Carolyn said. "What's his motive?"

Officer White found the nerve to speak again. "Maybe he doesn't like probation officers."

The detective shook his head. "Was that a joke, idiot?"

"No, sir," White said, his face blanching. "I thought . . ."

"After three months on the force," Hank told him, "you don't think, speak, or so much as take a piss without my consent. Listen, watch, and learn. Got it? If not, you'll be looking for another job by next week." He turned back to Carolyn. "Did anyone know you were going to be at that motel tonight?"

"Not that I know of," she said, recalling the earlier conversations she'd had with John and her brother.

Hank Sawyer pointed to the door and White shuffled off in that direction. The detective lingered behind. "You're a smart lady. Why are you standing up for a murderer?"

Carolyn held her breath until the detective had left. He was shrewd all right. She should have learned something when he'd come down so hard on the rookie officer. Never offer information unless it benefits you.

Was Hank's wisdom worth contemplating? She'd been tough on Daniel, even though she'd only been doing her job. He wasn't the same as other parolees, though. Would he have had enough time to set up something as complex as a timed explosion? Could her harsh demeanor have incited him to the point where he'd want to kill her? His clever inventions aside, Daniel Metroix was a convicted murderer. Was he also a devious psychopath?

Another chilling thought entered her mind. For all she knew, everything that Daniel had told her could have been either a lie or a delusion. The drawings and computations she'd seen in his room looked impressive, yet under closer examination, they could turn out to be meaningless.

Climbing out of the hospital bed, Carolyn yanked the I.V. out of her arm, found her clothes in a plastic bag taped to the foot of the bed, dressed, and walked out to find a pay phone to call a cab. When she realized she'd left her purse inside the motel room, she placed her hands over her face and cried.

Chapter 7

Wednesday morning, Rebecca leaned over and shook her mother by the shoulder. "I'm sorry to wake you, Mom," the girl said. Her curly dark hair was parted in the middle and pinned back with barrettes. "John said there wasn't anything to make for our lunches. You'll have to give us some money."

Carolyn sat up in the bed, peering up at her daughter through red and irritated eyes. She'd finally caught a ride home with a nurse, collapsing in her bed before dawn. Damn, she thought, doubting if she'd ever see her purse again. At least she hadn't been carrying a lot of cash. Lately, she was lucky to keep a spare twenty on hand. In addition, her credit card was almost maxed out. Her salary paid the mortgage and put food on the table. Tapping it for tuition to law school had squeezed her dry. Now she'd have to go through the inconvenience of applying for a new driver's license, ATM card, and MasterCard.

Getting out of bed and slipping into her robe, she staggered to her closet and rummaged in the bottoms of all her purses. She found a crumpled five-dollar bill, several ones, and a handful of change. "I think there's eight dollars here," she told her daughter, placing the money into the palm of her hand. "You take half and give John the rest."

Rebecca was staring at the bandages on her mother's elbows. Carolyn's knees and legs had also been injured in her frantic escape down the concrete stairway, but the lower half of her body was hidden beneath her bathrobe.

"What happened?" the girl asked. "John said you were in some kind of accident. He wouldn't tell me anything else because he said you'd get mad at him."

Carolyn pulled the girl into her arms, inhaling the fresh scent of her hair. At least her son had kept his mouth shut this time. There was no reason to frighten his sister by telling her that her mother had almost been killed.

"I tripped and fell down a flight of stairs," she said, her eyes meeting John's across the room. "I'm fine, honey. Run along to school or you'll be late."

Rebecca seemed to be afraid to leave. "Will you be here when we get home?"

"I promise," Carolyn told her, deciding the night before had earned her a day off. She could work on her cases without going to the office, and she didn't have any scheduled appointments. Spouting off lies to Amy McFarland might have been tasteless, yet the four new cases Brad had claimed he'd assigned her had never materialized.

Carolyn was thankful that she'd left her briefcase in the car. If she'd taken it to the motel room with her, it would be lost as well. The only problem was getting her car back. She assumed it was in the parking lot of the Seagull Motel, unless the police had towed it.

She saw John standing in the doorway. "Paul Leighton helped me get the car home," he said, tossing a set of keys onto the bed. "I thought you might need it."

"Thanks," Carolyn said, holding the front of her robe closed. "How did your friend manage to drive two cars?"

"Paul thought it would be okay if I drove the Infiniti," he answered. "I knew you kept a spare set of keys in your drawer. It's not like I don't know how to drive, and it wasn't that far. You're not going to go off on me again, are you?"

"I thought I was supposed to call him professor," his mother said. "And I wasn't mad at you last night."

"Fine," John said, stuffing the bills his sister had handed him into his pocket. "We need to leave. I let you sleep as long as possible. You look awful, by the way. Try to get some rest, okay? I'll fix dinner tonight."

Rebecca hugged her mother and disappeared through the doorway with her brother. Carolyn returned to her bed, then grabbed the phone off the end table.

"I need to speak to Warden Lackner," she said when a female voice answered. "I'm Daniel Metroix's parole officer."

"Hold on," she said. "I'll transfer you to Warden Lackner's office."

Carolyn ended up speaking to half of the warden's staff before she finally reached his assistant, a man named Raphael Scribner. "How can I help you?" he asked politely.

"I'd prefer to discuss this with the warden," she said. "Tell him it's urgent. I spoke to him yesterday."

The warden's deep voice came on the phone. "This is Stephen Lackner."

Carolyn gave him a rundown on the events of the night before, along with some of the things she'd uncovered related to the original crime.

"I need to ask you a few more questions about this lab. You said Daniel was good at fixing things. What type of things did he fix?"

"I already told you, Officer Sullivan," the man said, his voice tinged with annoyance, "Daniel repaired various tools we use here at the prison."

Yesterday it was small appliances, today it was tools. "Metroix told me he invented a number of things during his incarceration," Carolyn said. "One of the earliest inventions he claimed he developed at your prison appeared to be a multiscreen monitoring system with recording capabilities. That's not exactly the same as fixing minor electrical appliances or tools." She heard the warden breathing heavy. "He also said he developed a walking suit for a guard's daughter who was partially paralyzed. He called this walking suit an exoskeleton, and said the United States military as well as research facilities around the world are working day and night to perfect it."

"Nonsense," the warden said emphatically. "The man's mentally ill. I'm glad you weren't seriously injured. Other than that, I can't help you."

"You allowed Metroix to work in the lab only if he agreed to sign over all rights to his inventions," she continued. "Is that correct?"

"There were no inventions," Warden Lackner said. "Everything we did was perfectly legal. Metroix called it a lab. It was only a workshop, part of a joint venture program. Some of the goods were used here at the prison, and others were sold to an outside vendor."

Carolyn was beginning to peel off another layer in Daniel's complicated life story. The warden may have written letters in Daniel's behalf to the parole board, only to find a way to circumvent them and covertly convince the board to deny his parole. A man who conducted himself fine behind bars could nonetheless pose a threat to society, particularly if the warden had exaggerated the dangers presented by his illness. The next few questions would be the most pertinent, but for some reason, Carolyn didn't expect the warden to answer them truthfully.

"Let me see if I understand this correctly." She could tell that he was annoyed. The inflection in his voice also indicated that he was nervous. She decided to turn the conversation around, hoping she could extract more information. "By law, the fruits of an inmate's labor go to the prison or whatever state governs the particular institution where he's incarcerated. Is that accurate, Warden Lackner?"

"Exactly," he said, sighing in relief. "Goodbye, Officer Sullivan."

"Don't hang up," Carolyn shot out, knowing it was time to play hardball. "Metroix hired an attorney who believes there's a legal issue involved as to the ownership of his work.

He wasn't merely repairing radios or making license plates. His designs and inventions have been professionally evaluated, Lackner. A great deal of money may be involved."

The line fell silent for several moments. Finally the warden said, "I'm a busy man. I have a prison to run."

Before Carolyn could say anything else, she realized he'd hung up on her. So, she thought, Charles Harrison might not be the only person who wanted to get rid of Daniel Metroix. She was certain the warden had lied to her. How many inventions were involved? Twenty-three years was a long time. Having gained some insight into his personality, she doubted if Daniel remembered even a portion of what he'd done. Setting the exoskeleton aside, if Warden Lackner had substituted his name on an invention that became a staple in every household, he could have a fortune at stake.

Realizing it was past ten o'clock, Carolyn dialed Brad Preston's direct line.

"What the hell went on last night?" he barked. "Your picture's on the front page of the newspaper. Hank Sawyer has already called me twice, demanding to know what we're going to do about Metroix."

Carolyn rearranged the pillows behind her head, trying to get comfortable. "I'm not going to issue an order to violate his parole," she said. "If the DA's office wants to file charges, that's their prerogative. Until I investigate this more thoroughly, my position is that Metroix was an innocent victim. This is far more complex than you could ever imagine, Brad. The warden at Chino might even have hired someone to knock off Metroix."

"What is it with you and this man?" Brad asked, his voice so loud that Carolyn had to hold the phone a few inches away from her ear. "We've got a psycho who tried to blow up a motel with you in it. And you're trying to tell me this guy's not in violation of his parole! Not only that, you're making accusations against a prison warden. I'm beginning to wonder who's crazier, you or Metroix."

"I have a massive headache, Brad," she told him, closing her eyes. "Why don't you start by lowering your voice."

"I assume you're not coming in today. Fill me in on what's going on."

Carolyn told him what she'd learned so far about Daniel Metroix's case, along with a few details regarding her conversation with Warden Lackner. "The more likely scenario is that Charles Harrison contracted to have Daniel killed after his release from prison."

"Since you seem to be certain that Metroix didn't cause his son's death, then why isn't Harrison convinced? He's not an ignorant man, you know."

Carolyn carried the portable phone to the kitchen to put up a pot of coffee. The hangover, she decided, must have been caused by a combination of morphine and stress. The mellow, floating sensation she'd experienced the night before was gone. Every step made her feel as if her knees were going to crack open. To the staff in an emergency room, anything that wasn't life-threatening was considered minor. Whatever injuries she'd sustained weren't going to kill her, but they were most assuredly painful.

"You know how people are in situations like this," she told him. "This was Harrison's only child. The man has tunnel vision, Brad. He's fixated all his grief and hatred on Metroix because Liam Armstrong and Nolan Houston swore he was responsible. Remember, I dated Armstrong. He was a bully and a coward. I also went to school with Houston. I don't remember much about him, though, other than the fact that he's good-looking and black. Once I wrestled with Armstrong in the backseat of his car, I tried to stay away from football players."

"Why are you convinced that Metroix didn't set off the explosion? The warden verified he had a lab. Maybe Hank is right and he did possess the skills to pull something like this off."

"If I hadn't dragged him out of that room," Carolyn said forcefully, "Metroix would be dead. I had to fight him as it was. He didn't want to leave the designs for his inventions."

"Now he's an inventor."

"I saw some of his work," she continued. "Warden Lackner tried to tell me he was making tools or appliances in some kind of joint venture program. I don't believe him."

"You keep forgetting that Metroix is a schizophrenic."

"So what?" Carolyn shouted, slamming the coffeepot down on the counter so hard she cracked the glass canister. "His illness is probably what made him a target for Armstrong, Houston, and Tim Harrison. These boys were nothing more than high-class thugs. You know what Metroix told me?"

"No," Brad said, "but I'm certain you're going to tell me."

"They taunted him, beat him, and then urinated in his face. Nice guys, huh?"

"Why didn't any of this come out at the trial?" he asked. "No matter what these boys did, they did it over twenty years ago. We've got people running around shooting and maiming innocent citizens as we speak. Those are the bastards we should be worried about, not some parolee from years back who's already served his time. Let's say Metroix did get shafted. Nothing's going to change that now."

Carolyn removed the broom and the dustpan from the pantry closet so she could clean up the glass on the floor. "We're not talking ancient history anymore," she told him, bracing herself against the kitchen counter. "Someone tried to kill Metroix last night. If this person or persons wasn't hired by Charles Harrison, our next probable suspect is the warden. The DA can ask for the death penalty in a murder for hire."

"It's not a murder until the person is dead."

"Keep giving me the runaround and it will be."

"You're really serious about the warden?"

"Dead serious," Carolyn told him. "How can we get our

hands on the release papers Metroix signed for his inventions?"

"We don't have any jurisdiction at Chino," Brad told her. "We'd have to get the state attorney general to issue a court order. Even if your man did invent something valuable, which I think is highly unlikely, the only releases you're going to find are the ones issued to the prison or the state."

"Why can't we do a patent search under Stephen Lackner?"

"Be my guest," he said. "I'll put a hundred dollars on the table that you're not going to find anything. Think about it. Lackner has to possess some degree of intelligence, or he would never have been made warden of a major prison facility. Keeping a large population of convicts under control means you have to understand how the criminal mind works."

Carolyn stared out the kitchen window. She needed to mow the grass this weekend. She couldn't ask John, as the poor kid was already doing more than his share. She wished it was December instead of April; then she wouldn't have to worry about the lawn. "You mean he would have put the patents under another name?"

"You got it, babe," Brad said. "You're the one who's studying to be a lawyer. Even I could figure that one out. Lackner could have used a relative, a friend, a guard's wife, or simply created a corporate identity, then sold the invention to a major corporation. You're never going to catch this man, and that's assuming Metroix actually invented anything of value. Even then, why would the warden have to kill him? The way you tell it, he's gotten away with this for years."

"Simple," Carolyn told him, bending down and sweeping some of the glass fragments into a pile. Realizing she was barefoot, she cautiously made her way to the living room and flopped down on the sofa. "As soon as Metroix was granted parole, the warden had to realize that it was only a matter of time before he showed his work to people on the outside. Anyone who saw one of his inventions would want to know what else he'd done. As an example, how would you like to own the patent on the VCR?"

"This is the most ridiculous thing I've ever heard. Do you really believe Metroix invented the VCR?"

"No," she said, checking the soles of her feet and plucking out a tiny glass sliver. To make certain she didn't bleed on the carpet, she placed her legs on the coffee table. "But he may have invented the first multiscreen television set with recording capabilities. That's got to be worth a few bucks."

"Whatever," Brad told her. "Let's forget about the warden and Metroix's inventions for the time being and deal with the immediate problem. If I get an order to violate Metroix's parole, are you going to refuse to sign it?"

"Yes," she said. "And tell Hank if he has any questions, he can call me here at the house."

"He thinks the DA may file attempted murder charges."

"They won't file until they have a provable case," Carolyn told him. "The motel was already wired for demolition. The first thing they have to prove is that the building didn't blow on its own. For all we know, the demolition company was at fault." She reattached one side of the tape to her bandaged right knee. "Our illustrious DA, Sean Exley, is up for reelection this year, in case you've forgotten. Exley would never let one of his prosecutors file an attempted murder case with this many holes in it. Outside of Daniel Metroix, the man they want to charge, I'm their only victim. At present, they have to consider me a hostile witness. Trust me, Exley wants to win every case. What I've described is a prosecutor's worst nightmare."

"You know something," he said, realizing her points were well taken.

"I know a lot of things," Carolyn quipped, bristling with confidence.

"I wish you'd never gone to law school," Brad told her. "You used to be a good probation officer. Now, whenever I talk to you, it's like talking to another attorney. As if we don't have enough of them as it is."

Carolyn smiled. In a way, Brad was right. She did look at her cases differently since she'd enrolled in law school. "Too late now," she said, clicking the phone off.

Chapter 8

Daniel Metroix was huddled in a corner inside his cell at the Ventura County Jail. It was Wednesday. He hadn't slept since the night before. He remembered the explosion, the hospital, the police officers, but he wasn't certain if any of it had been real. He needed his injection. The voices were raging inside his head like a demonic symphony.

A vision of his mother appeared. A heavyset woman with dark frizzy hair, Ruth Metroix had legs as large as tree trunks. She was wearing her stained pink satin bathrobe.

"My precious baby," the apparition said. "What did you do now?"

"I didn't do anything," Daniel shouted. He glanced over at the bars in his cell, consumed with anger and confusion. Memories assaulted him. He clenched his eyes shut, spinning back in time. He was in his old bedroom at the Carlton West apartments.

The phone rang in the small kitchen. Daniel could hear his mother's voice speaking to his psychiatrist.

"I'm sorry to disturb you at home, Dr. Gershon," Ruth Metroix said. "Something is terribly wrong with Daniel. He hasn't come out of his room for two days. I tried to go in there. He must have something blocking the door. He hasn't been eating. He hasn't been going to his classes." She paused, listening. "How do I know if he's been taking his medication? Wait, let me see if I can get him to talk to you. Please honey," she yelled, "come and talk to Dr. Gershon. I have him on the phone."

When Daniel didn't answer, he heard her heavy footsteps on the wood floor. "If you don't come out, I'll have no alternative but to call the police and have them break down the door. They'll want me to put you in the hospital again."

He shoved aside the heavy dresser that was blocking the door and flung it open. "Why are you doing this to me?" he said. "I'm studying. I have final exams next week."

Ruth swallowed hard. "But you haven't been going to school."

His hands were shaking violently, he hadn't shaved in almost a week, and the room reeked of body odor.

"Come to the kitchen and talk to Dr. Gershon," she pleaded, reaching out and trying to grab his hand. "If you do this for me, I promise I'll leave you alone."

Daniel reluctantly did as his mother asked. As soon as she heard him speaking on the phone, he saw her dart inside his room.

"Get out!" Daniel yelled, rushing down the hall and shoving her aside.

Ruth gestured toward the pictures that lined the baseboards. Photos of family members: aunts, uncles, cousins. Shots of Daniel as a toddler riding his bicycle on the sidewalk in front of the complex. "What are you doing? What's the point of this? Why did you take the snapshots out of our photo album?"

He glared at her, refusing to answer.

"Aren't you going to tell me what Dr. Gershon said?"

"He said I should increase my medication," Daniel answered. "Now, will you get out of my room so I can study?"

"Doesn't he want to see you?"

"Dr. Gershon's going on vacation for two weeks," he mumbled. "I made an appointment for when he gets back."

When Ruth saw the open Bible on the floor, she gasped.

Even though she was a devout Christian, Dr. Gershon had instructed her to remove all religious symbols and books from the apartment, even the cross that had been over Daniel's bed for most of his childhood.

Daniel could remember when the nightmare had begun, but he would never understand why. At a school dance, he'd felt compelled to baptize Gracie Hildago in the town reservoir. Without realizing what he was doing, he'd held her head under water too long. The poor girl had almost drowned. He'd spent the next three months at Camarillo State Mental Hospital, a legally sanctioned torture chamber.

Ruth bent down to pick up the Bible and remove it from the room. Daniel wrestled it away from her, then slammed the door in her face. To make certain she didn't try to come in again, he shoved the dresser back in place.

"Idiot," the voice inside his head said. *"You'll never step onto that stage to get your diploma. By June, you'll be dead and buried."*

"No," Daniel said, covering his ears with his hands. "I refuse to listen. You're only a figment of my imagination."

He dropped down on his knees, crawling around the room as he stared at the photographs. He had to remember who he was, somehow stay in touch with reality. Dr. Gershon had told him to increase his medication. He had already upped his daily dosage several days ago and the symptoms had only worsened. Tomorrow, he would take three pills instead of two.

He needed research books from the library. For his science class, he'd designed a prototype of a water purification system that his teacher had thought was excellent. He needed more information, but his mother insisted that he come straight home from school every day. Although he was seventeen, his illness had caused her to treat him like a child.

He remembered that Ruth had already told him that she wouldn't be home until late the following day. His grandmother was ill, and his mother had to drive her to the doctor.

Daniel decided he would go to the library tomorrow to get the books he needed. He liked studying in the library. Being surrounded by books made him feel secure.

"If you leave this apartment, they'll get you," one of the voices told him. *"They're waiting for you. You're a worthless piece of shit."*

Tears were streaming down his face. Why wouldn't the voices leave him alone? Why did they constantly berate him? Couldn't the doctors find a way to cut them out? If slicing off his arm would make the voices stop, he'd go out and buy a chain saw.

He didn't aspire to be wealthy. He'd already let go of any hopes that he might one day get married and have a family. Even if he had an opportunity to have sex, his medication made it impossible. All he wanted was to live his life with some semblance of normalcy, get up every morning and go to work, do something productive.

Daniel pounded the floor with his fists. "Is that too much to ask, God?" he wailed. "Must I suffer? Isn't there some way out? Why am I being punished?"

"What do you know about God, momma's boy? If you wait until tomorrow, you can meet him in person. You're dead, you disgusting asshole. You'll be back in a padded cell. That's a little like dying, isn't it?"

Daniel's fingers trembled as he frantically whipped through the pages in his Bible. He chanted the scriptures aloud, his eyes leaping from one section to another. The portion of the New Testament that was highlighted in red blurred, then melted into a river of blood. His blood. Demon blood. Damaged blood.

He walked to the closet and removed something from the top shelf, placing it in the center of the room. The large Bowie knife slowly began spinning on the floor. If he held his breath, he could hear it speaking to him, hissing like a snake. *"Pick me up, loser. You want an answer to your prob-*

lems, don't you? I'm the answer. Slit your wrists and it will all end."

Daniel pressed his thumbs hard against his eyelids, trying to make the hallucinations stop.

"You know there's only one way to stop it. All you have to do is pick up the knife. Maybe you should slit your throat. That way, you'll die faster."

"H-help me, God," he stammered, pressing his palms together in prayer. It was as if he'd been pulled into hell. His furniture turned into abstract blobs of brown. The walls closed in on him, trapping him in a tight box. He choked on his own saliva. Without thinking, he placed the knife at his throat, directly over his jugular vein.

A sudden breeze from the open window distracted him. He watched as the pages in the Bible fluttered. Almost as soon as the breeze came, it stopped. His gaze locked on the open page.

God was sending him a message.

Daniel read, beginning from Ecclesiastes 4:10: "For if they fall one will lift up his companion. But woe to him who is alone when he falls, for he has no one to help him up. Though one may be overpowered by another, two can withstand him. And a threefold cord is not quickly broken."

Daniel's eyes sprang open when he heard the jailer turn the key in the lock. The scripture had been right. The three awful boys had been waiting in the alley for him.

"Stand up," the large man said. "We're moving you to another cell."

Daniel stood, pushing the past away. Why was he in jail? He'd lost all his work. Was there really a reason to keep living? He'd fallen into the pit again.

When he didn't move, the deputy came inside and seized him. "Get your butt moving, Metroix," he said. "Are you deaf?"

* * *

After consuming three cups of instant coffee and two bowls of Lucky Charms, Carolyn threw on a pair of jeans and a T-shirt to head out to the bank. Once she got some cash and had them issue her another instant teller card, she would go to the jail. With the two agencies disagreeing as to how to proceed, the paperwork on Daniel's release might not be processed until the following day. She could imagine how he must feel. Only two weeks after his parole from prison, and he was once again behind bars. Not only that, the man had lost a lifetime of his work. He was probably more concerned with the loss of his inventions than the fact that he was incarcerated.

Grabbing an old brown handbag and her car keys, Carolyn exited the front of the house. When she saw her car in the driveway, she suddenly halted. Both the front and rear windshields of the Infiniti were shattered, and the side and rear panels had been bashed in as well. For a moment, she wondered if the car had been damaged from falling debris during the explosion. She knew this couldn't be true as John wouldn't have been able to see to drive the car home the night before. She also doubted if her son would fail to tell her about something this disturbing.

Moving closer to the car, she saw a gray, letter-sized piece of cardboard held in place by the windshield wipers. Careful not to cut herself from the shards of broken glass, she plucked it out by the tips of her fingers, hoping whoever had written it had left fingerprints or some other form of identifying evidence. The words were written in large block letters with a black magic marker:

METROIX IS A MURDERER. MURDERERS
HAVE NO FUTURE. HELP HIM AND YOU WILL
DIE WITH HIM.

Carolyn felt her breath catch in her throat. At eleven forty-five in the morning, the sun was high in the sky and the temperature in the mid-seventies, but she felt as if a dark cloud had formed over her head. She stared at the menacing words. Not only was her own life in jeopardy, but also the lives of her children.

Most of the people on the block worked, and their children attended school during the day. Why hadn't she heard anything? The crime had to have been committed some time after eight o'clock that morning, when John and Rebecca had left. Someone could have trashed the car while she was in the shower as her bedroom was located at the rear of the residence.

Carolyn carried the note back inside the house. She set it down on the kitchen table, then placed it inside a plastic sandwich bag. Burying her head in her hands, she tried to decide what to do next. She had to report the crime to the police. If she didn't, her insurance wouldn't cover the damage. The problem was she didn't know whether she could trust Hank Sawyer, or anyone else related to the Ventura police, the same department where Charles Harrison had once been chief. Jurisdiction was jurisdiction, however, and she had no other course of action.

After she notified the police, she called her brother. "Neil," she said when a groggy male voice answered, "I need to borrow your van."

"What time is it?"

"It's past noon," she told him. "John tried to call you last night. You'd already turned off your phones. I was involved in an explosion. This morning someone came to the house and vandalized my car. They also threatened to kill me."

She heard him whispering to someone. She assumed it must be the model with the face and body of an angel. "I'll borrow Melody's car and come right over," he told her. "You can't use my van. We've got it loaded with my paintings for the show. I promised the gallery I'd drop them off this afternoon."

"How is that going to help me?" Carolyn blurted out, her

nerves frazzled. "I need transportation. Your model friend, or whoever Melody is, isn't going to let me use her car for the next week, is she? The police are probably going to impound the Infiniti for evidence. Then I'll have to get it to a body shop."

"Can't you use a county car?"

"The pool cars are death traps, Neil," she told him. "The last time I drove one, the brakes went out on the freeway. I almost went through the windshield. Don't you remember? I spent two days in the hospital."

"Melody is going to hang out here this afternoon," her brother told her. "We'll figure things out when I get there. Calm down, sis. You're bombarding me with all this shit and I'm not even awake yet. Make me some coffee."

"I broke the coffeepot."

"What didn't you break?" he said, groaning. "Forget it. I'll be there in ten minutes."

Carolyn saw two police units pull up in front of her house, as well as the unmarked black Ford Crown Victoria driven by Hank Sawyer. She went outside to talk to them.

While the crime scene tech snapped photos and another officer began writing his report, Hank and Carolyn moved to the other side of the yard so they could converse privately. She leaned back against a large weeping willow tree.

"You're going to violate Metroix's parole now, I hope," he said, tilting his head in the direction of the Infiniti. "Didn't I tell you last night that you're walking on the wrong side of the track?"

Carolyn's emotions had gone from shock to anger. She narrowed her eyes at the detective. "Maybe you wrote the note and had one of your men take a crowbar to my car."

Hank laughed caustically. "Listen," he said, becoming serious again, "I might not agree with you on this Metroix fellow. I don't make threats and I certainly don't arrange for police officers to destroy private property. I realize you've been through the wringer, but you're out of line."

"Think about it," Carolyn said, running her hands through her hair. "Metroix certainly didn't smash up my car and leave a death threat. The man's in jail."

"Like I said last night," he told her, "he may have a crime partner. We're going to check and see if anyone else was released around the same time. A lot of these cons pair up when they leave the joint."

Police and corrections officers worked in the same arena, yet their areas of expertise differed. "How long has it been since you visited a prison?" Carolyn asked. "My guess is Chino released fifty inmates the same day they released Metroix. Everyone's all hot and heavy to lock these guys up. No one gives much thought as to where we're going to put them. Half the prisons in this state are so overcrowded they're under state mandate to release people prior to the completion of their sentences. The whole thing is turning into a farce, a revolving door."

"Metroix didn't do a quick turnaround," Hank reminded her, unwrapping a toothpick and sticking it between his teeth. "He was in long enough to have an entire prison gang behind him."

Carolyn crossed her arms over her chest, then stomped on a snail on the sidewalk to release her frustrations. Out of the corner of her eye, she saw a man standing near the curb. At first she assumed it was Neil, even though she hadn't expected her brother to get there that fast. Ten minutes to Neil generally meant an hour.

Carolyn stared at the man. She estimated his height at around six feet, and from what she could tell, he was slender and fit. He wasn't muscular like Brad, but his clothes hung nicely on his body. Wearing a white, loose-fitting shirt and gray slacks, his salt and pepper hair was pushed behind his ears. It must be naturally curly, she thought, seeing a few ringlets on his neck and forehead. His skin was fair, an interesting contrast against his dark hair. As he moved closer, she noticed that his eyes were a pale shade of blue. This had to be her son's new pal, the esteemed Professor Leighton. Even though he had a broad smile on his face, he squinted in the bright sun. She doubted that he spent a great deal of time outdoors.

Why was he home during the middle of the day, she wondered? John had told her he taught at Caltech. Not only that. Why, she asked herself, had he bought a house in Ventura? Caltech was located in Pasadena, almost a two-hour drive away.

Carolyn moved only inches from the detective's face. "Metroix served such a long sentence because someone made certain of it. Don't patronize me, Hank. You know what's going on here. Maybe when Charles Harrison heard that I refused to violate Metroix's parole, he hired some goons to bash my car in to scare me off."

"Proof, Carolyn," the detective said. "You can't throw those kinds of accusations around without backing them up. Harrison's a respected man in this city."

"I had my doubts about Metroix," Carolyn said, deciding not to tell him about her phone call to the warden until she did more research. "With the way things are shaping up, I'm almost certain he was railroaded. Are you covering for Harrison, along with every other cop around? The way you're acting, I'm beginning to think you are. Give Harrison a message, okay? Tell him the next time anyone steps foot on my property, their brains are going to end up on the pavement instead of my windshield."

Hearing a voice behind her, Carolyn spun around.

"You must be Carolyn Sullivan," the man she'd seen earlier said, extending his hand. "My name is Paul Leighton. Your son—"

Carolyn cut him off, not wanting the detective to get the idea that John was involved. "Nice to meet you," she said, forcing a smile. "Excuse us for a moment, Hank."

The detective shook his head in amazement. "This man may have seen the people who wrecked your car. Now you're going to try to keep me from talking to a possible witness."

"I'm sorry, Officer," Leighton said politely. "I didn't see anything worth mentioning. I assume you're a police officer," he added, glancing over his shoulder at the two other men. "You must be a detective, I guess, since you're not wearing a uniform. Forgive me. I'm not well-versed in police matters."

"Detective Hank Sawyer," he said, squeezing the man's hand and pumping it. "As you can see, Mr. Leighton, we're investigating a crime here. Any information you could provide us would be appreciated."

"I did hear a lot of racket around ten o'clock," Leighton offered. "I thought it was the garbage truck. To be honest, I forgot what day of the week it was." He massaged his hand, as if Hank's handshake had been painful. "When I'm working, I tend to tune out interference."

"I see," Hank said, sizing up Leighton. "What type of work do you do?"

"Well," he said, obviously not an overly talkative person, "right now I'm attempting to finish a book."

"I gather it's not a detective novel," Hank said, chuckling.

"No, no," Leighton said, laughing. "I'm on sabbatical. I teach physics over at the university."

Any mention of physics was enough to send the detective off to speak with the other officers. Carolyn gently took the professor by the elbow, leading him toward the front of her house. Physicists and inventors, normally a rarity, were suddenly in abundance. She wondered if Leighton did most of his writing by hand, the reason he'd cringed when Hank had given him one of his bone-crunching handshakes.

"It was really nice of you to look after John and Rebecca last night," she said, taking a seat in one of the white wicker chairs on her front porch, then gesturing for Leighton to do the same. "As soon as I get a handle on things, we'd love to have you and your daughter over for dinner."

"Oh," he said, lowering himself into the chair next to her. "I was happy to help out. Who do you think did this to your car? Was it related to the incident at the motel or a random act of vandalism?"

She shrugged. "No one knows at this point."

"I wasn't aware there were any problems in this neighborhood," he said, brushing his finger under his nose. "I have a home in Pasadena. I decided that distancing myself from the university for a while might make my work move along faster. You know," he added, lowering his eyes, "when you've been affiliated with an academic community for as long as I have, people have a tendency to intrude on your privacy."

Her son had been right, Carolyn told herself. From what she could tell, Leighton appeared to be an interesting and decent man. And of all days for her to meet him. She looked like a bum off the street. No makeup, her hair dangling in wet strands from the shower, and she was dressed in a drab gray T-shirt and a pair of John's baggy Levi's with rips in the knees. She'd plucked them out of the laundry basket, hoping the rips would minimize the pressure on her injuries.

Carolyn had to admit that there was an aura of elegance about the professor. Maybe she was attracted to him because he was the antithesis of Brad Preston.

"My brother is on his way over. I'm going to have to make arrangements to rent a car," she said, watching as the police loaded the Infiniti onto their flatbed to transport it to the crime lab. "This really is a good area. After last night, you must think I attract trouble."

"I understand you're a probation officer," Leighton stated, swatting a fly out of his face. "That means you deal with criminals on a regular basis."

"More or less," Carolyn told him. "But I've never ended up with them in my driveway. Hopefully, this will be the first and last."

Paul Leighton sat quietly, staring into space. Obviously, he possessed another rare trait—he was comfortable with silence.

"John really enjoyed visiting with you," Carolyn spoke

up. "I'm certain he told you about his aspirations to attend MIT."

"I have an extra car," the professor said. "I'm saving it for when my daughter gets her driver's license. You're free to borrow it until you make other arrangements. All it's doing is gathering dust in my garage. Running the engine would keep me from having to recharge the battery whenever I get around to driving it."

How sweet, she thought. "I couldn't really," she answered. "You've done enough. Anyway, thanks again."

"No, please," Leighton said, his voice elevating. "Lucy was angry at me for making her switch schools. Rebecca introduced her to all her friends the other day. Lucy wants to have her spend the night when they'll have more time together." He paused, rubbing his hands on his thighs. "It's not easy raising a child by yourself. Of course, according to your son, we're in the same predicament."

Carolyn felt comfortable, as if Leighton were an old friend. "If you're absolutely certain," she said, "I might consider taking you up on your offer. Because my purse was destroyed in the explosion, I have to reconstitute my identity. I don't think I'll need the car for more than a day. I'm adequately insured in case something happens."

"Come with me," he said, standing. "You can take the car now."

"My brother and I may be able to figure something else out," Carolyn said, removing a piece of paper and a pen from her purse. "Write down your number. I'll call you if I need to use your car. Are you sure I'm not imposing?"

"Not at all," Leighton said, flashing a broad smile. "What are neighbors for?"

Chapter 9

Neil arrived forty minutes late, roaring into Carolyn's driveway in a burgundy Porsche.

The police had already left and she was waiting on the front porch. At six-three, her brother resembled her father—large, expressive dark eyes, a narrow face with chiseled features, unkempt black hair, and a boyish way about him that made women either want to mother him or jump into bed with him. Neil was so slender he looked as if he hadn't had a decent meal in months. Carolyn wished she shared his metabolism. He ate everything in sight and never gained a pound.

She glared at him. "What took you so long?"

"Oh, you know," Neil said, a sly grin on his face, "unfinished business from last night."

"Unfinished business named Melody, I assume," she said, rocking in the white wicker chair. "When you were a baby, Mother used to say you had your days and nights mixed up. You used to cry all night and sleep all day. You haven't changed. The only difference is you paint all night and have sex all day. I wish I could live the way you do. My life's a disaster."

"Let's go inside," he said. "What's this about an explosion?" He glanced back at the driveway. "Where's your car? I thought it broke down."

"The police towed it," Carolyn answered. "Didn't you listen to anything I told you on the phone?"

"Not really," Neil admitted, opening the door to the house for her. "I didn't go to sleep until seven o'clock this morning. I dropped everything when you insisted I take John and Rebecca out to eat last night. Melody and I were supposed to meet some people for dinner. Instead, she ordered a pizza and watched a movie by herself. I had to make it up to her. That's why I took so long—"

"Spare me the details," Carolyn said, conjuring up images of Neil and Brad sitting around discussing their sexual escapades. How could a woman who had the face and body of an angel also own a Porsche? It wasn't fair.

Once they were inside, Neil draped an arm around her shoulder. He patted her on the back, then yawned. "Everything's going to be all right. Make me a cup of coffee."

After reminding him that she'd broken the coffeepot, she made him a cup of instant. He took a few sips, then dumped the rest in the sink. "Come on," he told her. "We'll go somewhere and have breakfast."

"I don't have time," Carolyn told him, describing the events of the past twenty-four hours. "I need to rent a car, Neil. My purse was in the hotel room. I don't have any money, credit cards, even a driver's license. You can use your credit card to rent me a car, but if you list me as a second driver, I'll have to show them a valid license."

"Where do you have to go?" he asked. "I'll drive you. I have to be back by three to drop off the paintings at the gallery in L.A. I didn't want to bring the van for fear someone would rear-end me."

Carolyn thought of Daniel and how desperate he'd been to save the designs for his inventions. She was angry the police had arrested him without her consent on a parole violation. "One of our neighbors offered to loan me his spare car.

I guess I'll have to take him up on his offer. I might get tied up at the jail. It's past one already."

Neil had a curious expression on his face. "Is someone trying to hurt you or something? You look okay to me."

"I shouldn't have bothered you again. I know you're busy. Everything will be fine, like you said."

"Hold on," he said, raising a palm. "I admit I've been anxious lately, but if someone's causing you a problem, all you have to do is tell me how to find him. I'll go over and set him straight. Nobody messes with my sister."

He pulled Carolyn into his arms, hugging her tightly. She probed his abdomen with her finger. "I can feel your ribs, Neil. Have you been eating?"

"Like a horse," he told her. "Forget about me. Tell me who's bothering you. I can have Melody drive the paintings to L.A. Let's take care of this sucker."

Carolyn stood on her tiptoes, kissing his forehead. They'd always looked after each other. She stroked one of his hands, separating each of the fingers. They were large, almost brutish. She saw the paint stains on his fingernails, and smelled the distinctive odor of turpentine. Years ago, she'd bought a book of Michelangelo's paintings and sculpture, marveling at the artist's ability to depict the raw strength in the hands of a working class man. She'd told her brother he had Michelangelo hands. Her mother had mistakenly thought she was referring to Neil's paintings, one of the reasons she'd started telling everyone that he was the contemporary Michelangelo.

"You're not going to slug anyone with these hands," Carolyn said, releasing them. "I carry a gun, remember? If they come back, I'll shoot them."

Her brother smiled mischievously as he headed for the door. "I had fun with the kids last night, but you still owe me a pie."

Carolyn laughed. "Does it have to be homemade? I can buy you three pies if you want."

"Hey," Neil said, winking, "a deal is a deal."

* * *

At two-fifteen Wednesday afternoon, Carolyn pulled Paul Leigton's ten-year-old blue BMW convertible into the parking lot at the government center complex. Walking in the direction of the jail, she fingered her county ID in the pocket of her jeans. Luckily, she kept it in her briefcase instead of her purse. The bank had taken only fifteen minutes to issue her a new instant teller card. Getting a duplicate driver's license and a new MasterCard would be more time-consuming.

"I'm here to see Daniel Metroix," she said at the window, holding her ID up to the glass so the jailer could see it.

"He's in the medical wing, Sullivan," said Chris McDougal, a black deputy in his late twenties. "You'll have to interview him another day."

"Why's he over there?" she asked. "Because of injuries he sustained last night?"

"Hold on," the deputy told her, opening another file on his computer. "Says he was transferred in from Good Samaritan. According to our records, there's nothing physically wrong with him. He went psycho or something this morning."

"No!" Carolyn exclaimed, assuming Daniel had come unglued when he'd found himself back in jail. She also wondered if it was time for his monthly medication. Even a psychotic break was possible under the circumstances. She tried to recall what he'd told her about the new drug he'd been taking. All that stood out in her mind was that the drug was administered by injection. A chemical that went directly into your bloodstream could cause serious problems if the patient suddenly stopped taking it. "I have to see him," she said. "He's my parolee. I have a right to see him even if he's in the infirmary."

"Look," McDougal told her, "when this guy went berserk, it took five of our people to subdue him."

"Get your supervisor," she said. "And as soon as you call him, I need to see Metroix's booking jacket."

A number of jailers were milling around behind the glass partition. McDougal left and returned a few moments later with a metal folder. He dumped it into the bin with a loud ting, then placed his mouth in front of the microphone. "Sergeant Cavendish is coming down to talk to you."

"I'll be waiting," Carolyn said, opening the file and flipping through the paperwork. She took a seat in a long row of interconnected plastic chairs used by visitors, opening her briefcase and pulling out a release sheet.

As she'd anticipated, the DA had failed to follow through and file charges. An arresting officer could book a subject on probable cause, but he had to back it up with a formal complaint, and the prisoner had to be charged and arraigned in front of a judge within twenty-four hours. She'd finished filling in the particulars when she looked up and saw an enormous man with a square jaw peering down at her. "You Sullivan?"

"Yes," she said, standing. "Here're the release papers on Daniel Metroix. I'd like them processed as quickly as possible."

Sergeant Cavendish looked surprised. "You're not going to violate him?"

"No," Carolyn told him, clasping her briefcase and the metal file to her chest. Cavendish had to be over six-five and couldn't weigh less than three hundred pounds, all of it solid muscle. He reminded her of a Neanderthal. She sensed that he got a kick out of intimidating people, especially small women officers like herself. "I understand there was a problem this morning," she said. "Metroix's a schizophrenic. He needs his medication."

"Listen, lady," Cavendish said, "half the guys in here have some kind of head problem. Your boy assaulted one of our officers. We can file charges against him ourselves."

Carolyn thrust her shoulders back. "That wouldn't be wise, Sergeant."

"Oh, yeah," the sergeant said, one corner of his lip curling. "And why is that?"

"Because he was illegally booked," she told him, hoping she might be able to bluff him into releasing Daniel. "I was with him when the building blew last night. He's my parolee, and no one can violate his parole except me or a superior at my agency. I informed Detective Sawyer and Officer White that I wasn't prepared to violate his parole. Not only that, regulations state that an inmate has the right to receive proper medical treatment. Metroix was supposed to have an injection either this morning or last night."

"Did a doctor order this injection when the prisoner was transferred from the hospital?" Cavendish asked, not quite as aggressive as before. " 'Cause if we don't have an official order on file, we can't administer it."

"I need to go to the bathroom," Carolyn said, rushing off in the direction of the ladies' room.

As soon as she entered a stall, she pulled down the toilet seat, sat down, and opened the metal file. Finding the release papers from the hospital, she saw that the area where follow-up instructions were to be inserted had been left empty, more than likely because Hank had placed Daniel under arrest before the emergency room physician had gotten around to finishing the paperwork.

Carolyn wrote an order that the patient had to be administered an injection by six o'clock that morning. She couldn't recall the exact name of the drug Metroix had told her he was taking, but she remembered jotting down the letters DAP. Before she left the bathroom, she caught a glimpse of herself in the mirror.

"Not only do you look like a bag lady," she told herself, "you're turning into a criminal." Since Daniel Metroix had come into her life, her world had turned upside down. She'd forged an official document. She hoped the man was the victim she perceived him to be. If not, she had less of a brain than Cavendish.

"I'm sorry," she told the sergeant, feigning embarrassment. "When nature calls, you know." He reached for the file, and she quickly stepped back. Until she knew Daniel was going to be released, she didn't want to commit to her deception. If things didn't go the way she planned, she'd have to make another emergency trip to the bathroom.

"He's taking an antipsychotic medication," Carolyn told him. "It wouldn't be unusual for him to have a violent reaction in withdrawal. You can proceed any way you deem fit, Sergeant. I'm certain your assault charges won't stick, though, since you failed to follow through on the doctor's orders. In reality, the county could be sued and—"

Sergeant Cavendish sighed. "That's enough," he said. "I'll release this man on one condition."

"Okay," she said. "I'm listening."

"You have to take custody of him," he told her. "Can you handle that? You ain't that big and this inmate stirred up a lot of trouble this morning."

And you aren't that smart, you big oaf, Carolyn was tempted to tell him. "You've got yourself a deal."

"Give us about thirty minutes and the problem's yours."

As Cavendish turned around and headed toward the security door, Carolyn wondered how an undertaker would ever get a man his size inside a coffin. His muscles were so overdeveloped, she didn't think it was possible for his arms and legs to lay flush against his body.

She glanced at her watch. John and Rebecca would be getting home from school in less than an hour, and she was in such a morbid state her thoughts had turned to undertakers. Worse—what was she going to do with Daniel? He'd gone up against five jailers, and if the events of the night before had caused him to become psychotic, he might be as dangerous as everyone kept insisting. She thought about her gun, then realized this was another item that had been lost during the motel explosion.

Carolyn pulled out her personal cell phone and called her house, leaving a message on her answering machine. The phone issued by the county had also been in her purse. She felt guilty as she'd promised Rebecca that she'd be there when she got home from school. John had said he would cook dinner. Unless she came up with another plan fast, they'd be setting an extra plate at the table.

Chapter 10

B y four o'clock Wednesday afternoon, Carolyn had Daniel Metroix in the passenger seat of Professor Leighton's BMW. His clothes reeked of smoke and were in tatters, and a day's growth of stubble covered his face. He hadn't said a word since they'd left the jail. She noticed that his right arm was jerking in some type of spasm.

"What's the name of the drug you're taking?" she asked, glancing over at him.

"Decanoic acid phenothiazine," Daniel told her. "I was supposed to take my monthly injection several days ago. The infirmary at prison used to give it to me. I lost track of time. My medicine, along with the rest of my stuff, was in the motel room. Do you have it?"

"No," she said, wondering how she could obtain this type of medication. People didn't hand out psychotropic drugs, and what he was taking probably wasn't even that common. If she wasn't mistaken, she recalled him mentioning that the drug had only recently been approved by the FDA.

"Why did they arrest me again?"

Carolyn's hands locked on the steering wheel. The look out of his eyes was frightening. He was probably exhausted and confused, in addition to the fact that he hadn't taken his injection. No way could she allow him around her children.

"They made a mistake," she told him. "I took care of it, didn't I? You're not in jail anymore."

"What happened to my work?"

"I'm not certain," she said, although she knew it was lost forever. Perhaps what she saw on his face was despair. Finally his life had taken a right turn, only to end up back where he'd started. "Let's deal with the most urgent problem first. We have to find a way to get you a new prescription."

"My work's important," Daniel told her, becoming agitated. "I might not be able to regenerate even a fraction of what was in that room. Those papers represented years of my life. I wish you'd let me die last night. All I've ever had was my work."

"I understand," Carolyn said, keeping her voice low and consoling. "We need to find a psychiatrist. No one outside of a psychiatrist would be able to prescribe that type of medication. I only know one person we can call," she added, thinking of Dr. Weiss. "He doesn't see patients anymore. Besides, I'm sure a new doctor would want to evaluate you before he prescribed anything, maybe even admit you to a hospital."

Carolyn felt as if she were talking to herself. Daniel had his head turned, and didn't appear to be listening. She thought about dropping him off at the local mental health facility so she could go home and get some rest. Not only was his life in jeopardy, she appeared to be linked to him by association. She had to keep tabs on him for her own protection. In addition, she needed more information.

"What happened at the jail?"

"I don't remember."

His voice was muffled, and he was still staring out the window. "Look at me," she said. "Did you hit anyone?"

"I don't think so," Daniel told her, clasping one of his hands with the other to control the tremors. "I need my medicine."

"I understand," Carolyn said, suddenly remembering that she made a copy of the prescription to put in his file. "You had your prescription when you came for your intake inter-view. Where is it now?"

He became quiet, then suddenly started talking rapidly. "I dropped it off at the drugstore near the motel so I wouldn't lose it."

"Do you remember the name of the pharmacy?"

"Rite Aid," he said, a sense of urgency flashing in his eyes. "Can you take me there?"

"That's where I'm headed now," she answered, making a U-turn and steering the car onto the 101 Freeway. "You need to stay calm and trust me. Once we get your medicine, I'm going to see if I can rent you another motel room. You must do exactly as I tell you. We don't want a repeat of last night."

"I have money," he said. "My attorney, Mr. Fletcher, had me open up a bank account. The bank's right down the street from the drugstore."

"You'll need identification," Carolyn told him. "Not only that, most hotels require a credit card. We may run into trou-ble. My purse and all its contents were destroyed."

Daniel reached into his pocket and pulled out a new black leather wallet. "I have everything," he said, flipping the wal-let open and displaying a California identification card, as well as numerous credit and bank cards.

She no longer had to worry about verifying his story about the money he'd inherited. "Was that in your pocket last night?"

"Yes," he said. "Mr. Fletcher set me up, like I said. I've never used any of the plastic cards except for the motel."

"Did you tell this attorney where you were staying?"

"Of course," he said, looking at her as if he didn't under-stand why she'd asked him such a foolish question.

Carolyn almost collided with the car in front of her. "I thought you said you didn't give anyone except me the phone number to the motel."

"I didn't," he told her.

"But you said you did."

"No," Daniel said. "I said I *told* him where I was staying. That didn't mean I gave him the phone number."

Carolyn felt the hairs prick on the back of her neck. Since he'd told his attorney where he was staying, her premise that no one outside of herself knew that he was renting a room at the Seagull Motel had flown out the window. "Has everything you've told me been the truth?"

"Yes," he said. "I don't lie."

"I called the warden at Chino. He referred to your lab as a workshop. He said you and some other trustees repaired small appliances and made tools. Is that what you were doing?"

"No," Daniel said, the spasm in his right arm getting worse. "Did Warden Lackner really say those things?"

"He said you made up the stuff about your inventions, that you'd never invented anything. I'm trying to help you. I have to know the truth."

"I thought the warden liked me," Daniel said, looking dejected. "I did everything he told me to do."

"Did he make you sign a release for your inventions?"

"Yes," he told her. "No one ever believes me. They didn't believe me when I told them those boys attacked me. They didn't believe me in the jail this morning."

"What happened at the jail?"

"I slipped and fell. One of the other inmates slugged a guard, then everyone got into it. As usual, they blamed me."

Carolyn made a sharp left when she saw the Rite Aid sign. "We're here," she said, relieved. "Let's go inside and get your medicine."

"I need paper, the large kind."

They got out of the car and headed into the store. "You're not going to school," Carolyn said, losing her patience. "Get the damn prescription filled so I can go home."

"My work," Daniel said, crestfallen. "I want to try to reproduce my work. I lost things I've been working on since I was a teenager."

"Be thankful you're not in jail," Carolyn told him. "I'll

call you tomorrow morning. You have to promise me you'll stay in the motel. This is serious, understand?"

"Is someone still trying to kill me?" Daniel asked as they headed down the aisles toward the pharmacy. "Is that why you're helping me?"

"They may be," she said. "There's another problem. I'm in danger and so is my family. If you know anything you're not telling me, you better cough it up right now."

"I need books," Daniel said. "Get me anything you can find on thermodynamics. I was studying thermal electron generators. I also need information on hydrogen power cells."

Carolyn glanced down and saw that his shoelaces were untied. "Tie your laces," she told him. He also needed clean clothing, deodorant, a toothbrush, a razor. Brad's assigning her a parolee to supervise had ticked her off, but nowhere to the extent of what she felt now. "I'm not your personal shopper. Get what you need while they're filling your prescription. Then we're leaving, got it?"

Carolyn remembered that she also had to watch him give himself the injection. Her children were home alone. She was the one who needed to see a shrink.

By nine-thirty Wednesday evening, Carolyn felt as if she were about to pass out from exhaustion. She'd spent over an hour helping Rebecca with her homework, then cleaned up the kitchen so her son could complete his studies. Finally she tucked her daughter into bed. As she was heading down the hall, she ran into John.

"Paul called while you were in Rebecca's room," he said, trailing behind his mother as she continued toward the master bedroom. "I wanted to come and get you. He told me not to bother you. Why didn't you tell me someone broke the windows out in the Infiniti? Paul said he loaned you his other car, that blue BMW I saw in his garage. He called to make certain you didn't have any problems with it."

Not wanting to alarm the children, Carolyn had parked the professor's car on the opposite side of the street. She also didn't want to tell her son that it was far more than the windows on the Infiniti that had been damaged. The professor must have seen his BMW and feared she'd had some kind of mechanical problems.

Sitting down in the blue velvet chair across from her bed, Carolyn draped her arms over the sides and stretched her legs out in front of her. "I didn't want to scare you," she said. "I guess I should have told you about the car. After last night, I thought we needed some time to regroup."

John's face twisted in anger. "Some of my friends saw the article in the paper about the explosion. Why didn't you tell me that man had been convicted of killing a kid?" He pointed an accusing finger at her. "Someone's messing with you again because of him."

"No one hurt me," Carolyn told him, too tired to argue. "Think about it, honey. I was in the house alone when the damage to the car occurred. If they'd wanted to hurt me, why didn't they do it then?"

"Wrong!" John said, closing the door to his mother's room so his sister wouldn't overhear. "Whoever these people are, they're warning you. You were with that stupid guy again tonight, weren't you? That's why you were late. Jesus, Mother, why are you doing this? I feel like you're the kid and I'm the parent, like you've suddenly decided to hang out with the wrong crowd. Are you in love with this creep or something? Tell me, okay? Because I don't understand." He stopped speaking, then a moment later erupted again. "Don't you know how I feel? You're going to get us killed."

"Don't raise your voice to me," Carolyn said. "I'm ethically bound to help this man if I suspect he's been a victim of injustice. Well, let me tell you something. This isn't a little mistake someone made. Daniel Metroix has lost most of his adult life. And I know a lot more about life than you do, *son*." She paused, letting her last word linger in the air.

When his mother used a generic reference such as *son,* John knew it was time to shut up and listen. It was her way of reminding him where he stood in the pecking order.

"Everything that's happened over the last two days only confirms my suspicions that Daniel Metroix was framed. What's going on right now may not be related to the Harrison boy's death. There's a possibility that it has something to do with his inventions."

John didn't understand what his mother meant by inventions. All he knew was now was not the time to ask questions. "Fine," he said, slapping his hands against his thighs. "What do you want us to do?"

"Be extremely cautious," Carolyn advised, repositioning herself in the chair. "From now on, I don't want Rebecca walking on the street alone. Either I'll drive her or you'll have to walk her to school and pick her up at the end of the day." She knew what she was asking of him was an additional inconvenience. Life wasn't easy. "As to your own protection, try to stay in a group when you're not here at the house. I'll buy both you and Rebecca a cell phone tomorrow. That way, you can call either me or the police if you notice anything even slightly suspicious." She paused, letting her previous statements sink in. "I'm not going back to law school until this problem has been resolved. That way, you won't be alone as much as you have in the past. You'll also have more time to concentrate on your schoolwork."

"Why would you drop out of law school because of this man?" John asked. "You've worked so hard."

"I didn't say I was dropping out for the entire semester," Carolyn told him. "I may miss a few classes, that's all. I can catch up. Besides, I'm not giving up my school or anything else for *this man,* as you keep calling him."

She bent down and plucked one of the bandages off her right knee. The stitches would dissolve, the doctor had told her. Too bad problems didn't dissolve as easily. "When I became a probation officer," she said, "I took an oath to uphold the law and protect society. Daniel Metroix is every bit as deserving of my time and efforts as Professor Leighton down the street or any other resident of this county. This may sound overly simplistic, John, but bad things happen to good people. Never forget that one of those unfortunate people could one day be you."

The wisdom of his mother's words struck home. John knelt on the floor in front of her and gently removed the bandage from her other knee.

"I can't back off now, anyway," she whispered, knowing whoever was trying to kill Daniel had probably already learned that she'd arranged his release from jail. "I'm in too deep."

"Why don't you take off those jeans," John told her, gazing into her eyes with respect and tenderness. "I'll get some hydrogen peroxide and some new Band-Aids. The cuts aren't that deep. You should keep them covered, though, so they won't get infected." He reached over and rolled up her sleeves, removing the bandages and studying the cuts on her elbows. "They didn't even need to stitch up this one," he told her, clasping her left forearm as he examined the wound. "Stay here while I get the first-aid kit from the kitchen. Then you have to go straight to bed."

Before he got back on his feet, Carolyn tossed her arms around his neck and embraced him. His words had been echoes of her own. Funny, she thought, remembering all the childhood injuries, colds, viruses, and flus she'd nursed over the years. Once children matured, they treated much of the wisdom they'd acquired as if it had magically appeared, seldom giving credit to the parents who'd implanted it.

"Are you sure you don't want to become a doctor?" Carolyn asked, letting her arms slide down his muscular shoulders. "You'd make a good one."

"Never know," John said, smiling as he hurried out of the room.

* * *

Carolyn drove both Rebecca and John to school Thursday morning, then headed to the government center complex. The night before, she'd made a list of the various people she needed to contact regarding Daniel and the events surrounding Tim Harrison's death. The situation with the warden might have to wait until she obtained more specific information about his inventions. She couldn't tell if someone held or had applied for a patent until she knew precisely what had been invented.

Brad was probably right. If Warden Lackner was corrupt, he would have been sophisticated enough not to register the patents under his own name.

Modern technology had provided many benefits to criminal investigators, yet it had also placed barriers around those they needed to contact. Due to constant soliciting, hardly anyone had a listed phone number, even in a town the size of Ventura. In reality, there was no such thing as a small town anymore. The entire universe was electronically connected. Being in law enforcement, Carolyn could obtain an unlisted number without a problem, but she couldn't prevent a person from blocking a call or not picking up the phone unless they knew the caller. Probation and parole officers now spent untold hours trying to perform what had once been one of the most simplistic aspects of their job—calling and checking up on their offenders. Months could pass before an officer could confirm that a probationer had actually absconded or was merely hidden behind a wall of security, either on their jobs or in the homes where they resided. Some measure of proof was necessary to file the appropriate court documents, and although surprise visits sounded good on paper, appearing at a probationer's door without notice could either be a waste of already overburdened officers' time, or place them in grave danger.

Carolyn ran into Veronica in the hallway. "You look terrible," the woman exclaimed. "I thought you were going to become famous defending criminals, not getting yourself blown to pieces." When Carolyn glared at her, she quickly added, "I'm joking, okay? Can't you smile every now and then? Seriously, are you okay? Everyone's been talking about you and this Metroix fellow."

Veronica took Carolyn's hand and pulled her into one of the interview rooms. "You're not carrying on with him, are you? I mean, the newspapers said you were in his motel room."

"Please," Carolyn said, too pressed for time to listen to her habitual jabbering. "How could you even think such a thing? I wasn't able to collect all the information I needed from him at the office. Metroix is a supervision case. It's required that we check their living environment. Right now, his home is a motel."

The woman pointed at her chest. "Don't blame me, honey. I'm your friend. People talk, that's all. Preston is looking for you, by the way, and he doesn't look very happy."

Carolyn poured herself a cup of coffee from the break room, then carried it back to her desk. The first thing she did was call the records division to see if they could furnish her with the phone numbers and addresses for Liam Armstrong and Nolan Houston. As soon as she hung up the phone, Brad strode into her cubicle, red-faced and furious.

"The least you could have done was check in with me this morning," he yelled at her. "You weren't able to come to work yesterday, but you felt good enough to get Metroix out of jail. Hank Sawyer went ballistic a few minutes ago. He demanded that I force you to tell me where you stashed him."

Carolyn continued making notes to herself on a yellow pad, not so much as raising her head. Finally she tossed her pen aside, mad that she had to fight her own agency as well as the police to do what she felt was her job. Brad had never questioned her judgment before, nor had any of the district attorneys or judges. The only people who ever complained about her were defense attorneys. Did Brad really believe she would protect a man who posed a threat to the community, or more specifically, someone who was out to harm her or her family? "Hank Sawyer has no right to know Daniel Metroix's whereabouts. No criminal charges were filed. I'm the officer you assigned to supervise this man. The only person he's required by law to keep apprised of his whereabouts is me."

"Sometimes I forget how hardheaded you are," Brad said, yanking a chair from the other desk and straddling it backwards. "Look, why go to war over this? We're supposed to work in concert with the PD. Hank has a right to interrogate a witness to a crime. And what happened at that motel wasn't a minor incident. Not only that, he says someone left you a threatening note and smashed your car up yesterday. Why didn't you tell me?"

Carolyn stared out the window, her anger dissipating as she fell deep in thought. Like a jigsaw puzzle, the case seemed to be scattered in pieces. The time element was a major problem. Somehow she had to find a way to resurrect the events of the past, then successfully connect them to the crimes of the present. She also had to consider that this might be a puzzle that could never be solved.

Carolyn recalled awakening at four in the morning when she was a teenager. She'd gone to the kitchen for a glass of milk and found her father working at the kitchen table, stacks of papers in front of him, all covered with complex equations. He used to concentrate so intently that Carolyn and Neil had placed bets as to who could distract him. They'd rattle pots and pans, blast their radios, even stand in front of him and scream that someone was breaking into the house. Carolyn had been shocked when her father had stopped working that morning and talked to her. He'd explained that he was attempting to solve the Riemann hypnosis, the Holy Grail of mathematics. After his death, her mother told Carolyn and Neil that their father's obsession with this unsolved problem was the reason he'd been unemployed for so many years. As she grew older, Carolyn had become more like her father. She now realized how hard it must have been for him to let go and take a teaching position so he could support his family.

Pulling herself back to the present, Carolyn asked, "Did Hank know if the crime lab found any fingerprints or other evidence on the note left on my car?"

"Since you're convinced Charles Harrison is behind this, did you really expect them to find any incriminating evidence?" Brad stood, shoving the chair aside. "The least you could do is look at me when I talk to you."

"I refuse to respond when you yell at me," Carolyn said calmly. She swivelled her chair around to face him. "I'm not only smarter than you, Brad, I'm more professional."

"I'm not sleeping with Amy McFarland."

"Right," she said. "Don't try to bluff at poker. Is she good in bed?"

"Not since you told her I'm engaged."

Carolyn locked eyes with him. "Guess you'll have to buy her a ring."

It took a while before Brad realized she was teasing. They'd bantered back and forth for years, making an otherwise unpleasant job more bearable. A person who overheard some of their conversations would assume they despised each other. Nothing could be further from the truth.

"You're beginning to sound like yourself again," he said. "I'm not sleeping with Amy McFarland, okay? The girl wants to get married and have babies. I don't have it in me to change dirty diapers."

"I was afraid they wouldn't find anything worthwhile on the note," Carolyn said, returning to the business at hand. "It was written on cardboard. You know, the kind of heavy, coarse paper they put inside men's shirts at the dry cleaners." She fiddled with a strand of hair. "At least we know something about this person."

"What's that?"

"They're not poor," she said. "Poor people don't send their shirts out to be washed and ironed. Maybe Charles Harrison wrote the note himself."

"And showed up in your driveway with a crowbar?" Brad argued. "That's absurd, Carolyn. I called around. Harrison's on his last leg. The booze got to him. His liver is shot and he's waiting for a transplant."

Carolyn gave him a coy smile. "So he hires classy thugs."

Brad laughed. "Yesterday you were ready to go after a prison warden. Now Harrison's back in the hot seat."

"I haven't had a chance to check out the patent situation," she explained. "Lackner would have to work awfully fast to trash my car only a short time after I got off the phone with him." She stared at the center of his chest. "That's the most hideous tie I've ever seen, Brad. Are those headless naked ladies?"

"You're losing your eyesight," he said, laughing. "They're bowling pins." After all the trouble she'd encountered, Carolyn Sullivan was gutsy enough to keep her sense of humor, one of the reasons he generally catered to her demands. As much as they squabbled, he not only cared for her, he respected her.

"We have to cooperate with the police," he said, serious again. "Be reasonable, Carolyn."

"I'll cooperate," she told him, holding her ground. "I'm not willing to cooperate right now."

"What do you want me to do?" Brad asked. "Can you afford to be suspended without pay? Maybe you should give your children some thought before you answer. Don't forget, I have to report to Robert Wilson. He knows you dropped the ball on Downly."

"My children and I are fine," Carolyn said. "I'm going to make an appointment to speak to Judge Shoeffel."

Brad raised his voice again. "You're taking this to Arline Shoeffel? You've got balls. I wouldn't have the nerve to present a case this weak to any judge, let alone the presiding judge herself." He paused, then remembered. "Oh, you know Shoeffel from law school, right? She teaches one of your classes."

"Don't you understand my problem, Brad?" Carolyn said. "I don't know who to trust at the police department. I'd like to think Hank isn't involved, but how can I be certain? The only way to clear this up is to go straight to the top."

"Hank was a rookie when Metroix was sent to prison," Brad told her, thinking she was being paranoid. "And some of the officers at the PD weren't even born."

"I don't care," she said, "I refuse to allow this man to be assassinated."

"You really believe things could go that far?"

"Absolutely," Carolyn said, touching the tender spot on her right elbow. The rest of the injuries she'd sustained the night of the explosion were healing nicely. Daniel had been lucky, as he'd been wearing Levi's and a long sleeve shirt. "Didn't you tell me Harrison was on his deathbed? What kind of punishment can you hold over a dying man's head? He may be determined to take Metroix with him. I'm not going to let him."

"You know," Brad said, belching, "you're going to give me a damn ulcer. You want to play lawyer, I'm sure between the PD and the DA's office, we can come up with hundreds of botched cases. That's not your job. What's the status on the Sandoval shooting?"

"I've already interviewed Lois Mason," Carolyn told him, having no idea where she'd even placed the paperwork. "The report isn't due for two weeks."

"What about Eddie Downly?" Brad asked. "Even with the rape charges, you have to officially violate his probation. Of course, once he's convicted, you'll be assigned to handle the pre-sentence investigation."

On this case, there would be no disagreements. "What's the latest on the girl?"

"She's still at Methodist Hospital," Brad told her. "The lab found tissue and blood under her nails. A bloody fingerprint from her neck appears to be Downly's, but it's the DNA that will nail him. Three witnesses from the neighborhood picked him out of a lineup. He'd been stalking her for five or six days. At least the sick fuck didn't kill her."

"Do you know which DA will be prosecuting? I'd like to see how many counts they're going to file." Carolyn gritted her teeth. "I'd be more than happy to pay Downly a visit. What I'd really like to do is to take him out and shoot him."

"A meat grinder would be more appropriate," Brad told her, stretching his lanky frame. "Against my better judgment," he continued, "I'm not going to interfere in the Metroix case. You've got one day. But if Hank or anyone from the PD calls me again, I'm transferring the call to you. You want to be in the field alone, then that's where you're going to be."

Carolyn cleared her throat. "My gun was in the motel room," she said. "I'll need another one, as well as a shoulder holster. My holster was in my car, and the PD impounded the car for evidence. Oh, and I also need a new cell phone. Right now, I'm using my own for agency business."

"I'll write the requisitions," Brad told her. "You can pick them up from Rachel. My suggestion is you head over to the supply clerk immediately. Try not to kill anyone. And for God's sake, don't let this man we're all supposed to be protecting play around with your gun. I'd like to see you pass the bar exam, not help your kids pick out a casket."

Chapter 11

At eleven-fifteen that morning, Carolyn was flipping through the pages of Fast Eddie's file. Although she had been assigned to supervise him, another officer had investigated the case prior to sentencing. The indifference represented in the report was appalling. The victim's statement consisted of only a few sentences. Putting on her headset, she dialed a number.

Once she concluded the call, Carolyn removed a pair of heels from her file cabinet, stepped into them, then left her flats under her desk and walked briskly toward the ladies' room.

Standing in front of the mirror, she searched her makeup bag until she found a tube of bright red lipstick. After she put on several coats of mascara, she looked in the mirror. Something was missing. Ah, she thought, removing a black pencil to line her eyes.

Finished with her face, she rolled her skirt up at the waist until the hemline was several inches above her knees. Placing the makeup bag back into her purse, she unbuttoned the top of her blouse, wanting her cleavage to be visible. Luckily, she didn't need a Wonder Bra, what some women thought was the greatest invention of the twentieth century. In the breast department, nature had been more than generous.

Carolyn took the elevator to the first floor, left through

the back door of the building, and continued around the corner to the men's jail.

"Visiting hours aren't until three," Deputy Herschel Wells told her, a tall man with short brown hair and an olive complexion.

Carolyn filled out a form requesting to see Eddie Downly, placing it along with another document into the metal bin. "I'm Edward Downly's probation officer. I need to see him."

"You must be shitting me," Wells said, his tongue sweeping across his lips as he gawked at her chest. "You aren't planning on going inside like that, are you? We'll have a riot on our hands."

"Get the damn prisoner," Carolyn said gruffly. "I don't have time to stand around here all day. I'm placing a hold on Downly for violation of probation. I gave you the paperwork."

"It's almost lunchtime," Wells told her. "If I pull him now, he won't get to eat."

Carolyn's eyes narrowed. "Downly raped an eight-year-old girl. He doesn't deserve to live, let alone eat. Have one of your men park him in an interview room."

Wells pulled up the inmate's booking sheet on the computer, then looked back at Carolyn. "You're asking for trouble, you know. Can't you get whatever information you need from Downly through the glass?"

What the deputy was referring to was the regular visiting area of the jail. A bulletproof sheet of glass separated the inmates from anyone who came to see them. They used a phone to communicate. Probation officers, police officers, and attorneys had the option of what they referred to as a face-to-face interview. For security reasons, the inmate and visitor were locked inside a room by a jailer. Many of Carolyn's fellow officers refused to place themselves in such close contact with a violent offender, knowing they could be attacked or used as a hostage in an escape attempt. The more serious the crime, however, the greater importance Carolyn placed on a face-to-face interview. Her goal was to get the offender to trust her, hoping he would provide information she could use to justify a longer term of imprisonment. She didn't use a tape recorder as most officers did, nor did she take notes. Inmates would seldom open up when they knew their words were being recorded.

Compiling an accurate criminal history was crucial. Carolyn had handled offenders with a ten-page rap sheet who were presented to the court as first-time offenders. The law stated that unless the prior offense resulted in a conviction, the incident could not be considered at sentencing. With the deluge of cases flooding the courts throughout the country, dispositions were not always reported. Plea bargains presented another problem. An arrest for assault with a deadly weapon could end up as a conviction for theft, rapes could appear as breaking and entering, and vehicular manslaughter could be knocked down to a misdemeanor traffic violation. If the offender supplied the details of the actual offense, however, the information was then admissible with or without a formal disposition. Carolyn did everything humanly possible to provide the court with a detailed and usable criminal history.

She loved to see the look on a criminal's face when the judge handed down a lengthy prison term, knowing the guy had expected to receive no more than a few months in jail. What enraged offenders the most, though, was the realization that they'd brought this on themselves by talking so openly to the pretty probation officer.

Carolyn had suffered only one frightening experience. It had happened not long after she'd been hired. The old jail, located in Oxnard, a sister city to Ventura, had been a dark, dilapidated structure. Since there were only two interview rooms, they occasionally used a large open room that had at one time been a shower. The man Carolyn had been assigned to submit a pre-sentence report on had been a Hispanic male facing sentencing on five counts of residential burglary. Of course, had she been dressed as she was today, she felt certain the man would have raped her. As it was, he'd chased her around the room for almost two hours, ripping her blouse and slamming her head against the concrete floor. Carolyn had screamed for help, but no one had heard her. Because it was shift change, the officer who'd locked her inside had forgotten to tell anyone that she was there.

The new jail was a marvel of modern technology. When she hit the buzzer, a jailer usually responded within a matter of minutes.

"Get the prisoner," Carolyn told Deputy Wells. "I know how to take care of myself."

Once she passed through the security doors, Carolyn stopped and stored her purse and her new gun in a locker. An older deputy with balding hair and a bulging stomach appeared to escort her through the corridors.

"Looks like it's show time, Sullivan," Alex Barker said, having watched Carolyn in action for years. "You know what the inmates call you these days, don't you?"

She didn't really care, but she liked Barker. She occasionally asked him to do favors for her. "The Wicked Witch of the North?"

"Worse than that," the deputy said, talking over the din of wolf whistles and profanity coming from the men in the cells. "Not these idiots, of course," he added. "The men in this block are pre-trial. It's the guys serving time who call you the Angel of Death."

"Sounds good to me," Carolyn said, smiling.

"The story goes that a drop-dead gorgeous broad pays a visit, and the next thing they know, the inmate disappears. They're too stupid to figure out that the guy has been shipped off to prison."

Barker unlocked the door to a small, windowless room. "This your man?"

Carolyn nodded, seeing a slender young male slumped in a chair. A probation officer held an advantage over the investigating police officers. She didn't have to read the prisoner his Miranda rights. Her duty was to determine whether or not he had violated the terms and conditions of his probation. In order to do this, she had to address the issue of the pending offense.

"Hi, Eddie," she said, once Barker had closed the door and locked it. "Long time no see. Sorry I cut into your lunch hour."

"The food here isn't worth eating," Eddie said, scowling. He tilted his head to one side, squinting as he peered up at her. "You're my probation officer, right? You look different."

Carolyn took a seat at the table. They needed to establish whether or not Eddie was a pedophile. Not all men who raped a child fell into that category. Many were merely sexual predators. Overpowering their victims aroused them, and age was not always a factor. She'd known rapists whose victims ran the gamut from women old enough to be their grandmother to teenagers and children.

Eddie glanced at her breasts, then furtively looked away. A rapist would have been turned on by the seductive manner in which she was dressed. If Eddie was a pedophile, there could be other victims. He'd strangled Luisa Cortez and left her for dead. The police would have to check all missing persons reports on prepubescent children.

Now Carolyn had to play a different role.

She braced her head in her hand. "Sorry," she said, yawning. "I'm really bushed today. I spent the night at my boyfriend's house. I forgot to bring a change of clothing. We went to the Rolling Stones concert at the Staples Center. I didn't get much sleep."

"You like the Stones?" Eddie asked, relaxing. "They're old, man."

"My boyfriend's a fan," Carolyn told him. "Anyway, I didn't come to talk about myself. What's going on, Eddie? The police charged you with rape. I thought you'd be married by now. Everything seemed to be fine the last time I saw you."

"I didn't do it," he protested, his face flushing. "Do I look like someone who'd have to rape a kid? Girls go crazy over me. The cops locked me up and let the twisted asshole who did this get away." He swiped at his mouth with the back of his hand. "Have you talked to them? You know, the police? What kind of evidence do they have? Did the girl die? They wouldn't let me watch TV last night."

"Luisa Cortez survived," Carolyn said, biting the inside of her mouth to keep from jumping across the table and gouging his eyes out. She remembered the phone call, waiting for the most opportune moment. "Where were you at the time of the crime?"

"I was with my friends," Eddie said, coughing. "The cops have already talked to them. I have an airtight alibi."

Carolyn opened the file. "Are you referring to Teddy Mayfield and Sam Howard?"

"Yeah," he said, excited. "I've been trying to call them. They cleared me, didn't they? The cops promised me they'd talk to them."

"Both of these men are in jail in San Francisco. They were arrested in a hit and run accident the day before the rape." Carolyn watched as he squirmed in his seat. "Mayfield and Howard also had an active warrant for possession with intent to distribute. I think you picked the wrong people to cover for you, Eddie. I assume you bought your drugs from them."

Eddie shot her a black gaze. "You're lying. You came here to trick me, make me say something incriminating." He moved his right hand up and down. "That's why you came here with your tits hanging out."

"I thought you were smart," Carolyn said, opening the file again and pulling out the crime scene photos Hank Sawyer had sent to her. "Drug dealers aren't very reliable." She turned the pictures around so he could see them.

Luisa Cortez was covered with blood and dirt. Abrasions encircled her small neck. She was nude and her legs were spread open, her pencil-thin arms limp at her sides. Between her legs were purplish bruises and streaks of dried blood. A few feet away were a torn flower print dress, a pair of white cotton panties, and two socks decorated with kittens. The girl's sneakers had not been recovered, leaving the police to believe that she'd been raped at another location, then thrown out of a moving car. One of the first things Luisa had inquired about when she'd regained consciousness at the hospital was her new shoes with heart-shaped cutouts. Carolyn suspected Eddie had kept the shoes as a souvenir.

His mouth fell open as he stared at the images. She saw his hand shaking as he tried to push the photos aside. This was the part pedophiles didn't want to remember—the terrible reality of their actions. They somehow convinced themselves that they cared for the children they attacked. She'd caught one man when he'd showed up for his seven-year-old victim's parent/teacher conference.

Carolyn slammed her fist down as hard as she could, flattening his hand on the table.

"Stop," Eddie cried. "You're hurting me."

"Am I really hurting you?" Carolyn asked, hissing the words through clenched teeth. "Look at the pictures, Eddie. Did you enjoy what you did to Luisa Cortez? You like little girls, don't you? I talked to Maria Valdez today." She watched the shock register on his face. "Maria's sister, Rosita, lied when she reported you to the police. She did it to protect her seven-year-old sister, save her from the trauma of a trial. You molested Maria, not Rosita. You can't get it up with a real woman."

Sweat was poring off Eddie's face. "You're off your rocker. I don't know what you're talking about. Rosita was my girlfriend."

"Let me give you some free legal advice," Carolyn told him. "Plead guilty to kidnapping, rape, and attempted murder. The DA has more than enough evidence to convict you. Remember when you registered as a sex offender and went to the lab so they could collect a DNA sample? You might have kept Luisa's shoes as a souvenir, but we have something of yours that's going to cost you your freedom. Your DNA has been matched to evidence found on Luisa's body. Not only that, she can identify you. You might as well have left your phone number and address."

Eddie yanked his hand away, tears gushing from his eyes. He started to speak, then decided against it, scooting his chair to the back of the room.

"As part of the plea bargain," Carolyn continued, "insist that you serve your prison time in protective custody. If you don't, the inmates will kill you. Being in prison doesn't mean these men don't have sisters, daughters, or nieces." She took a deep breath, then continued, "If there are other victims, maybe in other states, you could stay out of prison longer if you cooperate and tell the truth. You know how the system works. You have to be tried in whatever city holds jurisdiction. Then when everyone is finished with you, they ship you to prison. Once you get to the joint, you're a dead man."

Carolyn stood, stepping backward toward the door, fearful he might try to retaliate. Eddie was staring into space, though, contemplating what she'd told him. She hit the buzzer, relieved when she heard the key turn in the lock. As soon as Alex Barker opened the door, she spun around and stepped through.

Carolyn was about to dart into the ladies' room on the first floor when Brad Preston saw her. Most of the people in the building had gone to lunch, and the corridor where the public bathrooms were located was tucked underneath the stairwell.

He walked over and took her by the arm, steering her into the men's room, then leaning against the door so no one could enter. "Who are you trying to nail?"

"Let me go," Carolyn said, wrenching away from him.

"You asked me to violate Downly, didn't you? He's a pedophile. The victim in the underlying offense was almost the same age as Luisa Cortez." After describing her phone conversation with Maria Valdez and her older sister, Rosita, she added, "Call Hank and tell him they need to search for additional victims. Check missing persons on girls under twelve. Make sure they send out a national bulletin. Since I failed to keep tabs on Downly for the past year, there's no telling where he's been living."

"You look terrific," Brad said, smiling as he pulled her into his arms. "I forgot what a great little body you have." He cupped his hands under her breasts, then kissed her on the lips.

Carolyn stared at his handsome face, his amazing eyes, his incredible smile. Without thinking, she let her hands open. Eddie's file and her purse fell to the floor. She had convinced herself that she was over him. Obviously, she'd been mistaken. No man had ever aroused her the way Brad did. She held his face in her hands. "We could lose our jobs, you know."

"You worry too much," Brad told her. He switched places so Carolyn's back was against the door. Pinning her hands over her head, he kissed her mouth, her neck, then trailed his tongue down the center of her chest. She closed her eyes and moaned.

How long had it been?

She heard a noise and glanced over at the urinals. What if a man was inside one of the stalls? She held her breath and listened, her heart racing in excitement. Brad had intentionally chosen the men's room. What they were doing seemed even more decadent. She felt herself slipping. The floor was slick and her heels made it hard to keep her balance. She kicked off her shoes, then unbuttoned his shirt, moving her hands over his bronze skin as she marveled at his taut muscles. "You're so beautiful," she whispered. "Men aren't supposed to be beautiful."

Brad laughed, "I'm not sure if that's a compliment or an insult."

"Neither am I," Carolyn said, moving a few feet away.

"You aren't going to make love to me?"

"No," she said, fighting her desire.

"My house is only a few miles away," Brad told her, his eyelids still heavy with lust. "All we have to do is be discreet, make certain no one in the office finds out we're seeing each other again. Stop by my house after work."

"You have lipstick on your face." Carolyn reached over and wiped it off with her finger. "What we did today was a long way from discreet."

"Oh, yeah," he said, grinning. "Maybe that's why you liked it so much."

"I don't want a relationship where we have to sneak around," Carolyn told him. "We wouldn't be able to go out in public. You're a fantastic lover, but I want more. I have to think about John and Rebecca. They need a man in their life, someone they can look up to as father."

"What's going on with Frank?"

"Nothing," Carolyn told him, leaving him to guard the door while she went to the sink to wash off the heavy makeup and repair her clothing.

"He's supposed to be supporting your children," Brad told her. "Have you filed against him? They'll throw him in jail."

"We don't know where he is right now," Carolyn explained. "He changes his phone number all the time. I reported him for nonpayment of child support three months ago. They haven't found him."

"He must not be working, or they'd trace him by his social security number." Someone jiggled the door handle. Brad leaned against it with his right shoulder. "I'm a plumber, guy," he yelled. "Use the john upstairs. I'm up to my ears in shit."

Carolyn placed her hand over her mouth to muffle her

laughter. As soon as they heard the man's footsteps receding, she said, "Has anyone ever told you that you're insane?"

"All the time," Brad said, arching an eyebrow. "What else did you get out of Downly?"

"Not much," Carolyn said, falling serious. "He might plead guilty and save us the expense of a trial. The most important issue is to find out if there are other victims. He got sloppy with Luisa Cortez. Serial rapists or serial killers don't usually start making mistakes until the third or fourth crime. If there are other victims, they're probably dead. I keep thinking of the families, not knowing if their child is dead or alive."

"At least we caught him," Brad said. "What about his girlfriend? Didn't he tell you he was engaged?"

"He would have used her if she existed. The men who were supposed to provide him with an alibi are drug dealers. They were in jail in San Francisco when he raped Cortez. He must have told me he was engaged to keep me from finding out he was a pedophile. Fast Eddie isn't interested in adult women."

"Disgusting," Brad said, shaking his head.

"We can't do this again," Carolyn told him, her eyes drifting downward.

"Why not?" he argued. "Okay, I admit we shouldn't play around at work. That doesn't mean we can't see each other."

"I have to go on with my life, Brad," Carolyn said. "Even before you were promoted, I knew our relationship wouldn't last. You don't want to raise some other man's kids, come home every night to the same place and deal with domestic problems."

Brad was upset. "I care about you."

Carolyn kissed him on the forehead. "I care about you too." She cracked the door to make certain no one was around, then quickly left before he could stop her.

Chapter 12

Carolyn sweet talked Arline Shoeffel's assistant, Raul Morales, into getting her in to see the presiding judge during the afternoon recess. Unlike some of the other judges, Shoeffel didn't indulge in three-martini lunches paid for by ass-kissing attorneys at Ventura's finest restaurants. She'd won her position due to her impeccable ethics, her uncanny grasp of the law, and her ability to supervise high-level individuals. One of the most important duties of a presiding judge was moving the calendar. With the number of cases Ventura County processed, her job could be compared to stopping a runaway train.

Carolyn felt lucky to have spent time alone with Arline the evening her car broke down. People at the courthouse seldom saw her, unless they spotted her in her silver Lexus either entering or leaving the restricted underground parking garage. Only a few details about her personal life were known to the general public. The judge had never been married, she never attended social functions, and she carried her lunch to work every day in a brown paper bag. In many ways, she was like a phantom. Only the judges who worked directly under her had contact with her on a regular basis.

Before her one-thirty appointment with Arline, Carolyn drove to a Verizon store across the street to purchase cell phones for Rebecca and John. She was delighted when she learned the phones were free, but her excitement withered when she realized that she'd have to sign a six-month contract with the phone company. She waited anxiously while the store clerk activated the phones, then left and tossed them into the trunk of Professor Leighton's BMW. She almost ran a red light in her rush to get back to the courthouse, fearful if she was late, Arline would refuse to see her.

"Did I make it?" Carolyn said, trying to catch her breath as she burst through the door to the judge's outer office.

A former New Yorker, Raul Morales slowly pulled his eyes away from his computer screen. An attractive, stuffy man in his early thirties, Morales probably knew more about the law than most attorneys. His blue-striped dress shirt was crisp and starched, and he was wearing a black vest and charcoal slacks, his shoes polished to perfection.

"Barely," Morales said, looking in distaste at Carolyn's disheveled appearance. "Have you been jogging? Perhaps you should comb your hair." He reached over and handed her a tissue as she whipped her brush out and ran it through her tangled hair. "You're perspiring as well. I hear it's warm out today. Must be the Santa Ana winds again. Last week I had to wear a jacket. This morning it felt like summer."

"You're not in New York anymore. In California, we have a different season every week." Carolyn blotted her forehead and upper lip, listening as he called the judge on the intercom.

"I only promised you five minutes," he said, gesturing toward the closed door. "She has another appointment in fifteen and she needs time to eat her lunch. I suggest you talk fast."

Arline Shoeffel didn't raise her head until Carolyn was standing directly in front of her desk. "Have a seat," she said, removing her glasses. "I was concerned when you didn't attend class last night. I heard about the explosion. How are you?"

Carolyn didn't answer her question. She remained standing. "I have a volatile situation on my hands," she told her. "If I didn't think someone could lose their life, I wouldn't be here." She quickly outlined the most recent developments in the Metroix case.

"What you've told me does sound worth pursuing," the judge said, her words carefully articulated. "Put together everything you have and send it over. We'll have a light dinner together after class next week. We can discuss Metroix then."

"This can't wait," Carolyn told her, walking over and placing her hands on the edge of her desk. "I'm not returning to school until whoever is behind this has been apprehended. I can't risk leaving my children home alone. These people know where I live. They've been to my house."

"I see what you mean," the judge said thoughtfully. "Wouldn't Mr. Metroix be better off in protective custody?"

"No," she told her. "He already got into an altercation at the jail. It wasn't his fault, according to what he told me. Not only do I think he was falsely convicted, ironically Metroix seems to be a talented inventor. Some of his inventions could be valuable, to the extent that a prison official may be personally profiting from them."

"What led you to believe Mr. Metroix was an inventor?" Arline asked. "I thought you said he was mentally ill."

Not this again, Carolyn thought. The same problem applied to people with cerebral palsy or Lou Gehrig's disease. Those who didn't know better sometimes thought they were retarded. "Have you ever heard of John Forbes Nash?"

"The name sounds somewhat familiar," the judge answered, leaning back in her chair. "What does this man have to do with Mr. Metroix?"

"Nash was schizophrenic," she told her. "He also won a Nobel Prize." She let her words sink in, then continued, "Metroix's working on something that could benefit national security. I'm not competent to evaluate it. For that, we're going to need a major research facility. My father taught math, though, and my mother has a master's in chemistry. I know enough to tell you that what I saw was impressive."

"Complex," Arline commented, her eyes drifting toward the ceiling. "What you've told me not only seems worthy of the court's attention, it has some interesting legal aspects." She reached behind her and picked up the California Penal Code off her credenza. Raul stuck his head in the door.

"Judge Alcott will be here in fifteen minutes."

"That's fine," she said.

"But you need time to eat your lunch."

"You're not my mother, Raul," Arline told him, peering up at him over her glasses. "Don't interrupt me again. If Alcott shows up, he can wait."

"Do you want me to go?" Carolyn asked, seeing Raul giving her a dirty look, as if it was her fault that his boss had snapped at him.

"No," the judge answered. "The law tends to be concrete, even tedious. Assigning cases and supervising other judges isn't as challenging as one might think. Regarding the prison," she continued, "as per section 2812, it's unlawful for a prison to sell anything made by an inmate unless the articles are legally sanctioned by law." She flipped to another page. "Now, 2717.1 states that the Director of Corrections can enter into what's referred to as a joint venture program with an outside organization or entity."

"Warden Lackner mentioned something about a joint venture program," Carolyn interjected. "But Metroix said the warden not only made him sign away the rights to his inventions, he also insisted that he work specifically on the exoskeleton."

"If this warden is personally profiting in any way," Arline told her, "or even had the intent to sell Mr. Metroix's inventions, he would be in violation of section 2708." She looked up and smiled. "You may have caught yourself a rat. This man could be criminally prosecuted if what Mr. Metroix told you is true."

"What should I do?" Carolyn asked, excited.

Arline was studying another section. "Would you say this video monitoring system that Mr. Metroix claims he invented provided exceptional assistance in maintaining the safety and security of the prison?"

"Absolutely."

"Take a look at section 2935 when you get back to your office," she said. "Mr. Metroix should have received a year off his sentence. I'll go over the rest of the particulars as soon as I receive them. Don't call me, though. I'll call you once I determine how we should proceed."

"Thanks, Arline," Carolyn gushed, feeling as if she'd argued her first case as an attorney. "This means a great deal to me."

"Good day, Carolyn," the judge said, coolly dismissing her.

Fast Eddie was curled up on the lower bunk in his cell. He was weak from hunger. He'd always been a picky eater. The slop they tried to feed them at the jail made him sick to his stomach, and he hadn't eaten in twenty-four hours.

Some of the things Sullivan had told him had been bold-faced lies. When he'd raped the girl, he'd worn a rubber. He wasn't stupid enough to leave behind that kind of evidence.

As small as she was, though, Luisa had put up quite a struggle. She had scratched him, but the injuries were so mild, they were barely visible. Her little fingernails had been paper thin. Sullivan had been trying to intimidate him. All they had to connect him to the crime was the girl. It wasn't uncommon for children that age to fall apart on the witness stand. When a defense attorney started drilling them, they got flustered and confused.

He hadn't planned on strangling her. He'd intended to place a plastic bag over her head and suffocate her. He didn't like to do anything sexual while his victims were thrashing around. When he'd tossed the girl out of the car in the vacant lot near her house, he'd been certain she was dead.

Luisa Cortez had been special. Eddie had been considerate of her family, leaving her where he knew they would find her. If he had known she would live to possibly identify him, he would have buried her in a remote location. Her body had been still and cold. He'd used a washcloth to make sure there were no hairs or other evidence that could be traced back to him. Listening to her chest, he had mistakenly believed the sound he'd heard was his own heartbeat instead of hers.

Luisa would have led a lousy life anyway.

A wave of pleasure passed over him. She'd looked so sweet, with her silky black hair and pretty dress, singing to herself as she skipped down the sidewalk.

He heard a deep voice call his name, then the electronically controlled door to his cell swung open. "Edward James Downly," a tall guard said, "get your ass in gear. Your bondsman posted your bail."

Eddie bolted upright in the bed. Was he dreaming? The judge had ordered him held without bail. Not only that, Sullivan must have a hold on him for violation of probation.

"You coming or what?" the guard asked, smacking on a wad of chewing gum.

Eddie leapt to his feet, snickering under his breath as the jailer led him through a maze of corridors to the release section of the jail. He waited behind a painted line until a deputy in a room that resembled a cage called out his name.

Fast Eddie stepped forward to the window.

"We've got one pair of Levi's, one brown knit shirt, one pair of jockey shorts, two socks, and a pair of Nike tennis shoes." The officer inside the room stacked everything in a neat pile. "Next we got one men's wallet containing sixty-three dollars, fifty cents in change, one pair of sunglasses, and a Nokia cell phone." He stopped and handed Eddie a form. "Sign at the bottom and you're good to go."

As soon as Eddie scribbled his name, the guard pointed to

a room where he could change. If it was a dream, he was loving it. Five minutes later, he stepped outside into the California sunshine. Slipping on his sunglasses, he pulled his cell phone out and depressed the button to activate it. The damn battery on the phone was still charged. This was one hell of a lucky day, Eddie thought. Might even be one for the history books. He wasn't much of a gambler or he'd head straight for the racetrack.

Daniel overslept and missed the free breakfast buffet at the Comfort Inn. After showering and dressing in the Lakers T-shirt and sweatpants he'd purchased at Rite Aid the night before, he spent the morning attempting to duplicate his latest work on the exoskeleton.

Regenerating his computations regarding the electrical components could easily take years, and even then, he would have to test them to make sure they were functional. He'd almost perfected the device that would improve locomotion to the exoskeleton, in addition to a compact power converter and actuator. No one that he knew of, though, had yet developed the perfect material for the suit. Most of the exoskeletons he'd seen in technical or military magazines had been nothing more than cumbersome, robotic, man-wearable hardware. He wasn't interested in augmenting the performance of soldiers. Daniel wanted to provide a way for paralyzed or crippled individuals to become mobile again.

Laying down his pencil, he told himself he couldn't allow the loss of his work to destroy him. He'd battled his illness and served his prison sentence. Then again, perhaps he deserved everything that had happened to him and his torment would continue into eternity.

When his stomach started growling, Daniel noticed that it was one-thirty. Carolyn had said she would call him that morning. She'd instructed him to stay in the room and order his food from room service. The items on the menu didn't interest him. He decided to walk over to Saul's Bagels across from the Seagull Motel. He'd eaten there several times and enjoyed it. He needed some fresh air anyway. What good was it to be out of prison if you stayed cooped up in a motel room?

Remembering to take his key and put the DO NOT DISTURB sign on the door as Carolyn had instructed, Daniel rode the elevator down to the lobby. He wasn't entirely certain where he was, so he stopped and asked the desk clerk for directions. The bagel shop was about twenty blocks away. If he ran, he might feel less anxious.

As he jogged along, he occupied his mind by trying to decide what he wanted to have for lunch. His mouth started watering for a hot pastrami sandwich and a side order of delicious coleslaw. To have something to snack on later in his room, he'd also buy some bagels and donuts. Every now and then, he developed a hankering for something sweet. The food in prison had been awful, and it was always cold.

Overall, having a decent meal was probably one of the things Daniel had enjoyed the most, particularly since his grandmother had made it possible for him to have enough money to eat whatever he wanted.

He saw the large neon sign that read Saul's Bagels up ahead. The bagel shop was one of those hole-in-the-wall places that more than likely served only bagels when they'd first opened, then as they'd amassed a regular clientele, they'd started adding donuts, sandwiches, and other items.

When Daniel ran, he had to be careful, as he wasn't used to watching out for cars. At Chino, he'd jogged around the yard during afternoon exercise. All he had to look out for at the prison were other inmates, and the majority of them stayed clear of him.

Prison was a strange place, a world within a world. During his first year, the inmates had ganged up on him. He'd suffered through some ordeals too terrible to mention. Even before Warden Lackner took a shine to him, however, most of the inmates had begun to avoid him. By that time, rumors had circulated that he was mentally ill. Even the most hardened inmates didn't want to tangle with a crazy person.

Daniel stopped, keeping his legs moving as he waited for the signal light to change. Several cars drove past. Then a black SUV pulled up close to the curb and he caught a glimpse of a man's face leaning out the window.

He never saw the gun.

The explosion reverberated inside his ears. Daniel felt a searing pain in his upper abdomen, only inches away from his heart.

Images raced through his mind. He saw a beautiful little girl smiling up at him, then extending her arms for him to pick her up. Her face was so sweet and tender, looking at her made him want to cry.

He remembered the Christmas his father had given him his first watch. He'd run straight to his room and taken it apart. Then he saw their new TV disassembled on the living room floor. Ruth's bloated face frowned at him as she beat him with a belt.

"Why do you do these things?" his mother screamed at him. "Why do you tear everything apart? Your father saved for a year to buy us a new TV." The belt cut into his legs. "I'm not going to stop whipping you until you answer me. You tried to take Mrs. Clairmont's washing machine apart last week. People think I have an idiot for a son."

"Please, Mother, don't hit me again," Daniel had sobbed. "I want to find out how things work."

As the pain from the gunshot wound intensified, the memories from the past retreated.

Several vehicles slammed on their brakes when they saw a man standing in the middle of the road, blood gushing out of his abdomen. Another driver began honking his horn. A woman got out of her car and waved her arms around, shouting for someone to call an ambulance.

Daniel's body contracted at the waist in a violent muscle

spasm. He didn't realize he'd been shot until he looked down and saw the blood oozing out around his fingers. Then he recalled the look of hatred on the man's face as he'd leaned out the window with his arm outstretched.

He staggered forward a few more feet, then slumped to the pavement, a pool of blood spreading beneath his motionless body. He blinked several times, struggling to remain conscious.

The woman who'd called for help knelt down beside him, rolling up something that looked like a beach towel and pressing it against the bullet wound. She was heavyset and resembled Daniel's mother. "Hold on," she said, breathless from running. "You've been shot. You're going to be all right. Try to stay calm until the paramedics get here."

"Are . . . you . . . going to hit me again?"

"No," the woman said, tears gathering in her eyes. "Don't talk. I'm going to pray for you. God will send his angels to help you."

Daniel suddenly felt at peace. The woman wasn't his mother. Ruth was dead, buried with the rest of his family at the Queen of Angels Cemetery. He'd taken the bus to Los Angeles, gazing at the vacant plot that his grandmother had purchased for him. In life, there had never seemed to be a place for him. At least in death, he told himself, he'd have a permanent home.

Chapter 13

After her meeting with Arline Shoeffel, Carolyn picked up a file and went into a room to dictate her report on the Sandoval shooting.

Lois Mason, the sixty-seven-year-old victim, had recovered from the bullet wound in her shoulder, but emotionally and mentally, she would never be the same. During the interview, the woman had sat with her hands folded neatly in her lap, answering most of Carolyn's questions with a yes or a no as if she were on the witness stand.

In a pre-sentence investigation, when a victim wasn't able to provide information, the probation officer would turn to the closest relative. The woman's daughter had cried when Carolyn spoke to her on the phone.

"My mom wasn't afraid of anything. Now she won't leave the house, she isn't eating, and we can't even get her to communicate with us. We may have to put her in a home."

The only reassurance Carolyn could provide was that Carlos Sandoval would go to prison for life. A violent act perpetrated against an elderly female was tantamount to a homicide. She didn't have the heart to tell Mrs. Mason's daughter that a life sentence did not mean the prisoner would never be released. Life without the possibility of parole meant what it said, yet Sandoval's crime legally didn't merit such a sentence.

Regardless of what kind of punishment her attacker received, Lois Mason knew there were other men like Sandoval in the world. As tragic as it sounded, death might come as a relief.

After dictating her report, Carolyn glanced at her watch. It was a quarter to three and she hadn't checked in with Daniel yet. Not only that, she'd planned on leaving the office early and picking up John and Rebecca at school. Once they had the cell phones, she could relax somewhat. She'd have to call the school, though, and arrange permission for them to keep the phones on during class in case she needed to reach them in an emergency. She also had to rent a car. She couldn't keep Leighton's BMW forever. Her indebtedness to this man was substantial. Cooking him a meal wouldn't do it—she'd have to find some other way to repay his kindness.

Using the Internet, Carolyn found contact information for Liam Armstrong and Nolan Houston. Armstrong was a commercial real estate agent in Los Angeles, and Houston owned a chain of golf stores called Hole in One.

She pulled up an article from the Ventura paper about Nolan Houston from years back—the typical "hometown boy makes good" story. The former football player had switched sports and ended up playing on the P.G.A. tour. Since Carolyn didn't follow golf, his success had passed without her knowledge. Houston had retired from golf five years ago, trading on his name to establish a twenty-one-store chain of retail stores.

Carolyn was attempting to find out more about Liam Armstrong when her phone rang.

"Your man's been shot," Hank told her. "I'm at the crime scene. The shooting occurred around two-fifteen."

Carolyn's adrenaline surged. "Metroix?"

"Who else?"

She shoved her chair back from her desk, clasping the phone with both hands. "How bad?"

"Don't know yet," Hank said, yelling over the background

noise. "Way it looks, the shooter was aiming for his heart. Ended up hitting him in the stomach instead. Metroix has earned my sympathy this time. I've been down that road myself. A bullet starts dancing around inside your gut and you've got nothing but misery ahead of you."

"Where did it happen?"

"On Anchors Way, near the Seagull Motel. From what the witnesses say, it may have been a drive-by. I'm sending Trevor White to the hospital now. Since White was with me when we arrested Metroix, he'd rather see your face than one of ours."

Why hadn't she remembered to call him? Daniel must have become restless. Carolyn felt lightheaded and had to brace herself against her desk. "I told him not to leave the motel room."

"What motel room?" Hank asked. "Did he go back to squatting again at the Seagull? Good grief, woman, why didn't you stash him somewhere else?"

"I did," Carolyn said defensively. "I drove him to the Comfort Inn from the jail. Why would he go back to the Seagull? He doesn't drive and it's miles away."

"How would I know?"

"Did they take him to Good Samaritan?" Carolyn asked, devastated that Metroix had once again been victimized.

"No," Hank said. "Ambulance took him to Methodist. Couple of surgeons called in sick today at Good Samaritan. They're diverting anything that requires surgery to Methodist."

Carolyn grabbed her water bottle off the desk and took a long swallow, her throat suddenly parched. "Who did this, Hank?"

"All we know is the vehicle was a dark-colored SUV, more than likely black, but possibly a deep shade of green. Our best witness says she isn't a car person. She claims she can't tell one SUV from another. She thinks the license plate had a three in it, and the first letter might have been either a G or an O."

"Was Metroix conscious?"

"For a while," the detective said. "Mrs. Olson didn't think to question him. You can't fault her on that. Her clothes were covered in blood, and she said Metroix kept asking her if she was going to hit him. They'll have to cut the bullet out and sew him up. Everything depends on what kind of ammo the shooter used and how much damage it caused. Getting him into surgery will take time. He might come to, though, and be able to give you a description of the suspect and the vehicle." He paused and then added, "You don't have to waste your breath convincing me that someone wants Metroix dead, Carolyn. I'm going to back you up a hundred percent on this one. I don't give a shit if Charles Harrison used to be head of the CIA. If he's behind this, he's going to pay the same price as any other criminal."

"I'll call you later," Carolyn told him, grabbing her purse. "I'm on my way to the hospital now."

"Go get your kids before you do anything," Hank instructed her. "Oh, and I told White to stand guard over Metroix. I'm beginning to get bad vibes about this thing. Harrison's a sick man. And I'm not merely referring to his liver problems. Hired killers are vicious. They don't care who dies. All this kind of scum cares about is payday."

Carolyn rushed to Jefferson Junior High to pick up Rebecca, then swung by Ventura High to pick up John. Once they were both in the car, she told them what had transpired.

"Is he going to die?" Rebecca asked from the back-seat.

"I hope not, sweetheart," her mother said. "I know you and John must have homework. I don't want you to be alone. That means you'll have to come with me to the hospital. You can start on your schoolwork in the waiting room. I shouldn't be too long."

John cut his eyes to his mother. "I'm really behind at

school, Mom. We're having a calculus test tomorrow. Take Rebecca. I can't study in a hospital. There's too much noise."

Carolyn felt her pulse pounding. Both she and her children had been under too much stress. But this wasn't your everyday situation. Hank Sawyer was far from an alarmist. He wouldn't have cautioned her if he didn't believe his concerns were valid. "You have to do what I say, John," she told him, deciding to get everything out in the open. "I'd much rather see you fail an exam than have you end up in the morgue."

"Isn't a morgue where they take dead people?" Rebecca asked.

"Can't you shut up for a change?" John asked his sister, craning his neck around. "Mom and I are trying to talk." He took a breath, then turned back to Carolyn. "I'm sorry this guy got shot, okay? Look at this logically, though. Whoever did this has solved their problem. Why would they hurt us now? They were only mad at you because you got in their way. I'll be fine. Take me to the house."

Carolyn shook her head, shocked that he would defy her this way. "I'm the one who makes the decisions in this family," she told him, pulling over to the side of the road. "I refuse to let you stay home alone."

John slapped back against the seat. "Why is everything always so hard for us? Why can't we be like other families? I'm doing everything I can to make something out of my life. You should be worried about me instead of some stranger who just got out of prison." He opened the car door and took off down the sidewalk.

"Stay here," Carolyn told her daughter. "I'm going to lock the car when I get out. I won't go where you can't see me. Is that all right?"

The girl nodded, pulling her backpack onto her lap.

"How dare you walk off like that!" Carolyn shouted, once she'd caught up to her son. "You think life is easy for me? I barely have time to keep up with my job, let alone the extra pressure of trying to get my law degree. Your father hasn't given me a dime in years. You want to go to MIT. None of the other schools are good enough for you. I need to save for Rebecca's education too."

"I thought Neil was going to take care of our college tuition," John told her. "He opened a savings account for us last year. I remember signing the signature cards."

"Your uncle's paintings were selling very well then," Carolyn explained. "The economy has taken a nosedive. When their businesses are failing, people don't buy art. Neil set up college funds for you and Rebecca, but he only put in a small amount. It will take years for the accounts to mature. Neil may settle down one day and have his own family. All I'm trying to say is that we shouldn't depend on other people."

John had been staring at the ground. He slowly raised his eyes to his mother. For a long time, they remained silent, both of their chests heaving with emotion. "What about dropping me off at Turner's house? It's five blocks away and his mother doesn't work. Not only that, his two brothers are as big as tanks."

"That's acceptable," Carolyn told him. "You still owe me an apology."

He walked over and draped an arm around her shoulder. "I'm sorry," he said quietly, stepping back. "Let's not waste any more time. If you want me to get a scholarship, I can't afford any days off."

Carolyn felt certain John would succeed. He not only possessed the intellect, he had the drive. It didn't make up for his disrespectful behavior, however. He could become the richest and most accomplished person in the world, but if he didn't learn to respect those around him, he would ultimately be despised. "Can you spend the night with Turner?"

"Sure," John told her. "He has an extra bed. His mother told me I was welcome to stay there anytime I wanted."

"Good," Carolyn said bluntly. "I accept your apology. We need to put some space between us, though." Without waiting for him, she spun around and marched back to the car.

By the time they made it to Methodist Hospital, Daniel Metroix was being prepped for surgery. With Rebecca at her side, Carolyn spoke to a pretty black nurse named Ann Brookings, suited up in green scrubs.

"The bullet didn't damage any major organs," the nurse said. "The physician performing the procedure, Dr. Silver, isn't anticipating any serious problems. Mr. Metroix appears to be in fairly good physical condition, which generally helps."

Carolyn glanced over at Trevor White leaning back against the wall. All four of them were standing behind a red line and the words DO NOT ENTER printed on the floor. Carolyn leaned forward and whispered, "Make certain the police officer doesn't leave his post. This isn't only for the patient's safety. Tell the rest of the staff that if they see anything even slightly suspicious, either advise Officer White or dial 911 immediately."

Brookings started to pull her mask down over her face in preparation for entering the operating room. Instead, she moved a few inches closer. "You really think we should be that concerned, Ms. Sullivan?"

"Yes," Carolyn told her, raising her arm so that she could see how tightly she was holding onto her daughter's hand. "How long will he be in surgery?"

"Two hours, minimum," she said. "He'll be in recovery for at least two more hours, if not longer. If I were you, I'd take my girl and go home."

"A detective named Hank Sawyer will be here shortly," Carolyn told her. "If Metroix says anything you think might be related to the crime, please write it down and advise the police. We need to know if he saw the man who shot him."

"The patient's going to be on heavy narcotics for several

days," Brookings said. "He'll be alert off and on tomorrow. When he's awake, he'll be screaming or talking gibberish from the dope." She paused and smiled. "I don't make it a habit to speak so candidly. I'm trying to tell it like it is, you know. You seem like a nice lady." Before she slapped open the double doors leading to the operating room, she added, "Your man probably did see the person who shot him, unless the shooter wore a mask. Masks aren't in style these days."

They were discussing a violent act. "In style . . ."

"I grew up on the street," she said, placing one hand on her hip. "Remember carjackings? How long has it been since you've handled a carjacking? This may have been a drive-by, like the cute little officer over there said. As for me, I personally don't buy it. Drive-by shootings aren't that popular either."

"What's makes you think he saw the shooter?"

Ann Brookings gave a warm smile. "Frontal wound."

Back in the BMW, Rebecca turned to her mother. "At least I won't have to worry about my homework," she said. "I did most of it in the car. You know, while you and John were fighting."

"We weren't fighting," Carolyn said, inserting the key in the ignition. "We had a disagreement, that's all."

"Humph," Rebecca said, fastening her seat belt. "Sure looked like a fight to me. Where are you taking me now? To the morgue or something? And is a bunch of bad guys really chasing us, or are you having a nervous breakdown?"

Her mother took several deep breaths before answering. "I'm going to pretend I didn't hear that." She gunned the engine, then instead of putting the car into reverse, she drove forward and struck the concrete divider. Getting out, she felt as if her children had suddenly turned into monsters. The chrome bumper of Paul Leighton's BMW was dented. Now she'd have to pay to have it repaired. She couldn't count on her insurance, as she had a thousand-dollar deductible. She glanced up at a large tree, expecting it to come crashing down on her head.

"You want to know where we're going?" she said once she was in the driver's seat again. "The first thing we're going to do is rent a car."

"A little food would help," Rebecca told her. "If you feed me, I might not be so grumpy."

"Touché," her mother said, patting her hand. She saw a Carl's Junior on the corner, and steered the car toward the drive-through.

Once they picked up their hamburgers, fries, and milkshakes, her mother pulled into a parking spot. Rebecca asked her, "I thought a touché was something women use on their private parts."

Carolyn's tension disappeared as she burst out laughing. When you were ready to dump your kids out on the nearest street corner, you remembered how dull life would be without them. "Are you talking about a douche?"

"Yeah," the girl said, taking a bite out of her hamburger. "It's called Messenger or something. They advertise it in all the magazines. Allison's mother has boxes of that stuff in her bathroom. One is called Baby Powder Fresh. Since you don't use it until you grow up, why would you want your private parts to smell like baby powder?"

Her mother attempted to answer, but she couldn't stop laughing.

"It's not funny, Mother," Rebecca said. "When you get married, does your husband sniff your butt like a dog? That's disgusting. I'm never going to get married."

"The word I used starts with a T," Carolyn told her. "Touché is a French word, honey. It's associated with the sport of fencing. When a person scores a point against their opponent, they called it a touché. I think the company who makes the product your friend's mother uses is called Massengill, not

Messenger. We'll have a long talk about these types of things when I get some free time."

Carolyn steered the BMW out of the parking lot. Girls Rebecca's age seemed so sophisticated compared to those from her own era. She'd assumed that her daughter knew whatever there was to know regarding the facts of life. As usual, she'd been mistaken. The girl was far more naive than she'd realized. Overall, however, Rebecca's innocence was reassuring.

They spent the next hour at Hertz filling out the necessary paperwork to rent a car, Carolyn having to use her position as a probation officer to convince the rental agency to let her take a car without a credit card. They required a thousand-dollar deposit, so she wrote a check and hoped she had sufficient funds in her checking account to cover it.

"Do you have Professor Leighton's phone number?" she asked Rebecca as they searched through a row of cars in the Hertz lot. "I wrote it down, but I left it in the house."

"Why?"

"Because I don't know what to do about his car," Carolyn answered. "I need to return it before something else happens."

Her daughter reached into her backpack and pulled out a flower covered address book, opening it to the page where she'd jotted down Lucy Leighton's number. "I like Lucy," she said, handing the open book to her mother. "She's nice and she has all kinds of cool stuff. She even has a TV and DVD player in her bedroom. She probably won't talk to me now that you wrecked her father's car."

"I didn't wreck it," Carolyn told her. "I only dented the fender." She finally saw the bronze Toyota Camry parked in slot twenty-two, and gestured for her daughter to get inside. Before they left, though, she called Paul Leighton, explaining what had occurred.

"Don't worry about it," he said. "I think that dent was already there. As far as picking up the car goes, I can come and get it now. Have you eaten? Why don't you let me buy you dinner?"

"God, no," Carolyn answered. "I've caused you enough trouble."

"Don't be silly," he said, laughing softly. "I'm sure Lucy will end up spending more time at your place than she does here. Trust me, she's a handful. She takes after her mother."

"I'll agree to let you pick up the car," she told him. "But only if you promise you'll let me take you out to dinner. Rebecca and I have already eaten tonight. Why don't we plan on Saturday? That is, unless you have other plans, or something else goes wrong on this end. Oh," she added, "I know you're fibbing about the dent. I checked the car out before I drove it. I'll make arrangements to have it repaired next week."

"Take your time," Paul said, deciding it was useless to argue with her. "Don't worry about how we're going to get the car back. I'll bring my housekeeper, Isobel. We'll discuss the dent over dinner tomorrow evening. What time would you like me to pick you up?"

Carolyn noticed Rebecca giving her a strange look. "Around seven, I guess."

"Sounds great," he said. "Leave the keys to the BMW at the Hertz counter. Advise them we'll pick up the car within the hour."

Carolyn closed the cover on the cell phone and slipped it into her purse. "Why are you looking at me like that?" she asked Rebecca. "We've been driving this poor man crazy. The least I can do is take him out for dinner."

"Are you going to have to buy douche now?"

"No," Carolyn said, leaning over and kissing her on the cheek. "We do need to have that talk, though." She turned the key in the Camry and used caution navigating her way out of the lot, then stopped in front of the office to drop off the keys to the BMW.

"Can't we go home now?" Rebecca pleaded. "I'm tired."

"I need to stop at the store, honey," Carolyn told her. "I broke the coffeepot the other day."

One of the girl's barrettes had disappeared, and her hair was dangling over her right eye. "Why do you have to buy a stupid coffeepot tonight? Can't you get it tomorrow?"

"Because I want to stay awake," Carolyn explained. She figured that whoever had shot Daniel was more than likely the same person who'd left the threatening note and damaged her car.

"Why do you want to stay awake?" Rebecca asked. "All I want to do is go to bed."

Carolyn had her gun, but she needed to remain alert to protect herself and her daughter. "I have to catch up on my work for law school," she lied, stopping in front of Von's supermarket. "Getting my law degree means a lot to me."

A moving target was harder to find. Carolyn had tried not to remain in one spot for longer than thirty minutes. Changing cars had also been a priority. She'd considered staying at Neil's house, or driving to her mother's condominium in Camarillo. But law enforcement officers' addresses weren't listed in the computer systems at the department of motor vehicles, so either someone on the inside had given out her address, or someone had followed her. The last thing she wanted to do was lead them to her mother's doorstep.

Carolyn knew that Daniel Metroix's shooting meant one of two things—the situation was either winding down or escalating. What she feared the most was that in the world of professional killers, everything up to this point had been nothing more than foreplay.

Chapter 14

"I have bad news," Brad Preston said, his anger sparking over the phone line. "The jail accidentally released Eddie Downly!"

Carolyn was in the checkout line at Von's supermarket. She dropped the box containing the coffeepot. The glass shattered inside as it struck the floor. Seizing Rebecca by the hand, she rushed out of the store.

"You broke it, Mom," the girl said. "You have to pay for it. We can't—"

"I'll come back tomorrow," her mother told her as they got back in the Camry and locked the doors. "Be quiet now, honey. This is an extremely important phone call."

Brad continued, "Okay, a man was arrested today named Edward James Downy. The computer assigned him the same booking number as Fast Eddie. The deputy on duty must have typed in the name wrong. Even the middle name was the same, and the prisoner had the same DOB as Downly. The sheriff is trying to say it was a computer glitch of some kind because their system is programmed not to assign the same number if a prisoner is already in custody."

"The same DOB!" Carolyn said, shaking her head in denial. "That's too big of a coincidence. Something horrible is going on, Brad. I saw Downly myself. I ran into you after I left the jail. Do you remember what time it was?"

"Around twelve," Brad told her. "The other guy was booked thirty minutes later. The deputy you saw at the front desk took his lunch around then. He doesn't handle bookings anyway."

Carolyn felt as if her head were spinning. "We're talking a major conspiracy inside the criminal justice system."

Brad was calmer now that Carolyn appeared to be on the verge of hysteria. "Let's not get carried away until we know all the facts. This happened twice last year. Not all coincidences mean there's a conspiracy. The people I feel sorry for are the girl's family."

Because her daughter was with her, Carolyn was making every attempt to control her emotions. She felt like putting her fist through the windshield. "Have you notified Hank?"

"The jail did."

A despicable act had been committed that she might have prevented had she done her job more thoroughly. Now a violent rapist was back on the street. A man she thought was innocent after twenty-three years in prison had been shot—a crime that may have been contracted by the second-highest-ranking police officer in Los Angeles, Deputy Chief Charles Harrison. Who could she trust?

"Listen," she said. "Call Hank. If you can't find him, call the captain, the lieutenant, or anyone else at the PD. I'm sure they're broadcasting that Downly was mistakenly released. Tell them they have to go public with any evidence they have tying Downly to the rape. If Fast Eddie believes he has a chance to walk if the girl isn't around to testify, he'll try to kill her."

"Don't you think the PD is aware of that?"

"Metroix and Downly aren't the only cases the PD is handling," Carolyn argued. "Small town, small police department. They can't forget about the robberies, burglaries, wife beatings, gang shootings, traffic accidents, or whatever might be happening right now or in the next few minutes."

"You're right," Brad said. "Calm down, okay? The PD even

called out their reserves. They'll catch the bastard. They caught him before."

"Who's Edward James Downy?"

"A guy with too many traffic tickets," Brad told her. "He arranged to have a bail bondsman post his bail. Fast Eddie walked at one-fifteen. The jail didn't discover the error until Downy started raising hell a few hours ago. That's when they found out they'd released the wrong man."

Placing her head down on the steering wheel, Carolyn said, "I can't talk about this anymore. Rebecca's with me. I need to go home."

"I called the watch commander at the PD and instructed them to keep an eye on your house. What's the status on Metroix? Is he out of surgery?"

"I don't know," she said. "Call me later." She started to end the call, then added, "Fast Eddie has a cousin who lives in Compton. He might try to hide out there until he gets enough money to get out of town."

"Is the cousin's address in the file?"

"Yes," she said. "If I think of anything else, I'll notify the PD."

"Keep telling yourself it's just a job, baby," Brad said. "You were right on something else. You should have been promoted instead of me."

Carolyn saw that Rebecca had fallen asleep, her head slumped against the passenger window. "Thanks," she whispered, cupping her hand around the phone so she didn't wake her.

"Forget law school. We need you with us, not defending criminals. I miss you, Carolyn."

Tears streamed down her face. "I miss you too."

They were only a few blocks from the supermarket when Carolyn saw headlights in her rearview mirror and checked the speedometer to see if she'd been speeding. It wasn't a traffic cop, she decided, as the vehicle didn't have emergency lights. Whoever it was, they were tailgating.

She searched her memory for anything she might not have noted in Downly's file. She knew him better than anyone else. She'd seen the man once a month for three years. At present, however, her mind was mush.

The vehicle behind her suddenly swerved to the left, gunned its engine, and pulled up alongside of her. Since she was traveling on a two-lane roadway, she assumed the driver was attempting to pass. The car was a black, late model Corvette with dark tinted windows.

Carolyn reduced her speed, but the car continued to pace her instead of moving forward. It was only inches away from the Camry. She reached over and squeezed her daughter's arm. "Get my gun out of my purse!" she shouted. "Hurry!"

The girl was half-asleep. "What's going on? Where are we?"

"Do what I say," her mother yelled, flooring the accelerator. "Open my purse and hand me the gun. It won't go off. The safety's on."

Rebecca grabbed her mother's purse, but they were traveling at over eighty miles per hour now, and the handbag slipped off the seat onto the floorboard.

"Keep your head down," her mother said over the roar of the engine. "The minute you hand me the gun, call 911 on my cell phone. Tell the dispatcher we're traveling east on California Street. We've already passed Elkwood. Someone's trying to run us off the road. They may be armed. Once you get the police on the line, I'll give you an update on our location."

"I don't want to die," Rebecca cried, pulling out the Ruger and handing it to her mother.

Carolyn's eyes darted from the car alongside her to the right side of the road. The Corvette was traveling on the wrong side of the street, in the direction of oncoming traffic. She tried to think clearly. She couldn't turn right as they were approaching a large park and a bank of tall trees. At this speed, if they slammed into a tree, both she and Rebecca would be killed.

Carolyn slid down in the seat, firmly gripping the steering wheel as the speedometer inched its way past ninety-five. She spotted the white reflective paint on a street sign. Before she could make the decision to turn, the sign was behind her. At this speed, the side streets were coming up too fast.

"I can't dial the phone," Rebecca screamed, bent over at the waist in her seat. "You have to slow down."

"Sit up now!" Carolyn said, panting as she was forced onto the shoulder by the Corvette. She couldn't wait. She had to turn off the main road and take her chances. "Use both your hands and feet to brace yourself against the dashboard."

Out of the corner of her eye, Carolyn saw the passenger window of the Corvette opening. She couldn't take her eyes off the road long enough to get a look at the people inside, yet she thought she saw the barrel of a gun.

Removing her foot from the accelerator, Carolyn yanked the steering wheel to the right as soon as the next street sign appeared in her line of vision.

The Camry fishtailed, the rear colliding with the front of the Corvette. The Corvette skidded sideways, then began spinning. Rebecca was shrieking at the top of her lungs.

They were in a residential neighborhood lined with parked cars. Carolyn spotted a vacant lot between two houses. She drove over the curb, across the grass, and between the houses, then slammed on the brakes.

"Get out of the car!" Carolyn yelled to her daughter. "Start running."

Both of them leapt out at the same time. Carolyn raced over and grabbed Rebecca's hand, pulling her along as she darted down the alley behind the homes. She could hear the Corvette's engine in the distance. Whoever had been pursuing them had been a skilled driver, or the car would have rolled or failed to pull out of the spin.

From the way the Camry had handled, Carolyn knew it must have incurred damage to the rear end. Thank God, she thought, the car had been driveable, or she was certain both she and her daughter would have been slain.

Seeing an open garage door, Carolyn darted inside and slid under a pickup truck, pulling on the edge of Rebecca's blouse until the child's entire body was concealed. The garage was dark and she couldn't tell if anyone was inside the house.

"Please, Mom, I hurt my ankle."

Carolyn reached over and pressed her hand over her daughter's mouth. "We can't talk," she whispered. "Be perfectly still until I tell you it's safe."

She heard police sirens on a nearby street. She held her breath and listened for the sound of the Corvette's engine. Her fear returned as the noise of the sirens receded. In her haste to get away, she'd left her gun, purse, and cell phone in the car. The police didn't know their location as Rebecca hadn't been able to complete the call. Someone had either reported the speeding vehicles, Carolyn decided, or the police were responding to another crime.

She removed her hand from her daughter's mouth. "Are you okay, honey?" she said, stroking the girl's sweaty brow. "I'm sorry I had to do that to you. I couldn't take a chance. I didn't want you to make any noise."

"My ankle hurts really bad," Rebecca told her, trying to keep her voice low. "Aren't the men in the car gone now?"

"I'm not sure," Carolyn said, bumping her head on the undercarriage of the truck. "They may be looking for us on foot. You have to be brave. Try to talk as little as possible. We also have to worry about the people who live here. They could mistake us for burglars."

"Then they'll shoot us, right?" Rebecca said, collapsing

onto the concrete. "It's hard to breathe under here. And there's some repulsive slimy stuff all over my hands and face."

"It's okay," her mother said. "The truck must have an oil leak."

Carolyn refused to leave their hiding spot, fearful the men in the Corvette were canvassing the neighborhood. She had to assume they were the same people who'd shot Daniel that afternoon. All they had done was swap vehicles. She'd failed to get a look at the license plate, though, and chastised herself for not being more alert. The car was probably stolen anyway, as was the SUV used that afternoon in the shooting. The people they were dealing with were pros, as Hank had mentioned. Nonetheless, once they dumped the vehicles and the police picked them up, they'd have a lot more to go on than they did at present. Forensic science had solved an untold number of crimes. Even the most accomplished criminals left behind some type of evidence.

Rebecca had fallen asleep, and her mother curled up next to her to keep her warm. She had no idea how much time had passed. She was wearing her watch, but it was pitch black under the truck. Next time, she decided, she'd buy a watch with an illuminated dial. She also swore if they made it out alive she would start carrying her gun in the shoulder holster. Preston had warned her, but she'd been too obstinate to listen.

She heard a noise in the alley and her body stiffened. Moments later she heard what sounded like a baby crying, then relaxed when she realized it was only a fight between two cats.

How had the pursuers recognized her in the rented Camry? They must have followed her. Where had they first picked her up? Was it when she'd left the courthouse, or had they followed her from the hospital?

Carolyn had tried to exercise every precaution. She hadn't

gone home, knowing they knew where she lived. Her thinking was that the shooters would have laid low, waiting to see if their victim was dead. The argument with John had delayed her, then it had taken more time to drop him off at his friend's house. By then, the killer could have called the hospital and discovered that Daniel was expected to live. Had they come to finish the job, then spotted Carolyn at the hospital, deciding to get rid of her so she didn't cause them any more problems?

Eddie Downly came to mind. He'd been arrested Monday and mistakenly released several hours before Metroix was shot. The intelligence information she'd gathered had led to his arrest. That, coupled with her visit to him at the jail, could have given Fast Eddie numerous reasons to want her dead. More important was the fact that he couldn't be certain what else she knew. The places and people Eddie had used in the past would be off limits now.

Carolyn found it difficult to believe the two situations were related, since Eddie had been in custody at the time of the explosion. The only plausible scenario that would link Harrison to Downly was that Harrison had somehow arranged his release so he could follow through and kill Daniel.

Would a deputy chief put a child rapist back on the street? If he had, Carolyn suspected that Harrison intended to use him, then kill him. With the kind of charges hanging over Downly's head, he could order him to kill Daniel without even paying him.

Deciding to sneak out and see if it was safe for them to leave, Carolyn crept to the edge of the garage and peered out into the dark alley. Except for a few lights burning inside one of the houses, it was as quiet as a graveyard. She didn't even hear a dog barking or a radio playing. The two cats she'd heard fighting earlier had gone on their way.

Fairly certain the men in the Corvette had given up and left, Carolyn dived underneath the truck and woke Rebecca.

"Stay beside me," she said once they'd exited the garage and started making their way down the alley. "If I squeeze your hand, drop to the ground and don't move."

"My ankle," the girl said, whimpering. "I don't think I can walk, Mom."

Carolyn was a fairly small woman, but her maternal instincts provided a burst of renewed energy and strength. She hoisted the girl into her arms. When she saw the Toyota Camry parked in the same spot where she'd left it, she realized the hours they'd spent in their cramped hiding place might have been for nothing. The men in the Corvette must have sped past without seeing the car tucked in between the rows of houses.

She placed Rebecca in the front seat. Carolyn caught a glimpse of the girl's swollen left ankle and knew she needed medical treatment. She certainly wasn't going to take the child to Methodist Hospital. Being in proximity to Daniel Metroix or anything related to him had proved far too treacherous. She would take Rebecca to Good Samaritan. Thank goodness, John hadn't been with them.

She circled to the other side of the car and opened the door, finding the Ruger resting on the seat. She wouldn't have been half as terrified if she'd remembered to bring along the gun. Opening the glove box, she pulled out her new shoulder holster, strapping it on her body and inserting the gun into the pocket.

Daniel might have to fight his own battles for the time being, she decided, yet Carolyn was determined to put an end to the terror she and her family had been experiencing. As Rebecca's pain-filled eyes gazed over at her, she removed the Ruger and checked the magazine where the ammo was stored. Before she replaced the gun back in the holster, she released the safety. She knew it was dangerous. She also knew a situation could develop where a moment lost could cost her or her daughter her life. Years before, police officers didn't use seat belts because it reduced the time it took for them to get out of their patrol cars. As soon as they were home, she'd engage the safety again.

"Whatever you do," she told Rebecca, turning the key in the ignition, "don't touch my gun. If you pull the trigger, the gun will fire. I know you're hurting and tired. What I'm telling you is very important. Do you understand?"

"Yes," the girl said, a somber look on her young face. "What if the same thing happens again? You asked me to get your gun, remember."

"The next time I ask you to get my gun," Carolyn told her, "I may want you to use it."

Rebecca understood what her mother was implying, but she was frightened. "I don't know how to shoot a gun. What if I shoot the wrong person? You've always told us how much you hated guns."

"I know," Carolyn said, images of her uncle's blood splattered all over the living room walls surfacing. "When your ankle is better, I'll take you and John to the pistol range. A gun is a terrible thing, honey. I'm sure you realize by now that someone is trying to hurt me. A bad person will sometimes hurt the people you love if they can't hurt you. I'm not going to let that happen." She sighed, checking the rearview mirror as she backed the Camry onto the street.

"Didn't your uncle kill himself with a gun?" her daughter asked. "You said you wished all the guns in the world would disappear, that a little gun like the one you have had no good purpose except to hurt people."

"I guess even a terrible thing like a handgun has a purpose," Carolyn answered. She never imagined she would be making such a statement to her twelve-year-old daughter. Circumstances had a way of changing a person's perspective. "Garbage is garbage. When a person starts shooting or hurting innocent people, Rebecca, they're nothing more than human garbage."

Chapter 15

Hank Sawyer climbed behind the wheel of his department-issued black Ford at six o'clock Friday morning, heading out to Denny's as he did every morning for breakfast. Once he'd wolfed down two eggs, toast, and guzzled three cups of coffee, he slapped some bills down on the table and spent a few minutes chatting with the waitress, a middle-aged blonde who was several pounds overweight, but had a pretty face and an affable disposition.

"When are you going to let me take you out to dinner, Betty?" Hank asked, grabbing a handful of toothpicks at the counter.

"You know my number, Hank," the woman said, leaning over the counter. "You always say you're going to call, but you never do. How long has it been now? Two years."

"You like to dance?"

"Sure," Betty said. "I used to go dancing all the time. There's a place that has great country music on Saturday nights. They even have dance lessons if you're rusty. They also have some of the best barbecue in town."

"I'm tied up right now," the detective told her. "Maybe next week I may be able to break away for the evening. I might step on your toes, though." He glanced down at his bulging stomach. "That's if you can get close enough to me to dance."

"Stop eating bacon," Betty said, laughing. "I'm teasing,

sugar. I like a man with a healthy appetite, and not just for food. One of these days, you're going to have to quit talking about it and give me a call."

"Next Saturday," Hank called out as he headed to the door. "You got yourself a date, Betty. I'll call you Friday to confirm."

"Believe it when I see it," the woman said, rushing off to take care of another customer.

Hank felt his spirits lift. The job had been his life since his wife had left him. Of course, his work had been one of the reasons his marriage had failed. Maybe it was high time for him to break out of his shell.

He called Carolyn at home. When he didn't get an answer, he called her cell phone. "Are you awake?"

"I am now," she mumbled grumpily. "Did they pick up Downly?"

"Where are you?"

"I'm at my brother's," Carolyn whispered. "We didn't get out of the hospital until four this morning. I decided to stay over here rather than go home."

"Give me your brother's address," Hank said. "I'm coming over. I want to see you before I drive to Los Angeles to talk to Charles Harrison."

Once Carolyn told him where her brother lived, Hank said he could be there in ten minutes.

"We'll have to talk in your car," she said, carrying the portable phone into the living room. "Neil works at night and sleeps during the day."

"Sounds like Dracula."

"He'd like that," Carolyn said. "Have you been drinking this early in the morning?"

Hank hit the off button on his cell phone, embarrassed that people hadn't forgotten the days when he'd done battle with the bottle. He'd been sober now for five years.

When he pulled into the driveway, Carolyn was waiting with a thermos of coffee and two cups. She was dressed in a paint-stained sweatshirt and a pair of running shorts that reached almost to her knees.

Her brother must have some bucks, Hank thought. The house was located in the foothills, and had a panoramic view of the ocean. He watched as Carolyn tiptoed barefoot down the cobblestone walkway, then opened the door and climbed inside the passenger seat.

"Nice pad," he said. "What does your brother do for a living? Rob banks?"

"Why are you picking on my brother?" Carolyn asked. She offered the detective some coffee. When he passed, she poured a cup for herself, setting the thermos on the seat beside her.

"I don't drink anymore," Hank told her, staring out the front window. "Did you think you had to sober me up with coffee?"

"I wouldn't mind a stiff drink myself," Carolyn said. "There's no reason to get bent out of shape, Hank. As to my brother, he paints. And not houses. Neil's an established artist."

"What were your babbling about last night?" he said, referring to her late night call from the hospital. "You don't really think Charles Harrison arranged to spring Fast Eddie from the jail to kill Metroix, do you?"

"Honestly, I don't know what to think anymore," Carolyn said. "The times fit except for the explosion. Maybe Harrison had someone else handle the motel job. They're not the same type of crime."

Hank didn't want to admit it, but she was right. Pointing a gun at someone and pulling the trigger was not the same as detonating an explosive device. The motel job required a certain amount of expertise. Any street punk could point a gun out the window of a car and pull the trigger.

"There's also Warden Lackner," Carolyn reminded him. "Did you have your people search Metroix's room at the Comfort Inn?"

"Of course," he said. "We didn't find anything but a stack of papers and an old photograph."

"Has it already been booked into evidence?"

"Nah," Hank told her, reaching into his pocket for a toothpick. "There wasn't anything related to the case, so I thought I'd drop his things off at the hospital. Metroix will need something to wear when they release him." He stopped speaking, wondering why she looked so anxious. "He came through the surgery fine, if that's what you're worried about. He's not coherent enough yet for us to question him."

"You said there was a stack of papers," she said, turning sideways in the seat. "Was there anything on the papers, like designs or equations?"

"Yeah," Hank said. "I couldn't make sense of it, though." He pointed his thumb toward the back of the car. "Stuff's in the trunk if you want to look at it."

"Get it," Carolyn said, her eyes blazing with intensity. "All of Daniel's work was supposedly destroyed in the explosion."

Hank returned with a plastic sack.

She tossed the few items of clothing into the backseat, then pulled out what appeared to be approximately thirty pages of paper and a single snapshot encased in a plastic evidence bag. Rolling down the window, she hoped the brisk morning air would keep her awake as she tried to understand the complex equations. Some of it she'd seen before. This wasn't the original, though, nor was it a copy. Daniel had been desperately trying to reconstruct the work he'd lost in the explosion. Leaning closer to the detective, she held up one of the papers. "This is a design for an exoskeleton."

"I think I saw something like that in a science fiction movie," Hank said, uninterested.

Carolyn jerked the paper away in frustration. "I told you," she said sharply. "The military has been working on perfecting exoskeletons for years. All these other papers are computations for energy sources and other devices you need to make the exoskeleton function properly."

Hank shifted the toothpick around in his mouth. "How do you know that?"

"Because my parents were educated in science and math," Carolyn told him. "I got pregnant, Hank, or I might have gone into the same field. My father almost went nuts trying to solve this one problem. He finally gave up and took a job teaching math at the high school. When I was growing up, we ate, slept, and breathed this stuff."

The detective peered over her shoulder.

"Some of the physics is over my head, but Daniel may have solved an essential problem." She slapped the papers down in her lap. "We're talking big money here."

"How big?"

"Millions," Carolyn told him. "Don't get me wrong. I can't say definitely that Daniel's a genius, or that what I'm holding is worth killing someone over. All I know is, he told me that he'd been working on this for years." She cleared her throat, then took another sip of her coffee. "I spoke with Arline Shoeffel the other day and she thought it was plausible that the warden might be involved. Daniel said he designed what he called a walking suit for a guard's daughter who'd been paralyzed from the waist down. The suit, an exoskeleton, didn't work that well because he didn't have access to the right materials. The girl did walk in it, though. That was years ago. Since then, he's improved it."

Hank was impressed. "This guy invented something that made it so crippled people could walk?"

"Not necessarily," Carolyn said, raising a finger in the air like a pencil. "Whether the exoskeleton he developed works correctly doesn't really matter. Don't get me wrong. It'd be sensational if it did. That's not really the point. Say the warden showed Daniel's work to someone outside the prison, maybe a private research facility, or anyone who recognized its value. The way these things evolve is the following." She paused, waiting for the detective to absorb what she'd told him before continuing. "Okay, a scientist or inventor develops a prototype. He's either hired by a large company or he sells his invention outright. Then they put their own people to work on it. If Warden Lackner sold Daniel's designs, he can't afford to let anyone else see his work. He could be criminally prosecuted, even if he only had the intent to sell them. And this is straight from the horse's mouth."

"Judge Shoeffel, right?"

Carolyn nodded.

"Then maybe Lackner is behind this, instead of Chief Harrison."

"That's what I've been trying to tell you," Carolyn said, screwing off the cap on the thermos and refilling her coffee cup. "Let me finish. The prison may have entered into what's referred to as a joint venture program. If so, then it wouldn't be illegal. Lackner mentioned this kind of program when I talked to him on the phone. I think he might have been trying to throw us off. He's nervous, let me tell you. He even hung up on me the last time I called."

Hank smirked. "Ever consider the warden is too busy to spend time talking about an ex-con?"

"Maybe," Carolyn said. "I can usually tell when someone is lying. There's a slight possibility that the prison is working with the military. Like I said, I don't think this is the case."

"Hold on a minute," Hank said. "How is a prison warden going to claim he invented this exoskeleton or whatever you're talking about?"

"Under the table deals are done every day," Carolyn told him, "especially with something this valuable. All Lackner has to do is offer a piece of the pie to a guy who knows something about math and physics. The dupe studies the work and presents it as his own, claiming he can't take it any further because he doesn't have the right equipment or resources. Either that, or the warden convinces them his dead cousin had these papers in a box in his attic."

"Incredible," Hank said, shaking his head. "Get some rest. We'll talk later. I need to get to L.A. Chief Harrison's been out on sick leave for the past two weeks. I have his home address. I personally think you're in left field with the prison warden."

"Can I keep these?" Carolyn asked, gathering up the papers in her hands. "I know someone who may be able to give us an intelligent evaluation."

"Sure," the detective said. "How's Rebecca doing?"

"They put a cast on her ankle," Carolyn told him. "She's more scared than hurt. John spent the night with a friend. Should I let him go to school today?"

"He's probably safer at school than he would be with you," Hank said, although he hated to be put on the spot. He didn't know Carolyn's children. They had a mighty fine mother, he thought. The woman hadn't had a decent night's sleep in days, and she was still plugging away, doing everything she possibly could to protect her family as well as the community.

"Do you think it's safe for Rebecca and me to go home?"

"I've instructed patrol to drive by as often as possible," the detective said. "You know we don't have the manpower right now to put a patrol unit in front of your house twenty-four hours a day. I could pull White and his relief officer from the hospital. We've also got a team of officers standing guard over Luisa Cortez until we catch Downly. The mayor's even involved."

"Don't worry about me," Carolyn told him, opening the car door. "I can handle myself. I don't want anyone to hurt my children."

Hank swung by the station and picked up a uniformed officer named Mike Russell for backup. He couldn't, however, envision a man like Charles Harrison shooting another cop on his own property. Besides, it wasn't even nine o'clock, and the thought that Harrison himself had been personally committing all the crimes was ludicrous.

The situation with Eddie Downly was a disaster. The story had been plastered on the front page of most California newspapers, and with the Internet, even people in other countries had probably read about it. Hank was relieved that his department had not been involved. He didn't buy Carolyn's notion that Harrison was involved in Downly's release, or that he'd hired the man to assassinate Daniel Metroix. Eddie Downly had committed only two crimes that they knew of—the earlier child molestation and the rape of Luisa Cortez. Back when the criminal justice system, along with the rest of the world, wasn't run by computers, mistakes like this seldom happened.

Nonetheless, anything was possible. Downly had been on the street until Monday. Carolyn didn't know that Hank was aware that she'd stopped seeing Downly prior to the termination of his four-year probation. The detective was meticulous about his work. With a crime this serious, he'd read every word in Downly's file. Why destroy the reputation of an otherwise outstanding officer like Carolyn when he knew how overburdened she'd been?

Hank had made poor decisions himself throughout his career, and not only when he'd been drinking. He pursued the most dangerous criminals, and the cases that had the greatest chance of reaching prosecution. The others got pushed to the back of the file cabinet. That was the reality.

Mike Russell was a large, stoic man, a former marine who didn't waste his breath unless it was important. Hank had Russell drive so he could rest his eyes and decide what approach he should take with Harrison. Even if his hired goons were around, which was unlikely, he knew from experience that they wouldn't pose that great a threat.

The majority of criminals were nocturnal. They wreaked havoc all hours of the night, and generally didn't come to life until their stomachs started growling around lunchtime. Law enforcement had used this fact to their advantage for years. Raids conducted during the early morning hours were usually successful, and far few officers were injured.

Hank had been on the force only two years when Charles Harrison had been promoted to chief. He recalled how much the men had looked up to him, and not only due to his position. Harrison hadn't cared about the politics, as many police chiefs did. He'd been loyal to the officers, determined to elevate their standard of living and find ways to ensure their safety.

At present, the investigation of the incident at the Seagull Motel seemed to be going nowhere. The demolition company, Barrow and Kline, admitted that the room had been wired along with the rest of the motel, yet they swore they weren't responsible for the explosion. According to Ralph Kline, one of the partners, an unknown person had disconnected some of the wires from the main system, reconnecting them through a device inside the phone, which was set to activate whenever it rang. A sharp electrician might have been able to rig up something along these lines, but Kline doubted it. In his opinion, the person probably had training in explosives. Hank wondered if he had been a former member of a police bomb squad, maybe an officer who'd worked under Harrison in the past.

Basically, Kline hadn't told him anything that he didn't already know.

"We're almost there, sir," Russell told him, checking the numbers on the curb. "The address is 5036 Eagle Drive, right? This is 5034, but I can't find 5036." He stopped in front of what appeared to be a vacant lot, dense with trees and overgrown shrubbery. "What do you think? Are you certain they gave you the right address?"

"Yes," Hank answered. "I checked it twice." There were no numbers on the curb and no mailbox. Pulling out a pair of binoculars, he spotted a house through the thick foliage at the rear of the lot. Obviously, Harrison didn't want to be found.

Hank looked up at the sky as they climbed out of the Ford. The day was overcast and gray. Living this close to the ocean, he'd hoped it was only morning fog. The fog generally burned off by late morning or early afternoon. Nope, he thought, shaking his head. He didn't think they were in for another rain shower. He was fairly certain, though, that the sun wasn't going to put in an appearance for the remainder of the day.

Hank had been divorced for ten years. Martha, his former wife, had later remarried and moved to Florida. He had vowed to live the rest of his life alone. His wife leaving had been a blow, but her remarriage had shot him down several more notches. That's when he'd dived into the bottle. Betty was a nice lady. He couldn't handle the dating scene. As far as he was concerned, Martha would always be his wife. The waitress might make a pleasant companion. A little sex now and then would spice up his life. Use it or lose it, one of his buddies had reminded him the other day.

When you went to visit a dying man, Hank decided, a gray day almost seemed appropriate. Even if the deputy chief had nothing to do with the recent crimes, the detective knew it would do him good to see a man who'd failed to know when it was time to stop drinking.

Officer Russell walked ahead and held back the tree branches and shrubbery leading to the front of the house. The detective rang the doorbell while Russell stood to one side with his hand on his service revolver.

When no one responded, Hank looked up and saw a light burning in an upstairs bedroom. He depressed the doorbell again and refused to let up until he heard the faint sound of footsteps. Turning quickly to Russell, he said, "Stay out of sight unless I need you. We don't have a warrant. This will only work if Harrison thinks I'm here on an unofficial visit."

A small, olive-skinned woman cracked the door. "Go away," she said, immediately closing it.

"Open up," the detective shouted. "Your boss and I are

old friends. I heard he was sick. Tell him Hank Sawyer from Ventura is here to see him."

A short time later, the woman reappeared. He could tell now that she was Hispanic, and assumed she was Harrison's housekeeper.

"Do you have a warrant?"

How fast they learned, Hank thought, wondering how long she'd worked for Harrison. He had heard rumors that the deputy chief's wife was in a mental institution, that she'd suffered a breakdown after their son was killed. Harrison tried to tell people that she had some type of chronic illness. Everyone knew he was covering up the truth. Perhaps the diminutive woman with the silky dark hair and shapely body was more than Harrison's housekeeper.

"I don't need a warrant, lady," he told her, his voice softening. "Like I said, Charles and I go way back. I came to cheer him up, talk about old times."

The woman placed a hand over her mouth, her shoulders shaking as she began crying. A few moments later, she collected herself, wiping her eyes with the edge of her blouse. "You can't see him."

"And why is that?" the detective asked, reaching in his pocket for a toothpick.

Again, the woman's face twisted in anguish. "Chief Harrison died last night. Now, will you leave us alone?"

Hank spat the toothpick out of his mouth, caught off-guard by this new development. "Is his body inside?"

Mike Russell took up a position next to the detective.

"No," the woman said, raising her eyes to the tall, uniformed police officer. "The funeral home picked him up last night. We're making arrangements, contacting his relatives. Please, can't you respect our privacy?"

"Is Mrs. Harrison here?"

"Mrs. Harrison is in a hospital in Los Angeles. She knows about her husband. If you want to speak to her, you'll have to call Fairview Manor."

"Then who is *we?*" Hank said, stepping closer so he could get a look inside the house. "Who else is inside this place?"

"Only Mario," she said, refusing to budge from her position.

"Who's Mario?"

"The gardener."

The detective was appalled. "You trying to tell me that you and the gardener are arranging Charles Harrison's funeral?"

"We're taking care of whatever has to be done," she said, thrusting her chin forward. "Chief Harrison left specific instructions. Can't you go and leave us alone?"

"Were the police here earlier?"

"No," the woman said, a puzzled look on her face. "The funeral home said it wasn't necessary to call the police, since Charles . . . I mean Chief Harrison . . . was under a doctor's care."

Either they were lovers, as Hank had suspected, or the woman was shacking up with the gardener and they thought they could continue to live it up in Harrison's house. The detective brushed some leaves off his shoulder. He noticed that Russell had several scratches on his hands. For all Hank knew, Harrison was inside and had concocted this story to buy himself time.

"I'll leave, okay?" he said. "But not until you tell me the name of the funeral home."

"Arden Brothers."

"Is he going to be buried or cremated?"

"Cremated," she said, sniveling again. "He didn't want to pay the extra money."

"My ass," Hank barked, spinning around to leave. The funeral business was the worst racket in town. Guys who played with dead bodies all day could be bought for a few grand. After two aborted attempts to kill Daniel Metroix, Harrison sends his thugs out to knock off Carolyn Sullivan, who persistently gets in his way. Then when he fails again, he stages his own death and skips town, either satisfied because Metroix was shot, or leaving whoever he'd hired behind to finish the job.

Hank tripped over a tree stump and landed hard on his right knee, the same knee he'd had surgery on two years before. Russell reached down and pulled him to his feet. "Thanks," he said. "All Harrison needs is a pond filled with piranhas."

Russell laughed. "Guess he didn't like visitors."

When they reached the car, Hank glanced back at the overgrown yard again. Harrison's coconspirator was more than likely the man named Mario. He knew one thing. Mario sure as hell wasn't doing anything even remotely resembling gardening.

Chapter 16

"**Y**ou're not imposing," Paul Leighton said, sitting across from Carolyn and Rebecca in his living room a few minutes after ten o'clock Friday morning. "Can I get you something to drink? We have coffee, tea, milk."

"We're fine," she answered, placing her hand on top of her daughter's. "I was going to leave her at my brother's house." She started to explain that she was afraid that Neil would fall asleep, since he'd been working when she'd knocked on his door at four that morning. She'd slept only a few hours herself, but she'd had no choice. As an artist, her brother was also sensitive when it came to people invading his space. He could handle the models and girlfriends. Children were different.

"My mother could look after her," Carolyn continued, "but after last night . . ."

The professor held up a palm. "You already explained when you called, Carolyn."

Paul's home was sparsely, yet comfortably furnished. He had removed the carpeting and refinished the original hardwood floors. In addition, he'd knocked down the wall separating the dining room from the living area, creating an open space which made the house seem larger. A maple-colored leather sofa and several matching chairs were positioned in the center of the room, along with a coffee table laden with books and magazines in neat stacks. Where the formal dining room had been was now a combination library and office. Floor-to-ceiling bookcases lined all three walls, except for the space required for the two windows. His desk seemed unusually small, similar to the student desk Carolyn had purchased several years ago for John. The surface contained a lamp, a pencil holder, a framed photo of his daughter, a pad of paper, and nothing more.

In one corner was another small desk and chair with a computer and printer. As she'd expected, the professor was extremely neat. He also had the luxury of a full-time housekeeper.

"Isobel will fix Rebecca's lunch," Paul told her. "Lucy has a collection of DVDs she can watch. I'm certain she'll be pleased to find Rebecca here when she gets home from school." He looked somewhat embarrassed. "I don't want you to get the impression that my daughter is spoiled. One of the reasons Lucy has so many DVDs is that I don't pay as much attention to her as I should. Time gets away from me when I'm working."

"The doctor said for Rebecca to keep her foot elevated," Carolyn told him, pulling a prescription bottle out of her purse. "You can give her one of these every four hours if she has pain. The X-ray showed a hairline fracture. She should be able to go back to school Monday."

"Don't worry," Paul said, smiling at Rebecca. "We'll take good care of her."

Carolyn glanced anxiously at her watch. "I have to meet my supervisor at the office. It shouldn't take me more than a few hours. Do you plan on going out today? If so . . ."

"No," he said, grasping the seriousness of the situation. He tilted his head toward a glass gun case, letting her know that he had the means to protect Rebecca should the need arise. "And as far as my work goes, I've been staring at a blank page for almost a week now."

Carolyn removed Daniel's papers from her backpack. "I'd really appreciate it if you could take a look at these and let me know what you think."

Paul seemed somewhat annoyed. "Is this your son's—"

"No," she said, cutting him off. "I can't tell you the man's name. He's attempting to perfect a design for an exoskeleton."

"An exoskeleton," he said, taking the papers from her hand. He glanced at some of the drawings and equations, then jerked his head up. "Is this classified material? Did it come from the Department of Defense?"

"Of course not," Carolyn told him. "I don't have any connection with the DOD."

"Then why can't you tell me the man's name?" Paul asked. When he realized he wasn't going to get an answer, he set the papers down on the coffee table.

"I don't want anyone to know Rebecca's here," Carolyn said, glancing over at her daughter. The garages of all the houses on their block were located in the back. Leaving the rented Camry at her brother's, Carolyn had taken a taxi to Leighton's. The driver was waiting outside to take her to the government center. After her meeting with Brad, she'd have no choice but to borrow a car from the county motor pool.

She stood to leave, kissing Rebecca on the cheek. "Oh," she said, reaching into a sack and handing the girl one of the cell phones she'd purchased the day before, "if you need me, all you have to do is push number one on the auto dial. Number two is the police department. If it's an emergency, call the police first before you call me."

"Cool," the girl said, eagerly snatching the phone out of her mother's hand.

"I didn't buy this for you to chat with your friends, young lady."

Rebecca's face fell, then quickly brightened. "Don't you have to pay a certain amount every month? One of the girls at school has a phone and she says she gets an hour or something free." She thought a moment and then added, "It's called air time."

Carolyn saw Paul smiling from across the room. "Kids are too smart these days," she said, turning back to her daughter. "You can make a few calls. Don't go overboard. When this is all over, I'm taking the phone back."

Rebecca's eyes narrowed. "Are you going to take John's away too? He thinks you're going to let him keep it."

They'd stopped off at Turner Highland's house where John had spent the night. Carolyn wanted to drop off the phone and caution her son after the events of the night before. She'd instructed the cab driver to use the side streets, keeping her eyes peeled to make certain no one was following them. Turner's mother offered to pick the boys up after school.

With the responsibilities her son carried, Carolyn might consider letting him keep the phone. He wasn't the type to abuse such a privilege. John was too busy with his schoolwork to waste time talking nonsense. She wondered how Rebecca had figured it out, or if John had said something.

"Why don't you watch a movie like Professor Leighton suggested," Carolyn told her. "Since you didn't get much sleep last night or the night before, maybe you should take a nap. Paul, do you mind if she rests on your sofa?"

"Make yourself comfortable in Lucy's room, Rebecca. That's where the DVD player is anyway. If you have trouble working anything, call me on the intercom." He turned and peered into Carolyn's weary eyes. "When you finish whatever you need to do, take some of your own advice. You know, get some sleep. Your daughter will be safe here. Don't come back until six. And bring John with you. Isobel will make us all a nice meal. We can postpone our dinner out until next weekend. By then, perhaps all this will be behind you."

Carolyn watched as Rebecca hobbled down the hallway

to Lucy's bedroom on her crutches. Paul was standing next to her now and she could smell his aftershave, something musky and masculine. There was also a unique calmness about him, a comforting contrast to the frenzied pace of the last few days. As the light struck his face, she noticed how beautiful his eyes were—a pale shade of blue. Today he was wearing his reading glasses. Instead of detracting from his appearance, they made his eyes more noticeable and gave him a distinguished look. No, she corrected herself, this was a man who didn't need to *look* distinguished. He *was* distinguished.

Then another thought passed through Carolyn's mind. John was one of the few teenage boys who actually prayed. They didn't talk about it much, but he'd mounted his rosary on a hook over his desk. Had he been praying for his mother to fall in love with their new neighbor? Of course, John's aspirations to become a physicist may have led him to seek any help available.

More important reasons could also exist. Her son might want his mother to establish a relationship with the professor beyond obtaining a recommendation to MIT. Her former husband had virtually abandoned his children. In many ways, Frank's absence in John and Rebecca's life was a blessing. To think that her son longed for male companionship and guidance, however, was troubling. On the other hand, the solution might be standing right in front of her.

"I don't know how to thank you," Carolyn said, a slight flutter in her voice.

"I'm beginning to feel like we're family," Paul said, smiling. "It's kind of nice. When I'm teaching, there're more people around. Writing a book is a solitary task." He stopped speaking, then added, "About this man's design for an exoskeleton . . ."

"I guess I'll see you at dinner then," Carolyn said, smiling pleasantly. "I can take the papers back if you're too busy to look at them."

"No," he said, scowling. "I'd like to know whose work I'm evaluating."

"I'll call and check on Rebecca in a few hours."

"Sleep," Paul said, his tone more of a command than a suggestion. "You look dead on your feet."

"I promise I'll use the time wisely."

Carolyn glanced over her shoulder at him as she walked out the door. A physicist of Paul Leighton's caliber might be intriguing, but she sensed he could also be controlling. She'd rather have a clandestine affair with Brad than end up as a constant in one of the professor's social equations.

Chapter 17

"I guess I'll have to reassign the Sandoval shooting," Brad Preston said, leaning back in the black leather chair behind his desk. "This thing last night doesn't make sense, Carolyn. Your parolee was in the hospital, so why would someone try to run you off the road? Are you sure this wasn't a couple of crazy teenagers? Maybe they wanted to race you."

"In a rented Camry?"

Brad flashed a smile. "Never know."

"This isn't a game, asshole."

Brad's assistant, Rachel, had taken the day off, so they knew they wouldn't be interrupted. They were killing time, waiting for Hank Sawyer to call. He sat upright. "Yesterday, you said I was a fantastic lover. Today I'm back to being an asshole. Why don't we compromise and consider ourselves friends? If that doesn't work, try remembering every now and then that I'm your supervisor."

"I get mad when you don't take me seriously." Reclining on the small sofa in his office, Carolyn was wearing black slacks and a blue cotton top. Her hair was tied back in a ponytail. Before taking Rebecca to the professor's, she'd darted into her house and changed clothes, then grabbed a clean shirt and pants for her daughter. "I figured out why you pulled me into the men's rest room the other day."

"Oh you did, huh?" Brad said, a mischievous look in his eyes.

"I'd look like an idiot if I tried to report you for sexual harassment," Carolyn told him, extending one of her legs in the air. "You could claim you were going about your business when I barged into the men's room and tried to entice you to have sex with me. We didn't have intercourse, so you didn't do anything out of order."

"Forget about the other day, okay?" Brad said, eager to change the subject. "About last night—"

"Think about it," Carolyn said. "Daniel Metroix was in jail when they smashed my car and left the threatening note. And these weren't kids trying to run me off the road last night. I'm almost certain they intended to shoot me like they did Metroix."

"Did you see a gun?"

"I'm not really sure," Carolyn answered. "Only seconds before I managed to turn off the road, the passenger in the Corvette rolled down the window. I remember seeing something protruding. It was dark, though. When you're traveling almost a hundred miles an hour in a residential neighborhood, you don't have a lot of time to do anything other than drive."

"That's too bad about Rebecca's ankle," Brad said. "She's a sweet kid."

"Yeah," Carolyn said, sitting up. "You don't have to reassign the Sandoval case. I dictated the report yesterday. All that's left is to proofread it and submit. Don't give me anything new, though."

Brad rubbed the side of his neck. "We're up to our eyeballs right now. The stress is killing me. I think I've got another herniated disk. This thing with Eddie Downly has the whole city in an uproar."

"I'd die if something happened to my children," Carolyn told him. "This is too close to home. I'm scared, Brad."

The call they'd been waiting for finally came through. Brad punched the button for the speaker phone, tossing his feet on top of the desk.

"Charles Harrison is dead," Hank told them. "I just left Arden Brothers Funeral Home. They claim he was cremated early this morning."

"When did he die?" Carolyn asked, moving closer in order to hear better.

"Last night," Hank said in his gravel voice.

"Great," Brad said. "Now it's too late to do an autopsy."

"Don't you know how it works?" the detective asked, his tone bordering on sarcasm. "Because Harrison was under a doctor's care, all his housekeeper did was call the funeral home to pick up the body. I guess you guys in probation don't handle deaths."

"Only murders," Brad said, placing his palms on the desk.

"By law," the detective continued, "no one outside of the funeral home is required to even *see* the body. The death certificate hasn't been signed yet. The mortuary is sending one of their people over to Harrison's doctor's office sometime this morning."

Carolyn and Brad exchanged tense looks. She couldn't believe what she was hearing. It placed her speculations about the former police chief in a new light. "Charles Harrison is really dead?"

"That's what they say," Hank replied. "Sounds a tad too convenient, if you ask me. Metroix is shot around two yesterday. Then, last night, someone comes after his parole officer. Metroix survives . . . Carolyn escapes. And don't forget the explosion at the Seagull. These people are batting zero."

Carolyn placed a hand over her chest. "Are you implying that Harrison could have faked his own death?"

"I might fake my death too if I'd hired some goons and they botched things up this bad, leaving me wide open to take the heat." He stopped to take a breath. "I'm certain Harrison was a sick man, okay. In reality, his health problems would give him even more of a reason to stage his own demise. Who wants to spend their last days in a cell?"

"Let's backtrack a minute," Carolyn said, trying to get all the facts straight. "Even when they cremate someone, isn't there a way to identify them? We need a positive ID, Hank."

"Arden Brothers is a first-rate joint," he said. "Mrs. Harrison is in a mental hospital. She probably wouldn't have been able to attend her husband's funeral even if he'd planned on having one. Do you think the hospital wants Arden Brothers to mail the poor woman her husband's ashes?"

"What's the point, Hank?"

"They got rid of them," he said. "Most people don't want the ashes, or at least that's what Anthony Arden told me. They used to dump them in a bin out back. Now they have an arrangement with Ivy Lawn cemetery. They send whatever remains they have on hand to the cemetery and they bury them in a common grave. This morning happened to be their regular day to clean house. Morticians even have their own vocabulary. They refer to what's left as cremains."

Carolyn recalled reading something in the newspaper. "Wasn't there a lawsuit several years ago about this type of thing?"

"You guys still don't understand," Hank told them, becoming even more agitated. "The case you're talking about was a company that promised to scatter the remains at sea. I don't think they owned a boat or even a crematorium. They had bodies stashed all over the place. Arden Brothers didn't do anything wrong. When no one claims the cremains, and no specific arrangements have been made for some type of vault, urn, or any kind of service, the funeral home burns them and buries them in the common grave."

"Seems like a good way to get away with murder," Carolyn tossed out. "What about his teeth?"

"If you want to fish through that stuff and see if you can find a bridge or something that didn't disintegrate, be my guest. Our best bet is to try to track Harrison through doctors and hospitals. He'll need medical treatment if he's alive."

"Why would he give his real name?" Carolyn asked, walking around the room. "Harrison was a deputy chief. He wouldn't be that stupid. He's either left the state or he's holed up somewhere in L.A. under an assumed name. You can certainly have your department check various doctors and hospitals. Personally, I think it's a waste of time."

"Let's say Harrison did die." Brad's expression hinted that he thought the situation might be as it appeared. "For all we know, he had nothing to do with the recent events. That means we have to consider other suspects. Did you come up with anything on either the Corvette or the SUV?"

"Not yet," Hank said. "We're running the partial plate the woman witness gave us every way possible. Knowing the make of the car would have helped, know what I mean?"

"Both of the cars were probably stolen," Carolyn told him, flicking the ends of her fingernails. "My bet is they've already dumped them. Are your people checking abandoned vehicles?"

"Sure," the detective said. "You know how many vehicles are abandoned every year in this city? And what makes you think they ditched the cars in Ventura? Not only that, people who kill for money know the ropes. They leave cars in supermarket parking lots where weeks or even months can pass before anyone notices them. Either that, or they sell them to salvage yards. Those guys don't report half of the vehicles they strip. There's too much profit in stolen auto parts."

"We may never catch these guys," Brad said. "Isn't that what you're trying to tell us, Hank?"

"More or less."

"What about Daniel?" Carolyn asked. "Has anyone spoken to him?"

"No," Hank said. "White said he's been out cold all morning. I plan to go over there myself this afternoon."

"Well," Brad said, standing and stretching, "our agency has done all we can."

Carolyn sat down on the sofa. "Why was I a target to begin with? I understand about Daniel." Her voice elevated with excitement. "There're two men whose lives could be destroyed if the truth ever comes out about Tim Harrison. And since I'm the only one who's been trying to get the case reopened, getting rid of me would put an end to their problems." She raised her arm in the direction of her supervisor. "Look how you're acting, Brad," she said. "You think Daniel and I are no longer in danger, that we should forget about everything that's happened. Even if you remove Daniel and Harrison from the picture, it doesn't change the fact that someone may have tried to kill me on two separate occasions."

"Calm down," Brad said. "Anyway, you've lost me as to the two other men."

"You haven't lost *me*," Hank's voice boomed over the speaker phone. "Guess it's time we paid a visit to Liam Armstrong and Nolan Houston. Can we even prosecute these men, though? The statute of limitations on perjury expired years ago."

"Perjury was the least of their crimes," Carolyn told him. "I wouldn't worry about the statute of limitations. We're talking murder, Hank."

"How do you get to murder?" the detective asked. "From what I know about the original crime, the Harrison boy's death may have been an accident."

"Daniel Metroix went to prison for second degree murder," Carolyn said, feeling certain they were on the right track. "If either Houston or Armstrong shoved Tim Harrison in front of that car, then they can be prosecuted for the same crime. There's no statute of limitations on murder. Don't you see? We've been coming at this from the wrong direction."

The line fell silent, then, a few moments later, Hank

began speaking again. "You might be right, Carolyn. You know what happens when you start looking under rocks."

"I've already tracked down Houston and Armstrong," she said, speaking rapidly. "Just their businesses, though. Their home numbers are unlisted, and I didn't have time to trace them. I want to be with you when you see them. It's harder to kill someone once you look them in the eye."

"I don't want to interview them at their homes," Hank told her. "It's doubtful if they'll tell us anything worthwhile with their wives and children around. Let's call it for today, and plan to pay Armstrong and Houston a visit Monday. Meet me at the PD around eight o'clock."

Carolyn left Brad's office to get the information she'd compiled on the two men so she could go directly from her home.

"Smart lady," Hank told her supervisor. "We could use a few like her at the PD. You're going to miss her when she gets her law degree."

"Let's hope she lives long enough," Brad Preston said, punching a button on the speaker phone to end the call.

Chapter 18

Arriving at her house at two-fifteen Friday afternoon, Carolyn staggered down the hall and fell face first on her bed. Knowing her children were safe, she could relax. Paul Leighton had been right. If she didn't get some sleep, she was going to end up hospitalized for exhaustion.

She awoke when she heard her son's voice.

"Where's Rebecca?" John asked, standing over his mother's bed. "I tried to call you about thirty minutes ago. No one answered the phone."

"I guess I didn't hear it," Carolyn said, feeling as if her eyes were glued together. She reached over and grabbed the clock on the end table, seeing that it was almost five o'clock. "Rebecca's at Paul's house. I had some important things to take care of at the office."

John placed his hands on his hips. "What's more important than your kid? She breaks her ankle. She gets the crap scared out of her, and you run off and leave her with Paul. The man's trying to write a book. He's not running a baby-sitting service."

Carolyn sat up on the edge of the bed, a sharp tone to her voice. "Are you criticizing me again?"

"All these terrible things have been happening," the boy explained, punching the air for emphasis. "You make demands on me. Why can't I say anything when you—"

"Stop right there," Carolyn told him. "I don't want to get into another argument. We're having dinner at the professor's house tonight. I thought you'd be pleased."

Her son's frustrations seemed to vanish. "Really?" he asked. "How did that come about?"

Carolyn felt disgusting. She scratched her head. She hadn't washed her hair in several days, and she even caught a whiff of body odor. In her rush to get out of the house that morning, she'd forgotten to put on deodorant.

"Like most things," she told him. "He asked and I accepted. I need to get cleaned up. I suggest you do the same." She paused and then added, "Play your cards right and you might get a recommendation to MIT. Your judgment is pretty good when it comes to men. I like this one."

"Wow," John said, turning around in a small circle, his eyes bright with excitement. He started to dash out of the room, then stopped. "What should I wear? What are you wearing?"

"I can't believe you're concerned about your clothes," his mother said, although she was wondering the same thing. "I'm sure as long as we're clean, we'll be acceptable. Wear jeans and something other than a tank top."

"This is so great," John said, placing his hand on his head. "I have so many things I want to ask him."

"So do I," Carolyn said, hoping the professor could give her some answers regarding Daniel's work. "We're supposed to be there at six. I suggest we get moving. The first shower is mine. I'll try not to use up all the hot water."

"I already showered at Turner's this morning," John said, grinning sheepishly. "Take as much time as you need. You want to look pretty, don't you?"

Carolyn walked over and threw her arms around his neck. "Don't get too carried away about me and this man. Because I find him interesting doesn't mean he feels the same. Nothing may come of it." She didn't want to take away John's happiness by telling him that Paul might be too demanding for her. His friendly demeanor could mask a number of unpleasant traits. "Your professor friend may not be in the market for a girlfriend, anyway."

John laced his fingers together, then lifted them into the air in a gesture of triumph. "You're wonderful," he said. "You're beautiful, smart, strong, brave. Not only that, you're my mother! How could any man not go nuts over you?"

Carolyn felt a rush of pleasure. She reached up again and tenderly stroked the side of his face. "Those were awfully nice things you said," she told him. "A few minutes ago, you accused me of neglecting your sister."

"I didn't mean it that way," John told her. "I've been worried this past week. Sometimes I feel like Becky and I don't have a father, that I have to take his place."

"Her name is Rebecca," his mother reminded him.

"I'll never understand girls in a million years," he said, shaking his head. "Whether your realize it or not, Mom, you and *Rebecca* are a lot alike. Big things zip right over your head, then you go through the roof over a stupid word or a name."

"You might be right," Carolyn said, never having thought of it that way. "We may have our differences now and then, honey, but I wouldn't trade you for the world. I'm proud to have you as my son."

"Yes," John said, turning his eyes toward the ceiling. "There must be a God, don't you see? Finally, something good might happen around here."

At about the same time Carolyn, John, and Rebecca were about to sit down for dinner with Paul Leighton and his daughter, Hank Sawyer was standing at the bedside of Daniel Metroix. He'd been moved from intensive care to a regular room on the seventh floor of Methodist Hospital. Advising Trevor White's relief officer to take a break and get himself something to eat, he quietly entered the room.

An orderly brought in a dinner tray. Hank looked it over, seeing a cup of broth, milk, a container of juice, a single slice of bread, and some type of pudding. Although he couldn't recall much from the days directly following his own shooting, he seriously doubted if Daniel would be eating anything. If they'd brought something even moderately appealing, the detective would have helped himself. He'd skipped lunch and he was starving.

Daniel's skin was as pale as a corpse, his face knotted in agony. When the detective reached down and touched his shoulder, his body stiffened and his eyelids sprang open. "Are you the doctor?"

"No, pal," he told him. "I'm Detective Sawyer, with the Ventura PD."

Daniel's eyes closed again.

"I know how you feel," Hank continued. "Hurts like a bitch, doesn't it? A murdering piece of shit put a slug in me a few years back, in about the same spot as you were hit." Seeing that Daniel was now awake and listening, he added, "It's the cramping that gets you. That and the gas pains. Every day will get better. Hang in there. You know, try to ride it out. Nothing else you can do anyway."

"Who shot me?"

"We were hoping you'd be able to answer that question," Hank said. "Can you recall the make of the SUV or the license number?"

"No," Daniel said, his right hand closing on the bedrail as a violent muscle spasm ripped through his abdomen.

"It helps if you breathe," the detective said, grimacing as he waited for the spasm to pass. Once Daniel's head slumped back against the pillow, he started asking questions again. "What about a physical description? Did you see the shooter's face? Can you tell us his age, hair color, any distinguishing facial features?"

"He was white," Daniel told him.

"That certainly narrows it down," Hank said caustically.

"Anything else? Like eyes, chin, mouth, teeth, scars. Since he was in a car, I don't expect you to describe his clothes or build."

"Dark sunglasses," he said, staring at the ceiling. "I think he had blond hair. Either that, or he was wearing some kind of light-colored cap. I'm not certain. Everything happened so fast."

"Tell me about this desk clerk at the Seagull Motel," Hank said. "You said a man on the bus from Chino wrote down the address and told you it was the best place to stay. Was he another parolee?"

"No," Daniel answered. "At least, I don't think so. It wasn't a prison bus. A number of people were released the same day. I don't know where they went. One guy said he was going to try and stay in the area and get a job. Most of them wanted to find a bar and get drunk."

"What did the man on the bus look like?"

"Older guy," Daniel said. "I think he was in his forties. Seemed straight."

"In what way?"

"I don't know," he said, pressing the button on his morphine pump as another muscle spasm seized him. Once the drug reached his bloodstream, he added, "He acted sort of like you, or maybe some of the guards at prison. Tough guy, sure of himself, wearing one of those nice knit shirts."

"Could he have been one of the guards?"

"If he was, I don't recall ever seeing him," Daniel answered. "And what would a prison guard be doing on a Greyhound bus? All those guys have cars."

The detective picked up the slice of bread off the tray, holding it so Daniel could see it. "You gonna eat this?" When the man shook his head, Hank tore the plastic and shoved the bread into his mouth. Then he pulled up a chair and took a seat. "I have an acidic stomach," he explained. "Kicks up a fuss when I don't eat. What did the man who rented you the room at the Seagull Motel look like?"

Daniel remained silent a while, searching his memory. "Skinny, white," he said. "Not too bright. Oh, and he had tattoos on his knuckles. I don't know what the letters were, so don't ask me. All I recall is that they were fancy writing, the same kind they use to write graffiti on walls."

Hank leapt to his feet. Eddie Downly had the same type of tattoos on his knuckles. Of course, so did hundreds of other thugs and gangsters. Carolyn's suspicion that Fast Eddie might have been involved, though, had became more believable. The office at the Seagull Motel had been wiped clean prior to the explosion. The crime lab wasn't able to retrieve a single print.

"How many times did you see this man?" Hank asked. "You know, the clerk, the guy with the tattoos on his knuckles?"

"Twice, I think," Daniel told him. "I checked in Monday about four. The guy was real antsy. I thought he might be on speed or something. He also had sores on his arms and face."

Certainly sounded like a speed freak, the detective thought. When a person used amphetamines over a long period of time, the toxic chemical practically oozed out of their pores. Damn, he thought, Carolyn wouldn't know if Fast Eddie had been a serious drug user; she hadn't seen him for twelve months. A year in the life of a criminal wasn't the same as that of a normal person. For all they knew, Eddie could have killed someone, raped numerous young girls, and robbed a dozen liquor stores.

Hank asked, "When did you see him again? You said you saw him twice."

"The hot water didn't work," he told him. "I went down to the office to ask them to give me another room. The clerk claimed they were booked. He told me I'd have to wait for their repairman. I knew the motel couldn't be full, as there were hardly any cars in the parking lot." He stopped and pushed the button for more morphine, then closed his eyes to fight the pain.

"I wouldn't be pressing you if it wasn't for your own protection," Hank said. "The captain wants me to pull the guard off your door. I need to know everything you can tell me about this room clerk."

"He started yelling at me," Daniel said, speaking with his eyes closed. "I decided taking a shower wasn't important, so I left. There's nothing more to tell. I never saw the guy after that."

The detective stepped out of the room, called dispatch, and advised them to have a patrol unit get the photo lineup they'd shown to the girl Eddie Downly had raped over to the hospital right away. The problem was, Metroix was so heavily drugged that any identification he made wouldn't carry much weight. All Hank wanted to do was make certain they weren't wasting their time trying to tie Downly into the incident at the Seagull. Every law enforcement agency in the country had already been alerted that a dangerous criminal had escaped.

On the Metroix case, however, they were all over the map. Hank knew they had to somehow pull everything together.

"Let's talk about Chino," the detective said. "Charles Harrison's dead, by the way. That doesn't mean he didn't hire someone to take you out. He only croaked last night. We need to consider other suspects. Did someone have it in for you at the prison?"

"Not that I know of," Daniel told him, more alert now. "I can't believe Charles Harrison is dead. The way that man felt about me, I thought the hate alone was going to kill me. I never thought I'd outlive him."

"You almost didn't," the detective pointed out. He tossed the plastic bread wrapper into the trash, then reached in his pocket for a toothpick. "You've got to be honest with me if you want us to arrest the person who shot you. Everyone makes enemies inside prison. Were you affiliated with any type of group or prison gang?"

"No."

"Did you have a lover?"

Daniel looked shocked. "You mean a man?"

"Yeah," Hank told him. "Not a lot of girls at Chino. First, let's get something straight. If you got your jollies off with a man means nothing right now. I might bang a guy too if I'd been locked up as long as you were. No one's going to put it in the newspaper. We don't have one solid lead on this case. Zilch, understand? The shooters are well aware of this fact."

"How?"

"No one's knocking on their door. Since they got away clean, they may come back to finish what they've been paid to do. My job is to keep that from happening."

Daniel suddenly became animated. "Carolyn? Is she all right?"

Carolyn, huh? Hank thought, rocking his chair back on its hind legs. Daniel had placed his parole officer on a first-name basis. Of course, after Metroix's experience at the Seagull, Hank could see how he might feel their relationship extended beyond the normal professional boundaries. For all practical purposes, Carolyn Sullivan had saved his life.

"Forget about *Officer Sullivan* for the time being," Hank said. "You didn't answer my question. Did you have a lover inside prison?"

"No," Daniel said, looking the detective straight in the eye. "I've never had a lover, male or female."

Hank brought his chair to an upright position. For a long time, he gazed down at the floor. How many forty-one-year-old virgins were there? More important, how many men would admit such a thing? And sex was only one aspect of life that Metroix had never been given a chance to experience. He wasn't a bad-looking man. He could have married, had a few kids, got himself a first-class education, even sold all those inventions. Carolyn thought his work was valuable, and he respected her opinion. The woman had the brains to know.

A young patrol officer stuck his head in the door, clasping a manila envelope. "I was told to deliver this to you, sir," he said, placing the package in the detective's hands. "Do you want me to hang around?"

"No," Hank said, removing the contents of the envelope. "We already have enough men here at the hospital. We need you back on the street."

As soon as the officer left, the detective released the railing on Metroix's bed, then leaned over to show him the images. "Do you recognize any of these men?"

"That guy looks a little like him," Daniel said, struggling to focus his eyes as he placed his finger on one of the pictures.

The detective sighed. The man he'd picked wasn't Eddie Downly. "Are you certain?"

"I think so," Daniel said, reaching out and pulling the photos closer to his face. "This one looks even more like him. He had weird eyes."

Bingo, Hank thought. He'd fingered Eddie Downly as the clerk at the Seagull Motel. It couldn't be classified as a positive ID, but at least it was a start.

"Take it easy, my friend," Hank told him. Considering the hardships Metroix had endured, his childlike sincerity would tug on even the hardest of hearts. "In a few days, when you're feeling better, I'll stop by a restaurant and bring you a decent meal. Way I see it, you've been on the receiving end far too long. Between me and the lady, we're going to do our best to turn things around for you."

Chapter 19

Before they sat down for dinner Friday night, John discussed his desire to go to MIT with Professor Leighton in the living room while his daughter gave Carolyn a tour of the house. Rebecca followed on her crutches.

Lucy was a skinny girl with straight blond hair that fell to her shoulders. Several inches taller than Rebecca, she had braces on her teeth and deep dimples in both cheeks.

Because Paul had converted the formal dining room into a combination library and office, he'd added another room off the kitchen, furnishing it with a table large enough to seat twelve people, along with an antique breakfront filled with china and silver. The room was illuminated by a beautiful crystal chandelier.

"Most of the antiques belonged to my mother," Paul told them as he took his seat at the head of the table. "All the tacky modern stuff, I picked out myself. A decorator told me I had to choose between the old and the new. I told her to get lost." He lovingly ran his hands across the polished mahogany surface. "This is the same table I ate on when I was a child. Some things you want to keep forever."

"That sounds like my mom and her cuff links," Rebecca said, seated next to Lucy. "They belonged to my great-grandfather."

The family's housekeeper, Isobel Montgomery, was a

wiry, attractive black woman in her late fifties with closely cropped hair. She served lasagna, salad, and homemade bread sticks soaked in garlic.

"Aren't you going to eat with us?" Lucy asked anxiously.

"No, sweetheart," Isobel said, untying her apron and placing a hand on the girl's shoulder. "I'm going out to dinner with a friend. Don't forget the chocolate cake we made this afternoon."

"Isobel's been with us for eighteen years," Paul explained after the woman left. "She's one of the reasons Lucy decided to live with me instead of her mother."

"My real mom can't cook," Lucy said, passing the salad bowl to John. "She has a housekeeper, but I don't like her. She doesn't speak English and she isn't Isobel. Besides, my mother and stepfather are never home."

John took a few bites of his salad, then reached for the large platter of lasagna. "This is great," he said, wolfing it down.

Rebecca was munching on a bread stick. "I wish we had someone to cook and take care of us."

"Mom and I take care of you," John told her, knowing she'd hurt his mother's feelings. "You talk like you're an orphan or something."

"I do not," Rebecca snapped. "And the stuff you make tastes like dog food."

"Oh, yeah," he said. "You're almost thirteen. Why don't you cook your own food?"

Paul stood, smiled, then rubbed his hands together. He picked up a bottle of wine that had been chilling in the ice bucket. "As long as your mother doesn't object," he said, sensing Carolyn's offspring were about to get into an argument, "I think you guys should have a little wine. In Europe, children are allowed a glass of wine with their dinner."

"You never let me drink wine before," Lucy said.

"Tonight is special," her father answered. "We're going to

make a toast to our new home and our wonderful new friends. What do you say, Carolyn?"

"It's okay," she said, admiring his ingenuity. "Half a glass, though. No refills."

After they finished their meal, Rebecca and Lucy headed to the kitchen to prepare their dessert. Paul got up to clear the plates, but John insisted on taking care of it.

"You should keep your foot elevated," Carolyn told her daughter.

"I've been sleeping all day, Mom," Rebecca protested, leaning on her crutches. "My ankle doesn't hurt anymore. Even the swelling has gone down."

"Can Rebecca sleep over tonight?" Lucy asked, setting her father's chocolate cake down in front of him. "She wants to watch *The Mummy Returns* with me. Isobel said Rebecca could go to church with us in the morning, then to the cemetery to visit Otis. For lunch, you could take us to Dave and Buster's."

Her father sighed. "You'll have to ask Ms. Sullivan."

"Not tonight, Lucy," Carolyn said. "Maybe next weekend you can spend the night at our house. Your father needs to concentrate on his book. We've imposed enough."

The girls went into the living room. John asked his mother if he could go home. "Paul told me a way I could solve this problem I've been having trouble with. Everyone thinks Mr. Chang will use it on our final exam."

"I'd rather you stay," Carolyn told him. "We'll be leaving soon." She heard the girls giggling in the other room.

"They get along well," Paul said. "Can I get you another glass of wine, coffee? John, we have sodas."

"No, thanks," he said, sulking.

"Coffee," Carolyn said, knowing she had another sleepless night ahead of her. She could let John keep watch the next day.

"If you forget what we talked about," the professor told

John, "you can stop by tomorrow morning and we'll go over it again."

"Really?" John asked, perking up. "Are you certain? I'm sorry I caused a scene at dinner. I thought you'd never want to see me again."

"Come with me," Paul said, gesturing toward the living room. The girls were sitting on the floor next to the fireplace. Lucy was showing Rebecca pictures from the dance camp she'd gone to the previous summer. John took a seat on the sofa next to his mother.

The professor opened the hall closet and removed several large rolled-up sheets of paper. "I've been fascinated with roller coasters since I was a kid. One of my friends works for Arrow Dynamics. They designed 'X' for Six Flags. I bet him fifty bucks that I could come up with something better."

"Who won?" Carolyn asked.

"They finished building it, but I still don't know if I won the bet or not. The coaster is supposed to be up and running in three weeks, then we'll have to wait and see what the critics think." Paul ran his fingers through his hair, his face flushed with childish excitement. "Anyone want to see?"

"I love roller coasters," John said, rushing over and watching as he spread out the drawings on his desk. "This is the coolest thing I've ever seen. It's a four-dimension roller coaster."

"What does that mean?" Rebecca asked.

"Unlike traditional coasters where trains only parallel the track," Paul explained, "riders race in vehicles that can spin independently, three hundred and sixty degrees forward or backward on a separate axis."

"Look at this, man," John said, pointing, "it's a twenty-foot-wide wing-shaped car. You go down headfirst, face-down. This right here is called a vertical skydive. Then you've got a twisting front flip, three back flips, and four raven turns."

Paul smiled. "I'm impressed, guy. You really know your roller coasters."

"You bet," the boy said, leaning over so he could see better. "This is how I first got intrigued with gravity. How old was I, Mom?"

"Second grade, I believe," Carolyn said, glancing over at the professor. "He had the same problem you must have had, Paul. He was too small to ride on them, so I didn't want to spend the money to get into the park. We'd find a place outside the fence and sit there for hours watching."

"What are you going to call it?"

"All the good names are taken," Paul said. "You know, Colossus, Medusa, Talon, Twister, Vortex. Besides, I just put it together as a hobby. They're going to call it Super X. I preferred Ultimate X, but I think they're trying to compete with Bolliger and Mabillard, the guys from Switzerland. They designed the Superman coasters and are reported to be the best in the business."

"You mean you didn't get paid for this? It must have taken you years to figure all of this out." John looked over at Rebecca. "He used physics. See, I told you it wasn't boring."

"The company paid me," Paul said. "That didn't mean I got to name it, though."

"There's this computer game," John told him. "It's called World's Greatest Roller Coasters in 3D. There's another one called Roller Coaster Tycoon, but this one is better. You get to build the coaster, the park, even the concessions."

"I've seen the last one you mentioned," Paul told him. "It's interesting. They never had things like that when I was growing up."

The girls as well as Carolyn peered over John and Paul's shoulders. "I'm never going to get on that stupid thing," Lucy said, punching her father's arm. "Dad says I'm a chicken. He tricked me into going on Superman Ultimate Flight. I was so scared, I almost died. You guys think I'm exaggerating, but I'm not. They took me to the hospital in an ambulance."

"You didn't almost die," her father said. "You fainted. I

promise, you don't have to ride on this one. Half the adults I know wouldn't ride on the kind of coasters we're building today."

"Wow," Rebecca said. "I'm not afraid. I can't wait to ride it."

"Great," Paul said, "because you're all invited to come as my guests to the opening. The park's closed to the public, kind of like a private party. You can go on all the other rides as well."

Carolyn's cell phone rang. "Excuse me," she said, stepping into the kitchen.

"Ready for another mindblower," Brad Preston said. "I'll let Hank tell you. I've got him on a conference call. Where are you?"

"At the neighbor's house. What's going on?"

Hank spoke up, "The clerk at the Seagull may have been Eddie Downly."

Believing she hadn't heard him correctly, Carolyn closed the door. "Repeat what you said." Once he did, she placed her forehead against the wall.

"If Downly was the clerk at the Seagull, then he had to be working for Harrison," Brad said. "Who else but a deputy chief would be able to spring a scumbag rapist like Downly and make it look like an accident? That means it was an inside job. Try to find this Downy guy with the parking tickets. The whole thing was a setup. We're being played for fools on every corner."

While Brad was merely reacting, Carolyn was thinking.

"Don't go through the roof, okay?" Hank said. "Metroix was pumped full of morphine when he picked Downly out of the photo lineup. Not only that, Downly wasn't the first man he identified. How many guys do you know with tattoos on their knuckles, for Christ's sake?"

"He was your probationer, Carolyn," Brad said. "What did the tattoos say?"

"The left hand said 'love' and the right hand said 'hate,' " she told them. "Fast Eddie either tried to have them removed, though, or whoever tattooed him was an amateur. I only know what they spelled because he told me. The letters are almost impossible to read."

Carolyn's mind was still churning when she returned to the living room.

"Something wrong?" Paul asked. "I was going to have a glass of brandy. Want to join me?"

"You've been a wonderful host," Carolyn told him. "It was very kind of you to invite us to the opening of the ride you designed. I'm sure John and Rebecca will be counting off the days. We need to get home, though. Something's come up regarding one of my cases."

John caught the tail end of her sentence. "You're not going out tonight, are you? I thought you didn't want us to be alone."

"I'm not going anywhere," his mother reassured him. "I need to review some things." She thought of Daniel. "Did you have a chance to look at the papers I gave you this morning?"

"It's good work," the professor said, walking them to the back door. "Some of it's engineering, the rest physics. I didn't have a chance to study it in depth. You only gave me the papers this morning. I faxed them over to a colleague at Caltech. He called me before dinner and asked what kind of credentials this person has. There's a slot opening up next year in the physics department."

"None," Carolyn said, tossing her sweater over Rebecca's shoulders.

"A doctorate in physics might not be necessary."

"You don't understand," Carolyn told him. "He doesn't even have a high school diploma. All he has is a GED."

"Impossible," Paul said, his eyes expanding. "This is a joke, right?"

"No," Carolyn told him, not in the best mood after what she'd heard about Eddie Downly. "I didn't give you permission to fax or share this man's work. Call whoever you sent it to and tell them to destroy it. I gave you the originals. May I have them back, please?"

"Certainly," Paul said, leaving and returning a short time later with the stack of papers.

Carolyn saw John and Rebecca making their way across the lawn. Lucy wasn't around, so she assumed the girl had gone to her room. She quickly leaned over and kissed Paul on the cheek. "That was rude of me," she said softly. "I apologize. The papers are evidence in a criminal investigation. I shouldn't have given them to you. I thought you'd be able to tell me if they have any value."

"They definitely have value," Paul Leighton answered. "And the person I faxed them to is not only a trusted friend, he's a fine physicist. I'll follow your instructions, but if you want, I can arrange a private consultation at the university."

The night air was chilly. Carolyn wrapped her arms around her chest to stay warm, then called out to John and Rebecca. They were passing under a light on the right side of the professor's garage. She didn't want them to go inside the house without her. "Wait right where you are," she shouted. "I'll be there in two minutes."

"We need an engineer as well as a physicist," Paul explained. "The problem with something like an exoskeleton is that you can't always tell if a problem has been solved until you build it and test it."

"I'll have to get back to you next week," Carolyn said, tucking the papers under her arm as she hurried across the lawn to her children.

"There's someone in our house!" Rebecca said, her voice shaking. "Look through the window. You can see his back in the mirror."

"Get down," Carolyn shouted, whipping her Ruger out of her purse. Shifting the gun to her left hand, she grabbed her cell and hit the auto dial for 911. Before she started speaking, she recognized Frank as he walked into the hallway leading into the kitchen. She told the emergency dispatcher to cancel the call, then disconnected. How did he get a key to the house? She'd changed the locks years ago.

"It's Dad," John said, walking around in a circle. "I'm not going inside, Mom. He's probably strung out and came here to hit you up for money."

"Maybe he wants to see us," his sister argued. "He's not a monster. He won't hurt us or anything."

By the time they unlocked the back door and went inside, Frank was sprawled out on the living room sofa watching TV. He pushed himself to his feet. "There's my girl," he said, smiling as he held his arms open for his daughter. "Come here, gorgeous. What happened to your ankle?"

"I tripped," Rebecca told him.

"Give Daddy a big hug." Once he released her, Rebecca took up a position beside him, glaring at her brother.

"Aren't you even going to say hello, slugger?"

"Hello," John said flatly. "Now leave. This is our house. Mom pays the bills. How can you walk in here like you own the place?"

Carolyn sat down across from her former husband. Frank had dark circles under his eyes and his cheeks were concave. His pants appeared several sizes too large. He must have lost twenty pounds since she'd last seen him. She was certain he was under the influence. "How have you been, Frank?"

"Things are tough. I thought I might crash here on the sofa, if that's all right." He glanced at a cell phone on the coffee table. "I'm waiting for an important call. A lead on a job."

Carolyn laced her hands together. She knew he was lying. He must be waiting for a call from a drug dealer. It was a delicate situation. Rebecca now had her hand on her father's shoulder. "I'd prefer you didn't stay, Frank. Get in touch with me next week and we'll talk about scheduling a visit so you can spend some time with Rebecca."

"I have my school picture," the girl said. "I told Mom to send it to you. She said she didn't have your new address. Want me to go get it?"

Frank ruffled her hair. "Sure, pumpkin. I'd love to have your picture."

Rebecca picked up her crutches and headed off to her room. John was standing by the doorway, a sullen look on his face. "Mom asked you to leave."

"Hey," Frank said, "there's nothing to get worked up over. God knows what your mother's been telling you about me."

A tense silence fell over the room. Carolyn and John remained motionless. Rebecca returned, handing her father the picture and a thick stack of letters. "Are all these for me, angel?"

The girl looked anxiously over at her mother. "Mom said they were returned from your old address." She saw the cell phone when her father picked it up. "I thought you didn't have a phone anymore, that you couldn't afford one."

"I meant a regular phone." He rummaged around until he found a pen and then tore off a scrap of paper from a magazine, scribbling down some numbers. "Now you can call Daddy anytime you want."

John went to his room in the garage and slammed the door. Carolyn pretended to watch TV until Rebecca got up to go to the bathroom. "What you're doing is cruel," she whispered. "Rebecca loves you. So does John. He's angry because he knows you stopped seeing them rather than pay child support."

"Shit, woman," Frank told her, flopping back against the sofa, "you sent the dogs after me. I can't pay child support until I get a job. I can't get a job if I'm in jail, know what I mean?"

"How did you get in?"

"I crawled through a window," he said. "I remembered the alarm code."

Rebecca came back into the room. "He can't stay tonight,"

her mother said. "You've got his number. You can call him tomorrow."

"Well," Frank said, his lip curling in anger as he stood to leave, "I guess I'll be on my way. You're cold, Carolyn. What's the big deal if I sleep on the sofa? All I'm asking for is one lousy night. My car's almost out of gas and I'm a little short on cash right now. Besides, my daughter wants me to stay." He began swaying, grabbing hold of the back of the sofa to steady himself.

Carolyn caught the scent of alcohol. When he got high on cocaine, he started drinking to come down. He staggered toward the door. Rebecca started crying. "He shouldn't drive," she told her mother. "He might have an accident."

Removing a twenty-dollar bill from her purse, Carolyn walked over and pressed it into his hand. Frank leaned down and tried to kiss her. She gently pushed him away. If she pushed too hard, he'd fall over backward. "The money I gave you is for cab fare," she said. "Your twelve-year-old daughter is smart enough to know her father is too drunk to drive. I'll call the cab now. It should be here in five or ten minutes."

"Thanks, baby," Frank said, shoving the twenty in his pocket.

Somewhere buried inside the slovenly, reeking shell of a man standing in front of her was the handsome, kind, and genuinely talented writer Carolyn had married. Here and there, she caught glimpses of his former self. He was still young. Most novelists didn't surface until they were in their mid- to late forties. Frank could teach again if he pulled himself together. He had a degree. Perhaps he could find his way back before it was too late.

"Get sober and find a job," she told him, speaking low so Rebecca wouldn't hear. "I'll put the child support case on hold for a few more months so you don't end up with an arrest record. You were a good teacher, Frank. You've got the rest of your life to work on your writing. It's not easy finding a publisher for your first book. Even Hemingway and

Fitzgerald were rejected at one time." Her choice of authors had been a mistake. Both men had been alcoholics. "You're not only destroying yourself, you're hurting the children. If you keep using drugs, you're going to die."

Carolyn watched through the screen door as he made his way down the walkway to a battered black Mustang convertible, then fumbled around for his keys. The canvas top was torn so severely that he'd stopped using it. The red seats had stains and mildew on them from exposure to the elements. She had given him the car as a Christmas present twelve years ago, making the monthly payments out of her paycheck. The spiffy new convertible had made him so happy. Every Saturday, he would put on his bathing suit and wash and wax the car in the driveway. He'd looked so much like John in those days—tall, tan, and muscular. She had always been afraid that she'd lose him to another woman. The affairs really didn't matter. She'd lost him to cocaine.

Carolyn went to the kitchen to call a cab. She would have to get locks installed on the windows. She wondered if Frank had been the one who'd vandalized her car, angry that she'd filed a formal complaint against him for nonpayment of child support. It wasn't worth the aggravation. From what she'd seen tonight, he'd have to undergo months of rehab before he could hold down a job.

When Carolyn went outside to check on him a few moments later, he'd already sped off. She stood there a while, the wind blowing her hair back from her face, sad that what had once been so good was now seemingly lost forever. Turning back toward the house, she saw a small white object on the sidewalk. Picking it up, she cupped her hand over her mouth. Inside the house, she opened her purse and slipped Rebecca's school picture inside a side pocket.

She found the girl in the hallway, looking out the window through her tears. "Don't cry, honey," Carolyn said, lifting the items out of her hands. "I gave your father some money. He'll be fine."

"No, he won't," Rebecca shot out, sliding down the wall as she sobbed. "I might not be as smart as John, but I'm not stupid. I saw him drive off from my bedroom window." She threw a wrinkled up piece of paper at her mother. "I tried to call him. It's not a working number. He lied to me. He doesn't ever want to see us again. John was right. All he wanted was money."

Carolyn sat down on the floor and rocked her in her arms. What could she say to comfort her? Her father could have an accident and be dead within an hour. She should report him to the police for fear he might kill an innocent person. "Sleep in my bed tonight," she said, trying to sound cheerful. "I'll make us a cup of hot chocolate. Maybe we'll stay up late and watch a movie."

Carolyn found John studying at the kitchen table. "He broke out a window in the dining room," he told her. "I taped up part of a cardboard box until we can get another piece of glass installed. Why didn't the alarm go off?"

Carolyn stood at the sink, staring out into yard. Too much time had passed now for the police to stop him. She would check for accidents in the morning. She hoped he'd run out of gas. "I had the locks changed. I forgot to change the alarm code."

"Dad's brain is fried," John said. "How did he remember?"

His mother sighed, turning around to face him. "I used our anniversary. He gave your sister what he said was his cell phone number. She called it and found out it wasn't a working number."

"Bastard," he said, standing and grabbing his books off the table. "Do me a favor, okay?"

"What?" Carolyn said, filling up two cups of water and placing them in the microwave for the instant hot chocolate.

John walked toward the door leading to the garage, then glanced back over his shoulder. "Forget the anniversary. I wish you'd never married him. As far as I'm concerned, I don't have a father."

Chapter 20

The corporate office for the chain of golf stores owned by Nolan Houston was located in a high-rise office building off Wilshire Boulevard in Los Angeles. Wanting to make certain Houston was available, Hank had called Monday morning and made an appointment to see him at ten, claiming he was an Internal Revenue agent.

"Works every time," he told Carolyn, a sly smile on his face. "Tell them you're a cop, and they give you the runaround. Mention IRS and they piss their pants."

Once they were on the road, Carolyn removed her compact from her purse and dabbed on some lipstick. "Remember the physics professor? The man who bought the house down the street? I asked him to take a look at the papers from Daniel's room at the Comfort Inn. He faxed them to one of his colleagues at Caltech."

"Oh, yeah?" the detective said, adjusting his rearview mirror.

"I didn't tell him whose work it was," Carolyn continued. "But get this, they thought he was a candidate for a professorship."

"You're shitting me."

"Paul wants to set up a meeting with some of the faculty members at the university. To evaluate Metroix's work, not to consider him for a post at the university. What do you think?"

"I saw Metroix at the hospital Friday evening," Hank told her. "Granted, he was in pain and doped up on morphine. Don't get me wrong. I feel sorry for the guy, but I don't think he's a genius. I'd be surprised if he could find his way out of a paper bag, know what I mean?"

Typical reaction, Carolyn thought. Daniel's unique abilities were beyond the average person's comprehension. His illness and the time he'd spent in prison also put a dent in his credibility. "All I want is your permission to allow Caltech to evaluate his work. If nothing comes of it, then at least we know where we stand regarding the situation with Warden Lackner."

"It's Metroix's property," Hank told her. "Don't you think you should get permission from him instead of me?"

"This could turn out to be evidence," Carolyn said. "I know the warden isn't one of our primary suspects. What if we rule out Armstrong and Houston, along with Harrison and Downly? Then we're back to square one."

"So find out what it's worth." The detective exited the freeway and took the off-ramp leading onto Wilshire. Locating the building, they pulled into an underground structure and parked.

"What do you make of this?" The photo that had been with Daniel's papers had fallen out on the seat when Carolyn had opened her purse. She handed it to the detective.

Hank shrugged. "It's a snapshot of two kids. Why? Do you think it has some bearing on the case?"

"Probably not," Carolyn said after they'd parked and began walking toward the building. "Rebecca found it on my nightstand yesterday and thought the girl was me."

They made their way to the twelfth floor where the corporate offices for Hole in One were located. "I'm glad you decided to talk to Houston first," she told him. "I had a bad experience with Liam Armstrong."

The detective looked surprised. "You know him?"

"I used to," Carolyn told him, taking in the large gold letters on the glass doors. "I went to high school with Houston and Armstrong. This is a fancy place, Hank. Look how I'm dressed." She was wearing a plaid shirt, jeans, and a studded denim vest. "I look like a cowgirl. I doubt if what I'm wearing is customary attire for Internal Revenue agents."

"Don't worry about it," he said. "We're going to tell Houston we're cops once we get our foot in the door."

Nonetheless, Carolyn could tell Hank was also intimidated. They entered the lobby where two attractive young receptionists were seated behind a long console, both of them wearing headsets and speaking on the phone. A distinguished-looking man in an expensive suit, carrying a black leather briefcase, was seated on a sofa thumbing through the pages of a glossy magazine.

A tall, handsome black man dressed in a green golf shirt with the Hole in One logo emblazoned on the front, his arms bulging with muscles, burst through the doors and walked briskly down one of the side corridors.

"We're here to see Mr. Houston," Hank told a receptionist, pulling out his badge, then placing it back inside his jacket before she had a chance to read the words Ventura Police. He watched as the woman's eyes darted toward the corridor where the man had gone, confirming his suspicions that the individual who'd whisked past them had been Nolan Houston.

A slender blonde with large blue eyes, the woman held up a finger for him to wait until she had concluded her phone call, then moved the microphone away from her mouth. "Do you have an appointment with Mr. Houston?"

"Sure do," Hank said, winking at Carolyn as he leaned sideways against the counter. "We're with the Internal Revenue. I suggest you call your boss and tell him we're here. And you might want to mention that we don't care much for waiting."

While the woman called Houston, the detective stepped

aside with Carolyn. "I don't know about Armstrong," he whispered in her ear, "but this guy has one hell of a lot to lose."

With floor-to-ceiling windows behind him overlooking the Los Angeles skyline, Nolan Houston glared out at them from behind an ornate desk. His office walls were covered with oil paintings, and several bronze sculptures stood on white marble podiums.

"I could sue you people for misrepresentation," Houston said, furious. "I was scheduled to play in a charity golf tournament at the Los Angeles Country Club. You may not consider something like that important, but golf is my business."

"I don't think suing us would be in your best interest," Hank told him, one corner of his lip curling. "We're here to discuss the death of Tim Harrison."

Carolyn watched Houston's face, looking for his reaction. He didn't so much as blink. Due to all the years that had passed, she hadn't expected him to remember her. This was a cold, calculating man, she decided. It wasn't surprising that he'd become successful in the business world. Houston might not remember a girl he'd attended high school with, yet how could he forget the tragedy of a young boy's death? He reached for a silver pitcher sitting on a tray, along with four cut crystal glasses.

Nolan Houston poured himself a glass of water, but made no move to offer the same to his guests. "Tim Harrison died twenty-some years ago," he told them, holding the glass so it obscured the lower half of his face. "Isn't the man who killed him in prison?"

"Right now he's recovering from a gunshot wound," the detective said, reaching inside his jacket for a toothpick. "You wouldn't know anything about that, would you?"

"Of course not," Houston said, a flicker of fear surfacing. Moments later, the steely look returned. "Was it in the newspaper? I don't recall reading anything. I don't generally follow that kind of thing. Besides, I haven't lived in Ventura for fifteen years."

Hank stuck the toothpick in his mouth, then moved it from one side to the other, wanting some time to pass before he spoke again. "What makes you think he was shot in Ventura?"

Houston made a jerky movement, causing his chair to squeak on the plastic mat beneath it. His brows furrowed and there was a slight tremor in his hand as he set the crystal glass down on his desk. Carolyn noticed a coaster, but Houston hadn't used it. She exchanged glances with Hank, wondering if he'd picked up on it as well. Little things occasionally revealed more than a person realized.

"I assumed, okay?" Houston said, hissing the words through clenched teeth. "Why are you here, Detective? Certainly you don't think I have anything to do with this man's shooting." He paused and sucked in a deep breath. "To be perfectly honest, you're not going to find any sympathy here over this Metroix fellow. They should have never kicked the bastard out of prison."

Carolyn decided it was time she stepped in. "Do you remember me, Nolan? We went to Ventura High together. I dated Liam Armstrong."

"You dated Liam?" he said, placing his hand on his throat as if he were having difficulty swallowing. "What's your name again?"

"Carolyn Sullivan," she said. "I'm Daniel's Metroix's parole officer. I believe the same person who shot Metroix tried to run my daughter and me off the road last night. Not only that, Metroix's motel room was wired with explosives. I was there when they went off."

Hank asked, "Have you seen your friend Liam Armstrong recently?"

"I saw him about two years ago," Houston said. "Are you going to pay him a visit too?"

Neither the detective nor Carolyn answered. She felt certain Houston would call and alert Armstrong the moment they left his office. What they wanted to know was whether the men had worked in concert, or if only one was responsible for the recent events. Houston clearly had the funds to contract a murder for hire, but would a man of his caliber be callous enough to try to kill a female probation officer? She corrected herself. Success didn't equate to honor and decency. Only a short time and even she had become bedazzled by Houston's opulent surroundings.

Carolyn tried to reach into the past and envision the night of Tim Harrison's death. Liam, Nolan, and Tim Harrison were three of the most popular boys at Ventura High. Because his father was a police chief, the Harrison boy had enjoyed a certain status. As she recalled, all three drove nice cars, wore good clothes, and the girls were all dying to go out with them. The very nature of the game of football may have additionally played a role in the crime. It was an aggressive sport in which players were taught to take advantage of their opponents' weaknesses. They might never know what had happened in the days preceding Tim Harrison's death. Maybe one of the boys had taken a tongue lashing from a coach, or something else had occurred to make him feel inferior. What better way to pump up a wounded ego than to pick on a mentally ill individual like Daniel Metroix, whom fate had placed in their path?

She seriously doubted if Liam or Nolan had intended to kill their friend. Overall, however, their actions had been despicable. After beating and degrading Metroix, the situation must have gotten out of control. Daniel had recalled the three boys fighting, even claiming that he thought it was Harrison who set them off, upset that his father might find out what they had done. An elbow here, a misplaced slug, or a charge like she'd seen on the football field—it wasn't hard to imagine how Harrison could have gone flying into the dimly lit street, not providing an oncoming driver with adequate time to brake. Not only was she convinced that Liam

Armstrong and Nolan Houston had failed to tell the truth about their assault against Daniel, she believed they'd allowed the man to sit in prison for twenty-three years for a death they had more than likely caused.

For Houston to say he had no sympathy for the person he'd used as a scapegoat made Carolyn feel like ripping his throat out. Once again, she glanced around his office, deciding he didn't deserve so much as the glass he'd selfishly sipped his water from.

"What about Charles Harrison?" Houston said weakly, the prolonged silence from the officers having served its purpose. "If anyone wanted Metroix dead, it was Tim's father. Liam and I were worried he might shoot the guy in the courtroom."

"Right," Carolyn said, giving him a look of contempt. All these two boys had been concerned about was themselves.

"Chief Harrison is dead," Hank said. "He died Friday night."

"I'm sorry to hear that," Houston told them, staring at a spot over their head as he struggled to regain his composure. "What about his wife? Did she ever come around? She had a nervous breakdown. Tim was their life. Right after he got killed, Mrs. Harrison had to have a hysterectomy. After that, she was never the same. Maybe if they'd been able to have another child, it would have been easier to accept what happened."

Hank stood, then tilted his head toward the door, letting Carolyn know it was time for them to leave. They were halfway across the room when he turned around, catching Houston already reaching for the phone. "New information has come to light," he said. "Daniel Metroix swears you, Tim Harrison, and Liam Armstrong attacked him that night. He even recalls the Harrison boy arguing with you after you beat up Metroix."

"That's a damn lie," Houston barked, a line of perspiration popping out on his forehead.

"Since someone has attempted to take Metroix's life, as well as Ms. Sullivan's," the detective continued, "the investigation has been officially reopened. Of course, now there're three new crimes involved. You're an intelligent man, Houston. Didn't you think the truth was going to come out eventually?"

Nolan Houston froze, the phone clasped in his hand. The blood drained from his face. "I need an attorney," he mumbled without thinking.

Hank flung open the door, then waited for Carolyn to pass. He leveled his finger at Houston. "If anything else happens to Carolyn Sullivan, I'll come gunning for you myself. Are we clear, Houston?"

Once they were in the elevator, Carolyn asked the detective, "What do you think?"

"Dirty," he said, popping his knuckles.

"Are you certain?"

A bell pinged as the doors to the elevator opened on the ground floor. "Nothing in life is certain," Hank told her, his face softening into a fatherly expression. "At least we accomplished something. If Houston is guilty, he'll think twice before he tries to hurt you or your family again."

Chapter 21

Hank turned to Carolyn when they reached his police unit after leaving the building on Wilshire. "Let's stop somewhere and have lunch. I don't think I've ever seen you put anything in your mouth outside of those stupid protein bars."

"Don't be silly," Carolyn said. "I eat all the time. I thought we had a one o'clock appointment. It's already past twelve. Where are we meeting Armstrong?"

The detective smiled. "About five blocks from here."

"How did you arrange that?"

"I told him that's where I wanted to lease ten thousand square feet of commercial real estate for my new investment banking firm." Hank pulled into a strip shopping center. "I don't want to waste time. We need evidence. Kevin Thomas at the DA's office should have the requests for warrants ready by the end of the day."

They entered a popular spot called the China Garden, taking a seat at the counter rather than waiting for a table. The restaurant was packed and noisy. They ordered their food, then Carolyn looked over at the detective. "If Houston called him, Armstrong probably won't show."

"He'll show," the detective said, handing her an egg roll as soon as the waiter set down the plate. "Trust me, all Armstrong was thinking about when we talked were dollar signs. What difference does it make if he's tipped off that we're cops? The cat's already out of the bag. I know where to find him." A platter of rice mixed with shrimp arrived, and he spooned a large portion onto her plate. "Anyway, eat your food. You might be able to get away with only a few hours' sleep, but you can't live on air."

Carolyn spotted Liam Armstrong as soon as they stepped into the lobby of the Wilshire West Towers. "That's him," she whispered to Hank.

Armstrong wasn't as tall and fit as Nolan Houston. He walked stiffly and appeared to have a problem with his left leg. His face hadn't changed that much. A few lines shot out around his eyes and mouth, and his hair was sprinkled with gray. Carolyn recalled how excited she'd been when he'd asked her out on their first date. Even now, he was an attractive man. Wearing a pin-striped suit, a royal blue shirt, and a matching tie, he was carrying a briefcase and had a cell phone plugged into his ear.

"Are you Liam Armstrong?"

"Excuse me," he said, glancing at Hank's inexpensive suit and scuffed shoes. "I'm in the middle of a conversation."

Hank reached over and jerked the earpiece out of Armstrong's ear. Flashing his badge, he said, "Detective Hank Sawyer with the Ventura PD. Where can we go to talk privately?"

Liam Armstrong gave Carolyn a curious look. "I don't understand," he said, turning back to the detective. "You must have the wrong person." He reached into his pocket and handed them both his business card. "I'm waiting for an important client. He should be here any minute. What's the problem, Officer?"

"Your appointment has arrived," Hank told him, tossing Armstrong's card into the closest trash can. "We're investigating a number of serious crimes. They all seem to be connected to the death of Tim Harrison."

People were streaming through the double doors, returning from lunch. One of them bumped into Armstrong and almost knocked him to the ground.

"Tim's been dead for years," he told them, limping to the far corner of the lobby. "The man responsible was sentenced to prison for life. Whatever crimes you're investigating can't have anything to do with me."

"We can either talk here or take a ride to the police station," Hank told him. "It's your call, pal."

Armstrong's phone emitted a high-pitched sound. He reached in his pocket and turned it off. "I guess we could talk at the site," he said. "The previous tenants have already moved out. This is a prime spot, the entire eighth floor. Space like this seldom becomes available along the Wilshire corridor."

Hank had told him who they were and why they were there, yet he acted as if he thought they were still interested in leasing space. Houston had been rattled, Carolyn thought, but Armstrong was either suffering from a serious case of denial, intoxicated, or high on drugs. She moved closer, attempting to see if he had alcohol on his breath. If he was a drinker, he must use a lot of mouthwash.

"It's been a long time, Liam," Carolyn said once they were in the elevator. "I'm hurt that you don't remember me. We dated when we were in high school."

"I'm sorry," he said, shaking his head. "I saw a lot of girls when I was in high school. What's your name?"

"Carolyn Sullivan," she told him. "My father taught math."

They finally got a reaction out of him. "Certainly this isn't about—"

"No," Carolyn said, reaching over and hitting the button for the eighth floor.

They waited while Armstrong opened his briefcase and

fumbled around for a key, then placed it in a slot in the elevator. "I'll turn the air conditioning up," he said, pulling his collar away from his neck. "It must be eighty degrees in here."

"I'm comfortable," Hank said. "What about you, Carolyn?"

"I'm married, you know," Armstrong said for no apparent reason. "I have three children."

"Where were you this past Monday night?" Hank asked.

"Home with my family," he answered. "Why? Why are you here? Why did you pretend you were a client? Whatever questions you needed to ask me, you could have asked me over the phone." He turned his attention to Carolyn. "Are you a police officer now?"

"I'm with the Correction Services Agency," she told him. "I was assigned to supervise Daniel Metroix."

"You mean he's out?"

"Yeah," Hank said. "You didn't know? Didn't your buddy Nolan Houston call you?"

"Jesus," Armstrong said, "I haven't talked to Nolan in years. How could a man sentenced to prison for life be back on the street?"

Hank walked over to the windows, then turned around. Armstrong was perspiring now. "What about Wednesday? Can you account for your whereabouts between ten and three?"

Armstrong gulped. "I was seeing clients, I believe. My secretary will have to check my schedule for that day. These crimes you mentioned, where did they occur?"

"Ventura."

"Were they serious?"

"I'd say an explosion and a shooting were serious," Hank answered. "Do you agree, Carolyn?"

"Absolutely," she said, resting her back against the wall. There was no furniture, so they had no choice but to remain standing.

"But I don't understand why you suspect me of being involved, regardless of what types of crime were committed," Armstrong protested. "I've never been arrested for anything in my life. I work hard, provide for my family. I can give you dozens of references. Don't you need some valid reason for intruding on my life this way?"

"You're not under arrest," Hank said. "We're trying to determine what really happened the day Tim Harrison was killed."

Armstrong's eyes glistened with tears. "Five years ago," he told them, "I lost my left leg to cancer. I thought that was behind me. Yesterday my doctor told me he saw something suspicious on my X ray. Tomorrow I'm going in for an MRI." He paused, collecting himself before continuing. "I told everything I knew about Tim's death on the witness stand. I'm fighting for my life right now. If you want to ask me any more questions, you'll have to call my attorney." He opened his briefcase again, then handed them another card.

If Armstrong was involved, Carolyn thought, he should win an Academy Award. His story touched her to the point where she almost shed a tear. Lack of sleep wreaked havoc on a person's emotions, she told herself. She'd passed out on the sofa Sunday, but the kids kept waking her up. Rebecca and Lucy were becoming inseparable. They'd wanted to go to the movies, then watch TV. Carolyn had finally fed the girl dinner and sent her home.

"We're questioning everyone who was involved in the original incident," Hank said, rubbing his chin, "hoping it might shed some light on these new crimes."

Armstrong looked even more bewildered. "It would help if I knew what you were looking for, Detective. Who was shot?"

"Daniel Metroix," Carolyn told him, knowing he could pull up the events of the last few days over the Internet.

"I can't help you on that," he told them. "All I know is, Tim's father was torn up over his death. Chief Harrison is a powerful man. He was tough on Tim. He thought he could become a professional football player if he applied himself. Tim was a great quarterback. Ran like the wind and the best hands around. I doubt if he would have made it to the pros, though. College ball was a given. All the scouts were courting him."

Carolyn was curious. "When you say Tim's father was tough, what precisely do you mean?"

"Oh," Armstrong said, "I don't know all the particulars. Tim was scared of him. Once when he partied too much and fumbled the ball, he turned up the next day with a fractured jaw. He told everyone he was injured in the game. I thought it was strange because he hadn't mentioned anything in the locker room the day before."

"You think his father hit him?"

"Possibly," he said, his eyes trained on the floor. "After Tim was killed, I quit the team. I don't even watch football on TV. Tim Harrison was my best friend."

"Call us if you think of anything," Hank told him. "Good luck on your tests."

Liam Armstrong shook Carolyn's hand, then limped to the other side of the room, motioning for her to join him. The detective was already waiting by the door. She assumed it was more than Tim Harrison's death that had caused the real estate broker to lose interest in football. For a former athlete, losing a leg must have been devastating.

"I'm ashamed at how I acted that night," Armstrong told her. "I was young, you know. I thought the world and everything in it was mine for the taking. I appreciate that you didn't tell your father or the police. In a way, it might have been better if you had. Then I would have got my act together a lot quicker."

Carolyn didn't know what to say. "It sounds like you have a wonderful family, Liam. I'm sure they're very supportive. I'll keep you in my prayers."

Armstrong smiled for the first time. "Still the good Catholic girl, huh?"

"I don't know how good I am," Carolyn told him. "That wasn't a line, though. I do pray."

Chapter 22

Carolyn, Hank Sawyer, and Assistant District Attorney Kevin Thomas were seated in Judge Arline Shoeffel's inner office at four-thirty on Monday.

Hank had placed the case in the hands of the DA as soon as he'd learned of the possibility that Downly might be involved. After reviewing all the pertinent facts, Thomas had said he was willing to prepare search warrants for the residences of Charles Harrison, Nolan Houston, and Liam Armstrong. He wasn't certain, however, if they could convince a judge to sign them. The attorney was elated when he learned that Carolyn had already pitched the case to the presiding judge. That is, until he heard her reaction.

"I understand perfectly, Mr. Thomas," Arline Shoeffel said coolly, her glasses perched low on her nose. "However, the events of this past week may have no bearing whatsoever on the original crime. I refuse to allow you to execute these search warrants until you bring me more substantial evidence that Mr. Houston and Mr. Armstrong were involved. These men appear to be law-abiding citizens. Neither one of them has a criminal record. A certain amount of discretion must be exercised when you're dealing with prominent people in the community."

Carolyn said, "With all due respect, because Houston and Armstrong are successful businessmen doesn't mean they aren't guilty. Their success goes toward establishing motive."

Judge Shoeffel's mouth compressed into a thin line. Obviously, she didn't take well to people questioning her judgment. Kevin Thomas wisely kept his mouth shut. Arguing against one of the other judges was one thing. Getting on the wrong side of a presiding judge could destroy his career.

Arline adjusted her glasses, then thumbed through the pages of the file again. "Regarding Mrs. Harrison," she said, her voice so low they had to strain to hear her, "is she a voluntary or involuntary commitment?"

Thomas turned to Hank, who slowly shook his head.

"Can one of you please respond?" the judge asked, her frustration level rising another notch.

"We don't know," Hank finally admitted. "I didn't see any reason to contact the hospital. Mrs. Harrison has been institutionalized for almost twenty years. She's too sick to even attend her husband's funeral."

The judge closed the file, then placed her hands on top of it. "For one thing, Detective," she said, removing her glasses. "I was informed that Mr. Harrison wouldn't be having a funeral, that his remains had already been disposed of by the funeral home. Is that correct?"

"Well, yes," he answered, fidgeting in his seat. "People still have services, though."

"But Mr. Harrison isn't having a service."

"No," Hank said. "He made arrangements prior to his death for the funeral home to pick up his body and cremate it. His housekeeper said he wanted to keep the costs down."

"Do you believe Mr. Harrison is dead or alive?"

He shrugged. "We're not sure."

"Neither am I, Detective," Judge Shoeffel told him, picking up her glasses and shoving them back on her nose. "Although I'm not prepared to issue warrants regarding Houston and Armstrong until more evidence is produced, I will sign the one for Charles Harrison's residence." She pulled out the form, signed it, and handed it to the district attorney, along with the file.

"Now," she continued, "let's use a little intelligent reasoning, shall we? You've consumed a considerable amount of my time without adequately investigating this matter. Was Mr. Harrison in control of his faculties until the time of his alleged death Friday evening?"

"According to his doctor," Hank told her, "Harrison's liver was shot, but his mind was fine."

"When did the doctor last see him?"

"Approximately two weeks ago," he advised, anticipating her next question. "Harrison's doctor said that unless he received a liver transplant, he'd die. The doctor was upset that the housekeeper didn't call him when she found him dead."

The judge propped her head up with one hand. "And why is that?"

"Because he didn't expect him to die right away. See," Hank said, scratching his chin, "that's why we aren't entirely certain the man's dead. His doctor said he may have lived another year, even longer. Then again, his liver condition could have taken a turn for the worse the other night and killed him. An autopsy would have helped, but that isn't gonna happen now."

"No one suffers more in the death of a child than the mother," Arline Shoeffel told them. "This is evidenced by the fact that Mrs. Harrison is currently in a mental institution, whereas her husband didn't suffer any mental impairment whatsoever. The woman not attending her husband's funeral is immaterial, since his precise instructions were that he not have a funeral. Are we in agreement on this issue, Detective Sawyer?"

"I guess so," he said, shrugging.

"What may be vital to this case is whether Mrs. Harrison is being held in a secure facility, or if she's able to come and go at will. Of secondary concern is what type of resources the victim's mother has at her disposal."

Hank did a double take, instantly grasping what Arline Shoeffel was suggesting. Carolyn also felt like an idiot. The district attorney slapped the file against his knee, then sprang to his feet, shooting a glance at the detective and Carolyn that said he wished he'd never agreed to get involved.

"You failed to do your homework," Judge Shoeffel told them, seeing all four of her phone lines blinking. "Don't approach anyone else on the bench, thinking you can slip something past me. Remember, every road leads back to this office."

Brad Preston walked Carolyn to her Infiniti at six o'clock Monday evening. "When did you get your car back?"

"The garage brought it over this afternoon," she said, examining the car to make certain she was happy with the repairs. "I also scraped the front bumper on my neighbor's BMW. Now I have to pay for that as well."

"Are you going back to school?"

"Not this week," Carolyn told him, shielding her eyes from the late day sun. "I'm afraid to leave the kids alone."

They stopped speaking until several people walked past them. "Veronica said you had a date with that physics professor. How did it go?"

"Great," she said, smiling. "John likes him. Rebecca and his daughter get along fabulously, and his housekeeper is a terrific cook."

Brad leaned against the side of the car, making it impossible for her to open the door, a downcast expression on his face. "Is this a romance or a friendship?"

"My God," Carolyn exclaimed, "you're jealous. The man loaned me his car. He let Rebecca stay at his house. Maybe I was wrong about Amy McFarland, but don't tell me you haven't been seeing other women."

"I told you how I felt about you the other day," Brad said

self-consciously. "Sure, I've been seeing other people. They're just girls, though. They don't mean anything to me."

"Then the professor is only a guy," Carolyn countered, baffled at how the male mind worked. He could sleep with a dozen women and calmly proclaim it meant nothing. The fact that she'd had dinner with a neighbor, however, had upset him. "We broke up months ago, Brad," she told him. "I'm ashamed I let things get out of hand the other day. I care about you, I miss being with you, I even miss making love to you. I refuse to get emotionally involved again. And I definitely don't want to lose my job because of you."

"Why don't you invite me to the house anymore? We were friends for years before we started dating. Are you going to throw everything away? John and I used to have fun together. Rebecca isn't as easy for me to get to know because she's a girl."

John had posed the same question, Carolyn remembered. It was hard to turn a love affair back into a friendship. Once you crossed the line, everything changed. "Frank surfaced the other night."

"How did it go?" Brad said. "Did he give you a check for the back child support he owes you?"

"Are you kidding? Even if he had the money, I don't know if I would take it. He looked awful, Brad. We came home and found him inside the house. He made a fuss over Rebecca, then gave her a phony number. How could a man hurt his child like that?"

"He's on drugs," Brad said, disgusted. "He lives in the Twilight Zone."

"I want him to go away."

"What about Harrison's widow?" Brad said, changing the subject. "Did Hank find out anything this afternoon?"

"Yes," Carolyn told him. "Arline Shoeffel is brilliant. The place Madeline Harrison is in is like a country club. She goes shopping, gets her hair done, goes to plays and ballets.

I guess she feels safe living there or something. Hank thinks the bills from the hospital might be one of the reasons Harrison was so concerned about money."

"Then it's doubtful she hired someone to take out you and Metroix?"

"After today," Carolyn said, pushing back a strand of hair, "I'm not going to speculate until I have all the facts straight. Arline was receptive to reopening the case until she found out we had our heads up our ass."

"Come on," Brad said, nudging her in the ribs. "Do you really think the Harrison woman had anything to do with this? Where would she get the connections and the money to hire someone to commit these crimes? We're talking an explosion, a shooting . . . and the incident with you and Rebecca. Pretty sinister stuff for an old lady."

"How do I know?" Carolyn said. "Maybe Harrison's wife has a secret bank account. The hospital claims she's in excellent health. She runs two miles a day. She's not even that old, Brad. She's only sixty-two."

"I know," he said, laughing. "She grabbed one of her friends from the loonie bin, rented a couple of cars, and instead of a shopping spree, they went on a shooting spree."

"Sometimes you act like a juvenile delinquent." Carolyn reached over and gently shoved him aside. "We can talk more in the morning."

Chapter 23

At a few minutes past nine Monday evening, Carolyn was cleaning up the kitchen when the phone rang. A male voice said softly, "Want to come over for a drink?"

"I can't believe you're still pestering me," she said, assuming it was Brad. When they'd been lovers, he used to call her late at night, trying to talk her into sneaking him into her bedroom.

Paul Leighton said stiffly, "Maybe I called too late. I'll check back with you another time."

"Forgive me," Carolyn said, "I thought you were someone else."

"I'm sorry," he said. "Were you in bed? I intended to call you earlier."

"I was finishing up my household chores."

"Then come over for a nightcap. Lucy's down for the night. If you're worried about leaving your brood alone, I can send Isobel. She may not look too intimidating, but if anyone even came close to hurting your children, they'd be the sorriest man alive. Say fifteen minutes," he added. "I'll be waiting on my patio in the backyard."

"Send Isobel," Carolyn said. "I can't stay very long."

After she brushed her hair and sprayed on some cologne, Carolyn riffled through her closet, pulling out a tight-fitting black knit top with a revealing neckline. She removed her

T-shirt and started to pull the top over her head, then placed it back on the hanger. Having dinner with the professor and their children Friday evening was not the same as a late night rendezvous.

The situation with Brad had to stop. During the entire time they'd dated, he'd never once mentioned marriage. The best way to put a relationship behind you, her mother had always told her, was to start a new one. She didn't want Paul to think she was trying to snag a husband, though. Almost as soon as the thought appeared, she had to ask herself if it was true. Some nights when sleep eluded her, she cried in her bed alone. People all over the world suffered through disastrous marriages and refused to give up hope. She didn't want to live the rest of her life alone.

Carolyn tossed on a white blouse with a feminine lace collar, then stepped into a pair of black slacks. She heard someone knocking on the back door and rushed to answer.

"I'm the security guard." Isobel was dressed in an orange pullover sweater and what appeared to be her pajama bottoms, her feet encased in furry slippers.

"This is really kind of you," Carolyn said, wondering if the woman had been asleep. "Would you like to watch television in the living room?"

She held up a paperback book. "I don't watch television," Isobel said. "Nothing on the idiot box but trash these days. Tell me where the kids I'm supposed to be protecting are, then put me somewhere with a comfortable chair and some decent light."

Once Isobel was situated, Carolyn poked her head into John's room in the converted garage. The boy was pouring over his studies at his desk. His hair was disheveled, and there were dark circles underneath his eyes. Several books were open and he was staring at a column of equations, tapping his pencil against his forehead.

"I'm going out for a while," she told him. "You can reach

me on my cell phone. Paul sent Isobel over. She's in the living room."

John didn't appear to have heard her, then he turned around. "Tell Paul I think I've solved the problem," he said, excited. "I may get an A in calculus after all. That class has been giving me trouble all year."

"What about your other studies?" his mother asked. "You have to do well all around if you want to score high on your SATs."

"All A's," John said, without looking at her. "My other classes are a breeze."

"Great," Carolyn told him. "Call me if you need me."

They were seated in two green cushioned recliners on his patio. Paul opened a bottle of Chardonnay and filled their glasses. "Did you get a chance to ask your superiors about the design you showed me on the exoskeleton?"

"Yes," she told him. "There's no need for a meeting. All I need is permission from the owner of the work. I should be seeing him in the next few days."

The night was clear and he caught her gazing up at the stars. On one corner of the patio was a large telescope situated on a tripod. "Want a closer look?"

"Sure," Carolyn said, carrying her glass of wine as she followed him. As soon as Paul adjusted the lens, she bent down and positioned herself in front of the eyepiece. "Can you name all the constellations?"

"Possibly," he said, "but I'd rather listen to you talk. Cosmology isn't my speciality."

She felt his warm breath on her neck as he moved behind her and pushed a button to reposition the telescope. When she stood up and turned around, their bodies were touching. "You're a beautiful woman," Paul said, reaching out and stroking her hair. "I'm glad you came over tonight."

"So am I," Carolyn said, her breath catching in her throat.

He placed his hand on the back of her neck, then pressed his lips to hers. She felt his other hand on the small of her back. The kiss didn't last very long, but Carolyn felt a rush of emotion. Impulsively, she grabbed his face and passionately kissed him. Then she abruptly pulled back. "God," she said, laughing, "what am I doing? We hardly know each other."

"This is how it happens," Paul said, collecting her into his arms again. "The first time I saw you, I wanted you. I haven't felt this way in years. I'm fairly certain you haven't either."

What she'd shared with Brad had been more physical than mental. How could she love a man whom she was almost certain would be unfaithful? She had already been down that road with Frank. "Maybe I didn't want to feel this way."

"Perhaps I didn't either," Paul told her. "I went to considerable effort to relocate here and distance myself from the university. Finishing this book is important to me. I won't be able to stay here forever."

Carolyn placed a palm against his chest. "But you can come back," she said. "Why have a house here if you don't use it?"

"A year passes quickly, particularly among people with responsibilities. Don't you want to find out where this is going to take us?"

"How about heaven?" she said, snuggling up to him again and reveling in the feel and smell of his body.

"I don't believe in heaven," Paul told her. "It's a figment of the imagination, like everything else regarding religion."

Carolyn moved away, the moment shattered. "Are you trying to say you're an atheist?"

"Why don't we enjoy our wine?"

"No," she said, grabbing his hand and pulling him back. "I want to finish our conversation."

"Fine," Paul told her, somewhat miffed. "I consider myself an agnostic. I can't prove that there isn't a God, any more than I can prove the existence of God or anything remotely supernatural. In reality, an atheist has a stronger position. I'm sorry. I didn't get the impression that you were all that religious."

"You never asked," Carolyn said, experiencing a sinking sensation.

"Does it matter?"

The concern on his face made her wonder if his position on religion had created substantial problems for him. Had this caused the demise of his marriage? "Don't get me wrong," she told him. "I'm not a religious fanatic. I do believe, though, and so do my children. John—"

Paul walked several feet away, leaning against the wood railing as he stared out into the night. "Your son is young," he said. "What he believes today will change, particularly if he pursues his desire to become a physicist."

Carolyn let her arms fall limp at her sides. "I don't want to hear this," she told him, her idyllic thoughts of falling in love rapidly evaporating. "I need to get home."

"Are you really this immature?" he said, rushing over to her. "Can't two people with opposing views care about one another, respect the other's right to believe whatever they choose? What if I liked steaks, and you were a diehard vegetarian? Would you refuse to see me? Couldn't I continue to eat steaks while you ate vegetables?"

"I don't know," Carolyn said, confused.

"Of course we could," Paul answered. "I'm not trying to steal your beliefs, nor the beliefs of your children. I wouldn't be wasting my time if I didn't think there was potential here. Potential for happiness, companionship, pleasure, maybe even a lifetime commitment. Do you think I'm looking for a one-night stand? I don't give most women the time of day. Why someone of your caliber buried herself in this town as a probation officer is beyond me."

Paul pulled her into his arms, kissing her forehead, her cheeks, the side of her neck. Her body arched backward and she let out a long sigh. She couldn't walk away. She wanted this man. Something about him made her feel complete, as if she'd found a missing part of her anatomy. He scooped her up in his arms and carried her to the lounge chair, laying her down on her back, then stretching out on top of her. His tongue probed inside her mouth, as his fingers undid the buttons on the front of her blouse. "Stop," she said. "We can't . . ."

"Why?" he whispered. "No one can see us."

"Not now," Carolyn answered.

"When?"

"I don't know," she said, getting up and adjusting her clothing.

"Meet me here at the house for lunch tomorrow."

"There's too much going on at work."

"Make time," Paul insisted. "The courthouse isn't more than a fifteen-minute drive. I want to see you."

Carolyn felt more alive than she had in years. She felt a surge of energy, as if she could run, leap over the fence, and keep running until she collapsed. Brad had satisfied her body, but Paul stirred her soul. This was a man she could fall in love with, maybe marry. Thoughts that serious didn't lend themselves to impulsive decisions. She wanted them to take it slow, get to know each other, let the relationship develop.

She might be able to sneak away for a few hours, particularly since she'd completed all her case assignments. She wasn't going to tell Paul, however. Physics was similar to a game in many ways, or more aptly, an intriguing puzzle. Perhaps she was nothing more than a fascinating puzzle wrapped in skin for the professor to break down into equations and solve. She might have buried herself in a small town like Ventura, yet after years of working with criminals, she knew how to stand her ground.

"How can you make me wait?" Paul said, slapping the edge of the recliner like a petulant child. "You'll drive me crazy. I won't be able to concentrate on my book. What am I going to do?"

"Try praying," Carolyn tossed out, laughing as she walked down the steps of the porch and turned in the direction of her house.

Chapter 24

Hank strode into Carolyn's cubicle at ten-forty Tuesday morning. Instead of one of her suits, she'd worn a lightweight black knit dress that hugged her body and emphasized her curves. Planning on calling Paul and taking him up on his offer to drop by his house for lunch, she'd also passed on her practical shoes in favor of heels and nylons.

"You look terrific," Hank said. "Did you get your hair cut or something?"

Men, she thought, even when they did notice a woman had done something to improve her appearance, they couldn't figure out what it was. "Thanks," she said, searching the Internet for information on inventions and patents. "I'm trying to work, Hank. Did we get a break on the case, or did you come here to annoy me?"

"I thought you might want to go with me to Fairview Hospital to speak to Madeline Harrison."

"When?"

"After we search Charles Harrison's residence. Kevin Thomas wanted to go over some things in his office first."

Carolyn spun her chair around. "Did the lab come up with any more evidence from the Seagull?

"Nada," Hank said. "No prints, no hairs. The place was as clean as an operating room. Was Downly a speed freak?"

"Not that I know of," Carolyn told him. "Since he didn't have drug terms, I never tested him. Why?"

"Metroix said the clerk at the Seagull had sores on his arms and face. Sounds like speed to me. That, or he had——"

"Don't even think it," she said, her thoughts turning to Luisa Cortez. AIDS was always a concern in rape cases. When she'd seen Eddie at the jail, he'd had on long sleeves. She couldn't tell Hank about the visit, though, for fear it might compromise their case. "If Eddie had sores from speed, he must have been using for years."

"Maybe that's why they called him Fast Eddie?"

Carolyn fell silent. How could she forgive herself for failing to supervise this man the past year? After the preliminary intake interview, though, a probation officer spent only a small amount of time with the offender. She didn't recall seeing any signs of drug use.

"Here's what I'm thinking," Hank told her. "Before the Luisa Cortez incident, one of LAPD's finest caught Downly either under the influence or dealing dope. This could have been how Chief Harrison recruited him. Instead of taking him to jail, the arresting officer delivered him to Harrison. Since Downly grew up in Ventura and knew the area, he was the perfect candidate to knock off Metroix." He pulled up a chair beside her, sitting down and sniffing. "You even smell great."

Carolyn ignored him. "Then the chief had to get him out of jail. He couldn't take a chance that Downly might spill his guts in exchange for a reduced sentence on the rape. No," she corrected herself, "the law precludes reducing a sentence in the rape of a child. That's not it, Hank. The chief was afraid of me, don't you see?"

"Why would he be afraid of you?"

Did Harrison know? Carolyn asked herself. She'd trusted Alex Barker to cover for her. Even if Barker had done what she'd asked, someone else inside the jail could have notified the chief that a woman had paid Eddie a visit. Harrison didn't know what she looked like, but he knew how the system operated. "Have you talked to the man with the traffic tickets?"

"Who?"

"You know," Carolyn said, flicking her wrist, "Edward James Downy, the man they mistook for Fast Eddie."

"No," Hank told her. "We sent someone to the address on his booking sheet. It's an apartment complex. They say they've never heard of anyone by that name. We also checked with the company who posted the guy's bail. A middle aged male came to their office, slapped down three thousand dollars in cash, and instructed them to post James Edward Downy's bail."

"What about DMV records?"

Hank shrugged. "The driver's license must have been a fake. They've got Downly, but no Edward James Downy with the same DOB."

"This other person didn't exist," Carolyn said, shocked at the amount of deception involved. "The jail knew they'd released a rapist, but they still let the man with the traffic tickets walk. How could he have traffic tickets if he didn't have a driver's license?"

"The tickets were issued to Fast Eddie."

"This is the most convoluted mess I've ever seen," Carolyn said, massaging her temples. Could Alex Barker have discovered that her visit had already been inputted into the computer? Then, trying to fix it, he'd mixed up the inmate's booking numbers. She couldn't be at fault, she told herself. Even though his identity had been false, a real man had been booked and later released from the jail.

"You didn't explain why Chief Harrison would be afraid of you."

"Oh," Carolyn said. "He knew I would be investigating the new offense. I have a reputation for getting these guys to talk. Harrison had to spring Eddie from jail before I saw him again. Once he arranged his release, he told Fast Eddie to finish off Metroix."

"Makes sense," the detective said. "We know there's more than one person involved. After the shooting, the chief would have given Eddie traveling money and told him to get out of town. Then who tried to run you off the road the other night?"

"Eddie," Carolyn said, swinging a black stockinged leg. She stopped when she caught the detective paying more attention to her body than what she was trying to tell him. "But if Eddie's not dead already, he will be as soon as Harrison's people get their hands on him. The chief didn't give this bastard any money. That's why the guy's so desperate. He needs a safe house. I know all his contacts. He's trapped in Ventura, with cops on both sides of the fence gunning for him."

"We need more facts and less speculation," Hank said, pushing himself to his feet. "Unless we find something major at Harrison's place, I plan on heading down to L.A. around three. You in or out?"

Carolyn tried to decide what she should do. Even if she did follow through on her plans to have lunch with Paul, she'd have to return to the office by late afternoon. She needed to think about something unrelated to her work, try to clear her head. She told the detective that she'd meet him at the PD at three as it was closer to the professor's house. Then she called Paul, telling him she was on her way over.

As soon as he opened the door, Carolyn smelled the delightful aroma of freshly baked bread. Plates of thinly sliced roast beef, potato salad, and slices of pineapples, oranges, papayas, and strawberries were set out on the dining room table.

"You look more delicious than the food," Paul told her, lifting her hair and kissing her on the side of her neck.

"Where's Isobel?" she said, not seeing her when they'd passed through the kitchen.

"Day off," he said, smiling mischievously.

"I see," Carolyn answered. "Her regular day off, or did you send her away after she prepared all this food?"

"You *are* clever," he said, chuckling. "I gave her an extra day off so I could be alone with you."

"You shouldn't have gone to so much trouble," Carolyn told him, taking a seat at the table. "I'm not used to eating lunch. I'm more of a breakfast and dinner person."

"Oh, really?" Paul said. "Why don't we let this wait for a while? I don't usually eat lunch myself until later in the day." He handed her a glass of wine. "Come with me. I have something I want to show you."

Carolyn followed him, wondering if he'd stumbled across something else important regarding Daniel's work. When she found herself in the master bedroom, he removed the wineglass from her hand and pulled her down on the bed. "I'm hungry," he whispered. "But not for food."

"I can tell," Carolyn answered, removing his hand from her leg. When he kissed her, though, she instantly responded, lacing her fingers through his hair. His lips were soft, his body lean yet muscular.

He slipped one side of her dress down, exposing her right shoulder. "God, you're beautiful."

"I thought you didn't believe in God," she said playfully.

"Only a word," he told her. "You didn't come over here to discuss religion, I hope."

"Not today." Carolyn traced the outline of his nose with her fingertip, deciding he was more handsome than she'd originally thought. She loved his hair. He must blow-dry it to smooth out the natural curl. Her father had similar hair. After a few hours, the curls reappeared. She wondered how old he was, but didn't feel it was appropriate to ask. His face was unlined, and his skin was soft and smooth. In profile, he almost resembled a boy.

She picked up one of his hands and studied it. The fingers were long and tapered, the nails neatly trimmed—obviously not a man who earned his living performing manual labor. Snuggling up against him, she felt serene and content. He seemed eager but unhurried.

Ten minutes later, they were thrashing around with the energy and abandon of a couple of teenagers, giggling and teasing. They'd kiss, then stop and stare at each other, trying to see who would be the first to blink. Then he'd try to touch her breasts and she'd quickly move away.

Carolyn finally closed her eyes as he began sensuously stroking her between her legs. His touch was unlike that of men she'd known previously. That a physicist might be an exceptional lover was something she'd never considered. Smart, yes . . . good in bed, not likely. Ah, she told herself, aware that she'd been seriously mistaken. In addition to physics, Paul seemed to have acquired a master's degree in female anatomy. He not only knew *how* to touch her, he knew precisely *where*.

"Stop," she said, removing his hand again.

"No," he said, his eyelids heavy with lust. "We haven't even started yet. Take off your nylons."

Carolyn glanced at his bedside clock. It was one already. She couldn't allow the time to get away from her. Besides, as much as she desired him, she couldn't have sex in broad daylight, particularly with a man she'd only recently met.

The sliding glass door on the far side of the room looked out over a small enclosed courtyard filled with greenery. Since he didn't have drapes, there was no way to shut out the midday sun. She'd known Brad for years before she'd started dating him, and only after six months had she allowed the relationship to advance to the next level. Once the newness had worn off, she had learned to relax and enjoy herself.

"Take this off," Paul said, tugging on her dress. "I want to look at you."

"I'm not taking off my clothes," Carolyn said, grabbing his hand and kissing it. "You don't understand."

He turned sideways and propped his head up with one hand. "What don't I understand?"

She knew if she stayed much longer, she would succumb to his advances. She sat up. "I have to get back to work."

"That's an excuse," Paul said, pulling her back down on the bed. "Why won't you let me make love to you? How long are you going to keep torturing me? Don't you want me?"

"Of course I want you," Carolyn said, embarrassed. "And you know I'm telling the truth."

He kissed her again. "Then you're staying."

"I don't have to be back until three," she confessed. "I could even pass on the trip to L.A. and take the afternoon off. I can't have sex with you during the day. I've always been shy about my body." She thought of the stretch marks from her two pregnancies. She was slender, but she didn't exercise. She gazed in envy at the women on the streets, dressed in miniskirts or pants that hung precariously on their hip bones and exposed their entire midsection. Women in California were fitness freaks. They spent hours in the gym every day. She didn't have buns of steel, or six-pack abs, nor did she budget in a yearly tune up at a plastic surgeon's office.

Paul's warm breath was on her face. "Do you have any contact with the Divine?"

"The Divine?" she said, puzzled. "Do you mean God? Why would you ask something like that?"

"An eclipse would be nice right now," he said, smiling coyly. "Then it would be dark and we could make love."

"Just because I said I believe in God doesn't mean I have a direct line," Carolyn told him. "Even if I did, how would I manage an eclipse?"

"Easy," he told her. "Throw everything in front of the sun."

Carolyn placed a finger over his lips. "I'll work on your

eclipse, but only if you promise to let me go. I'm not going to have sex with you today."

"You're merciless. If you're not interested in me, all you have to do is tell me."

"Nothing could be further from the truth," she said, disentangling herself from his arms.

When Carolyn stood, she felt lightheaded and had to steady herself against his dresser. She didn't need wine. The man himself was intoxicating. And she wasn't only struggling against his formidable will, she was fighting her own desires to slip back into his arms again.

"I'll call you tonight," she told him, stepping into her heels.

Paul fell back against the pillow in frustration. "No lunch?" he asked. "You're going to walk off and leave me again? I might as well toss my manuscript in the trash."

"Be patient," Carolyn said, kissing him lightly on the lips before she left. "I didn't come for the food, remember? When the time is right, we'll be together."

"Oh," he said, sitting up and putting on his glasses, "my friend at Caltech called again this morning. Your man's design for a light-weight power source for an exoskeleton looks feasible. The government has offered up to fifty million to any corporation or research facility that perfects a practical and fully functional exoskeleton." He paused, wiping the lenses of his glasses on the edge of the sheet.

Carolyn was shocked. "Did you say fifty million?"

"I sure did," Paul said, their passion forgotten as his scientific mind resurfaced. "Let me get this straight. The guy has no formal education. How long has he been working on this project?"

"Over twenty years," she told him. "He's invented other things as well. But all his designs were destroyed in the explosion."

Paul was stunned. "You're telling me this was done by Metroix, your parolee?"

Carolyn placed her hand on her forehead. She hadn't meant to reveal Daniel's identity. "Yes," she said. "He's invented other things as well. What I gave you he did in his motel room the night before the shooting."

She didn't have time to explain the other complexities involved in Daniel's work. Her next step as far as Warden Lackner was concerned was to find out if there had actually been a joint venture program involving Metroix at the prison. Obtaining this type of information would probably require the help of the attorney general's office. She couldn't call Lackner again.

"What you told me is impossible," Paul told her, getting up and straightening the bed linens. "No one could do this much work in one day. You must be mistaken."

"Because all of his work was destroyed, he was attempting to reproduce it," Carolyn told him, smiling. "I was concerned that he might not be able to do it. From what you've told me, that won't be a problem."

Chapter 25

John had stayed a few minutes late Tuesday afternoon to speak to Mr. Chang, his calculus teacher. He was placing some books inside his locker when he heard someone step up beside him. Most of the students had already left for the day, and the corridors were empty. "Didn't anyone ever tell you not to sneak up on people?"

"I need help," a young man said, a panicked look on his face.

John stared at him. He looked about eighteen, so he assumed he must be a senior. He asked himself if the guy was trying to score drugs. His sweatshirt was stained, and he smelled as if he hadn't showered that day. "What's your problem?"

"My father had a heart attack. I'm supposed to meet my mother at Methodist Hospital. I transferred here from Simi Valley last week. I don't know my way around the city yet."

"If you're looking for a ride," John said, closing his locker and spinning the combination lock, "you're barking up the wrong tree. I don't have a car. What's your name?"

"Wade," he told him. "Look, my mother was hysterical. This is my dad's third heart attack. She forgot to tell me how to get to the hospital." He slammed his fist into a locker. "They're taking my dad into surgery in fifteen minutes. He might not live through the operation. I have to see him." He scrunched up his face as if he were trying to stop himself from crying. "We had an argument last night. I said some awful things. I don't want my dad to die without telling him I love him."

"Try to relax," John said, caught up in the other boy's emotional outburst. He thought of his own father—the resentment he felt, the way he'd spoken to him. Would he feel the same if he knew he was dying? "I'll write down directions to the hospital. Give me some paper. You're only about ten minutes away."

"I'm too upset," Wade said. "I tried to find the hospital earlier. I got lost. Please, come with me. I have a car."

"I can't," John told him. "I have to pick up my sister from school. I'm already late. If I don't hurry, we'll miss the last bus."

"I'm begging you, man."

Rebecca's school was only two blocks from Methodist Hospital. Not only that, his mother had instructed her to wait in the gym until he arrived. Since the boy had a car, John would probably get to Rebecca's school sooner than if he walked. "Okay," he said. "I'll ride with you."

"Hurry," Wade said, glancing down an empty hallway. "We'll go out the side door. The student parking lot was full this morning. My car's on the street."

"It *does* look like a country club."

Carolyn was speaking to Hank as they approached the front entrance of Fairview Manor. The hospital was located in the hills overlooking the UCLA campus and the area known as Westwood. The structure itself resembled an old Hollywood mansion, with lovely terraced grounds, banks of blooming flowers, and an abundance of mature trees. People were seated on the various benches and lawn furniture, some sleeping peacefully, others reading, some conversing with one another. A group of men were playing checkers at a small table. They spotted a few staff members in white uniforms.

The patients at Fairview weren't dressed in pajamas and shuffling around in a drugged-out daze. Carolyn saw a few strange looking characters, but overall, the people seemed perfectly normal.

"Shades of paradise, huh?" Hank commented as a pretty redheaded nurse strolled past them and smiled pleasantly. "Maybe we should reserve a room. I guarantee when I retire, I won't end up in a place this luxurious. I'll be lucky to afford a one-room apartment. And I won't have dozens of little darlings like that redhead tending to my every need."

Carolyn's mind was on other things. "Even a deputy police chief doesn't make this kind of money, Hank. They must charge a grand a day, if not more. I don't know any insurance company in the world that would cover the expenses on a high-end hospital like this."

"Maybe Blue Cross would foot the bill for a few months," he speculated. "Like our department, though, the coverage provided by LAPD is through an HMO."

"Good Lord," she exclaimed, stopping and facing him, "Madeline Harrison has been here twenty years. How could her husband afford it?"

"Your guess is as good as mine," Hank answered, removing his jacket and flinging it over his shoulder. "Harrison had himself insured for a million dollars, listing his wife as the sole beneficiary. That may be another reason he staged his own death. He ran out of money."

"What about the housekeeper?" Carolyn asked. "Do you think she's lying? She could be prosecuted as an accomplice. Isn't she the one who found the body?"

"Ms. Sanchez claims he was dead for several hours before she found him," the detective related. "Something's fishy there, even if Harrison's a goner. We don't have grounds to arrest the wife, so, for now, we have to let the situation play itself out. I'm not getting much cooperation at the PD."

Carolyn never realized what he must be going through. "They don't want to work on a case involving another cop, especially a well-respected former chief from their own department. Am I right?"

"Smack dab on the money," Hank said. "It would have been nice if the search of Harrison's residence this morning had shed some light on his financial status. Sanchez must have swept the place clean before she called the undertaker. Even Harrison's closets were empty. She claimed she was only following his instructions to give everything to the Goodwill. My guess is Mario, the so-called gardener, walked away with a new wardrobe."

"Did you contact the Goodwill to verify her statement?"

"Nah," he said. "I don't really give a rat's ass what happened to Harrison's clothes and other personal belongings. What we're trying to determine is if the man withdrew a large sum of money."

They reached the visitors' entrance to the hospital. The detective asked one of the attendants to get Mrs. Harrison. While they were waiting, they sat down on a sofa in the lobby.

"Chief Harrison was a city employee," Carolyn said. "Finding out where he banked shouldn't be that difficult."

"Every month he cashed his paycheck at the credit union. The money trail stops right there. We don't even know the name of Harrison's accountant. He bought some kind of prepaid burial plan six months ago."

"How did he pay for it?"

The detective rubbed his fingers together. "Cash," he told her. "Same way he paid the housekeeper and gardener. What medical bills his insurance didn't cover were paid with a cashier's check. That was for his treatment. I don't know who paid for Mrs. Harrison's care. All I know is, Harrison went to a lot of trouble to keep anyone from prying into his affairs." He brushed his finger across one eyebrow. "Why would he do that if he wasn't hiding something? Even if he didn't pay Downly like you suggested, he still had to hire someone to pull off the job at the Seagull."

"I know," Carolyn said. "Look for a bank or trust fund under the name of Tim Harrison. The boy would have had life insurance through the department."

Hank thought a while before responding. "Why keep a bank account in the name of your deceased son?"

"I'm certain the chief had power of attorney," she told him. "That's where he stashed his money. Not only that, he could have put his son's death benefits in a trust. After twenty-three years, it would have added up to a hefty sum. Daniel's grandmother only left him ten thousand. He ended up with seventy thousand when he was released from prison."

"I knew I let you hang out with me for a reason," Hank said, messing up her hair.

She reached over and did the same to him. "I look bad enough," she said, watching as he whipped out his comb and ran it through the thinning hair covering his bald spot.

"Mrs. Harrison will see you now," the woman at the front desk told them. "Go down this hallway and turn left."

Carolyn and Hank saw a large open room that must serve as a library. Bookcases lined the walls, and on one side of the room was a fireplace and a grouping of upholstered chairs. Large windows overlooked the front of the hospital, bathing the room in sunlight.

Madeline Harrison was seated in one of the high-backed chairs. The look in her eyes was lucid but guarded. A tall, slender woman, she was dressed neatly in a pair of brown slacks and a tan knit sweater. Her blond hair was silky and clean, swept back at the base of her neck and secured with a clasp.

"Why are you here?" Mrs. Harrison asked, her arms draped over the sides of the chair.

Hank and Carolyn sat down across from her. "We're making some inquiries about your husband's death. I'm Detective Sawyer, with the Ventura police, and this is Carolyn Sullivan. Ms. Sullivan is a probation officer."

"Charles wasn't on probation," the woman said, her eyes appearing intelligent and clear. "My husband was an alcoholic. He died from chronic liver disease. What possible reason would you have to inquire about his death?"

Perhaps Harrison's widow had tipped over the edge in the months following her son's death, but at present she showed no apparent signs of mental illness.

Hank asked, "When was the last time you saw your husband?"

"I don't recall," she answered, picking a piece of lint off her slacks. "Charles and I were married in name only. We would have divorced except for his insurance benefits. I'm playing in a bridge tournament at four o'clock. I'd appreciate it if you would leave."

"Are you aware that Daniel Metroix was released from prison?"

"I am now," Mrs. Harrison said, narrowing her eyes. "I gather you're his parole officer, Ms. Sullivan. Is that correct?"

"Yes," Carolyn answered. "Someone shot him."

"Good," the woman answered. "Is the bastard dead?"

"No," she said. "But he was seriously injured."

Madeline Harrison's jaws locked in anger.

"We need to ask you some questions," the detective continued. "Were you here at the hospital Friday?"

"Of course," she told him. "I don't go out at night, Detective."

"But you go out during the day, right?"

She turned and gazed out the window. Mrs. Harrison reminded Carolyn of a stone statue. Even when she spoke, it was hard to detect any movement except for her lips. Finally, she faced them again. "I don't believe I went out last Friday. You're referring to the day Charles died, I presume."

"Yes," he said. "This past Friday."

"The hospital has a sign-out sheet," Mrs. Harrison told them. "You can check that if you feel it's necessary. One of the staff members would have also had to arrange a taxi for me. We use a van for certain activities, such as visits to medical doctors, trips to museums, shows, things of that nature. I had a cold last week. I spent most of the day in my room."

"Do you share your room with another patient?"

"I used to," she said, her voice tinged with irritation. "Next month, I'll celebrate my twentieth anniversary as a resident of Fairview. After all the money this establishment has made off me, the hospital administrator finally agreed that I'd earned my privacy." She looked at her watch, then stood, her back ramrod straight. "I'm sorry, but I have to go. You've already made me late. My friends are waiting."

Hank bristled, walking over and blocking her way. "Just a minute, lady. We're investigating a number of serious crimes, all of which seem to be connected to your son's death. We didn't travel all this way for ten minutes of your time."

"Get out of my way, Detective," she snarled. "Either that or arrest me. I don't think you're prepared to do that, are you?"

Carolyn watched as Madeline Harrison strode boldly out of the room, her gait and body conformation more like a person in her late thirties than sixties. Whatever additional information they needed, they would obviously have to obtain from the woman's hospital records. No matter how relaxed the atmosphere at Fairview appeared, it was still classified as a psychiatric facility, and getting a court order for this type of information was similar to accessing files at the Pentagon.

At least, Carolyn thought, they'd answered Arline Shoeffel's question—there was nothing to prevent a patient from leaving the grounds. A guard shack was situated at the bottom of the hill and a five-foot metal fence encircled the property, more to keep people out than to preclude them from leaving. The hospital had informed Hank over the phone that all patients at Fairview were there by choice. A small percentage of the population suffered from classic mental illnesses such as schizophrenia and manic depression. Nonetheless, they were still voluntary admissions and could ask to be discharged whenever they desired. The rest had checked themselves into Fairview for treatment of prescription drug addictions, eating disorders, hypochondria, along with various and sundry phobias. A limited number of patients had health problems, not severe enough to merit hospitalization in a long-term care facility. Many stayed because they had nowhere else to go, and like Madeline Harrison, they'd grown accustomed to the security and routine of their surroundings.

Carolyn had been told that Mrs. Harrison had once been diagnosed with chronic fatigue syndrome. From what they'd seen today, and what the staff had related regarding her exercise regimen, whatever fatigue the woman had experienced in the past no longer existed.

"Is it possible she's involved?" Carolyn asked as they walked toward Hank's unmarked police unit in the visitors' parking lot.

"Who knows?" he said. "I think the probability that she did the crimes herself is remote. Could she have hired someone? No doubt about it. That woman is mean. She could stick a knife in your back and not so much as blink. God forbid she misses her stupid bridge game. When they told her the old man had croaked, she probably kept right on playing."

Carolyn was amused that Harrison's widow had ruffled the detective's feathers. She'd found the woman aloof, but she didn't detect any evidence that she was cruel. Mrs. Harrison might prefer to live inside an institution for reasons they would never know. What had impressed Carolyn was her strength. She had every right to resent their questions. No matter what type of relationship they'd had, her husband was dead and they had stirred up painful memories regarding her son. The more powerful the man, the more threatened he became when confronted by a woman who refused to give in to his demands.

"Hey," Carolyn said, leaning over in his face, "bridge is a serious game. I bet she plays duplicate. She's probably a master. I used to play duplicate years ago."

"I can't believe it," Hank said, glaring at her. "You liked her, didn't you? You have me running my ass off trying to catch whoever shot your pathetic little genius. Then when we interview a possible suspect, you suddenly become a turncoat. Women are nuts."

"Try interrupting a bunch of men when they're watching the World Series or the Super Bowl."

"Can it," Hank said gruffly. "I'm tired, I'm hungry, and the traffic is probably backed up halfway to Ventura. If we don't come up with some solid evidence by next week, the captain is going to yank me off the case." Reaching the car, he tossed her the keys. "You drive. I'm going to take a nap and forget I ever heard the name Daniel Metroix."

While Hank snored in the passenger seat, Carolyn called her home to check on her children. She had spoken to John at school after leaving Ralph's house, advising him that she was going to Los Angeles and might be a few minutes late coming home. "Hi, honey," she said when her daughter answered. "Put your brother on the phone."

"He's not here," Rebecca told her. "He didn't pick me up at school today."

"Why didn't you call me?"

"Isobel gave me a ride," she said. "Nothing happened or anything. I thought you said we should only call you if it was an emergency. John is probably over at Turner's. You programmed the police's number and yours into my phone, but you never gave me John's."

Carolyn felt acid bubbling back in her throat. How could she have been so negligent? She'd had no business spending even an hour with Paul with all the things that were going on. "Do you have the number at Turner's house?"

"No," Rebecca told her. "What's wrong, Mother?"

Carolyn was stuck in rush hour traffic on the 101 Freeway. She slapped the detective on the shoulder, waking him up, then continued speaking to her daughter. "Go to Professor Leighton's house and stay there until I get home. Don't go outside. If John shows up or contacts you, call me right away on my cell."

"What's going on?" Hank mumbled, straightening up in the seat.

Carolyn ignored him and punched the auto dial for her son's cell phone. After ten rings, she hit the off button. They hadn't set up voice mail. Both of the children had been instructed to keep their phones turned on except when they were at home sleeping. She glanced at the wall of traffic in front of her. There must have been an accident, as they were at a complete standstill.

"You drive," she told the detective. "Something's happened to my son." They got out of the car at the same time, circling around to exchange places.

"For God's sake, are you going to tell me what's going on?"

Carolyn ignored him, dialing John's number again. "John's missing." She stared at the cars around her, feeling panicked and trapped. "He didn't pick up Rebecca at school, and he's not answering his cell phone."

Hank reached into the backseat and grabbed the emergency light, leaning out the window as he attached it to the roof of the unmarked police unit. Before he turned on the siren, he contacted the dispatcher over the radio, informing her to get a unit over to Ventura High as well as Carolyn's residence.

"I told Rebecca to go to Paul Leighton's house," she told him. "It's two houses down from ours on the right. The address is 518 Wilton Drive. They should watch both houses in case John comes home."

"Could he be at a friend's house? What about your brother?"

"Maybe," Carolyn said, her voice shaking. She called Neil and got his answering machine. He was probably at the art gallery setting up for the show. She tried her mother. "Have you seen or heard from John today?"

"No, darling," Marie Sullivan told her, her words carefully enunciated. "What's wrong? Why haven't you called me? I know Neil is engrossed in his painting, but I always hear from you."

"My job, Mother," Carolyn said. "I can't talk right now. I promise I'll call you either later tonight or tomorrow."

She closed the phone and shot a furtive glance toward the detective. "John spends most of his time with a boy named Turner Highland. I don't have his phone number and address with me. I know the street and I can describe the house, though. He lives on Oakhurst, and the cross street is Windward. The house is the fourth down from the intersection, and the only one with a circular driveway. The exterior is light blue. There's a balcony on the second floor. Oh, and his mother drives a white Ford Explorer."

Hank relayed the information to the dispatcher, then flipped on the light and siren. Several cars pulled over to the shoulder, providing them with an opening to reach the nearest exit. Punching the Ford's big engine, he sped over the surface roads. "Don't worry," he yelled over the noise of the siren. "He's probably goofing off somewhere."

Carolyn chewed on a ragged fingernail. The detective was trying to comfort her, so there was no reason to argue. John was a responsible young man. Something terrible had happened, or he would have called or picked up his sister.

John reached a blue Dodge Stratus on the street adjacent to Ventura High, then waited while Wade unlocked the passenger door. As soon as he turned to get in, Wade twisted both his arms behind his back and secured them with a thick strand of rope. He tried to escape, but the boy had his knee in the center of his back. Wade quickly shoved him into the car and slammed the door.

John screamed for help. He turned sideways and attempted to kick the window out. Once Wade was in the driver's seat, he removed a roll of duct tape from the glove compartment and used it to cover John's mouth.

"Don't try anything else," Wade said, "or I'll kill you."

They drove for approximately twenty minutes, finally pulling up in front of a rundown house in a residential neighborhood. The paint was cracked and peeling, and the yard was overgrown with weeds. Wade drove into the open garage. He wouldn't allow John to get out until he'd closed the door and bolted it.

The house was unfurnished and stank, a musky combination of mildew and sewage, along with other odors John couldn't identify. The kitchen sink had been ripped out, and the threadbare carpet was stained.

Wade shoved John down onto the floor, removing more rope from his back pocket and using it to tie up his legs. He then ripped the duct tape off his mouth. "Here's the deal," he said, a phone dangling from his left hand. "Give me your mother's number. I dial, you talk. Tell her to meet you in the lobby of Methodist Hospital in thirty minutes."

"If I do what you say," John told him, trying to free his hands from the ropes, "my mother will show up with a dozen cops. Is that what you want?"

"No, no," Wade said, walking around in a panic. "Tell her you got hurt and a friend is taking you to the emergency room."

John felt like an idiot for letting the guy lure him to his car. Daniel Metroix was at Methodist Hospital. Wade wanted to use his mother to gain access to Metroix. If he managed to kill Metroix, John reasoned, Wade would probably kill his mother, him, and no telling how many other innocent people. He had to find a way to stop him.

"I don't know how to get in touch with my mother," he lied. "She said she was leaving the office early today. She had to stop off at the grocery store."

"Call her on her cell phone."

"She doesn't have a cell phone."

"You're a damn liar!" Wade shouted, moving closer so John could see the phone in his hand. "Where do you think this came from, jerk-off? I lifted it out of your back pocket. Are you trying to tell me that your mother doesn't have a cell phone but her kid does? That's bullshit. Give me the number or you'll be sorry you were ever born."

"My mom has a cell phone, okay, but she isn't allowed to use it except for official business."

"If I call her, she won't answer?"

"You'll get her voice mail," John said. "She won't check it until tomorrow morning."

"I don't believe you, you little prick," Wade shouted, becoming even more agitated. "I guess the only way to get you to cooperate with me is to hurt you." He walked over and picked up a saw from the kitchen counter. "Maybe I'll start sawing off your toes and fingers."

John's mind was clocking at lightning speeds. His mother had called him earlier, mentioning that she was driving to Los Angeles that afternoon to check out something related to the Metroix investigation. He doubted if she'd return to her office at the courthouse. Wade was on either cocaine or speed. Because of his father, John knew how to spot it. The boy's eyes were darting all over the place, and his mannerisms were jerky and frenetic. He couldn't seem to stand still, and he kept licking his lips.

Staring at the saw, John decided to give him his mother's direct line at the office, praying he was right and Wade would reach her voice mail. With his hands behind his back, he couldn't see his watch. It had to be close to five. School let out at three-thirty and he'd stayed maybe twenty minutes longer.

"Here's the number to my mother's cell phone," John told him, rattling off her office number.

Wade punched in the digits, then held the phone in front of his captive's face.

After a few minutes, John said, "Listen for yourself. It's her voice mail. Do you want me to leave a message?"

"Fuck," Wade said, tossing the phone across the room. "What am I going to do now? Metroix has to be dead by eight o'clock tonight or I don't get paid."

"So you're a professional killer?" John said, thinking the longer he kept him talking, the more time he would have before Wade killed him. No matter how terrified he was, he forced himself to speak in a low, measured voice. "Who hired you?"

"The Easter Bunny, moron," Wade tossed out. "Like I'm really going to tell you who hired me."

"They'll catch you and send you to prison."

"Ooh, scary," the other boy said, mocking him. "Prison doesn't scare me. It's living and dealing with people like you that makes me want to puke. I could kill you right now and it wouldn't mean a thing to me. I was only fourteen when I killed the first time. It's the best high around." The drugs had made him loose-lipped. "They caught me last time because of your bitch of a mother. They'll never catch me again. I'm smarter now. You think I live in this dump? I only used it because it was vacant. I have fifteen different ID's. I never stay in one place longer than a few days. I stole the Dodge only an hour before I grabbed you." He spun around and faced John, tossing his hands out to his sides and smiling. "Look at this face. Does this look like the face of a killer? Shit, you went with me, didn't you?"

John had to admit it: With his neatly trimmed hair and the scattering of freckles across his nose and forehead, Wade didn't appear menacing. His clothes were somewhat slovenly, but that wasn't unusual among teenagers. He noticed some black spots on his knuckles, thinking they might be paint. "Are you a handyman or something? Are you supposed to be fixing up this house?"

Wade set the saw down where he'd found it, then crouching in the corner, stared off into space.

The guy's belief that he was invincible had to be drug induced, John decided. Wade would never have told him the things he had unless he intended to kill him.

He had to escape.

The minutes ticked off like hours. John watched as Wade stood and removed a beer from a Styrofoam cooler in the kitchen, popping the cap and sucking it down almost in one swallow. John thought if he could distract Wade and get his hands on the saw, he could cut through the ropes. Wade was scrawny. John had built up his body lifting weights. He thought he could take him.

"I've got another plan," Wade said, walking over and yanking John to his feet. Before John could ask him what the plan was, the boy had covered his mouth again with tape. John did his best to walk with his legs tied together as Wade pulled him along.

They reached the steps leading into the garage. On the floor by the door, John saw a small white sneaker. The shoe had some type of design on it, but he couldn't make out what it said. Hearts, he thought, straining to see. He saw another shoe a few feet away splattered with paint. Next to the second sneaker was a red-stained towel. When he realized he might be looking at blood instead of paint, he experienced a violent wave of nausea. A young girl had been raped. His mother had been the rapist's probation officer. But it couldn't be Wade. The police had already caught the man.

Something awful had happened here—the stench, the saw, the blood-splattered shoes. They were so tiny. Tears pooled in his eyes. He thought he heard the bloodcurdling scream of a child.

John felt Wade's hand on his head as he pushed him into the backseat. His touch was repugnant. He forced himself to look into his eyes. What he saw was the essence of evil. Another entity seemed to be peering out at him. How could anyone butcher a child? He struggled against his restraints. Wade slugged him, then used his foot to force him onto the floorboard. He tossed something over his face so he could no longer see. John heard the car door shut.

He heard what sounded like hammering, then a clanking noise. He felt as if he couldn't breathe. *Don't panic,* he told himself. He remembered the metal bolt at the base of the garage door. It must have jammed. The car door opened and closed. Music blasted from the radio.

They were moving.

John's body bumped up and down as they sped along the roads and careened around corners. When the car came to a screeching halt, he slammed into the back of the seat.

Wade opened the rear door, using a pocket knife to slice through the ropes around John's ankles. He ripped the tape from his mouth, pulled him to his feet, then tossed the oversized black-and-red ski parka, which had previously covered John's face, over his shoulders.

John saw the sign for Methodist Hospital. He'd managed to work one finger free, but the ropes were too tight around his wrists. Once they got inside the hospital, he'd scream for help.

"We're just a couple of buddies going to visit a friend," Wade told him. "Look happy and keep your mouth shut."

John felt something round and hard pressing against his side.

"You know what a gun feels like, don't you?" Wade whispered in his ear. "Do exactly what I say and we won't have a problem. Make a wrong move and you're a dead man."

They entered through the lobby and ducked inside the service elevator. Wade punched the button for the sixth floor. Once they exited, they continued down the corridor until they found a supply closet. Wade stripped off his clothes and dressed in green scrubs, also pulling on a pair of latex gloves. He used a towel to wipe down the gun, then switched it to his right hand and shoved it into John's ribs again.

Wade peered outside of the room to make certain no one was around. Leading John toward the service elevator again, he depressed the button for the seventh floor.

As soon as the doors opened, John saw a uniformed police officer sitting in a chair at the far end of the corridor, flipping through the pages of a magazine.

Wade viciously kicked him, causing him to collapse onto the floor. He adjusted the parka so it covered John's arms and upper body.

"He pulled a gun on me!" Wade shouted, running toward the room the officer had been guarding. "He won't stay down long. You better move fast."

Trevor White removed his service revolver and used the radio clipped near his ear to call for backup. Hearing the ruckus, several nurses huddled together behind the nurses' station. Because his back was turned, White didn't see the man in the green scrubs enter Metroix's room. He was cautiously approaching the suspect at the end of the corridor.

John's hands were concealed by the parka. He knew the

officer couldn't see that he wasn't armed. He started to roll over, then stopped himself, afraid the officer would think he was reaching for a weapon. Any second he expected a bullet to rip into his flesh.

John clenched his eyes shut and prayed.

Inside Daniel's room, Wade aimed the .357 at the bed, his finger floating above the trigger. As he moved closer, he saw the bed was empty. Deciding Metroix must be using the toilet, he spun around and trained the gun on the bathroom door. He had to kill Metroix, and if necessary, shoot his way out of the hospital. He'd checked the exterior of the building the night he'd tried to run Carolyn Sullivan off the road. There was no outside fire escape. A leap out the window from the seventh floor would kill him.

Wade was backed up to the edge of the bed when he felt something latch on to both of his ankles. The linoleum floor had recently been waxed and he fell forward onto his face, his gun flying out of his hand and ending up on the other side of the room. Wade began kicking to free himself but he felt as if his feet were locked in a vise. He screamed in pain when he felt something sharp cut into his left ankle, then a moment later, his right.

Trevor White flung open the door, leveling his firearm at the man on the floor. "Don't move or I'll shoot," he shouted, perspiration dripping off his brow. He scooped up the .357 and shoved it into the waistband of his pants, then reached behind him for his handcuffs. "Where's Metroix?"

"How the hell do I know?" Wade told him. "I'm an intern. That man pulled a gun on me. I came in here to check on the patient."

"He couldn't have pulled a gun on you," White said, bending down to handcuff him. "His arms were tied behind his back."

The lower half of Wade's body was still underneath the bed. When White reached for his arms, Wade yanked the gun out of White's waistband and pulled the trigger.

The gunshot reverberated throughout the room. The bullet entered Trevor White's throat. The officer was propelled backward, blood pumping out of the gaping wound at the base of his neck. He struck the wall, then slid onto the floor.

Wade scrambled to his feet and sprinted out of the room. He didn't see John, so he shouted to the nurses. "A police officer was shot! Did you see which way the suspect went?"

The nurses looked confused. Wade didn't wait for the elevator. He found the stairwell and ran down to the first floor. Wiping the .357 clean with the edge of his shirt, he dumped it into a trash container and walked calmly out of the building.

Three police cars with their sirens blasting were pulling up at the curb. Wade fell in step with a group of nurses heading toward the staff parking lot. "What's going on?" a short young nurse asked, craning her neck around to look at the police cars.

"Bomb threat," Wade said, looking down at the ground so she couldn't see his face. He stopped walking when he reached the spot where the Dodge was parked, waiting until the group of nurses continued on without him.

Once inside the car, he crouched down in the driver's seat and took off. He drove slowly until he was several miles from the hospital, then he parked in an alley behind what appeared to be a vacant building.

Before he abandoned the Dodge, Wade removed his shirt and used it to wipe down the steering wheel, glove box, door handles, radio, and any other surfaces he might have touched. Getting out and opening the back door, he removed the cords of rope and the duct tape, wadding them in a ball and shoving them in the pocket of his pilfered green cotton pants.

His ankles were bleeding and it was painful to walk. They

didn't allow animals in the hospital, he told himself, so it had to have been that freak Metroix. He must have heard the commotion outside and hid under the bed. Metroix had spent twenty-three years in the joint, so his survival instincts were better than the average person's. No wonder the people who'd hired him wanted the guy dead. He'd cut Metroix's feet off as payback before he killed him.

Wade limped along another block and a half. He spotted a late model Honda Civic with the windows rolled down. Ducking inside the car, he pulled wires in the ignition until he managed to make the right connection and the starter engaged.

As soon as he reached the city limits of Ventura, Wade pulled off onto a beach access road and parked, pounding the steering wheel with his fists in a fit of rage. Realizing he still had on the latex gloves, he ripped them off and tossed them out the window, along with the rope and duct tape.

Not only had he failed to kill Metroix, which meant he wouldn't get paid, but he'd shot a police officer. The cop had been a fool. He could tell by the way he'd handled himself that he must be a rookie. If the man lived, he doubted if he would remember enough to identify him. He had planned on killing Carolyn Sullivan's son, or he would never have run his mouth, telling him how he operated. The kid knew everything, and would have no trouble whatsoever identifying him.

The tempest finally passed.

Wade told himself all he had to do was skip town and lay low until things died down. The problem was, he'd shot a cop. When you shoot a cop, nothing dies down. The nurses weren't a problem. Sure, they'd seen his face, but hundreds of other people looked just like him. His looks were one of the reasons he'd only been busted a few times after committing more crimes than he could remember. Whether he got paid or not was no longer his biggest problem, although a chance still remained that he might be able to get an extension and complete the job.

The probation officer's kid presented the greatest threat. If he was arrested, tomorrow or six years from now, the boy's testimony would convict him. The cop died and he was looking at the death penalty. It might be risky, but he felt fairly certain he could take care of the problem. He didn't have a choice.

The kid had to die.

Chapter 26

Carolyn and Hank Sawyer heard about the incident at the hospital over the police radio. Trevor White had been rushed into surgery. If the shooting had occurred outside of the hospital, the officer would have more than likely bled to death. The bullet had sliced through his carotid artery and hit his spinal cord.

"Are you certain John's okay?" Carolyn asked, bending over at the waist as if she were about to vomit.

"Take some deep breaths," Hank told her. "John might have trouble walking for a few days, but he'll be fine. He's lucky, Carolyn. If that bullet severed White's spine, he'll spend the rest of his life in a wheelchair."

They were only a few miles from the hospital. Carolyn called Paul and explained what had occurred. He assured her that he would look after Rebecca. When he heard what had happened to John, he wanted to come to the hospital and leave Isobel with Lucy and Rebecca. Carolyn thanked him for his concern, then informed him that if he wanted to help her, he'd stay where he was and protect her daughter.

"Having one of those rifles I saw in the cabinet out and loaded would probably be wise," she told him. "Just don't say anything to Rebecca. Tell her we found her brother and he's fine."

When she concluded the call, Hank said, "You've gotten tight with the professor, haven't you?"

"He's been helpful," Carolyn said, recalling the time they'd spent together that afternoon. "Whenever I need him, he's there for me. That's more than I can say for Frank."

"Everyone needs someone," Hank told her. "Sounds like Leighton is a decent fellow. Man's got a good job, gets along well with your kids, and seems as if he's genuinely concerned for your well-being."

Carolyn cut her eyes to the detective, more concerned with catching the killer than discussing her relationship with the professor. "We're going to have to move Metroix. When do you think the hospital is going to release him?"

"Well," he said, "it's been five days since the shooting. He must be in fairly good shape or he wouldn't have been able to tackle the shooter. Besides, the hospital doesn't keep people the way they did in the past. Where are we going to put him? We can move him to the hospital wing at the jail now that he's out of the woods."

"That doesn't make sense," Carolyn told him. "Someone inside arranged Downly's release. If that person was working for Harrison, they could kill Metroix and make it look like an accident."

Hank realized she had a point. "What do you suggest we do with him?"

"Paul has a house in Pasadena," she said. "Maybe I can talk him into letting us use it for a while. I'm not only afraid they may come after Daniel again, I'm worried sick about my children. If Paul agrees, I could get a visiting nurse to come in and look after Daniel during the day. Then the children and I could take care of him the rest of the time."

"What about your job?"

"I have vacation and sick time," Carolyn said. "Brad has already reassigned most of my cases. I should be able to disappear for at least a week. Hopefully, by then you'll have made an arrest. No one's going to look for us in Pasadena. All we have to do is make certain we're not followed."

"Take him in an ambulance," the detective told her. "You and your children can go with him. Can they afford to miss school?"

"Not going to school for a week or two is better than risking their lives. I can get their teachers to give me their assignments in advance. John will pitch a fit." She thought about it, then changed her mind. "Maybe after what happened today, he'll be more agreeable." Her voice cracked with emotion. "God, Hank, my son could be dead right now. We have to put an end to this. I don't know how much more I can take."

They pulled up and parked behind the black-and-white police units. When they reached the seventh floor, Carolyn rushed to the nurses' counter. "Where's my son?"

"Are you Mrs. Sullivan?" Her name tag read Alice Nelson, R.N. She was a kind-faced, middle-aged nurse with short black hair.

"Yes."

"Don't worry," Nelson said. "We put your boy in a room to rest. We're icing his knee. He was badly shaken, so the doctor gave him a mild sedative. Other than that, he didn't incur any injuries."

John opened his eyes when he saw his mother. Carolyn leaned down and kissed him, then pulled away and clasped his hand. "I'm so sorry this happened," she said. "How's your knee?"

"I'll be okay," he said, wincing in pain. "They didn't catch him, did they? I knew he'd get away."

"They will," Carolyn reassured him. "Have the police talked to you?"

"Yeah," he said. "I gave them everything I knew . . . the car he was driving, what he looked like, anything I could remember. This guy's a maniac, Mom. He made up this sob story about his father having a heart attack and not being able to find the hospital. I should have never let him trick me. He looks young, though. I mean, he certainly doesn't look like a murderer."

"It wasn't your fault. "

After John finished telling his mother everything that had occurred, she said, "Why didn't you call your sister on her cell phone if you were going to be late? That's why I bought the phones."

"I knew you'd blame me," John said, defensive. "I'm not used to having a phone. I was thinking about this problem, trying to remember what Mr. Chang and I worked on after class. Once I agreed to go with him, the guy snatched the phone from me anyway."

"Forget about the phone," Carolyn said. "I'm just glad you weren't seriously injured. Did they tell you the police officer was shot?"

"Yeah," John said. "The cop almost shot me. He was pretty lame. He acted like he didn't know what to do. Either that, or he was just scared."

Carolyn gave him a stern look. "It's not right to criticize him. I'm sure Officer White did the best he could under the circumstances."

Hank Sawyer walked into the room. "You did good, John. When you hid in one of the patient's rooms, you probably kept yourself from getting killed."

Now that his panic was subsiding, more details were surfacing. "He called himself Wade," John told them, rolling over onto his side. "That wasn't his real name, though. He said he used all kinds of different names. He bragged that he'd killed someone when he was fourteen. He was so strung out on drugs, I don't know if anything he told me was true."

Hank asked, "You told the other detective that you saw some kind of spots or something on the man's hands. Could they have been tattoos?"

"I guess," John said, fear flashing in his eyes. "This was a pretty hairy scene, you know. It's hard to remember everything. He had a saw. He was ready to start cutting my toes off. The thing that scared me the most were the little kid's sneakers in the garage. I'm certain they had blood on them."

The description matched Eddie Downly. Carolyn tried to suppress her horror that her son had ended up in the hands of such a vile and dangerous man. To make certain, she drew a picture of what Downly's tattoos looked like, purposely distorting the letters. "Is this what you're talking about?" she said, holding the paper in front of him.

"Yeah," John said. "I saw one of his hands pretty good when he was tying me up. Now that I think about it, I believe it spelled 'love.' Pretty weird thing for a killer to put on his knuckles."

"We'll be right back," his mother told him. Hank and Carolyn stepped out of the room.

"Eddie Downly is left-handed. The tattoo that spelled 'love' was on his left hand," Carolyn told him. "Why didn't Downly go after Luisa Cortez, since she was here at the hospital? Those had to be her shoes. John was probably in the house where he raped her."

"They released the girl yesterday," Hank told her, pulling out a toothpick. "Do you think Downly really killed someone when he was fourteen?"

"If he did," Carolyn said, "he got away with it. I already told you to check for any unsolved homicides. There's no telling how many crimes Eddie committed. Like John said, he's young, white, and doesn't come across as a hardened criminal. I only supervised him. I wasn't with him twenty-four hours a day."

"Stop beating yourself up," the detective told her. "We never know who we're dealing with when we bust someone."

They returned to the room. John was sitting up in bed, pressing the ice pack against his knee. "I forgot to tell you," he said, excited. "He was supposed to kill Metroix by eight tonight. Otherwise, they weren't going to pay him."

"Did he mention anyone else?" his mother asked. "During

the time you were with him, did he talk to anyone on the phone or give you any indication whatsoever that he was working with a partner?"

"Not that I remember."

"Did he tell you who hired him?"

"The Easter Bunny," John told them. "Obviously, he was making fun of me." He fell silent, thinking. "I'm sorry I can't tell you more about the house. I was so scared, I didn't pay attention."

"Do you feel up to taking a drive?" Hank asked.

"I guess," John said, removing the ice pack and checking to see if the swelling had gone down. The nurse had cut his jeans, so the bottom half of his right leg was bare. "I already told you that I don't remember how I got to the house. I feel like an idiot. I can't remember the name of one street."

"You'll recognize it if you see it, though," the detective said. "Were you in the car for a longer period of time from the school to the house, or from the house to the hospital?"

"It seemed like it only took us a few minutes to get to the hospital," John said, standing and taking a few steps to test his knee. "I may be wrong, though. When we left the house, I was on the floor in the back. I couldn't see, you know. After I saw the little girl's shoes, I kind of lost it."

"Come on, we'll go now. That house is probably loaded with evidence."

Carolyn could tell that her son was exhausted. She knew he had to work with the police, though, as the situation was too serious. "There may have been more than one victim. You said he had a saw. Did you see any blood on the saw?"

"I don't think so," John told her, growing pale as he re-lived those terrifying moments. "There wasn't much light inside the house. The shades were closed. And there was this really bad smell. I thought it was sewage at first. It might be dead bodies, right?"

"Listen," Carolyn said, taking a seat beside him on the bed, "the man who called himself Wade raped and strangled an eight-year-old girl named Luisa Cortez. His real name is Edward Downly. He threw her out of the car in a vacant lot, thinking she was dead. She's alive, but that doesn't mean he might not have killed someone else. Do you understand?"

"I thought that guy was in jail," John said, staring at his mother in confusion. "You told me yourself. One of the teachers at school even mentioned it. How did he get out?"

"I'll explain in the car," Hank said, finding John's shoes and socks in the closet next to his bed. "Get ready to leave. I'll pick up a few more ice packs for your knee. We need to find that house."

A uniformed officer stuck his head in the door. "We located the Dodge over on Walker Drive, sir. The lab's sending a tow truck. The plate came back as a stolen vehicle."

"That's how he operates," John said, speaking even more rapidly now. "He steals a car a few hours before he does the crime. Then he leaves it somewhere and steals another one."

"Bring him home after you're finished," Carolyn told Hank. "I'm going to check on Daniel."

"Oh, my God," John exclaimed, "where's Rebecca? Did she get home from school? All this time and I haven't even asked about her. I really let you down, Mom."

"Your sister is all right," Carolyn told him "Paul is looking after her. You didn't let me down. By not allowing this man to lure me to the hospital, you may have saved my life as well as a number of others. You should be proud of yourself."

"I didn't want him to hurt you," the boy said, tears glistening in his eyes. "I love you, Mom."

Carolyn pressed his head against her chest. "I love you too, sweetheart. Everything's going to be fine. We're going to catch him. Once we do, he'll never hurt anyone again."

Daniel Metroix was propped up in his bed, a downcast expression on his face.

"Were you hurt?" Carolyn asked.

"I'm okay," Metroix said. "They removed the stitches this morning. How's the police officer?"

"Still in surgery," she told him. "He's going to make it, but it doesn't look good. The bullet lodged in his spinal cord."

"I wish I could have stopped him from getting shot," Daniel said. "When I saw the officer shove the guy's gun in the waistband of his pants, I knew he'd made a terrible mistake. Then he leaned over and practically placed the gun in the man's hand." He stared at a spot on the wall. The exertion had obviously drained him. "A prison guard would never have done something like that. Did the other officers tell you I bit the guy?"

"No," Carolyn said. "Where did you bite him?"

"On his Achilles tendons," Daniel said, reaching over and taking a sip of water from a cup on the end table. "There was nothing in here I could use as a weapon. I managed to take him to the floor, but I was afraid he was going to get away from me. In prison, you learn to use whatever you have. Find someone with bite marks on their ankles, and you've got your man. The forensics people can match the wounds against my teeth, right?"

"Sure can," Carolyn told him. "First, we have to catch him. We're going to have officers stationed all over the hospital tonight, even though I doubt he'd be stupid enough to come back. By tomorrow morning, I should have figured out a safe place where we can take you."

"Nowhere has been safe," Daniel said, lowering his eyes. "Maybe you should just send me back to Chino."

"I know things have been tough," she said. "I was with you when the motel exploded. My daughter broke her ankle, my car was destroyed, and my son was kidnapped today. This wasn't even my fight, Daniel. When things go bad, all we can do is try our best to make them right."

"I'm sorry," he said, rubbing his hand back and forth on the sheet. "It just seems like life was better for me when I was in prison. When I'm not able to work, I get depressed."

"Listen," she said firmly, refusing to allow a man with his intellect and abilities to crawl back into a hole, "you want to give up and spend the rest of your life behind bars, go right ahead. All you have to do is steal some hubcaps."

Daniel fell silent.

"I showed your work to a physics professor I know," Carolyn continued. "He was very impressed. He wants some of the other faculty members at Caltech to take a look at your design for the exoskeleton. All I need is your permission."

His eyes lit up. "Are you serious?"

"Yes, I am," she said. "He even told me the government was offering fifty million to any individual or institute who comes up with the best prototype."

"When you say the government," Daniel said, his enthusiasm waning, "what you mean is the military. I'm not interested in perfecting the exoskeleton or any of my other inventions to be used in warfare. Money doesn't mean anything to me. My dream was to work in the biomedical field. I want to help disabled people."

"I'll either come by or call you first thing in the morning," she said. "We're going to catch this man, Daniel. If you hang in there and let us help you, you might be able to work anywhere you want."

Daniel gave Carolyn a pathetic look, almost as if he couldn't stand for her to leave. The poor man had suffered through so much, she thought. He'd gone without love since he was a teenager. John's ordeal had left her in an emotional turmoil. She impulsively walked over to his bed and kissed him on the forehead.

Carolyn experienced a strange sensation. As she gazed at Daniel's face, her vision blurred. "The picture you had in your room," she said, removing it from her purse. "Is this you?"

"Yes," Daniel said softly.

"And the girl?" she asked. "Is she your sister?"

"I loved her very much," he said. "Her name was Jenny."

"You never mentioned a sister," Carolyn said. "Where is she now?"

"At the Queen of Angels Cemetery in Los Angeles," Daniel said. "She was five when she died. When you moved into our complex, I thought God had sent her back to me. You were the same age and you looked just like her. We used to play together. You don't remember, do you?"

"No," Carolyn said, wondering if this early tragedy had played a role in his illness. "I'm sorry about your sister. How did you recognize me after all these years?"

"Maybe because the time I spent with you was happy, and my sister had been sick from the time she was born, I had more good memories of you than I did of her. When I heard someone named Carolyn Sullivan was going to be my probation officer, I wasn't sure it was the same person. The moment I saw you, though, I knew."

Carolyn had to leave. "Whether I remember the past or not isn't important," she told him. "I'm glad you found me."

"No one has ever really cared what happened to me outside of my parents," Daniel said, giving her a look of gratitude. "You risked your life to help me. You're a wonderful person."

"So are you," Carolyn said, smiling. "This time, I promise I won't forget to call you. Please—"

"Don't worry," Daniel said, cutting her off, "I'm not going to leave the hospital."

Chapter 27

Carolyn and Paul were sitting next to each other on the sofa in her living room. It was almost midnight, and both John and Rebecca were asleep. After several hours in the car with Hank Sawyer, John had finally identified the vacant house where he'd been held. The police had cordoned it off as a crime scene and were still combing the house for evidence. They hadn't discovered another body, but they did confirm that the sneakers John had seen in the garage had belonged to Luisa Cortez. Once the crime lab removed and examined all the evidence, they might be able to tell if more crimes had been committed and make an attempt to locate any additional victims.

"I don't mind you using my place in Pasadena," Paul told her. "Going in an ambulance is a good idea. To be honest, though, I don't think the visiting nurse is the way to go."

"Why?" Carolyn asked, peering over at him. "Daniel will need medical treatment. A gunshot wound is a serious injury."

"I agree he needs someone to care for him while he's recuperating, but he doesn't need a nurse," the professor told her. "Not only that, neither you nor the children should leave my house in Pasadena until the killer has been apprehended. I'm going to send Isobel with you. She can do the shopping, cook, and take care of Metroix. Pasadena is a small town. A new face would attract attention."

"No, Paul," Carolyn told him. "I can't let you do that. Lending us your house is enough. You need Isobel to help you with Lucy, as well as handle your chores. I don't want to keep you from finishing your book."

"To hell with the book," he said, placing a finger under her chin. "I think I'm falling in love with you."

They kissed, and then Carolyn pulled back. "Isn't a statement like that a little premature? We haven't even had sex. I know how you men operate. You're desperately in love until you get the woman in bed, then everything starts to fade."

"Even if we never had sex, I'd still adore you. Look at all the excitement you've brought into my life." Paul rubbed his hands together. "I've changed my mind about writing another physics book. I've decided to become a crime fighter."

Carolyn nudged him in the side. "You're making fun of me."

"Somewhat," Paul said, smiling. "I doubt if I could do your job even if I wanted. I meant what I said earlier, though. I guess it just wasn't the right time to begin a love affair."

"Amen to that one," she said, resting her head on his shoulder. "I'm so tired I can't see straight. Tomorrow, I have to contact the kids' teachers and get their schoolwork together, pack some of our things."

"Let the schoolwork go," Paul cautioned. "For this to work, you can't let anyone know what's going on. Don't forget that John was deceived by Downly. He uses his youth and appearance to his advantage."

"I wasn't going to tell the school where we're going," Carolyn said. "All I intended was to make it so they could keep up with their studies. You know how serious John is about his grades. Not only that, what are they going to do pent up in the house all the time?"

"I'll send some of Lucy's DVDs with you," he told her.

"And your son can learn more from Daniel Metroix than he'll ever learn at school. I thought of sending some of the professors at Caltech over to talk to him since he'll be in the area." He saw the look on her face, then added, "Not too smart, huh?"

Carolyn yawned. "Stick to physics."

A few minutes later, Paul realized that Carolyn had fallen asleep. He picked her up in his arms and carried her to her bed. Instead of returning home, he called and asked Isobel to bring him his rifle. Tonight, he decided, it was his turn to play sentinel.

Arline Shoeffel called Carolyn at home at seven-thirty Wednesday morning. Paul had left as soon as she'd awakened. The children were packing their things for the trip to Pasadena. Carolyn was resting in her bedroom, knowing she had a long day ahead of her.

The judge had heard about John's kidnapping and the shooting at the hospital, as well as the possibility that Eddie Downly was the man who'd raped Luisa Cortez. Carolyn told her about their plan to stay at the professor's house in Pasadena until Downly had been apprehended.

"What should we do about Warden Lackner?" Carolyn asked. "For all we know, he hired Downly. He had the same motive to get him out of jail as Charles Harrison. He couldn't take a chance that Downly would roll over on him."

"The attorney general's office is launching an investigation," Arline informed her. "They've already determined that there was no joint venture program at Chino."

Carolyn bolted upright in bed. "Then Lackner lied?"

"Looks that way," she told her. "There's also no official record of any inmate having a lab or workshop along the lines of what Metroix described. Several guards have already verified Metroix's story, so Lackner must have taken down the lab as soon as you started asking questions. The

AG's office would like to depose Metroix as soon as possible."

"Don't they understand that someone's trying to kill him?"

"I told them he wouldn't be available for several weeks due to his injuries," Arline continued. "I tried to arrange federal protection, but the case isn't far enough along to warrant it. The one thing you can do, since you're going to be spending some time with this man, is to attempt to compile a list of whatever it is he invented during his time at the prison."

Carolyn hung up and called Brad Preston.

"Where are you going?"

"As far away as we can get," she told him. "I'll check in with you at the end of the week."

"What about Metroix?"

"I don't know," Carolyn lied. "My primary concern is my family's safety."

"You can't just walk off the job and not let anyone know where you're going, or when you're coming back."

"Right now," Carolyn said, "I don't have to tell anyone anything. You want to get me fired, go right ahead."

"You're not being fair," he said, stung by her sharp remarks. "I am concerned about you. I'm not trying to get you fired."

"I'm tired and I'm scared, Brad," Carolyn said. "No one has ever come this close to hurting my children. If you care about me, don't ask any questions. It's for your own good as well as mine. Tell Wilson I'm having an operation."

"I've been thinking about you a lot lately," Brad said, his voice soft. "Maybe we could try again. You know, put things back together. All you'd have to do is transfer to another unit. Either that or I'll take over field services."

Carolyn scooted farther down in the bed, imagining he was beside her. Paul Leighton offered her intelligence and stability. Just thinking about Brad made her toes tingle and her nipples harden. "Were you telling the truth about Amy McFarland?"

"There was never anything between us," he told her. "To be honest, I haven't even been dating. I guess I'm getting old or something. I don't know what's wrong with me. The other day, I thought about asking you to marry me."

"Yeah, right," Carolyn said. "And you're going to give up drinking and staying out all night, sell all those stupid race cars, just suddenly settle down and become a family man."

Brad laughed. "Maybe."

"Maybe not is more like it," Carolyn told him. "You just can't stand it because I'm seeing someone else. I'll check in toward the end of the week."

Chapter 28

By ten o'clock Wednesday morning, Carolyn, John, and Rebecca were sitting in a room at the Ventura Police Department. Hank had pulled her Infiniti into a service bay at the rear of the station, then had some of the other officers remove the boxes of belongings she'd brought along and load them into a white van.

"Here's the plan," Hank said, entering the room and taking a seat across from them at the conference table. "You and your children will ride to the hospital in one of our evidence vans. This shouldn't attract suspicion as Downly knows we'll be sending people over to Methodist to collect evidence from the crime scene. Metroix is scheduled for release at noon. The hospital records won't show he's been released until tomorrow. If Downly manages to get hold of the hospital records or calls to check Metroix's status, all he'll be told is that he's no longer a patient. There won't be any forwarding address. This will give you a full day's lead time. To extend it any longer would be too risky. We don't know everyone involved in this mess. We're going to cover today by putting a phony note in Metroix's chart that he's been transferred to the psych ward." He stopped and took a drink of his coffee. "We know Downly isn't working alone. Whoever shot Metroix was in the passenger seat. The same holds true regarding the people who tried to run you and Rebecca off the road."

Carolyn saw the fear in the girl's eyes as she recalled that night. "Don't you have any leads on Eddie Downly?" Carolyn asked, reaching over and clasping her daughter's hand. John was sitting beside his sister, a sullen expression on his face. He'd gone through the roof when his mother had told him she was taking him out of school. Then, when she'd told him that they were going to be holed up with Daniel Metroix, John had told her she was insane. She tried to explain that since the killer knew all three of them by sight, it made sense for them to remain together.

"We don't have anything on Downly's whereabouts at the moment," Hank said, pushing his chair away from the table. "Whether you realize it or not, John, Downly wants to get rid of you as much as he wants to get rid of Metroix and Luisa Cortez. Your testimony will convict him."

"Well, that sure makes me feel good," John said sarcastically. "The guy might as well kill me. I'm probably going to flunk out of school anyway."

"You're not going to flunk out of school," his mother said. "Hank's just trying to explain why we need to go away for a while." She turned back to the detective. "What about Nolan Houston and Liam Armstrong?"

"You've got to let us carry the ball now, Carolyn," Hank said. "The captain, along with Kevin Thomas from the DA's office, has a meeting scheduled with Judge Shoeffel this afternoon. After what happened yesterday, she's agreed to issue search warrants for both Houston and Armstrong." He tilted his head toward the door. "We need to get moving, folks. The ambulance is already at the hospital. We've got men standing around over there twiddling their thumbs. I'd like to get them back on the street so we can find Downly. We also want this move to go as smoothly as possible."

On the ride to Pasadena, Carolyn called Paul Leighton

from her cell phone inside the ambulance. "Thanks for staying last night."

"I forgot to tell you," he said. "There's no phone service at the house except for the two lines paid for by the university. One is a DSL line for the computer. The other jack is right next to it. I didn't want to turn the phones back on in case Downly or someone else hacked into the phone company's records and got the address. We'll communicate only on our cell phones. If your cell phone doesn't work for some reason, just plug one of the phones into the jack behind my computer."

Carolyn started to hang up when the professor continued speaking, "Do you know someone who drives a black Nissan?"

"No," she said. "Why?"

"I saw a person parked a few doors down from your house in a black Nissan. I assumed it was an undercover cop, but I decided it was worth mentioning. I checked with the neighbors. No one knows anyone who drives that type of car."

"I'll ask Hank if it was one of their men when I talk to him later. I didn't spot any strange cars when we left to go to the police department."

Paul had sent Isobel to Pasadena early that morning, to air out the house and stock the refrigerator. "Was this person there when Isobel left?" she asked, cupping her hand over the phone so the children wouldn't hear.

"Honestly," he said, "I don't know. I doubt if it's anything to be concerned about. I checked with the neighbors, but a lot of people weren't home. For all we know, the person in the Nissan could have been a friend of one of the teenagers who live around here. Maybe they stopped by to give them a ride. The car disappeared around eight-thirty. That coincides with when most of the kids head out to school." He paused and then added, "From what I could tell, the driver was female. Nothing you've told me indicates that a female is involved."

Carolyn instantly thought of Madeline Harrison. Daniel had described the shooter as having blond hair, and Harrison's widow was a blonde. Mrs. Harrison had an aura of sophistication about her, however. It was hard to imagine her parked on the street alone, lying in wait to kill them. Some things just didn't fit.

When Carolyn remained silent, Paul asked her, "You have your gun, I presume?"

"Yes," she told him. "Guns I have in abundance."

Hank had given her a small arsenal of weapons. They wouldn't have support from the Pasadena police, unless they ended up in a shootout or some other kind of crisis developed. According to the detective, the local police force spent most of their time trying to prevent the wealthy senior citizens of Pasadena, who made up the majority of the residents, from running over the college students.

In a canvas bag in the rear of the ambulance were three additional handguns, an AK-47 assault rifle, and enough ammo to hold off an army.

Once she'd concluded her call with Paul, Carolyn familiarized herself with the supplies the hospital had given her to care for Daniel. Inside a large plastic sack, she found bottles of Percodan, antibiotics, antiseptics, bandages, and various other medications. At the end of the week, according to the sheet of instructions they'd given her, Daniel would have to be checked by a doctor. He was still pale and weak.

Rebecca felt sorry for him, and struck up a conversation. Dressed in a white cotton shirt and a red-and-black checked skirt, the girl wore her curly brown hair tied back in a ponytail, with a few tendrils pulled down over her forehead. "What does it feel like to be shot?"

"Painful," Daniel told her, lying prone on the gurney. "How's your ankle?"

"I can walk on it now," she told him. "The doctor called this a walking cast. I only had to use the crutches for a few days."

So he would have something to wear, Paul had given Carolyn several pairs of loose-fitting sweatpants and a stack of white cotton T-shirts. She'd brought along the underwear and socks he'd purchased at Rite Aid, along with his injectable medication, on the day after the explosion.

Rebecca kept probing. "Were you scared?"

"You don't have much time to be scared."

"I bet you hate the guy who shot you."

"Hate is an ugly thing," Daniel told her. "All it does is eat you up inside."

"But aren't you mad about all that time you spent in prison?" the girl asked, doodling in a spiral notebook she was balancing on her lap. "My mom says you didn't do anything wrong."

"I'm lucky to be alive," Daniel told her. "If it hadn't been for your mother and brother, I might be dead. Your mother's a courageous woman. John," he said, propping himself up with his arms, "I really appreciate what you did the other day. I owe you one, guy. That was some quick thinking on your part to give Downly your mother's office number instead of her cell phone. Most people would have caved in under that type of pressure."

John had his nose in a book about Richard Feynman, the Nobel Prize–winning physicist he was writing a paper on for school. He ignored Daniel's comments and turned to his mother. "Feynman taught at Caltech. We're going to be in Pasadena. Maybe I can get a tour of the campus."

Daniel spoke up again, determined to break the ice with the aloof young man. "You're a Feynman buff, huh? Did you know one of his hobbies was cracking safes? When he was working on the Manhattan Project, he used to drive everyone nuts."

John's eyes flashed with interest. "You know about Feynman?"

"Of course," Daniel said. "No one interested in physics could bypass Feynman. He was a giant in the field, as well as a wonderful teacher. Many people can *do* physics. It takes a special knack to teach it."

"I'm interested in nanotechnology," John said, closing his book. "Did you ever read Feynman's talk about swallowing the surgeon? Can you imagine what we could do if we ever get machines small enough to perform surgery inside the human body? Wouldn't that be awesome?"

"Unfortunately," Daniel said, "we've got a long way to go in that respect. Are you thinking of entering that field?"

"What field?"

"The biomedical field."

"I've never really thought about it," John told him. "I know I don't want to build weapons of mass destruction. I'm more interested in the benefits of physics and the sciences in the practical sense."

The ambulance pulled up in front of a small house with wood shingles, the walls covered with climbing ivy. The driver, an undercover police officer named Stockwell, told Carolyn and her children to wait in the car while he made the necessary preparations. They watched through the front window as the officer rang the doorbell, then waited for Isobel to respond. Stockwell instructed her to open the garage door so he could back the ambulance inside.

Once everything was in place, the officer made certain Daniel was strapped onto the gurney. Hank Sawyer had insisted that John wear a uniform to make him appear as if he was also a paramedic. An emergency vehicle such as an ambulance was always manned by two individuals, as one had to drive while the other administered to the patient in the back.

Stockwell motioned for John to help him carry Daniel into the residence. Carolyn and Rebecca were told to remain inside until he gave them the okay to sneak into the house.

They placed Daniel in the guest room on the first floor, near the garage. Since Isobel had worked for the professor and his family for years, she had her own room across the hallway. The two rooms shared a bathroom. The hallway that divided the rooms led past the kitchen, then into the dining room and living room.

Three additional bedrooms were located upstairs. Rebecca found what had to be Lucy's room, while John settled into the professor's office. Paul had informed them that the sofa converted to a bed. John was pleased when he saw a desk with a computer, along with an X-Box, which he assumed the professor had purchased for his daughter.

"I wonder if he's got DSL," the boy said, immediately booting up the computer while his mother leaned in the doorway. "He even has Windows XP."

"What's does that mean?" Carolyn asked, not as up to date on computer technology as her children. They had good equipment at the courthouse, but the county didn't have the funds to update the entire system as soon as something new was released.

"Well," John said, "Paul doesn't have to worry about me messing with his personal files. Windows XP is a Microsoft operating system that allows you to set up your computer so a guest can use it without a problem. I asked you to buy this for me for Christmas last year. You said it was too expensive."

John tapped into the Internet and the images flashed on the screen. "It takes me forever at home with our modem. You have to get DSL, Mom. Everyone has it these days."

Carolyn wondered if she'd made the right decision, isolating them in another city. "If *everyone* has a high-speed Internet connection, they must have a thicker bank account than I do," she told her son. "At least you'll have something to entertain yourself with while you're here."

When Stockwell left, they'd be on their own. Hank had warned her. The captain had refused to deploy manpower to a city where they had no legal jurisdiction. In addition, they needed every officer they could get to conduct their manhunt for Fast Eddie and his accomplice.

Advising the Pasadena police of the situation hadn't appeared prudent. The point was that no one should know where they were hiding, and because of the circumstances, anyone related to law enforcement was still considered suspect. Charles Harrison's death had not been confirmed. Not only that, Carolyn was afraid of Warden Lackner, a man who possessed enough clout to obtain any information he wanted.

After Officer Stockwell had brought in their boxes and the canvas bag full of weapons, he spoke to Carolyn privately in the kitchen. "I should split as soon as possible," he said. "We want it to look like a routine transfer. Picking this particular town wasn't such a bad idea. From what I hear, they transport elderly patients back and forth in ambulances around here all the time. There's a lot of money in this place. The people who live here don't end up in nursing homes. They hire someone to look after them at home. Outside of the students at the university, half the city's population probably consists of professional caretakers."

"That's good, isn't it?" Carolyn asked. "As long as Isobel is the one who comes and goes, we shouldn't attract much attention."

"I'd keep that to a minimum as well," Stockwell told her. "And don't forget to keep the drapes closed. Have the housekeeper shut the garage door and lock it when I pull out. Did Professor Leighton advise his alarm company that you'd be staying here?"

"Yes," Carolyn said, shaking his hand. "Thanks for helping us."

"Glad to be of service," the officer said politely. "Try to stash the firepower somewhere where you can get your hands on it fast. Just make certain if anything goes wrong, Downly or whoever is working with him doesn't get to it first. When I put your stuff in the closet in the master bedroom, I found a drop-down ladder that leads to the attic. It's your decision, but that's where I'd put it. Just keep your service revolver by the bed."

* * *

Fast Eddie was not allowed to call his employer on his cell phone.

Didn't the stupid bitch realize that there were only a limited number of functional public phones left? In a few years, they'd be obsolete. He'd gone to six different locations. In one, the receiver had been missing. Another one, the box that held the coins had been smashed in with an industrial sized wrench. The thieves had left the wrench. Thinking it might come in handy, he'd tossed it in the trunk of the black Nissan he was presently driving. Here and there, he'd been picking up various tools as well as license plates. He'd swiped the plates from towing yards, selecting the least likely car to be claimed. Most of the towing companies subcontracted with the city. Their fees were exorbitant, quickly mounting up to the cost of the vehicle. He now had twelve clean plates.

Because he was wanted by every law enforcement agency in the country, with bulletins listing him as armed and dangerous, Eddie changed the plate on the Nissan every four hours. When driving, he never exceeded the speed limit, never changed lanes without using his turn signals, never followed too closely, and never failed to yield the right of way. Cops couldn't stop every black Nissan they saw, particularly without probable cause. They had to rely on license numbers. Regardless, in a day or so, the Nissan would be history.

As to his appearance, Eddie could no longer pass himself off as a fairly clean-cut teenager, what had easily deceived Carolyn Sullivan's son. One of his personal idols was the serial killer Ted Bundy. But even Bundy had made mistakes. He'd only killed women, and many of the women had similar features. A professional killer, like himself, knew never to establish any kind of pattern. No FBI agent would ever come up with a profile on him.

Admittedly, he'd screwed up with Luisa Cortez. He'd given thought to trying to eliminate her, but it was too great a risk.

Her testimony wasn't important if Sullivan had told him the truth. A DNA match was impossible to beat. He opened his shirt and looked at the faint red marks on his chest. All they needed was a hair follicle, a minuscule piece of flesh, a drop of blood, saliva, or any other kind of bodily fluid.

First, they had to catch him. After the rape, he'd made the mistake of setting up a meeting with a drug dealer at a barbecue joint where he'd bussed tables before Sullivan had stopped keeping tabs on him. Finding out the girl was alive had disturbed him and he'd wanted to get high. Anywhere he'd been before, he now had to avoid.

After the incident at the hospital, Eddie had switched to the look made famous by the white rapper from Detroit who called himself Eminem. He wore a blue knit cap pulled down low over his ears and forehead, a long-sleeved, oversized T-shirt and loose-fitting, low-slung jeans. He scribbled song lyrics with a ballpoint pen on his palm.

At least the lady allowed him to call collect. He dialed the number from memory. She quickly accepted the call by saying "yes" to the voice automated system.

"I haven't located Metroix yet," Eddie told her. "I called the hospital, pretending I was his brother. I chatted up a nurse and she told me the police had taken Metroix somewhere in an ambulance."

Madeline Harrison was sitting in a comfortable beige recliner in her room at Fairview Manor. "They moved Daniel Metroix along with Carolyn Sullivan and her two children to a private residence in Pasadena."

"When did this happen?"

"This morning, while you were sleeping or committing another despicable crime."

"Look, lady," he said, raising his voice, "I wasn't sleeping. My partner and I were parked on the street near Sullivan's house before eight o'clock this morning. For guys like us, that's pretty damn early. They must have left before we got there. After an hour, we had to take off or the cops would have spotted us. Since you seem to know everything, why didn't you tell me in advance that they were moving them to Pasadena?"

"Do you want to get paid?" Madeline Harrison said. "I refuse to tolerate disrespect from a disgusting worm like you. Go to Pasadena and take care of the man who killed my son. Once I have proof that he's dead, you'll receive a quarter of a million dollars in cash."

"What's the address?"

"I don't have the address," she told him. "If I knew the address, I wouldn't need you. I'd kill the man myself."

"Great," Eddie thought, slamming the receiver down on the hook.

Madeline called her husband in Boston. "How did it go with the doctor today?"

"Okay, I guess," Charles Harrison said. "I'm on the list for a liver under the new identity. I would have had a better chance if I'd stayed in L.A."

"You'll be fine," she answered coolly. "Have you spoken to Boyd Chandler?"

"Not yet," he said. "Is Metroix dead?"

"No," she said. "The police moved him to an unknown location in Pasadena. I just spoke to Eddie Downly, instructing him what to do."

"What about the life insurance companies? Are they giving you any flack?"

"Things are progressing smoothly. The attorney I hired, Carl Myers, called me today. The police have no evidence of foul play. He advised the insurance agent that I need the money in order to take care of my expenses here at Fairview."

"You're still going to meet me once this is over?" Charles asked anxiously. "I mean, that was our plan. I don't want to go under the knife alone in a strange city. I might never wake up."

Madeline sighed, pulling the lever to recline her chair. "Oh, Charles," she said, staring at a chip in her fingernail polish, "why is everything so melodramatic with you? People have successful liver transplants every day. The chances of anything happening are minuscule. If you were so afraid of undergoing an operation, you should have stopped drinking years ago."

Harrison erupted, "Maybe if you'd stood beside me as my wife instead of living at the fancy place they call a hospital, I would never have developed a problem with alcohol."

"Your father was an alcoholic, Charles," Madeline said. "I only asked one thing of you over all these years. All I want is that awful man to die. He stole our lives when he killed Tim. Then the prison gave him special treatment. How could you allow that to happen?"

"I can't control what goes on inside prison," Charles shot out. "I kept him behind bars for twenty-three years. Whether you realize it or not, that wasn't easy. I sprang Eddie after Boyd took off. Boyd did a decent job on the motel. He got Metroix inside and hired a demolitions expert to booby-trap the room. How did I know the Sullivan woman was going to be there to rescue him? Boyd had to leave town for a while until things died down. People know him. He used to be an officer at the Ventura PD."

"You have an excuse for everything," Madeline said. "Can you get in touch with Boyd?"

"Yeah, I've got a contact number for him. Are we sticking to the last plan?"

"Yes," she said crisply. "Once Metroix is dead, I'll instruct Eddie where to meet Boyd for the payoff. I want that man dead. He raped an eight-year-old child."

"You want everyone dead," Charles mumbled under his breath. He worshipped his wife, but she'd controlled his life ever since their son's death. She lounged around at the hospital, having people wait on her hand and foot. He was certain she manipulated patients as entertainment. She used to come home for the weekend and make love to him. She'd tried to get him to have Metroix murdered at Chino. He'd made a few attempts. His position made it difficult to work within the prison system. The local jails were easier. Eddie had been brought to him by an LAPD officer he'd known for years, after arresting him in possession of a large quantity of methamphetamine. He had given Eddie the option. He could either work for him or have his probation violated and serve a year in jail. How could they have known he would rape a child? Sure, he'd been busted for a sexual offense. He'd read the original report and wasn't even certain a crime had been committed. Eddie and his victim, the teenage girl who had lived next door, were only two years apart in age. His story that they were girlfriend and boyfriend had seemed plausible. And it had only been fondling. He hadn't had sex with the girl. Once he'd been arrested for the rape of Luisa Cortez, Charles had no choice but to arrange his release. He couldn't take a chance that Eddie would expose him. All he'd done in the motel job was pose as a clerk. Handing the DA a deputy chief might not have gotten him a reduced sentence, but it would have bought him something. Sean Exley, the Ventura DA, was up for reelection. A major story would have served him well.

"I've already talked to Boyd," Charles told her. "He's prepared to take Eddie out. The price is a quarter of a million, the same number we placed on Metroix's head. Do you have that much available in your personal account, or do we need to wait for the insurance to pay off? I paid Boyd, Eddie, and the demolitions man for the motel job. I have less than a hundred left from Tim's trust account. I'll have to pay for the transplant, remember? The hospital bills will be enormous, and that's not including the surgical team. I can't use my health insurance."

"Dead men don't have health insurance," Madeline said.

"Don't worry, Charles, I have more than enough money. Once Eddie kills Metroix, I'll meet Boyd and pay him half the agreed upon sum. Boyd will get the rest as soon as he kills Eddie. After that, it's finished. I'll get on the next plane to Boston."

Chapter 29

Their first evening in Pasadena was uneventful. Isobel made fried chicken, mashed potatoes, and homemade biscuits. Afterward, Rebecca sprawled out on the floor in the living room while she watched one of Lucy's DVDs.

Daniel ate in his room on a tray. Carolyn joined him for dessert, a delicious key lime pie. She was surprised when she saw John poke his head in the doorway. "If you guys are talking, I can come—"

"No," Carolyn said, eager to see John, warming up to the man he'd previously resented. "I was about to go upstairs to make some phone calls."

She quietly closed the door behind her, feeling a rush of exhilaration. Perhaps good things did come when a person least expected them. Climbing the stairs to the master bedroom, she plugged her cell phone into an electrical outlet to keep the battery from going dead and dialed her brother's number.

"My show's tomorrow night," Neil said. "You're going to pick up Mother, right?"

"Don't you ever read the newspaper?" Carolyn asked. "John was kidnapped yesterday. A police officer was shot."

"Why didn't you call me?" Neil said. "Is John all right? Where are you now? I'll come over."

"We're not at the house," Carolyn told him. "And I can't tell you where we are, just that we're safe."

"What do you mean you can't tell me where you are?" Neil exclaimed. "I'm your brother, for Christ's sake. The least you can do is tell me what happened."

Carolyn gave him a rundown of the events of the previous day. "Don't worry," she added. "They'll catch Downly. Be cautious, though, Neil. If he figures out you're my brother, he may come after you to get to me."

"Wow," Neil said, "that really makes my day. What does this guy look like?"

Carolyn described Fast Eddie. "I'll call Mother and tell her you'll pick her up at nine in the morning." Before Neil could complain, she disconnected and called her mother.

"Listen, Mom," she said, "something serious has come up with my job. Neil's going to pick you up at nine in the morning and spend the day with you. I won't be able to come to his show."

"You're not coming to your brother's show!" Marie Sullivan said. "Surely the probation department can't keep you from something this important. Your brother will be shattered. And what will people think?"

Carolyn was thankful her mother didn't subscribe to the Ventura newspapers. When she wasn't socializing with her friends, she spent her time reading science magazines, watching educational programs, and working on chemistry projects in her basement. "You know I wouldn't miss Neil's show unless I had to, Mother. We're going to be in and out, so don't worry if you can't reach us at the house. Until I tell you otherwise, call me on my cell phone. Oh, and don't believe everything you hear."

"What does that mean?"

Carolyn had hoped she could withhold the fact that her grandson had been kidnapped. Her mother was in good shape for her age, but she had a heart condition. She couldn't take a chance that one of her friends would tell her. She explained the situation, insisting that they were safe and that she needn't worry. "I'll call you after Neil's show, okay? He's going to pick you up tomorrow morning at nine."

"This is terrible, Carolyn," Marie Sullivan said. "I want you to quit that job. It's too dangerous. Promise me. You and the children can live with me until you locate some other kind of work. I have three bedrooms and the schools here in Camarillo are excellent."

"I can't quit my job, Mother," Carolyn said. "In a few years, I'll have my law degree. This was an isolated incident. It won't happen again. Call Neil, so you can figure out what to do about tomorrow. I know he's home because I just talked to him."

"When will I see you?"

"I can't say for sure," Carolyn said. "Hopefully, we can get together next weekend. I love you, Mother. Have a nice time at the show tomorrow. I wish I could be with you."

Carolyn went downstairs, surprised that Daniel's door was still closed. She found Isobel in the kitchen engrossed in a paperback novel. "I need to check the schedule for Daniel's medications."

"Don't worry about it," Isobel told her. "I'm right across the hall. I'll take good care of him."

Carolyn took a seat at the table, seeing Isobel closing her book as she prepared to retire for the evening. "What was Paul's wife like?" she asked. "You don't have to answer. I'm just curious."

"Penelope," Isobel said, scowling. "That woman thought she was a queen or something. She never thought about anyone other than herself, even little Lucy. Didn't deserve a good man like Professor Leighton. This is her house, you know."

Carolyn was taken aback. "You mean she still lives here?"

"Not anymore," Isobel said, walking over and returning with a platter of brownies and a stack of napkins. "Help yourself," she said, setting the plate down in the center of the table. "You're a skinny little thing. Need some meat on your bones."

Carolyn patted her stomach. "The meal was delicious," she told her. "Trust me, leave those brownies on the table, and my kids will make them disappear. You said this is Paul's ex-wife's house. I'm beginning to feel extremely uncomfortable, Isobel."

"Penelope hasn't lived here in years," the woman told her, taking a brownie and placing it on a napkin. "She inherited this house from one of her relatives. She grew up here in Pasadena. This was just a place for fancy friends to stay when they came to town. She lives in a mansion in Malibu now with her new husband, ugliest man you ever laid eyes on."

"Why did she marry him, then?"

Isobel ate the brownie, then swept the crumbs off the table with her napkin. "Money, honey," she said. "And the man's a plastic surgeon. Keeps her tuned up like one of those Rolls Royce cars she drives. Last time I dropped Lucy over there, her face was so tight, she couldn't even smile."

"But I don't understand," Carolyn said, bracing her head with her hand. "If she had money, why did she marry an ugly man? Certainly not just to have plastic surgery. She could have paid for that without getting married."

"Old money doesn't last forever," Isobel explained, a wise look in her eyes. "Half of the maids around here have more money in their savings accounts than the old fools who live in these big houses. People born into this kind of life don't work. They consider it beneath them. We call them coupon clippers. Meaning, they live on whatever their mommies and daddies left them. Their houses are usually paid for, so all they got to do is pay the taxes and upkeep."

"Some of these houses are worth millions," Carolyn said. "Why don't they just sell them?"

"The younger ones do, then they go through the money.

These people spend like there's no tomorrow. That's how they were brought up, see." Isobel paused, stretching her arms out on the table. "The older folks never sell. This town is their life. They're born here and they die here. To sell and move away to another city would be like you packing your family off to Siberia."

"Speaking of family," Carolyn said, having grown fond of the woman, "have you ever been married?"

"Oh, I was married," Isobel said, a slight catch in her voice. "My husband ran off after my son was born. Never heard from him again. That was it for me and men."

"Where's your son?"

She blinked several times before answering. "Otis is dead."

"I'm sorry," Carolyn said, remembering Lucy saying something about visiting a cemetery. "What happened, if you don't mind me asking?"

"Murdered," Isobel said, wiping a tear away. "I owned a nice little house in Los Angeles. I had myself a job working for the post office. You work for the government. You know those kind of jobs don't come easy. A man broke into my house in the middle of the night. He shot Otis in the back while he was sleeping. I used to blame myself 'cause I let Otis move the TV set into his room." She glanced down at the paperback book. "My parents didn't have television. Momma said the only way we'd ever get ahead in life was to learn how to read. She was right, you know. That's what helped me pass the civil service exam. Otis was all I had, so I spoiled him. You know what the sad part is?"

Carolyn took a deep breath, but she didn't speak.

"If the TV hadn't been in his room, my son might still be alive. That murdering thug shot my Otis for a lousy TV set. He shot him while he was sleeping to make certain he couldn't identify him."

"How old was Otis when he died?"

"Fourteen," Isobel said. "This coming Sunday would

have been his thirty-third birthday. After Otis was murdered, I quit my job and moved out of the city. I met Professor Leighton in the grocery store. I've been with him for eighteen years. He and Lucy are my family."

Carolyn wondered why Paul had placed Isobel in a situation where her life might be threatened. "Are you afraid? You know, because of what's been going on with us?"

"Listen, sugar," Isobel said, her face shifting into hard lines. "Nothing scares me these days. You couldn't have a better person looking after you. If a pin drops in this house at night, I hear it. Someone comes around looking for trouble, they're going to be mighty sorry."

"Thanks," Carolyn said, walking over and kissing her on the cheek. "Having you here makes me feel everything's going to be all right."

"Of course it is," Isobel told her, standing and stretching her back. "You're with the right people now."

Before she headed upstairs, Carolyn went to the living room to peek in on Rebecca. "Don't stay up too late," she told the girl, walking over and kissing her on the top of the head.

"Why not?" she asked. "We don't have to go to school tomorrow."

"You brought your books, didn't you?" her mother said. "You'll just study the next chapter in every subject."

"You've got to be kidding," the girl protested. "The teachers skip around. I might end up doing a bunch of work for nothing."

"Not for nothing," Carolyn corrected her. "Anything you learn is of value. I know you've got a reading list for extra credit. I'll send Isobel to the library."

* * *

John was seated in a recliner across from Daniel's bed. "I was fooling around on the Internet," he said. "In school, we've been studying the *Columbia* disaster. I never knew Richard Feynman was on the presidential committee that investigated the *Challenger* disaster. That kind of thing really wasn't his speciality. You know, aerospace."

"He was one of the best physicists around," Daniel told him, propping the pillows up behind his head, "even though he didn't have any experience with the space program or the shuttle itself. At the time, he was battling cancer. Are you interested in hearing the story?"

"Sure."

"Feynman was visiting a friend who was a car buff. The guy had a couple of carburetors on the table, and mentioned to Feynman that the carburetors leaked when it got cold. The two men then wondered if cold might have created a problem with the O-rings on the *Challenger.*"

"The temperature dropped too low on the day of the launch," John said. "NASA didn't know the temperature was going to affect the O-rings. Anyway, that's what I read."

"They weren't completely unaware there was a problem with the temperature," Daniel said. "They just didn't know all the facts. This is where physics gave them their answer. Feynman proved his point during a session of the *Challenger* commission using nothing more than a glass of ice water."

"You're kidding," John said, completely enthralled.

"All the generals and bigwigs were in the room, and they were passing around a cross section of the shuttle joint. Rather than just glance at it and pass it on like everyone else, Feynman took out his tools and dismantled it. He removed a piece of rubber from the O-ring, compressed it with clamps, and then dunked it into the glass of ice water. That's why I said this afternoon that he was a colorful character. Most people wouldn't have had the guts to start taking apart a piece of evidence, particularly not in that setting."

"My friends don't understand anything about physics," John said, impressed. "They think I'm some kind of weirdo, that all it amounts to is a bunch of stupid math."

"Physics is everything," Daniel said, adjusting his bed linens. "Of course, that's just one man's opinion."

John stood, tilting his head and smiling. "You're pretty cool," he said. "I can see why my mother went to bat for you. I'd like to talk to you some more while we're here, if you're sure you don't mind. I mean, you're supposed to be getting well. I don't want to bother you."

"You can talk to me anytime you want," Daniel told him. "There weren't many inmates at the prison who were interested in physics."

After the children went to bed, Carolyn jumped on the Internet in Paul's office to see what she could find out about Madeline Harrison. She assumed the couple were married in Ventura, so she checked newspaper articles a few years before their son had been born.

An article announcing their engagement popped up. She stared at the couple's faces. Charles Harrison had been a nice-looking man, but his future wife had been gorgeous. The writeup said that Madeline's parents were both doctors who practiced in Los Angeles, and that she'd graduated from Cornell University with a degree in anthropology. She wondered how a woman with her background had met and married a police officer. Love, she assumed. No wonder she'd seemed so sophisticated.

If Madeline's parents had been doctors, she might very well have money of her own. She'd have to call and tell Hank. It had seemed too far-fetched to believe Mrs. Harrison had hired someone to kill Daniel. They couldn't rule her out as a suspect any longer.

Carolyn became engrossed in the old newspaper articles. As she was scanning through the archives, she caught the name Madeline Milcher and quicky locked onto the article. Milcher had been Madeline's maiden name. The article said the Cornell graduate had been arrested for shoplifting by the Ventura PD. The arresting officer was listed as Charles Harrison, and the charges were later dismissed as unfounded.

She printed out the articles and left the room, calling Hank from the master bedroom. The line was busy, so she left a message on his voice mail for him to call her in the morning.

Chapter 30

Boredom arrived Friday night like a thunderstorm. Rebecca had watched every movie at least twice, John had surfed the net and talked physics until Carolyn and Isobel had to resort to pinning up visiting hours on the door to Daniel's room. Even Isobel, who'd left the house several times to run errands and buy food, informed them that she was leaving Sunday morning to attend church and visit her son's grave.

"Why can't we go out to the movies?" Rebecca argued, tossing pillows around in the living room. "We'll wear disguises or something."

It was six-thirty and Carolyn was seated on the sofa. John was slouched next to her, changing the channels on the television. When Rebecca hit her mother in the face with a pillow, Carolyn exploded. "I won't tolerate this kind of behavior, young lady. I told you when we came here that we'd have to stay in the house until the police apprehended the suspects. We haven't even been here three days."

"No one's trying to hurt us anymore," her daughter said, facing her mother in defiance. "I feel like I'm being held for ransom. I want to go home, be with my friends, go back to my school."

John turned the TV off. "She's right, Mother," he said. "These people have given up, don't you see? They think

Daniel left town. He's always been the problem, not us. I'll never get a scholarship if I don't go back to school by next week. What do you expect us to do? Spend the rest of our lives here?"

Carolyn placed her head in her hands. She'd known there would be problems, but she hadn't expected them to surface this soon. "I talked to Detective Sawyer today," she said wearily. "They may have a lead on Eddie Downly. A man identified him as a suspect in a crime committed in Los Angeles last night."

"See?" John said, tossing his hands in the air. "The guy's moved on."

"Downly robbed a supermarket at gunpoint," his mother said, cutting her eyes to him. "He even fired at a bystander. Luckily he missed." Now that she had their full attention, she continued, "He's just waiting, don't you understand? What reassurance do we have that he won't end up on our doorstep the moment we return to Ventura? This man is a killer. You spent time with him, John. Why don't you tell your sister some of the things Downly told you? Do you want Rebecca to end up in the morgue? Or maybe he won't kill her. There're other things a man like Eddie Downly might want to do to a young girl like your sister, a girl just on the verge of becoming a woman."

John was appalled. "I can't believe you're talking about this kind of stuff in front of Rebecca."

Carolyn's daughter was sitting perfectly still now, her arms limp at her sides.

"She's almost thirteen," Carolyn told him. "She watches the news, movies, TV shows. She knows what goes on in the world." She looked at Rebecca, rubbing her hands on her jeans. "I'm trying to explain why we have to stay here, honey. I would never frighten you for no reason. My responsibility as a parent is to protect you." She got up and walked over to the girl, turning her arm over and revealing a circular scar located near her wrist. "Remember when you were seven? You decided to play with the oven. You didn't just burn your arm. You also caught your hair on fire. You didn't think that was dangerous either."

"I have an idea," John said, realizing his mother's concerns were valid. "Isobel's sick or something. She left a tuna casserole in the refrigerator for us. I can't stand tuna. We can order a pizza and watch a movie. If this Downly guy is robbing places, maybe someone will shoot him or the police will catch him any day now. You said he was in L.A., so we're safe here."

"I've already watched all the movies," Rebecca said, frustrated to the point of tears. "Besides, Mom said we couldn't order a pizza because she doesn't want anyone to know we're living in Professor Leighton's house. Sitting around with nothing to do makes me think more about the bad guys. Last night, I had a terrible nightmare."

"Paul and Lucy may drive over tomorrow evening," Carolyn told her, embracing her. "They'll probably spend the night. Then you'll have some company."

"Why can't you go get us a pizza and some new DVDs?" Rebecca said, pulling away from her mother. "Isobel won't mind if you take her car. There's a Blockbuster and a Domino's pizza place in the shopping center on the corner. I can see the signs from my window. Wear a hat and sunglasses. If someone sees you, they'll just think you're a movie star."

"Why don't we play gin rummy?" Carolyn suggested. "I think I saw a deck of cards somewhere. We'll have a tournament. Whoever wins will get ten dollars."

Rebecca gave it some thought. "That's the same amount as my allowance. You can't buy much with ten dollars. Let's make it twenty."

"Fine with me," her mother said, smiling. "Go get your money. We have to put our money on the table."

"You always win," Rebecca said. "I only have five dollars."

"Then five it will be."

Carolyn searched the house, but failed to find the cards. Thinking Isobel had put them away, she knocked on her door. She should check on her anyway. Hearing the woman moaning, she turned the knob and entered.

Isobel was in bed, holding a large plastic bowl over her stomach. "I'm really sick," she said. "Must be that flu that's going around. It's been coming out both ends for hours. I almost didn't make it to the bathroom last time. Don't come close. I don't want to get you sick."

Carolyn ignored her, walking over and placing her hand on her forehead. "My God," she exclaimed, "you're burning up."

Isobel pushed her aside and raced to the bathroom across the hall. Carolyn took the plastic bowl into the kitchen and washed it out, then carried it back to her room. She wasn't sure how old Isobel was, but she appeared to be in her late fifties. With a younger person, she would feel safe letting them ride it out. She worried that Isobel might become dehydrated, especially since she was running a fever. She waited for her to come out of the bathroom, then helped her back to her bed. "Do you know any of the local doctors?"

"I'll be okay," she said, leaning over the bowl as if she were going to vomit again.

"Where's the thermometer?"

"Look in the cabinet in the bathroom."

Isobel again made a mad dash across the hall. "Call Dr. Clark," she yelled through the closed door. "He's taken care of me for years. His number is on the refrigerator."

Carolyn called the doctor, then punched in the number to her cell phone to page him. Once Isobel was in bed again, she took her temperature and discovered that it was 103 degrees. Heading to the living room, she found John and Rebecca seated at the dining room table playing gin rummy.

"I found the cards under a magazine on the coffee table," John told her. "Rebecca doesn't want to eat the tuna casserole either. I'm starving."

"I'm waiting for Isobel's doctor to call," Carolyn said. "I'll make some peanut butter and jelly sandwiches." Tuna didn't sound too appetizing after cleaning up after Isobel.

Carolyn had the sandwiches, sodas, and a bag of chips on a tray when the doctor returned her call. "Hold on," she said, carrying the phone to Isobel.

After she took the children their food, Carolyn returned to Isobel's room, picking up her cell phone off the end table. She reminded herself to wash her hands and wipe off the phone with disinfectant.

"He's calling me in some prescriptions," Isobel told her, holding a piece of paper. "Something called Lomotil for the diarrhea and Compazine suppositories for the vomiting. I'm supposed to use the second one before the first one."

"Where's the pharmacy?" Carolyn asked, her brows furrowing.

"Honey, I'm sorry," Isobel said. "I forgot you weren't supposed to go out. Don't worry. Maybe this will pass in a few hours."

"Is there a pharmacy that delivers? Forget it," Carolyn added, trying to decide what she should do. What if the killers were watching the house? She would have to disarm the alarm. They could hit the delivery man over the head and start shooting the moment she opened the door. Isobel's Impala was in the garage. With the windows rolled up, there was at least some degree of protection. Since Fast Eddie had already committed another crime in Los Angeles, he could be out of the state by now.

"I'm going out," she told John and Rebecca. "The drugstore is in the same center as Blockbuster. Make a list and I'll rent some new DVDs. Will you be happy then?"

"Yeah," Rebecca said. "Buy some Peanut M&M's too, one of those big bags."

Carolyn went upstairs to get her purse. She removed her Ruger from the nightstand, retrieved one of the extra Rugers

Hank had given her, then went back downstairs to Daniel's room. "Have you ever fired a gun?"

He was sitting in the mauve-colored lounge chair, going over some of his work. Every day, he got stronger. He was now walking at least fifteen minutes every morning and evening, his incision appeared to be healing nicely, and they'd begun cutting back on his pain medication. "No," he said, setting the papers on the end table. "Is something wrong?"

Carolyn explained that she had to go out to pick up Isobel's prescriptions. "I can either leave a gun with you or my son. I'd prefer to leave it with you."

Daniel didn't hesitate. "Leave it with me."

Carolyn pulled the extra Ruger out of her purse and handed it to him. "Using a gun is pretty basic." She extended her right hand and braced it with her left, then showed him how to release the safety. "I'll reset the alarm when I go out. If the situation is serious enough that you have to shoot, there're only two things I want you to think about before you pull the trigger. Make certain it's not Isobel or one of my children. If they say they're the police, don't believe them. I've already spoken to Hank Sawyer today. There's no reason for anyone to show up at this house during the thirty minutes or so I'll be gone." She stopped and reached into her purse again. "Here's an extra ammo clip just in case all hell breaks loose." She removed the magazine presently in the Ruger to show him how it was done, then gave him the spare. "You've got ten rounds in each." Before she left, she added, "Also, if Eddie Downly or anyone else breaks into the house, don't try to wound them. The best place to aim is right between their eyes. With the kind of people we've been dealing with, shoot to kill."

Carolyn didn't wear a hat as her daughter had suggested, nor did she feel it was a good idea to try to disguise herself with sunglasses. A person wearing sunglasses at night would attract attention, precisely what she didn't want.

Once she reached the shopping center, she darted into Blockbuster, leaving Isobel's red Chevy Impala parked in the front. She was searching through the DVD section when she heard a man call out her name.

Carolyn shoved her hand inside her purse, clasped her department-issued Ruger, then dropped to her knees as she prepared to take aim. Before she got the gun out, she saw David Reynolds walking toward her, a broad smile on his handsome face. So he wouldn't know she'd almost shot him, she'd pulled a DVD off the bottom shelf and retrieved the paper with the other titles on it off the floor.

"Hi," she said, standing up. "What are you doing in this neck of the woods?"

"We've missed you in Shoeffel's class," David told her, dressed in a black turtleneck and a brown leather jacket. "I thought you'd dropped out. Judge Shoeffel said there was a death in your family. Was it someone close?"

"An uncle," Carolyn said, closing the flap on her purse. "Don't you live in Thousand Oaks?" Thousand Oaks was a small city not far from Ventura.

"Yeah," David said. "One of my buddies goes to Caltech, though. He invited me to spend the weekend with him. Hey," he added, "if you have some time on your hands, why don't you stop by his house later tonight? A few of us are going to kick back, watch a movie, have a few beers, then soak in the Jacuzzi. These are nice people, Carolyn. You look like you could use a few laughs."

"Thanks for inviting me," she said, acting disappointed. "Maybe another time."

He ran his fingers through his long hair. "That was insensitive of me," he said. "You just lost a loved one. Did your uncle live here in Pasadena?"

"Yes," Carolyn said. "I've been staying with the family."

"Was he a young man? Did he have children?"

"No," she said, "he was in his sixties. No children. Heavy smoker, you know. I've been trying to help my aunt sort some things out. My kids are getting restless, so we're going to head for home." She didn't want to reveal too much, even to a classmate from law school. People didn't mean any harm, but everyone talked. One thing led to another. "I'll see you in class next week," she said. "Hopefully, I can catch up."

She saw David looking at the large stack of DVDs in her hands. "Because we're leaving," she lied, "my aunt asked me to pick up some movies. She won't even leave the house yet."

"Taking her husband's death pretty hard, huh?" David said, reaching out. "Here, let me carry those for you."

"Thanks," Carolyn told him, "but there's a few more movies on the list. Nice seeing you. Have a good time with your friends."

At least if she'd had to run into someone, they'd turned out to be harmless. To be extra cautious, Carolyn lingered in the aisles until she saw David exit out the front of the store.

"We found her," the man said, leaping into the passenger seat of a black Nissan parked near the Ralph's supermarket on the opposite end of the strip center. "It's a good thing we changed our minds about hitting the market. I'm pretty sure she's packing." He watched as Carolyn exited Blockbuster, then entered the Savon drugstore next door. "I knew she was lying about driving back to Ventura tonight."

"Why?"

"Easy," he said, pleased with himself. "If she was going home like she told me, why was she renting a bunch of videos and X-Box games? Crank the ignition, but don't go anywhere until we get a fix on what kind of car she's driving."

"Did she say why she was here?" Eddie Downly asked, crouched low in the seat.

"An uncle died," he told him. "An uncle who didn't have any children."

"Think it's true?"

"I know it's not true," his partner said, firing up a cigarette. "Why would her uncle's widow want a bunch of X-Box games?" He inhaled deeply, then flicked his ashes out the window. "We take out Metroix, we get paid. We're not doing this on spec, I hope. There's kids involved."

"There she goes," Fast Eddie said, flipping off the headlights on the Nissan, then waiting until Carolyn backed the red Chevy out of the parking lot and turned down Lake Street heading toward Paul Leighton's house. Eddie made certain to keep at least one vehicle between him and the Impala, in case Carolyn looked at her rearview mirror and realized she was being followed. There weren't many cars on the road, so keeping track of her until she pulled into the garage at Leighton's wasn't a problem.

Parking at the end of the street under a large tree, Eddie turned to his partner. "Get me a beer, Percy," he said. "We're not going in until everyone's asleep. Then we'll case the house first, try to see if there's a burglar alarm or a Doberman in the backyard. I hate dogs almost as much as I hate cops."

"Do we have to take her out too?" Percy asked, reaching into the backseat and pulling two Budweisers out of a paper sack. "The contract was only on Metroix. I kinda like Carolyn. She's a sexy chick. Do you know she has a fifteen-year-old son?"

"You're the biggest asshole who ever walked the face of the earth," Eddie told him, thinking all the pretty boys like Percy were idiots. "Of course, I know about her son. I used him as a decoy at the hospital to get to Metroix. How long is your attention span? Thirty seconds. I can't believe you managed to pass yourself off as a law student. You must be better at acting than you are at thinking."

"Fuck," Percy Mills said, crushing the beer can in his hand. "It just slipped my mind for a minute, okay? Give me some credit. I spotted her, didn't I? You were prepared to go back to robbing supermarkets and breaking into houses."

They both fell silent. Percy pulled out two more beers, taking one for himself and handing the other to Eddie. "I wish we could have scored some coke or meth," he said. "I've never killed anyone when I'm sober."

"You've never killed anyone period," Eddie said, laughing at him. "You really got off pretending you were David Reynolds, didn't you? Even when you hired someone to do your homework for you, you were about to bomb out."

Percy didn't answer, perspiring and jittery as he prepared himself for the crime they were about to commit.

"Did you really think you were going to become a lawyer?" Eddie pulled out his 9mm Kurtz, handing his partner a .357 Magnum. The Kurtz had been legally purchased by one of Downly's friends, and thus far had never been used in the commission of a crime. Personally Eddie favored the .357, as it was the same make of gun he'd used the first time he'd ever killed someone. Although 9mm's were more popular these days, Eddie had picked up the .357 during a residential burglary. Since the owner of the .357 had reported its theft to the PD, Eddie wanted to make certain Percy would take the heat if something went wrong.

"We'll kill anyone in that house who sees our face, got it?" Eddie said, a maniacal look in his eyes. "Kids, old ladies, I don't give a shit. We've got a quarter of a mil coming when we finish this job."

"I don't know if I can kill a kid," Percy said, guzzling down his beer. "I've only served time in juvenile hall. Even if they nail us for the robberies, I'll get out eventually."

Eddie turned sideways in the seat. "When we go inside

that house," he said, "I want to make damn sure you shoot anyone I tell you to shoot, understand? If you have any doubts, just think about what the inmates are going to do to a pretty boy like you inside the joint. You've never been in the big house. They'll rip your insides out. Your intestines will be hanging out of your asshole."

Chapter 31

At ten-fifteen, Carolyn became annoyed by the constant pinging sound generated by the X-Box game John was playing upstairs, and went into the kitchen to make a cup of hot tea. She felt chilled, and wondered if she was about to come down with the flu. Rebecca was watching the movie *Clueless* in the living room as she tossed Peanut M&Ms into her mouth.

The beeper on the microwave went off at the same time Carolyn's cell phone rang. "We finally caught a break," Hank said. "Liam Armstrong cracked."

Carolyn dropped down in a chair at the kitchen table. "So Armstrong pushed Tim Harrison in front of the car?"

"He claims it was Nolan Houston," Hank told her, his voice hoarse from an afternoon of interrogation. "Just like your man said, they jumped him in the alley. They'd seen Metroix around town before and knew he had a mental problem. When his backpack broke and his books fell out, Houston started kicking them, making a game of it. The two other boys joined in, and things got nasty. Harrison wasn't a lightweight in the incident, at least not until he realized what they'd done." The detective paused and cleared his throat. "I'm sorry," he said. "It's been a long day. Armstrong confessed when we showed up at his house with a search warrant at ten o'clock this morning. We had to wait hours for his attorney."

"Do you want to call me back later?"

"No," Hank said, sighing. "Once I get something to eat, I'm going to crash for the night. According to Armstrong, Harrison held Metroix down while Houston urinated in his face. All three of them beat him. When the guy started bleeding, Harrison went ballistic, afraid they were going to get busted. The chief was tough on him. The kid was a top-notch player. The old man thought he had a chance to play pro ball."

Carolyn removed her cup from the microwave, then opened the mahogany box of assorted tea bags sitting on the counter. She thumbed through it until she found one that didn't have caffeine, dropped it in her cup, and sat back down at the table. "Is this when they started slugging each other?"

"Armstrong claims Houston tried to butt him with his head. He stepped aside, Harrison took the hit and was propelled into the path of the oncoming car."

"Where was Daniel when Harrison got killed?" Carolyn asked, wanting to make certain the stories all meshed. Nolan Houston would counter by blaming it on Armstrong. The only way the case would hold up in court was for as many individuals as possible to agree as to what happened.

"Armstrong doesn't remember. He thinks he was hiding over by the trash can," Hank told her. "Houston had fumbled the ball during practice that day. The coach had reamed him out in front of the other players. The way it sounds, Houston went out that night looking for trouble."

"Thank God," Carolyn exclaimed, thinking the end of their nightmare might finally be in sight. "What caused Liam Armstrong to confess? How did his tests turn out? Did the cancer come back?"

"False alarm," Hank told her. "Armstrong seems like a

decent guy, other than the fact that he let Metroix rot in prison for twenty-three years to save his own neck. When we showed up at the house, he knew it was time to throw in the towel. He has a wife and three kids. He wanted to save his family the embarrassment of a trial."

Carolyn took a sip of her tea. "What about Chief Harrison?"

"As far as Armstrong knows," the detective went on, "Harrison is dead. He claims he hasn't talked to the man since Metroix's conviction. Houston, however, called him as soon as word got back to him that you were asking questions. Then when he found out Metroix had been paroled, he panicked."

Carolyn couldn't wait to tell Daniel. "Then Houston must have hired Fast Eddie to kill Metroix."

"Armstrong doesn't know," Hank stated. "He knows Houston is loaded, that those golf stores rake in a fortune. Armstrong earns a comfortable living selling commercial real estate, but he isn't rolling in money like his former football buddy."

"Did they arrest him?"

"His attorney is trying to cut a deal with the DA. No jail time would be a disgrace, if you ask me, even if the guy was only a witness who failed to come forward, which isn't the case. But this is an old crime. We have his statement. Without some type of solid evidence, which I'm not certain we can produce, the DA could refuse to prosecute. They're certain Houston is going to claim Armstrong was responsible."

"Did you call Arline Shoeffel?"

"Not yet," Hank said. "As soon as the DA makes a decision, we can arrest Houston. Even then, there's no telling what charges they may file. And at this point, we're only dealing with the original crime. I've already argued with Thomas. They won't even consider an attempted murder for hire charge with what we have now."

Carolyn stood and started pacing. "That's bullshit," she said.

"It's all right there. Just because the evidence is circumstantial doesn't mean it won't pass muster with a jury. I've seen people convicted on far less. No matter how high they set the bail, Houston has the funds to post it. This man has made our lives a living hell. I'll call Arline myself."

"Calm down," the detective said. "You're overstepping your boundaries. The solution is obvious. We have to pick up either Downly or his partner. Since we know there's two of them, we'll play one against the other. Someone needs to go on record as to whether or not Houston put out a contract on Metroix. We may be dealing with two separate crimes here. Think about it."

"I can't believe it," Carolyn told him. "Are you trying to say that Harrison or someone else hired these men to kill Daniel, that they went after me only because I got in the way? Houston's motive has been firmly established. I was almost killed in an explosion. My son was kidnapped. A police officer was shot. Nolan Houston should be brought in immediately and held without bail."

"I know you're attending law school," Hank said. "I also know you're wasting your time calling Judge Shoeffel. The more serious the crime, the more evidence is required to obtain a conviction. You take Houston to trial and lose, the game is over. Wait it out and he'll fumble the ball again just like he did on the football field. Don't you understand what I'm trying to tell you? This man's prominence is another factor."

"I see," Carolyn said, fuming. "Because Nolan Houston's got money, we have to tap-dance around him. In the meantime, I have to hold my breath that these men he hired don't finish the job. Why don't you listen to me for a change, Hank?"

"If the DA jumps the gun on this, Houston will walk," he said, raising his voice. "Want to know who's representing Armstrong? Clarence Walters, only the most prominent criminal attorney in Los Angeles."

"We may never catch Downly and his partner," she said. "You've told me that a dozen times. Houston has no reason to cancel the contract. Both Daniel and I are material witnesses as to the attempted murder for hire. The only reason he'd have to call off his dogs is if we turn this over to the media and put him in the spotlight."

"I'm exhausted," Hank said. "I'll call you in the morning."

"Fine," Carolyn said, clicking the off button on the phone.

The two men were crouched on the left side of the garage. "What if the garage is alarmed?"

"Nobody alarms their garage," Fast Eddie told him, his eyes scanning the street. "Are you sure there wasn't a dog in the backyard?"

"Yeah," Percy said. "Looks like there's only a few lights on. One upstairs and another one in what looks like the downstairs bathroom. I'm almost certain they're asleep."

"*Almost* doesn't cut it," Eddie told him. "Stay where you are. If you hear or see any movement inside the house, come and get me."

He circled to the front and tried to open the garage door. Damn, he thought. The house was so old, he hadn't expected them to have an automatic garage door opener. Real security freaks even had bolts, making it almost impossible to get in. That's one of the reasons he'd selected the last house he'd used. Damn house was a piece of junk, but whoever had lived there had wanted to make certain no one got inside.

He tapped along the wood, then decided to use his fingers. The door was divided into four-by-four-foot panels. Finding a ragged edge, he pulled his screwdriver out of his back pocket. The house must be worth some bucks, he thought, probably because of the land. The structure itself wasn't in good shape. The owner must have forgotten to have it inspected for termites. Either that, or he'd fallen for a con. Eddie had worked for an exterminating company the year before. Some of them had their men walk around with a spray can filled with water. They even charged more by telling the customers that the chemicals they used were odor free. It was a dynamite job for a burglar. He'd hit every house he'd serviced. He was digging into the rotting wood when Percy stepped up beside him.

"What's wrong?"

"Nothing," Percy said. "Why is it taking so long?"

"I should shoot you," Eddie whispered. "I'm trying to get in, idiot. If they have an alarm, we have to disable it. What did you think I was doing? You're supposed to be covering me. Get back where you belong."

He couldn't afford to make any noise, so it took Eddie almost an hour to dig out a hole big enough for him to crawl through. Patience and persistence, he thought, using another tool to pick the lock on a gray metal utility box. Once he had it open, he used a penlight to examine what was inside. The box contained the controls to the alarm as well as the phone lines. Most security systems were set up to automatically seize the phone line and dial the alarm company when activated. Using his pliers, he cut through the wires. He tried to find the breaker box to turn off the electricity. He decided it must be inside the house somewhere, more than likely in a closet or utility room on the ground floor. He was ready to fetch Percy and enter the residence when he heard someone groaning inside. A few minutes later, he heard what he thought was the toilet flush. He turned the knob on the door leading into the house. Finding it locked, he placed his head flush against the door. The footsteps were getting louder. That meant someone was walking toward him. He quickly slithered back through the opening in the garage door.

Carolyn was disappointed. What she'd thought had been the news they'd been waiting to hear was only a beginning.

Nolan Houston was a powerful man, as Hank had pointed out. She remembered Liam Anderson as a teenage boy. After he had tried to force her to have sex with him, he'd ended up whimpering like a baby. From what she'd seen the other day, she was worried he couldn't stand up to Houston. And if Armstrong had a prominent attorney, reason told her Houston would hire the best criminal defense team in the country. She decided to wait and see what happened over the next few days.

It was almost eleven and both the children were already in their rooms with their doors closed. Carolyn stripped off her clothes and ran a hot bath. While she was soaking, she heard a noise outside her window. Hoping the wind had blown over a trash can, she got out of the tub and threw on her robe. Walking over to the window, she peered out between a crack in the blinds.

Not seeing anything amiss in the yard, Carolyn turned around when a gunshot blasted through the window.

Shards of glass flew through the air. She prostrated herself on the floor when another shot rang out. Adrenaline coursed through her body.

Carolyn frantically crawled over to the nightstand to retrieve her gun before she remembered that she'd left her purse in the kitchen. She heard noises downstairs on the first floor—the sound of glass breaking.

They were inside the house!

Rushing to the closet, she yanked down the ladder leading to the attic, scampered up, found the strap on the duffel bag and hurled it onto the floor. Once she'd climbed back down, she reached inside the bag, pulling out two additional 9 millimeters similar to the one she'd given Metroix. Both guns were called a C-9 Comp; however, one was outfitted with a pressure-pad-activated red laser that would allow shots to be placed on target without having the sights. The other had what was referred to as a white light flashlight instead of a red laser, which enabled the shooter to positively identify the object or person they were shooting.

Shoving the gun with the white light feature in the left pocket of her robe, she placed the one with the red laser in her right. Disengaging the safeties on both firearms, she heard Rebecca screaming from the other room. She picked up the AK-47 assault rifle, resting it on her shoulder as she ran toward the children's bedrooms.

The light in the bathroom went off. She checked the switch in the hallway. The killers had turned off the electricity. She met John in the hallway. "Stay with Rebecca," she whispered, placing the 9mm in his hand. "The gun is ready to fire. It has a flashlight device on it so you can see who you're shooting. Get in the closet. Crack the door so you can see. Don't come out until I tell you it's safe. Whatever you do, don't point the gun at your sister."

John flung the door to his sister's room open, set the gun down on the dresser for fear it would go off, then swept Rebecca up in his arms and deposited her in the closet. Returning for the gun, he reentered the closet, making his sister curl up in the corner. He then positioned himself on the floor, his hands shaking as he aimed the gun through a small opening in the closet door.

"Call the cops," John said, panting.

"No time," his mother told him. "Don't move until I give you the okay. I have to go downstairs. If you have to fire the gun, make sure you know who it is you're shooting."

Carolyn's body was soaked in perspiration. She'd now placed a loaded gun in the hands of a schizophrenic as well as a teenager. She was terrified that everyone would start shooting at once. Flattening herself against the wall, she moved slowly toward the stairway. Several more shots rang out on the first floor. Rebecca began crying again, then suddenly stopped. John must have shut her up. She was terrified that Daniel and Isobel had been killed. She had to remain calm. If she panicked, they would massacre her children.

With the drapes closed, the house was a dungeon of darkness. She wished she'd taken the other gun with the flashlight instead of giving it to John. The house was too quiet. The killers were listening, trying to determine where their victims were hiding.

Carolyn felt the parquet floor under her feet. Every step she took would lead them to her. Should she remain where she was? They couldn't get up the stairs without her seeing them. She would kill them before they reached the children.

The minutes ticked off inside her head. She wiped the sweat off her face with the edge of her robe. What if they grew tired of waiting and began firing through the ceiling? Depending on what type of weapons they had, they might hit Rebecca or John.

Carolyn depressed the pad on the laser, pointing it down the hallway. The beam of red light wasn't strong enough to illuminate more than a small round circle. She had to take action. She had to know who was alive or dead. "Daniel," she shouted.

"I shot a man," he answered, his voice echoing throughout the house. "I can't find Isobel."

"Is the man dead?"

"I'm not certain."

"Shoot him again."

A few moments later, Daniel called out to her. "He's not breathing."

"Where's Isobel?"

"Not in her room."

Carolyn realized the surviving intruder wouldn't go after Daniel as he knew he was armed. She bent down and placed the assault rifle on the floor. The gun felt cumbersome and was designed to be used in tactical situations at greater distances. She needed to be more agile, since it appeared that Isobel had either somehow escaped, was dead in another part of the house, or was being held as a hostage. Bringing the

Pasadena police in without explicit knowledge of what they were walking into could end up in disaster.

Before descending the stairs, Carolyn tried to determine the location of the other intruder. Since Daniel had shot his partner, she assumed his was the first room they had entered. Daniel must have checked Isobel's room already, then returned to the guest room to make certain the man he'd shot was dead. She assumed he'd remained there. That meant the surviving suspect was either in the kitchen, the bathroom, or the living room. Logic told her he was lying in wait for her in the living room, the only place where he could see her coming down the stairs.

Carolyn felt as if she were teetering on the edge of a twenty-story building. Descending the stairs would be suicide. She dropped to the ground and crept to the opposite side of the stairway. She couldn't afford to communicate with Daniel again. Her voice would guide them to her.

They'd reached a standoff.

The killer couldn't come up the stairs for the same reason Carolyn could not go down them. As long as she remained where she was, she held the advantage. He wouldn't wait forever. Any second, she expected him to start firing through the ceiling.

She had two choices.

The window in Paul's office had an aluminum awning that slanted downward toward the yard. If she crawled out the window, she could slide down the awning and enter through the rear of the house, taking the suspect by surprise. All she would have to worry about with this plan was that Daniel might panic and shoot her when she came through the back door. He had her gun, and the probation department did not supply their officers with weapons with lasers and flashlights.

Her only option was to go down the stairs.

She remembered that the upstairs hall had a narrow carpet called a runner. Feeling around with her toes, she found the edge. Squatting down, she quietly grabbed the end of it, rolled it into a ball, then unfurled it down the stairs. She waited, fully expecting to hear gunfire. When nothing happened, she positioned herself on her stomach, the gun in her outstretched hands.

Carolyn inched her way down the wooden staircase, the carpet underneath her buffering the sound. She removed her finger from the pad that activated the laser. Darkness was now her best defense.

Time seemed suspended. Reaching the bottom of the stairs, she crawled across the floor, then flattened herself on the wall outside the living room. Only a few feet away, she heard the sound of muffled breathing. She began to perspire even more profusely. She couldn't understand why the suspect didn't announce that he had a hostage, unless he was using poor Isobel as a human shield to deflect bullets. She prayed for God to help her, making the sign of the cross over her chest. She wasn't a marksman, and her familiarity with firearms was limited.

Carolyn couldn't wait any longer. For all she knew, there could have been more than two intruders. Isobel might already be dead and the men were positioned on opposite sides of the room. If this was the case, she wouldn't stand a chance. She couldn't shoot at two targets simultaneously.

Her decision made, she placed one foot forward for balance. When nothing happened, she depressed the pad on the laser and pointed it toward the living room. She was about to open fire when a pinpoint of red light illuminated a portion of Isobel's face. Moving the gun around, she saw the housekeeper sitting on top of a body, her nightclothes soaked in blood.

Isobel raised her hands over her head and cried out, "Sweet Jesus, don't shoot me!"

Sweat had dripped down into Carolyn's eyes. She blinked several times, trying to focus. "Are you injured?"

"I'm alive," the woman answered. "I'm not so certain about this guy. I think I killed him."

Isobel was close to the front of the house. Carolyn moved the gun from side to side, searching for another possible intruder. Ninety percent sure no one else was in the room, she rushed over and yanked the drapes open. The light from the street allowed her to see a person with long hair lying face-down on the floor. When she saw the fancy silver tennis shoes, she knew she was looking at David Reynolds. She dropped down beside him and put her finger on his neck to check for a pulse.

"He's got a heartbeat," Carolyn said. "Did you shoot him? Where's the gun?"

Isobel lifted her right arm, displaying a bloody butcher knife. "I stabbed the sucker," she said. "Since they killed my Otis, I always sleep with a knife under the mattress. The bastard got me around the neck and dragged me in here. He didn't see the knife in my hand."

"Stay here," Carolyn told her, seeing a gun a few feet away on the floor. "I'm going to call the police and an ambulance."

Isobel jerked her head around. "I'm not going to no hospital. Nothing wrong with me."

"Maybe not," she said, "but the man you stabbed needs medical treatment."

"I've been sick as a dog all day," Isobel said. "Man come in my room in the middle of the night wanting to kill me deserves to be stabbed. I should sit on this rotten piece of meat until he bleeds to death."

Carolyn's stomach was still churning. She bent over, fearful she was going to throw up. When the nausea subsided, she straightened up. "Why didn't you let us know you were alive, Isobel?"

"I'm not stupid," the woman told her. "Could have been five murdering thugs in here for all I know. I got mine, then decided if the others wanted to kill me, they'd have to find me."

"You did good," Carolyn told her, still reeling from the fact that her handsome classmate from law school was a hired killer. "I need to check on the others. Just sit tight until the ambulance gets here."

Carolyn raced to the foot of the stairs. "John, Rebecca, it's safe now. Are you both okay?"

"Yeah," John called down.

"We're going to call the police. Just stay in your room until I come and get you."

Carolyn located the switch box and threw the breaker, turning the electricity back on. Entering the guest room, she saw Fast Eddie on the floor at the foot of the bed, a large brackish hole in his forehead and a pool of blood beneath him. "Did you call the police yet?" she asked Daniel, confirming that Downly was dead. "We're going to need an ambulance for the man in the living room. Isobel stabbed him. Tell them it's a stomach wound. I don't think it's fatal, but he's lost a lot of blood."

"I couldn't find the phone in the dark," Daniel explained, the gun still dangling from his hand. "Do you think our problems are over now?"

"Yes, I do," Carolyn said. "I'll bring you the phone so you can make the calls. I need to go upstairs and take care of my children."

Finding her cell phone on the kitchen table where she'd left it, she returned and handed it to Daniel.

"I've never called the police before," he said. "They aren't going to put me in jail again, are they?"

"No," Carolyn told him. "Liam Armstrong confessed today. You're going to be cleared, Daniel."

When she passed through the living room on her way upstairs, Isobel was still perched on top of David Reynolds, her elbows braced on her knees. "Told you everything would be fine, didn't I? When you're with the right people, the devil may set the boat to rocking, but Jesus won't never let you sink."

Chapter 32

At two o'clock Monday afternoon, Carolyn, Daniel, Isobel, John, and Rebecca were seated at the long conference table at the Ventura Police Department. Brad Preston, Hank Sawyer, District Attorney Kevin Thomas, Captain Gary Holmes, and several other investigators were also present.

"Well," Hank said, his eyes drifting from one person to the other, "as you all know by now, there's no doubt whatsoever that Eddie Downly was killed in an act of self-defense. If Daniel hadn't shot him, the state would have eventually executed him." He directed his next statement to Daniel. "I spoke to Luisa Cortez's parents this morning and they wanted me to personally thank you."

"How's the little girl?" Daniel asked timidly. Although he was relieved that things had turned out the way they had, all the attention he'd been receiving was making him nervous. He'd already given interviews to two newspaper reporters. *People* magazine had approached him, along with several science and technical periodicals.

"She's doing fine, considering what she's been through," Hank told him. "Knowing Downly isn't around anymore should help in her recovery." He turned to address the rest of the room again. "Unfortunately, we have a number of significant problems. Percy Mills, AKA David Reynolds, will recover from the stab wound. He's not going anywhere, though, outside of the jail."

Carolyn presented the question everyone wanted answered: "Who hired Eddie Downly?"

"Mills doesn't know," the detective said. "He admitted that Fast Eddie told him he'd been hired to kill Daniel Metroix. Problem is, Mills claims he has no idea who hired him. Downly was shrewd. He knew better than to trust a guy like Percy Mills. From the way things went down at Professor Leighton's house, Mills was a robber, not a killer." The detective took a deep breath, then slowly exhaled. Everyone involved was reaching the point of exhaustion. "Mills didn't have the cunning or the balls to pull off a homicide."

Isobel scowled in disgust. "At least that evil man who raped that little girl is dead. We don't have to worry that he'll hurt any more children."

"Wait," Carolyn said, holding up a palm to silence her. "Mills was armed. Why didn't he shoot Isobel instead of taking her into the living room?"

"Who knows?" the detective said, shrugging. "By then, Downly was dead. Mills probably thought the police had the house surrounded, so he decided to take Isobel as a hostage."

"Why did he enroll in law school under an assumed name?"

"To get close to you," Hank told Carolyn. "Mills stole the records from a UCLA law student who'd died of leukemia. Because the real David Reynolds was an outstanding student, Ventura accepted the transfer."

"But that doesn't make sense," Carolyn said, perplexed. "He transferred in several weeks before I was even assigned to supervise Daniel."

"Yeah, but Metroix had already been paroled."

Daniel confirmed the detective's statement. "I got out of prison on February twenty-fifth. I didn't come straight to Ventura. I spent a couple of weeks in Los Angeles."

"When you came to Ventura," Kevin Thomas interjected, "you checked into the Seagull Motel. The man on the bus told you it was the best place to stay. Isn't that what you told Detective Sawyer?"

"Yes," Daniel said, nodding.

Hank slid a photograph across the table. "Does this look like the man on the bus?"

"That's him," Daniel said, staring at the image. "I'm almost certain. He even had the same mole on his left cheek. He was older than he is in this picture, though."

"Do we have an ID on this person?" Carolyn asked, peering over Daniel's shoulder.

"He's a former police officer named Boyd Chandler," Captain Holmes said, a gray-haired man in his mid-fifties. "Harrison's housekeeper identified him as well. He and another man we suspect was Pete Cordova, also a former officer and known associate of Chandler's, made frequent visits to Charles Harrison's residence. Their most recent visit was after Metroix had been released and already assigned as your parolee. The bail bondsman also identified Chandler as the man who gave him the three grand."

"This means Harrison contracted the hit," Carolyn surmised. "Have we confirmed his death yet?"

Hank pulled out a toothpick. "No," he said. "Harrison hasn't surfaced anywhere. We managed to track down a brokerage account. He had over two hundred thousand stashed under his son's name. The money's gone. He moved it a week before his alleged death. Took payment in cash and cashier's checks. We've notified the banks and given them the numbers on the checks. These things are hard to track down. To a bank, a cashier's check is almost the same as cash." He thought a few moments, then added, "And don't forget, Harrison was a deputy chief. With those credentials, people tend not to ask questions."

"Who gets the money from the sale of his house?" Carolyn

asked. "And is the insurance company going to pay the million dollars to Madeline Harrison? Why would he leave the money to her? From what she said, she hadn't seen her husband in years."

"No other heirs," Hank tossed out. "The insurance company has to settle the claim. They can't hold back unless there's definitive proof of a hoax, which we don't have right now. Mrs. Harrison's attorney has already contacted them. Guess she needs the money to pay the bills at Fairview. The house hasn't sold yet, but the wife gets that money as well."

Carolyn gave them a rundown of the information she'd learned in reference to Madeline Harrison's past. Hank didn't believe it had much bearing on the case. All it did was explain why Harrison's widow had possessed the funds to remain in an expensive facility such as Fairview for such an extended period of time. Charles Harrison would never have been able to amass the two hundred grand in his brokerage account if he'd been saddled with his wife's hospital expenses.

"Great," Carolyn said facetiously. "For all we know, Harrison is alive and may try to kill Daniel again."

"The man had a serious liver condition," Hank said. "If he's not already dead, he could die any day. Eddie Downly is dead, Percy Mills will go to prison for attempted murder, robbery, burglary, and God knows how many other outstanding cases that might surface. I wouldn't spend much time worrying about Charles Harrison."

Carolyn asked John and Rebecca to step out of the room, handing them some bills and telling them to get sodas from the vending machine down the hall.

"Harrison needs a liver," she said, as soon as the children had left the room. "Once he gets one, he could live as long as anyone else. We know he has enough money to pay for the operation. We have to find him."

"Consider him dead," Hank said, not knowing what else to tell her.

"Not without proof," Carolyn said, shaking her head. "And you have no proof. By arranging his own cremation, Harrison made certain of that."

Daniel had a dismal look on his face. "I thought everything was over."

"You're being an alarmist," Captain Holmes said. "More than likely, Charles Harrison is dead. A person staging their own death is highly unusual. Not only that, Liam Armstrong has all but cleared Metroix. Once Harrison becomes aware that Metroix didn't cause his son's death, why would he want to harm him? His anger should be redirected toward the men responsible, Nolan Houston and Liam Armstrong."

"What if Harrison refuses to believe they're guilty," Carolyn said. "And the trial could take months, even years. Even if they are convicted, you know Armstrong and Houston will file an appeal. In the meantime, Daniel's on the verge of becoming a public figure. His notoriety may infuriate Harrison enough to hire another person to kill him."

"Let me ask you something," Daniel said, the events of that night playing over in his mind. "Did Liam Armstrong say Houston pushed Tim in front of the car?"

"Sure did," Hank said. "We talked to Houston and his two attorneys this morning. Houston is using the exact tactic we thought he would. He swears Liam Armstrong pushed Tim Harrison to his death, then coerced him into withholding the truth from the authorities."

"He's right," Daniel said, staring at the detective.

A tense silence fell over the room.

"I'm not sure I understood you," Hank said, shocked at what he was hearing. "Why don't you tell us what you believe really happened?"

Daniel became animated, gesturing with his hands. "Most of what you said is true. At least, how everything went down.

All you have to do is reverse a few things. I remember Liam Armstrong talking to the man who ran over Tim, claiming I had attacked them and shoved the boy in front of his car. He tried to tell the man that I had a knife, which was also a lie." He face blanched. "I did own a knife," he admitted. "I didn't have it on me that night, though. I swear, I never intended to hurt anyone with it. I was going to kill myself. I tried but I didn't have the guts to do it."

Carolyn reached over and placed her hand on top of Daniel's. Even before he'd been falsely accused, he'd been so severely tormented, he'd wanted to take his own life. Not only had he survived twenty-three years in prison, but he'd attained some remarkable accomplishments. The attorney general's office had discovered that Warden Lackner had patented a number of Daniel's inventions under his brother-in-law's name. The multiscreen monitoring and recording system had generated millions. The best news was that the bulk of the money was recoverable. Lackner had deposited the earnings in a brokerage account, pocketing only a few hundred thousand per year, most of it interest or gains from investments. The AG was preparing to prosecute him as well as his brother-in-law. The warden had already been relieved of his duties at the prison. In addition, several major research and development companies were interested in recruiting Daniel, and Mitsubishi Corporation had offered him a six-figure sum as an enticement. Whether he liked it or not, Daniel Metroix was on the road to becoming rich and famous.

"Go on," Hank said. "We'd like to know what you remember about Tim Harrison's death."

"Nolan didn't say much," Daniel continued. "Liam did all the talking. I remember Liam saying several times, 'Isn't that right, Nolan?' You know, the way a person talks when they're trying to get another person to agree with them."

All eyes were on him now.

Daniel waited a few more moments before speaking again, staring down at the table. "I wasn't certain if I was guilty or innocent during the time I was in prison. I didn't give it a lot of thought, to be honest. When a jury says you did something terrible, a person with an illness like mine tends to believe it." He paused and looked up. "Since we've gone over this so many times, things are starting to come back to me."

"How can you be sure it was Liam Armstrong instead of Houston?" Kevin Thomas said, taking a drink of water as his case took another unexpected turn.

"Liam's the white guy, right?"

"Yes," Thomas said.

"Well, it was the white guy who pushed Tim in front of the car."

"Humph," Isobel said, crossing her arms over her chest. "That's one for the record."

"The boys were fighting," Daniel said, speaking softly. "Tim was angry because he knew they were going to get in trouble. Nolan told him to shut up, then started hitting him. Liam was several feet away. He started running toward Nolan, but Nolan made this funny move, almost like a dance step. I guess football players learn to do that type of thing. Instead of slamming into Nolan, Liam hit Tim. That's when Tim went flying through the air and the car hit him."

Hank leaned forward. "Are you certain?" he asked. "When you testify, they'll bring up the fact that you were psychotic that night. And if you were, how do we know what you're telling us is the truth?"

Daniel gave them an innocent look. "Because it is," he said, rubbing the side of his face. "I'm certain. I remember almost everything that happened that night now. Even when I had my first breakdown and they sent me to Camarillo State Hospital, I remembered everything that went on. At least from my own experience, being psychotic and having delusions aren't the same thing. During the times when I've been psychotic, I do and say strange things, but I know what's going on around me. In that state, everything is magnified. When you're delusional, you're more or less in a dream world."

"And you were psychotic the night of the crime?"

"I must have been," Daniel said. "If I'd been suffering delusions, nothing that happened would have been real. We know that isn't true."

Carolyn recalled the lab's analysis of the medication found on Daniel's person the night of the crime. They couldn't reproduce the pills, but the information was in the computer files. "He was given the wrong medication," she told them. "My assumption is the pharmacy gave it to him by mistake. The drug was called Levodopa. It's used to treat Parkinson's disease. According to Dr. Weiss, one of our expert witnesses on psychiatric matters, this particular drug would have caused an acute psychotic episode if administered to a schizophrenic."

"Why didn't this come out at the trial?" Kevin Thomas asked. "This is the perfect foundation for a diminished capacity defense."

Carolyn gave the attorney a dirty look. "Didn't you even read the damn trial transcripts?" she snapped, leaning forward over the table. "Nothing regarding Daniel's illness was introduced during the trial. He fought for over ten years just to get the prison to administer medication. It wasn't just Charles Harrison or a few football players out for a good time who ruined this man's life. The entire system is responsible. Is the same thing going to happen again?"

"I don't have to listen to this, Sullivan," Kevin Thomas shot back, standing up and yanking off his tie. "I was only brought on board last week. I have five other cases I'm preparing for trial. I'm not the one who screwed this case up. Why are you ripping into me?"

Hank said, "Cut the man some slack, Carolyn. None of the other DAs would give us the time of day."

"Fine," she said, linking eyes with the district attorney. "I apologize." As soon as the district attorney sat back down, she picked up where she'd left off. "The evidence was suppressed. The obvious person is Charles Harrison. He was chief then, and since his son was killed, I'm sure most of the law enforcement community sympathized with him enough to do whatever he asked."

Kevin Thomas glanced at his watch. "I have to go," he said. "My son has a baseball game at four."

"What are you going to do regarding Armstrong and Houston?"

"Prosecute them," he said. "Get Dr. Weiss to prepare a psych report on Metroix. His testimony will be vital."

"What charges are you going to file?" Carolyn asked, sorry she'd lashed out at him.

"We haven't made a firm decision," Thomas advised. "I'm shooting for attempted murder, since that's the charge Metroix was convicted under. The perjury counts won't fly due to the statute of limitations."

"Daniel deserves a full pardon," Carolyn said. "What can we do to get the ball rolling?"

"Judge Shoeffel has taken on that responsibility," Kevin Thomas said. "These things take time. Under the circumstances, I doubt if there will be a problem." He walked over and shook Daniel's hand. "You couldn't have a better person in your corner. When Shoeffel wants something, she generally gets it."

"Were there other victims?" Carolyn asked. "Did anyone respond to the bulletin regarding Downly?"

"Yes," Hank said, saddened by the atrocities they suspected Eddie Downly had committed. "We're sending out DNA samples to four other agencies. The girls' bodies were recovered, but their killers were never brought to justice.

Their ages range between six and ten. Two were found in Arizona, one in Las Vegas, and the fourth girl disappeared from Los Angeles five years ago. LAPD only recently located her body."

"How do we know it was Downly?" Brad asked.

"The girls were all snatched off the street, taken to a remote location where they were raped, then their bodies were either tossed out of a moving car or buried in a shallow grave. The killer wore a condom. Downly wore a condom when he raped Luisa Cortez. The only exception was the girl from Los Angeles." He glanced through his notes. "The other similarities were that all four girls were wearing dresses and they all had on white cotton underpants."

Brad looked over at Carolyn. "You pegged Downly as a pedophile from the beginning. He certainly didn't fit the standard profile. Most of the time they're middle-aged men. Downly was only nineteen. How did you know there were other victims?"

"He got sloppy, remember?" Carolyn said. "He dumped Luisa Cortez out of the car thinking she was dead. The girl from L.A. must have been his first victim. If she disappeared five years ago, Downly would have been fourteen. That's when he told John he'd committed his first murder."

Without saying anything, Carolyn got up and left the room. Brad went out to check on her. She was standing in the hall crying. "I had him, don't you see? He was already a murderer when the court placed him on probation. I should have seen it. He was never engaged. Everything he told me was a lie. He was purposely trying to deceive me. Except for the girl from L.A., he must have killed the other three during the time I was actively supervising him."

"Listen to me," Brad said, taking hold of her shoulders. "None of this would have turned out the way it did without you. You've cleared an innocent man that no one else cared about. You served as bait to reel in Downly and Mills. The jail accidentally set him free. He might still be out there if it wasn't for you. When everything went to hell in that house in Pasadena, you handled the situation like a champ. You're not a failure. You're a hero."

"Then why do I feel so lousy?" Carolyn asked, removing a tissue from her purse and blowing her nose.

"Because like all of us, you want to put an end to the worst kind of violence there is, crimes committed against innocent children. We can't stop it, Carolyn. All we can do is fight it. And that's just what you did."

"Thanks," Carolyn said, linking eyes with him.

"There's only one thing I want."

Carolyn wondered if he was going to ask her to marry him. She'd already made her decision, at least as far as the immediate future was concerned. She liked Brad better as a friend than a lover. The aspects of his personality that made him exciting would probably make her miserable if they were married.

"Drop out of law school," Brad told her. "If you insist on continuing, promise me you'll take a job with the DA's office. I couldn't stand to see you representing criminals."

Carolyn smiled. "You've got yourself a deal."

Carolyn sent John and Rebecca home with Isobel. Now that everyone was clamoring for a chance to speak to Daniel, Brad Preston was suddenly his best friend. They were in the hall outside the conference room. A gang of reporters were camped out on the front lawn of the police station.

Brad suggested a corporate apartment complex located not far from the government center as a temporary solution to Daniel's housing problem. Using his cell phone, he called and made an appointment for them to come over in thirty minutes. Daniel was recovering nicely from the gunshot wound, but he looked tired and somewhat disoriented.

"The way things are shaping up," Brad told him, draping an arm over Daniel's shoulder, "you're going to have more money than God. This multiscreen monitoring device should support you for the rest of your life. Now, if the exoskeleton works right, the sky's the limit." He held up a palm. "I know freeing up the big money will take some time. I understand you have an inheritance which should hold you over for at least a month. I'm certain we won't have a problem getting a loan if you need money."

"A loan?" Daniel asked, perplexed. "Why would I need a loan?"

"Scratch that," Brad said, realizing that dealing with Daniel was not going to be as easy as he'd thought. "The first thing on the agenda is to get you a driver's license. Then I'll take you car shopping. A Ferrari might be too ostentatious. A used Porsche would make a nice statement. We could also consider a Jag. What's your favorite color?"

"I need books and paper."

Carolyn and Hank Sawyer were standing in the doorway to the detective bay, eavesdropping on the conversation. She leaned over and whispered in Hank's ear, "Looks like Daniel has an agent."

"We'll get you all the books and paper you need," Brad told him. "We need to work on your appearance. *People* may put you on the cover. There's a men's shop close to the apartment. We'll stop by later and get you some decent clothes. You need dress shirts, a few pairs of decent slacks, a nice sports jacket, and at least one or two ties. The representatives from Mitsubishi want to take you to lunch tomorrow. Your attorney should probably go with you. Just remember that lawyers charge by the hour. They may act like your buddy, but they're not. If you feel the need to talk, I'll be glad to oblige you."

"Preston is a case," Hank said, moving his toothpick to the other side of his mouth. "Aren't you going to rescue your man?"

"No," Carolyn told him, smiling. "Brad might do him some good. Daniel needs to become more worldly. They're kind of cute together."

"I don't need all those things," Daniel told him, looking down at his feet. "All I need is a new pair of shoelaces. These have blood on them from the day I got shot. I guess I could wash them."

"Your time's too valuable to spend it washing shoelaces," Brad told him, steering him by the elbow. "Oh, I almost forget. You'll need a cell phone."

"Why?"

"Because everyone has one. It's great. You can take care of things while you're sitting on the john."

Carolyn laughed, waving good-bye to Daniel.

Seated at an empty desk in the detective bay, Carolyn was picking through the boxes of evidence the police had removed from Charles Harrison's residence. She pulled out a thick stack of phone bills and began going through them page by page. One number kept reappearing. In each instance, the call lasted only a minute. She walked over to Hank's desk. The workstations were separated by partitions. "Did you check out this number?"

"Yeah," the detective said, adjusting his reading glasses. "Trevor White called it, I believe. The woman who answered didn't speak English. Must have been one of the maid's friends."

"Usually when you see calls of this duration, it's a code of some kind. I used to call my mother collect from college. I'd ask to speak to a fictitious, prearranged person. Mother would refuse to accept the call, then call me back on the pay phone in the dorm."

"That's defrauding the phone company," Hank said, staring at his computer screen.

"I know," Carolyn said. "But collect calls were almost twice as much as regular calls. Trust me, Hank, something's going on here."

"Don't they need you back at the probation department?" he asked, typing out a report on the death of Eddie Downly and the stabbing of Percy Mills. The Pasadena Police Department held jurisdiction, but Ventura had to submit reports outlining their involvement with the two subjects.

Carolyn wandered back to the desk. She decided to check it out herself. With this big a case, things sometimes fell through the cracks. She instantly recognized the voice of Madeline Harrison. Instead of speaking, she listened.

"Is that you, Charles? Did a liver come in?"

Carolyn covered her mouth, then mumbled something in a deep voice.

"I'll call you back at the hospital," Madeline said. "We must have a bad connection."

Carolyn hung up, shouting over the partition, "She has a private line!"

"Who?"

"Madeline Harrison," she told him. "She has a private phone line in her room at Fairview. And guess who she thought was calling her? Her dead husband. He's in a hospital somewhere waiting for a liver transplant."

Hank stood up. "Is this some kind of a prank?"

"Absolutely not," she said, her veins pumping with adrenaline. "If we hurry, we might be able to catch Arline Shoeffel before she leaves for the day. We'll need a court order to get her phone records released. As we speak, she's calling Chief Harrison. We have to get the name of the hospital."

"Give me the damn number," Hank barked, shaking his

head in disbelief. "It's a good thing Trevor White's in the hospital. That guy could mess up a wet dream. You call the judge. She can authorize it over the phone, then make it official later."

Hank got a supervisor on the line at Sprint, giving her the number and asking her to trace the call. "Boston Memorial," he called out to one of the other detectives a few minutes later. "Get the Boston PD on the line. We'll e-mail them everything we've got on Harrison. He must have been admitted under an alias. They'll have to move fast."

"Can't they tell what room number she called?" Carolyn asked when Hank disconnected.

"No," the detective told her, whipping his tie off and tossing it on his desk. "They can only trace it to the hospital. They can't trace it internally. I was planning to take a few days off. Looks like I'll be flying to Boston."

Carolyn was snuggled next to Paul Leighton Tuesday evening. They were seated in a canvas swing in his backyard, sipping wine as they gazed up at the night sky. Daniel, Lucy, Rebecca, John, and Isobel had gone out to dinner and a movie.

"So Madeline Harrison was running the show from the start?" Paul said. "Does it look like they'll be able to get a conviction?"

"Absolutely," she told him. "The DA is filing three counts of attempted first degree murder. Madeline and Charles Harrison are facing three life sentences. If they had succeeded, they would have been executed."

"What defines first and second degree?"

"A willful, deliberate, and premeditated act."

"Will they ever get out?"

"Doubtful," Carolyn told him. "Not when there are multiple victims, explosives, kidnapping, numerous firearms violations. I'm referring to Madeline. Her husband will more than likely die before the case ever gets to trial. Boyd Chandler cut a deal. As soon as Charles Harrison heard about it, he confessed. They don't expect him to live more than a few days if he doesn't get a liver. He's got three hundred people above him on the transplant list. If I was in his shoes, I'd confess too. Who wants to carry something like that to their grave?"

"From the way it sounds, he was pressured into all this by his wife," Paul said. "Can't he reclaim his former position on the list?"

"Nope," Carolyn said. "I'm sure there are far more deserving people. Harrison was a deputy chief. He and his diabolical wife plotted a murder that we managed to stop. I thought we weren't going to talk about my work tonight."

"It's dark," Paul said, smiling. "The kids won't be home for at least another two hours."

"Oh, really?" she said coyly. "Are you making a suggestion that we go inside?"

"Something like that," he said. "Of course, there's always the recliner."

Carolyn straddled him, wrapping her arms around his neck and kissing him on the mouth. The swing began moving, yet it didn't topple. She was wearing a white linen blouse that was held together at the top with laces. He undid the laces, then cupped one of her breasts in his hand. "Do you know how much progress I've made on my book?"

"No," she said, brushing his hair back from his forehead.

"None," Paul said. "You're on my mind when I get up, when I go to bed. I think about you incessantly. I can't work. I can't sleep. The only thing I can do is eat. I weighed myself the other day. I've gained five pounds."

"Good," Carolyn told him. "When I'm not trying to keep people from killing me, I think of you too. The five pounds you gained, I lost. It's great being so stressed out that your body starts to shrink. I haven't worn this outfit in years."

"Let's go inside."

"Let's wait."

"What?" Paul said loudly, lifting her off of him. "You're a tease. You're never going to sleep with me. I feel like I'm back in high school again."

"Nothing wrong with that," Carolyn said, stretching her legs out in front of her. "I don't want it to be rushed the first time. We've waited this long. Why can't we go away somewhere where we don't have to worry the kids will walk in on us?"

"When?"

"We could go to your house in Pasadena next weekend," she said, thinking it would give her a chance to take care of the kind of things men gave no thought to when they were eager to get a woman in bed—have her hair cut, get a manicure, shave her legs, catch up on her rest. "Isobel could stay here with the kids."

Paul thought a few moments, as if he were solving a complex problem. "Would we leave Friday or Saturday?"

"I don't know," Carolyn told him. "Why?"

He placed his arm on her shoulders again. "I want to know how long I have to wait. It's a few minutes past seven on Tuesday. If we leave Friday, I'll only have to wait sixty-five hours, or approximately thirty-nine hundred minutes. That's if we don't start counting until midnight tonight and we leave at five. Now if you could take off work at noon, I would only have to wait sixty hours. Of course, there's the drive to Pasadena and the Friday traffic which has to be factored in."

"Am I going to have to listen to this type of talk forever?" she asked, laughing. "You need to go back to work on your book."

He jerked his thumb toward the house. "We could always go inside now."

"Friday will be fine," Carolyn said, a feeling of warmth spreading throughout her body. "Isn't anticipation wonderful? Now we'll have something to look forward to all week."

Turn the page to read a preview of Nancy Taylor
Rosenberg's next thriller
SULLIVAN'S JUSTICE
Coming from Kensington in May 2005

Chapter One

Thursday, December 23rd, 12:30 P.M.

Death was waiting, crouched inside the garage of Suzanne Porter's beautiful home.

Her shoes slapped against the wet pavement only a few blocks away. The sky had been overcast when she'd left on her daily run. Now it was raining, and she was soaked. Because her hair was layered, its thick strands stuck to her face and annoyed her. The only way to tame it was to wear a baseball cap. She didn't like to wear hats, though, as they gave her headaches.

Trivial things couldn't upset her today. She loved Ventura when it rained. Crossing to the other side of the street, she glanced through an opening between the houses and caught a glimpse of the Pacific Ocean snaking its way along the shoreline, the whitecaps churning. *The surfers must be in heaven,* she thought, seeing their heads bobbing in the water as they waited to catch the next wave.

The town had grown around the historic San Buenaventura Mission, founded in 1782. Suzanne was delighted with her husband's hometown, framed on one side by the sea and the other by the mountains. She felt certain they would spend the rest of their lives here. Her parents were dead and she had become very fond of Ted's mother and father. In addition, they had a wide base of friends, some who had known Ted since childhood.

She was filled with anticipation. Several months back, she'd decided on the perfect Christmas gift for her husband. Actually, it was a combined birthday and Christmas gift, but she was too excited to wait two weeks to give it to him. Her husband restored cars as a way to relax from the stress of his job. Once they were finished, it could take several months to find a buyer. He was always eager to start on another project, but he couldn't due to lack of space. Three weeks ago, she had secretly sold off some of the stock she'd owned prior to their marriage and hired a contractor to expand their garage so it would hold four cars. She would show him the plans on Christmas Day. Ted would love it.

She had spent the last week preparing for the holiday. This was Suzanne's year to have Ted's family over, and she wanted everything to be just right. Her sister-in-law, Janice, was a gourmet cook. Rather than take a chance, she'd arranged to have the meal catered by La Orange, one of the best restaurants in Ventura. She'd threatened Ted that she would tell his mother he looked at pictures of naked girls on the Internet if he told anyone. So what if she was a lousy cook? She could make salads and spaghetti. Most of the time they ate out.

Before she married, Suzanne had been a bond trader on Wall Street. When her hair had started turning gray at twenty-eight, she knew it was time to shop for a husband. Ted had been in New York on a business trip. He brokered for Merrill Lynch. She was taking a break while considering new career options.

During the holidays, she lost her will power and ate everything in sight. The night before she'd wolfed down half a box of Godiva chocolates. Since she'd turned thirty the month before, she knew her indulgence would show up on her thighs. Her daily workout consisted of an hour lifting weights in her home gym followed by a two mile run. That morning, she'd forced herself to step on the dreaded scales. She'd expected three pounds, maybe four tops. How could she have gained eight pounds in two months? All her clothes were a size six. She decided to extend her run.

Crossing the street again, she picked up the pace. By the time she reached her house, she was winded. She'd only added one mile, for God's sake, she told herself. A few years ago, she could run ten miles and hardly break a sweat. She leaned over and clasped her knees, then started up the sidewalk. The rain had eased up, but the weather report had predicted another front would move in by evening. She missed snow.

Suzanne had grown up in Connecticut. She remembered the snowball fights in her family's front yard on Christmas Day, ice skating on Whitman Lake, and sledding down Black Canyon with her brothers. Sure the constantly sunny skies were nice, but when the average temperature ranged in the seventies, she sometimes forgot what month it was. And it didn't seem like Christmas without snow. At least the rain provided some atmosphere. She laughed, thinking she should throw white sheets on the lawn and turn up the air conditioner.

Seeing her neighbor's nineteen-year-old son pull into the driveway, she walked over to speak to him. Rap music blasted through the windows of his black Mustang. His mother had bought it for him on the condition that he only drove his motorcycle on the weekends. Franny was afraid he was going to get killed.

Suzanne waited until he turned off the car's ignition and then approached him. "Is Franny home from work yet? I'm planning a surprise party for my husband and I wanted to invite your parents."

"You have a phone, don't you?" Eric Rittermier said, getting out of the car and slamming the door. He was a tall, brooding young man with pale skin and dark eyes. He wore two diamond stud earrings in his left nostril, a blue knit cap pulled down low over his forehead, and a stained gray sweatshirt with low-slung baggy jeans.

She took several steps backward, watching as he disappeared inside the house. Maybe Ted was right about having children. She could certainly live without trying to parent some arrogant, moody kid. Babies were adorable, but they didn't remain that way. You never knew if they were going to become criminals or geniuses.

Reaching her front porch, she bent over and removed her key from underneath the mat. Ted had cautioned her to set the alarm and stop leaving her key where someone could find it. Old habits died hard, though, and she kept forgetting. She'd only been gone a short time. Their former house hadn't had an alarm. The type of security system they had now made it impossible to open a window without setting off the alarm. Every window and door in the house had to be locked before she could arm the system. She refused to be a prisoner in her own home.

When she unlocked the door, she was greeted by her tan basset hound, Freddy. His excitement was underwhelming but cute as he tried to jump, his legs not strong enough to support his body. He ran toward the door leading into the garage, barking.

"What's wrong, Freddy?" Suzanne said, clapping her hands. "Let's go upstairs, boy. Mommy's smelly. She's got to get pretty for Daddy."

She walked over and adjusted one of the animated ornaments on the Christmas tree—a miniature soldier beating a drum. Inhaling the delightful scent of pine, she mentally went through her shopping list, confirming that she didn't have any last minute gifts to purchase.

She wished they had a view of the ocean instead of the foothills, but she couldn't complain. The money they'd saved had gone into improvements, like the luxuriously appointed cherry closet and the two-story library where she spent most afternoons, reading and sipping tea with Freddy curled up at her feet.

Suzanne removed her shorts and T-shirt and draped them over the laundry basket to dry, then stepped onto the cold bathroom floor. Grabbing a plush blue towel with flowers embroidered on the borders, she tossed it over the shower enclosure before she entered. The warm water cascaded over her body, the heat causing the clear glass to fog. Tonight they were going out to dinner with Ted's best friend and his wife. She hadn't decided what she was going to wear yet, and she wanted to blow dry her naturally curly hair.

She dried off and opened the shower door. She heard Freddy barking again. Throwing on her robe, she headed downstairs and found him scratching at the door leading to the garage. When she opened it, she heard a noise near Ted's latest project, a Jaguar XKE, under a car cover. Did they have rats again?

She shrieked when someone came out of nowhere and grabbed her from behind. A forearm pressed against her throat. Struggling, she threw an elbow back in an attempt to get away.

"Calm down or I'll kill you."

Suzanne craned her head around, seeing a towering figure wearing a black motorcycle helmet with a mirrored eye shield. A gun was pressed against her left cheek. The assailant had her in a choke hold, clasping her left arm firmly through his leather gloves. Her heart pumped like a rabbit.

She prayed it was the boy next door. "Eric?"

The intruder remained silent.

It couldn't be Eric, she decided. His voice was different. She couldn't be certain, though, as the person was outfitted with leather clothing.

"Don't kill me," she pleaded, tears pouring out of her eyes. "I have almost a hundred dollars in my purse. Take it . . . take anything you want. I won't call the police. I swear."

"You think I'm a thief?" he said, pressing his arm harder against her throat.

Suzanne gasped for breath. The intruder dropped his arm and spun her around. She felt his eyes wash over her. He was going to kill her. She remembered the poor family that was killed not long ago. The killer was so brutal, he'd murdered a six-month-old baby. The newspaper said he'd also decapitated his own mother. A stream of warm urine ran down her legs.

Looking down at the puddle on the floor, she saw Freddy whimpering at her feet. The intruder kicked him through the open garage door, then closed and locked it. She remembered a self-defense tactic and locked her fingers on his arm, then dropped her body to the ground to break his grip. His arm felt like steel. He looked down at her and laughed.

Suzanne's teeth were chattering. She bit the inside of her mouth, tasting the salty blood. "Help me!" she screamed, hoping someone would hear her. "Call the police!"

The assailant used the end of the gun, moving her robe aside in order to expose her naked body. Her stomach muscles twitched as she recoiled in terror. "Take me to your bedroom," he said.

Suzanne climbed the stairs, the gun pressing against her back. Why hadn't she set the alarm? When they reached the master bedroom, her eyes went to the phone on the end table. She had to stall him, find a way to call 911.

"Put on your bra and panties."

He must be a sadistic pervert who got turned on seeing women in their underwear. Maybe that was all he wanted. She yanked open a bureau drawer and pulled out a white pushup bra, snapping it in the front, then turning it around so she could shake her breasts into it. Next she found a pair of lacy T-back panties and quickly stepped into them.

The assailant was standing perfectly still. The gun fell to his side. She could see his chest rising and falling. She didn't care if he raped her as long as he didn't kill her. Her mother had taught her to imagine the worst thing that could happen, then everything else would seem less frightening. She wiped her eyes with her hand, then straightened her back. She had to be strong. He might be one of those men who couldn't get an erection unless the woman was submissive. He couldn't rape her without an erection. If he didn't get what he wanted, though, he might kill her. She made the decision. She'd take an aggressive stance and pray he would back down.

"Why don't you take off your clothes?" she asked, trying to sound seductive. "Then we can party. I bet you're a better lover than my husband." She forced a smile. *Rotten bastard,* she thought. *You're going to burn in hell.* "My husband loves pretty underwear, too. I have drawers full of this kind of stuff. I can model it for you if you want." She grabbed a handful and tossed it in his face, then threw herself in the direction of the phone.

The intruder was too fast. She felt him on her back as she slammed face first onto the floor.

"Stupid bitch," he snarled, grabbing a handful of her hair and pulling hard until her face was visible. "You should have never opened the door to the garage."

"Jesus help me!" Suzanne cried, seeing him pull a plastic wrapped syringe out of his leather jacket. "What are you going to do to me? Oh, God . . . please . . . My husband can get you big money. Thousands . . . Let me go and I'll call him. He can be here in fifteen minutes."

The assailant placed the gun in the waistband of his pants, then used the toe of his boot to roll her onto her back. Bending down, he clasped both of her hands and dragged her to the bathroom. Her fear was so great, her entire body stiffened. Propping her up near the toilet, he grabbed her left arm and then slapped his gloved hand against her forearm.

"I'll do anything," Suzanne pleaded. "I'll suck you off . . . anything." She felt a prick and a stinging sensation.

She saw her husband's face, smiling at her on their wedding day. Then she spun farther back in time. She was with her mother at the park down the street from their house. She was swinging. The sky was beautiful, filled with puffy white clouds. She wanted to swing high enough to touch it. The tree beside her was full of birds. Their chirps sounded like a secret language. Her mother was sitting on a bench across from her, wearing a white sun dress. The wind whipped through her glossy dark hair and exposed the delicate skin on her neck. The next thing she knew, she had flown off the swing and landed in the dirt, her right arm bent backwards. She heard her mother's voice, soft and comforting. "You'll be fine, honey. Be a big girl now and stop crying. After Dr. Lewis fixes your arm, I'll take you for an ice cream."

Suzanne looked down and saw the needle slide out of her vein, wondering why it didn't hurt. There was a trickle of blood, but her mother dabbed it with cotton. Warmth spread throughout her body. She felt as if she were floating in a sea of pleasure, so intense that she couldn't bear it. Her vision blurred. Her head rolled to one side. Everything was beautiful and peaceful. She wanted to stay in this place forever. Her mother was holding her, stroking her.

Her stomach suddenly rose in her throat. She was choking on her vomit when she felt someone push her head down into the toilet. Her skin felt as if it were on fire. "It's just the flu, sweetheart," her mother's voice said. "Once your stomach settles down, I'll give you some aspirin for the fever."

Everything would be fine, Suzanne thought, the warm, comforting sensation washing over her again. She could go to sleep now. Her mother would take care of her.

More Books From Your Favorite Thriller Authors

More Thrilling Suspense From
Your Favorite Thriller Authors

BOOK YOUR PLACE ON OUR WEBSITE AND MAKE THE READING CONNECTION!

We've created a customized website just for our very special readers, where you can get the inside scoop on everything that's going on with Zebra, Pinnacle and Kensington books.

When you come online, you'll have the exciting opportunity to:

- View covers of upcoming books

- Read sample chapters

- Learn about our future publishing schedule (listed by publication month *and author*)

- Find out when your favorite authors will be visiting a city near you

- Search for and order backlist books from our online catalog

- Check out author bios and background information

- Send e-mail to your favorite authors

- Meet the Kensington staff online

- Join us in weekly chats with authors, readers and other guests

- Get writing guidelines

- AND MUCH MORE!

**Visit our website at
http://www.kensingtonbooks.com**